THE PYRES OF DESTINY

A "CALL OF DESTINY" NOVEL
BY

D.M. EARLEY

EVOLVED PUBLISHING™

www.EvolvedPub.com
Evolved Publishing LLC
Butler, Wisconsin, USA

DEDICATION

For my wife, family, friends, readers, and my publisher and editor, Dave Lane (aka Lane Diamond), whose words of encouragement and positive reinforcement keeps my believing in myself and allowing me to share a story that can allow us to escape everyday life.

PART ONE

SECOND CHANCE

PROLOGUE
In This Life...

IN THIS LIFE... (Continued from *The Temptation of Destiny*)

Jake took her hand as they lay basking in the warmth of the sun, enjoying the peace of their new life.

Dakota broke the silence. "It's getting hot. Let's take one more dip, and head back to the cabin." She jumped up and tugged Jake's hand.

"You are a glutton for punishment," he said. "Okay, last time."

They dove into the cold water, and Dakota swam to the small waterfall and stood up. As the gentle cascade flowed over her, she tilted her head back and pushed her hair into the flow of the waterfall.

Jake couldn't take his eyes off her. She looked so sensual, so exotic. Bright-colored leaves hit the water around her. Despite the cold water, he felt his dick start to rise.

He backed up to bring it out of the water. "Hey, my Indian maiden, I have something for you."

She looked at him, raising her eyebrows. "I thought he was cold?" She walked slowly forward, teasing him as she ran her hands across her hard nipples.

Jake caught a reflection behind her. For a split second he wondered what it could be.

"*Dakota, dive!*"

A shot rang out... and the world went into slow motion.

Dakota lurched forward, her eyes wide, blood spraying from her chest.

Jake screamed, "*Noooooooooo!*"

A second shot rang out, and Jake felt a searing burn in his chest, dropping him to his knees in the water.

He struggled to move towards Dakota as her body bobbed facedown and lifeless in the torrent beneath the falls. Crimson-stained water rushed past him.

A third shot rang out, and Jake recoiled backwards, still on his knees. He struggled to maintain consciousness. As Dakota's body floated towards him, he grabbed her for their final embrace in this life.

Honi ran to Jake, and a fourth shot echoed in the fall air.

Silence befell the mountain. The birds stopped singing, and the sky darkened. Bright-colored autumn leaves fell from the trees above, covering the three in a death blanket as they floated in the shallows. Jake took his final breath and drifted into blackness.

Alexi woke suddenly, having fallen asleep on her couch, and looked down at her feet.

Jake stood there, his appearance that of a much younger man. He looked at her with a familiar sparkle in his eye and smile on his face. He walked up to her head, reached out, and brushed her cheek, his touch warm and comforting. He nodded and backed away from her slowly, never taking his eyes off hers, and disappeared.

Alexi smiled as tears trickled down her cheek. Jake had not lied. She knew he would be with her until she took her final breath.

Jim worked down at the front gate, doing his final cleanup from tourist season.

A truck pulled up with two men in fishing gear. They jumped from the truck and approached Jim. "Excuse me, sir," one of them said. "Where is Hangman's Bridge?"

Jim pointed east. "Go back down the road, and make a right. It is about two miles."

The taller fisherman reached his hand out to shake Jim's. "Much obliged, sir."

Jim shook his hand and felt a small prick in his palm. He jerked his hand away and looked at the stranger. His vision blurred as he began to wobble. The earth spun around him and he crashed to the ground, then struggled to get to his hands and knees.

He looked up, laboring to breathe. "Dakota will—"

"No, Chief, Dakota is already on the other side waiting for you."

With his last breath, Jim growled, "*Nooooo*," and lurched forward into the dirt.

Joe kissed Jessica goodbye and left the remote cabin.

Jessica held up a piece of paper. "Hey, aren't you forgetting something?"

"Damn, good catch. I would have been pissed if I rode all the way into town and forgot the grocery list."

"Well, maybe all that good sex I give you makes you forgetful." She winked.

"That's very possible. See you in an hour."

Joe fired up his motorcycle and started his ride off the mountain. He looked out over the fall colors painting the valleys below and accelerated through a sharp turn. Suddenly, his front tire exploded. He fought to gain control but hit the guardrail head on, catapulting him and the bike over it. Both came to rest hundreds of feet below on the rocky ledges.

On the canyon above the winding road, Fiore lowered his rifle. "Well, Mr. DA, *you, sir*, are what we call collateral damage."

Mr. Smith pulled his phone from his pocket as a text alert came across:

Two Elk down on the mountain. Hunting was good.

A second text followed:

Fishing is good at Wind River today.

A third text read:

Fatal motorcycle wreck on the pass. Traffic is backed up.

Mr. Smith nodded and smiled. "Another happy client."

Mr. P pulled a burner phone from his desk and dialed.

"Yes sir," the voice on the other end answered.

"Are the pheasants ready to leave South Dakota?"

"Yes, sir, they're crated and on the plane."

"How many do we have?"

"Eleven birds, sir."

"Very good. Make sure *none* of their feathers get messed up. The client wants them perfect."

"Their feathers are perfect, sir. See you at the ranch."

Decker raised his scope one last time to look down at the bodies of Jake, Dakota, and the wolf. He dialed Sam's cell phone.

"Yea, Decker?"

"Sam, I'll meet you at the Six Gun Saloon in Dubois for pickup around nine."

"10- 4."

Decker hiked down off the ridge above, and strolled to the waterfall. He waded to the lifeless bodies of his targets and rolled them over in the water.

"Damn, Jake Michaels, you were a lucky bastard, banging her." He snapped several pictures of Dakota's naked body.

When Decker had been on the ridge waiting to take his shots, he'd noticed a small opening to an old mine. He decided it would be the perfect place to dump the bodies and belongings from the cabin. He thought it unlikely anyone would ever find them, theorizing that the police would track the ATV back to Jim. People would believe Jake pulled another disappearing act, and Dakota joined him.

He bent down to retrieve Jake's body, but something caught his attention out of the corner of his eye. He stood and looked towards the waterfall, but saw nothing.

Suddenly, the skies darkened, the winds howled, and the water in the pool turned choppy. A lightning bolt crashed into a tree to the left of him. He recoiled, lost his footing on the slippery creek bed, and fell beneath the surface.

He attempted to stand, but something held him under the water. The more he struggled, the more resistance he faced. He thrashed violently in a fight for his life, but there was little he could do to keep the cold water from rushing into his lungs.

The skies turned blue again, and the waters calmed.

Decker's body was drawn to a small whirlpool forming in the middle of the pool, where his body spun several times in the vortex before disappearing.

As the moon rose over the mountains, Jake, Dakota, and Honi floated lifeless in the silvery light, the quiet of the night broken by whispers around the waterfall.

The Ancient Ones surrounded the pool, their heads lowered.

The Faceless Indian stepped from the darkness of the woods and approached the bodies.

The Spirit of the Water rose from the depths. She knelt next to Dakota and cradled her head. She looked at The Faceless Indian and nodded before retreating below the surface.

The Faceless Indian looked towards the night sky. "Heisonoonin, ceixotoni hinee neeniit Mingan, Honi, noh Hurit."

His hands glowed as he touched Jake's, Honi's, and Dakota's heads.

Several seconds passed.

Jake opened his eyes and took a deep gasp for air.

Dakota did the same.

Honi yelped and stood up.

Jake knelt and pulled Dakota to him. Their eyes met as he pushed the wet hair off her face. He watched the exit wound in her chest slowly close. He glanced at his own chest then, but found no evidence of a gunshot wound.

Honi gained his senses and walked to them, licking first Jake's face and then Dakota's.

Jake felt an uneasiness course through his body. A voice, not his, came from deep inside. "Rowtag, why have you brought us back? Have we not fulfilled our punishment?"

Dakota, in an unfamiliar voice, added, "We have suffered for tens of thousands of years in mortal bodies. Is our punishment not over?"

"Mingan and Hurit, your punishment is fulfilled. Your host's Destiny is not. They must stop the evil your indiscretions set free."

Mingan barked, "Rowtag, mortals *cannot* fight them. They will suffer pain like they have never known. *Why* would you do that to them?"

Rowtag placed his hands upon Jake's and Dakota's heads. "Sleep, Mingan and Hurit. You will be called upon again."

Jake and Dakota regained their composure after the manifestation of souls inside them fell dormant.

"Your name is Rowtag?" Jake said.

"Yes, I am known by many names. That is what the First Ones called me."

"The presence inside Dakota and I, Mingan and Hurit... will they guide us in fulfilling our Destiny?"

"No, Jake, your guidance will come from the Spirit World, as it has on this journey. Mingan and Hurit will be called upon only by me. Your bodies are merely a vessel for them until such time comes. For now, Dakota and you may relax. Enjoy the love you have found. Your journey ahead will be challenging."

Rowtag walked into the darkness and faded from sight.

Jake looked at Dakota. "Well, Counselor, I guess Eternity will have to wait one more lifetime for them."

CHAPTER 1
DREAMS

Samuel Red Hawk woke suddenly. He gathered his senses and reached for the phone. His heart raced. He hoped it was not too late.

Anna looked at the caller ID. "Hello Father."

"Anna, is Jim there?"

"Yes, he is sitting outside with Jay, why?"

"I had a dream. Please let me speak with him."

"What kind of dream, Father?"

"A dream of evil white soldiers, like the ones that hurt our Lomasi."

Anna had learned her lesson the last time she did not listen to Samuel. She rushed the phone outside to Jim.

Jim saw the concerned look on his wife's face as she handed the phone to him. "Who is it, Anna?"

"It's Father. He had a dream. He needs to talk to you."

"Yes, Samuel, what is it?"

"Jim, I had a dream you will meet with two white men. They have been sent to kill you. Do not shake their hands. They will approach you at the gate."

Jim paused for a second rolling his eyes. "Okay, Samuel, I will be on the lookout for them. Why do they want to kill me?"

"You threaten their leader."

Jim thought for a second about the dream Samuel had the night of Dakota's attack, and swallowed hard. He would take this warning a bit more serious.

"Very well, Samuel," he said. "Thank you for the warning. Now, you get some rest. Anna and I will be there Monday to pick you up."

"Jim, there is an ancient evil on the earth. A great battle is coming."

"Okay, Samuel. Do you want to speak with Anna?"

"*No*, I must rest. I must have my strength for what the Spirit World will show me. I must prepare for the great battle."

Samuel hung the phone up. He lifted his ceremonial pipe to the sky, blessed it, and prepared for a visit to the Spirit World.

I must learn more.

Jim looked at Jay and Anna, and shook his head. "Samuel claims there will be two men at the gate sent to kill me. He said not to shake their hands, and that a great battle is coming to Wind River. It is amazing how some days he is clear as a bell, and others he fades into some other world."

Jay looked between the couple, and said, "Jim, I know you do not believe in the ancient ways as I do, but I saw things the day we arrested Jake Michaels. I saw the Ancient Ones on the Sacred Grounds. They were in great numbers. I heard Jake Michaels speak in the Ancient One's tongue at the police station. Maybe Samuel is right. Maybe there is a great battle coming?"

Jay's prophetic tone caught Jim's attention.

"Jim, remember Father's last dream," Anna quickly added.

Jim took a deep breath, shook his head, and chuckled. "Well, Jay, I was heading down to the gate to do a final cleanup of the area. It is surprising Samuel saw that. Do you want to do a little stakeout?"

Jay nodded. "Sure, but I am not cleaning up trash."

Anna said, "You two be careful down there, just in case Father is right. Neither of you are spring chickens anymore."

Jay wrapped his arm around Jim's shoulder and winked at Anna. "These two old Indians still have a fight or two left in them."

The men jumped in the old farm pickup and drove down to the gate.

Jay said, "Drop me off at the logging road. That will give me a good view of the gate, just in case Samuel is right."

"Damn, Jay, you really *are not* helping me pick up garbage, are you?"

Jay grabbed his right shoulder and rolled it, wincing in pain. "My bones are too old for that."

Jim huffed. "Oh, but you can fight a couple assassins?"

"My partner will handle that." Jay patted a .44 magnum on his hip, turned to walk up the logging road, and soon ducked into the trees.

Jim returned to the gate and started to pick up trash.

A few minutes passed, and a black pickup with dark windows drove up the road. It slowed as it approached Jim. He glanced towards Jay, who acknowledged his look with a nod before stepping behind the cover of the pines.

He looked into the blacked-out cabin, and could make out two silhouettes with cowboy hats on.

The door opened, and a tall redheaded woman jumped out. "Jim White Feather, you handsome devil, what are you doing picking up trash?"

Jim walked towards her with his arms extended. "Nice truck, Beth. What are you doing out this way?"

The two hugged.

Beth patted him on the shoulder. "My God, you're still as solid as you were forty years ago."

"And you are still as beautiful."

"Always the smooth talker, Jim White Feather. How is Anna?"

"She is good. You should take a ride up to see her."

Jay looked down on Jim and Beth, and noticed another vehicle pull halfway down the road and turn around.

"Jim, I would, but I'm taking my friend up to the Continental Divide trail. I assume the logging road is still drivable?"

"Yes, it is in good shape. In fact, if you look back there, wave to Jay."

Beth looked back and waved in the direction Jim pointed too.

Jay stepped out of the cover and waved back.

"Jim, why is he hiding in the bushes? Never mind. It's Jay... forget I asked." Beth laughed.

The two hugged again.

Beth jumped back in the pickup and drove up the logging road.

Jay watched as Beth paused the truck where he stood tucked in the brush.

"Hey, Jay," she called out. "If you're taking a piss, you don't have to be that bashful. I remember all two inches of that thing."

Jay stuck his hand through the thick cover with his middle finger raised. "Best two inches of your life."

"I love you too!" She rolled up the window and drove ahead.

Jay laughed to himself. He and Beth had dated for several years after he returned from Vietnam. He wanted to go back into the military and make a career out of it once the war ended, but Beth did not want to leave Wind River. When he retired and moved back to the Reservation, Beth had been married for the past twenty years. He often wondered what his life would have been like with her. She was smart and driven, absolutely determined to succeed in her veterinary practice, which she did. She owned four offices between Jackson Hole and Lander.

He snapped out of his daydream when the noise of another vehicle coming down the road caught his attention. It was the same vehicle he'd seen earlier.

Jim looked up from the garbage pile he was raking.

A four-door, cookie-cutter, black sedan approached him, stopped, and two fishermen got out. They approached Jim.

"Excuse me, sir, where is Hangman's Bridge?" the taller of the two men said.

Jim pointed east. "Go back down the road, and make a right. It is about two miles."

The taller fisherman reached his hand out to shake Jim's. "Much obliged, sir."

Jim looked down at the outstretched hand and did not shake.

"What's wrong, Mister, don't you shake hands?" The taller man said.

"No, I am a germophobe. Sorry," Jim said, and shrugged.

The shorter man stepped forward, and lifted his arm to pat Jim on the shoulder.

Jim blocked his hand with the rake.

"Hey, Chief, calm down," the taller man said. "We mean no harm. But I must say, you are starting to offend me."

Jim stared at them for a second, and said, "I think it is best you boys get back in that truck and leave."

The two men looked at each other and smirked.

"Well, Matt," the taller one said. "The man said we should leave."

Matt paused for a second, looking Jim in the eyes. "You know what, Sam, I don't think I'm leaving until he apologizes and shakes my hand."

The three men stared at each other until the unmistakable clicking of a revolver cocking broke the silence.

Jay stepped from the cover of the brush. "I believe the man asked you to leave."

Matt and Sam put their arms up as they looked over at Jay walking towards them with the .44 aimed head-high.

"Hey, Matt, Tonto has a big six-shooter," Sam said.

Jim watched Matt's eyes. As soon as they glanced towards Jay, he struck, landing a hard right across Matt's jaw and knocking him to the ground.

Sam reached into his vest.

Jim pulled out his sidearm and cocked it against Sam's cheek. "I would not do that."

Sam raised his arms.

Jim reached back and pistol-whipped him, knocking him to the ground.

Jay approached the downed men and tossed two sets of handcuffs on the ground. "Put them on."

"Fuck you, Tonto," Sam growled.

Jay lifted his foot up and crashed the heel of his cowboy boot across Sam's face. A gash opened on his cheekbone, spurting blood onto Matt.

Jay pressed his cocked pistol into Sam's bleeding face. "Again, I will ask you nicely, put the cuffs on."

Matt and Sam cuffed themselves.

Jim looked at Matt's right hand. "Take that ring off and put it on the ground."

"Fuck you, Chief," Matt barked.

Jay pulled his knife and pressed it against Matt's ear, drawing blood. "I do not think you heard him. I would listen to the man if you want to use this ear again."

Matt worked the ring off and dropped it on the ground.

Jim picked the ring up with a stick and examined it. On the outside of the ring portion, hidden on the palm side, was a small needle. He played with the face of the ring, and it opened to expose a small chamber with liquid in it. He showed Jay.

Matt looked at Sam with raised eyebrows.

"Who sent you?" Jay said.

"Fuck off," Matt hissed.

"Jay, grab their car and take them for a little ride down the canyons. I will follow you in the truck."

"10-4."

Jay pulled Sam and Matt's car up, opened the trunk, and ordered them inside. When they hesitated, he cocked the hammer on his gun.

The two men complied.

They traveled three miles into the canyons on Jim's property. Jay stopped the car and popped the trunk just as Jim arrived behind him.

The two assassins laid soaked in sweat and blood.

Jay reached in and yanked them out, one by one, and threw them to the dusty ground.

Jim and Jay drug them off the road and positioned them back-to-back on the ground. Jay then pulled a set of jumper cables from their car and tied the two together around the chest.

Jim knelt and looked Matt in the eyes. "Okay, one last chance. Who sent you here?"

Matt spit a mouthful of blood in response.

Jay walked over to the two captives, bent down, and looked at them hard while pulling his survival knife from his belt. "Many years ago, our ancestors had ways to make prisoners talk. Some found it barbaric, and we were forced into the laws of the white man. The old ways died. The bad thing for both of you is, we are on our Ancestor's land, and Jim and I still believe in the old ways."

He cut one of Sam's pants legs, exposing his thigh, and with a quick slicing motion, he filleted a one-inch piece of Sam's leg.

Sam jerked violently and his screams echoed through the canyons.

Jay moved around to Matt and forced the hunk of flesh into his mouth.

Matt spit the bloody, hairy piece of meat out and puked.

Sam thrashed, trying to get loose. "*You sick Motherfuckers, we will kill you!*"

In a calm voice, Jim said, "We will feed you each other, piece by piece, until you answer our question. Now, who sent you?"

"*Go to Hell,*" Matt hissed.

Jim looked down at Jay and nodded.

Jay stood, grabbed Matt's hair, pulled up on his scalp, and sliced the taut skin.

Matt screamed in pain and kicked his legs wildly.

"*Okay!*" Sam yelled over Matt's cries of agony. "It was Dibella, Vincent Dibella."

Jay stopped the scalping, and his eyes darted to Jim.

Jim said, "Dibella? Why would Dibella want me dead?"

"We don't know. We just take the orders," Sam said.

Jim nodded at Jay.

Jay bent down and drew the knife to Sam's ear.

"*Please no!* I really don't know," Sam pleaded.

With a quick slice, Sam's right ear fell to the sandy dirt, and Jay reached down and picked it up. He then shifted around to Matt and grabbed his mouth to open it.

Matt shook his head trying to avoid Sam's ear being shoved into his mouth. "South America, you bastards. *South Fucking America!*" Matt blurted, before the sand-crusted ear could be forced past his lips.

Jay stood and walked over to Jim, and they looked down on the two bloody assassins.

Jim pulled a phone from Sam's pocket and scrolled through the contacts, all listed in code.

"What contact is Dibella?" Jim said. "What is your confirmation message?"

"#Four, Fishing is good at Wind River today," Sam murmured.

"Who else has he ordered a hit on?" Jim said.

Sam, trying to maintain consciousness, mumbled, "I don't know. He keeps contracts and contractors separated."

Jay knelt next to Sam and raised the knife point to his eye. Sam did not flinch.

"Let him go Jay," Jim said. "I believe him."

"What are you going to do with us?" Matt said.

Jim tossed a canteen of water to the ground. "You are free to go. If you make it off the Sacred Lands tonight, you were meant to live. Tell your boss this is over. We will not be as hospitable next time."

Jay bent down and unlocked the handcuffs. He stood up and whispered, "Ha tcaciihi telhiiha."

Jim and Jay jumped in the two vehicles and left for the ranch, purposely taking a different route to mislead the two assassins deeper into the canyons.

Jim stopped his truck at Buzzards Gulch and got out.

Jay joined him between the vehicles. "What are you thinking?"

Jim said, "I say we leave the car here. I guarantee they were spooks. No one will come looking for them."

"I agree. Do you think Dibella will go after Dakota?"

"I was alone when I tried to force his asshole attorney Sellman into a deal. I would assume he thinks Dakota knows about South America. It would look too obvious if he killed both of us. Even if he made it look like an accident, or natural causes, it would raise red flags. She is with Jake at the cabin. Dibella's men would have a difficult time finding them out there. Still, to be safe, I am going to ride out tomorrow morning and talk to them. You want to go?"

"Yes, I will go with you. Does anyone else know about the plea you offered Sellman?"

"Yes, Joe does. Do you think he would go after a DA?"

"Think about how that would divert the attention off of him, if Dakota and you showed up dead. No one would connect Dibella to the death of the DA that prosecuted Jake."

Jim nodded his head in agreement. "We need to warn him, also."

"Jim, what happened in South America?"

"Dakota and I had a client being charged with embezzlement by his partners. He met an untimely death on a solo hiking trip. To make a long story short, his partners were connected to the Dibella boys, and a sexual assault and pornography charge in Belize. Those charges were dropped when the victim refused to testify. I threatened Sellman with exposing this during the trial, in hopes he would get Dibella to consider a plea. As you know, that did not happen. It appears I opened an old wound."

Jay paused for a second. "There is much more to this story for Dibella to order your execution. After watching the tape, we know the Dibella boys were human traffickers. Do you think Sellman or Vincent Dibella are behind a trafficking ring? They both have plenty of money. It would make no sense."

"Honestly, I think it's more than money."

Jay nodded. "Well, it appears this case is far from over, but... we cannot pursue it based on what we just did to these two goons. You will need to use the legal system and the evidence you have to move it forward."

Jim sighed. "When Dibella realizes I am not dead, he will send more people to stop me. Maybe Samuel is right, and there *is* a great battle coming to Wind River."

"We will be ready, Jim. Let's go home."

"Sounds good. I am sure Anna is getting worried. Hey, what did you whisper to them before we left?"

"Ha tcaciihi telhiiha."

Jim laughed. "The cannibal dwarfs Jay? Please tell me you do not believe in that old myth?"

"Do you believe in Samuel's visions now?"

Jim raised his brows and nodded. "Good point, my old friend."

Jake snapped his eyes open. Dakota's head laid across his chest. He gently stroked her hair as he analyzed the dream of their death. He looked past the field towards the butte above the waterfall.

"Dakota, wake up."

Dakota moaned. "Do I have to?"

"I had a dream. I need you and Honi to get back to the cabin. Lock the door, and make sure you have the rifle ready."

Dakota, hearing the seriousness in his voice, lifted her head. "What kind of dream, Jake? You're scaring me."

"Someone was sent here to kill us. There's a sniper on the ridge behind the waterfall. He has no shot on us right now. Get up and walk to the right side of the clearing back to the cabin."

"Who sent someone to kill us?"

"I don't know, but I'll find out."

"What are you going to do? You're naked and have no gun with you?"

"I'll loop around the left side of the falls through the pines. I leave a ghillie suit in a hunting blind there. He won't see me through the canopy. The noise of the waterfall will cover my footsteps."

"And then what, Jake? Are you gonna beat him to death with your dick? Come back to the cabin and get your gun."

"I don't need a gun. *Please*, just listen to me. The dream showed me one shooter. I know where he is, so I'll creep up on him. Now go. I'll tell you the rest of the dream when I get back."

She leaned forward and kissed him. "Jake Michaels, after all we have been through, you'd better not leave me alone on this mountain."

"In your words, trust the Spirits. Now go, and have the rifle ready in case I fail and he comes for you."

Dakota and Honi left for the safety of the cabin.

Jake slowly made his way through the pines, retrieved his ghillie suit, and moved forward. He reached the base of the ridge and surveyed the climb. If his dream vision had been correct, the sniper would be looking east. Jake's best approach would be to travel farther to the north spine of the ridge and move along the creek bed back to the shooter.

He reached the top of the ridge and crept along the stream for several hundred yards, and heard the sound of the waterfall in the distance. His dream showed the shooter posted on an outcropping to the right of the falls. He stepped up on a boulder and scouted the area. A movement caught his eye, so he slipped into the creek and bellied his way downstream. His special forces training had prepared him well for what he was about to do.

The shooter lay prone above the falls, his eyes focused in his scope at the area below.

Jake slithered out of the stream and crept behind the sniper. He held a grapefruit-sized creek stone in his right hand. "*Hey.*"

The sniper rolled over on his back and pulled his gun up.

Jake crashed the stone across his jaw, and quickly followed with a second blow to the shooter's right arm, causing him to lose the grip on his rifle. Jake looked down to see a survival knife on the shooter's hip. He pulled the knife from the sheath and pushed it against the shooter's throat. "Make one move, you cocksucker, and I will cut you ear to ear."

The shooter slowly rolled his head to the right and spit out a mouthful of blood.

Jake reached with his left arm, grabbed the rifle, stood, and pointed it at the shooter's head. "Who sent you?"

"Fuck you, Michaels," the shooter hissed.

Jake dropped to his knees, buried the six-inch blade into the shooter's thigh, and twisted it 180 degrees.

The shooter's cries echoed through the canyon.

"Get up on your knees, you piece of shit," Jake growled.

The shooter struggled to his knees using his left arm. His right arm dangled lifelessly at his side. Blood flowed from his mouth, and his camo pants quickly turned crimson from the knife wound. He wobbled on his knees trying to maintain consciousness.

"One more time, who sent you?"

"I don't know. We just get orders."

Jake glared at the shooter. "I don't believe you."

He moved behind the shooter, yanked his head back by his hair, and pressed the blade lengthwise across his mouth. With a quick slice, the blade split the shooter's cheeks from his lips to his jaw bone. Jake pushed him forward onto his stomach.

The shooter writhed in pain on the ground.

"We can keep this up all day, or you can tell me who the fuck sent you."

Jake dropped in front of the shooter again, pulled his head up and moved the knife towards him.

"Dibella," the shooter struggled to say.

Jake stood. "Why would Dibella want us dead?"

"South America." The shooter leaned forward to avoid chocking on his own blood.

"Give me your phone."

The shooter reached into his pants and threw the phone on the ground.

"Who is your contact and what is the confirmation message."

"Number One, two elk down on mountain, hunting was good."

Jake sent the message and looked down at the shooter. "I should let the grizzlies and wolves finish you tonight."

The shooter struggled to look up. "Fuck you and that Indian cunt," he forced out through his mangled mouth.

Jake nodded and squeezed off one round.

Jake climbed down the rocks and waded into the pool to clean the blood from his body. He saw Dakota running towards him.

The two embraced at the water's edge, holding each other tight.

Jake loosened his hug and looked at Dakota. "It was Dibella. He sent the shooter."

"Why, Jake, because of his *piece of shit* sons?"

"No, because of South America, but... there's more to this. Let's get back to the cabin. I'm freezing."

CHAPTER 2
MINGAN AND HURIT: THE BEGINNING

Jake and Dakota sat on the bear skin rug facing the roaring fireplace. She grasped his hand. "You're still shivering, love."

"I'll warm up in a few minutes. Thank God the Spirit World warned us, or we wouldn't be here."

"Jake, what exactly did they show you?"

Jake recounted the dream, leaving no detail out except one: his visit to Alexi. He ran his hand through his hair and shook his head. "There *has to* be more to this. Dibella will not stop once he finds out we're not dead. He'll send more goons."

Dakota shifted from Jake's side and faced him, placing her hands on his knees. "Destiny will not allow us to be separated. We *need* to visit the Spirit World tonight. We need answers from this Rowtag."

She paused. Her face tightened and eyes narrowed. "Could my grandparents be in danger also? We have no way of warning them from here."

Jake looked deep in her eyes as he placed his hands on her shoulders. "I thought about that as I walked back. The Spirits will warn them, probably through Samuel."

Dakota thought for a second, "You're probably right."

Jake reached over to the small table to his left and retrieved a pipe and a pouch. "Are you ready for some answers?"

Dakota nodded.

They drew several deep hits each, and stared into the dancing flames as the medicine gently flowed through their bodies, separating them from the physical world.

The couple stood outside the cabin. The hue of gold aspens illuminated the nighttime mountains. Light snow fell, and each flake twinkled like small stars. For the first time, Jake and Dakota stood fully clothed in the Spirit World.

In the distance, Rowtag meandered through the meadow.

The two interlocked hands and walked towards him.

He turned as they approached. Gone was the dark abyss that once formed his face. Steel blue eyes set in a chiseled, kind face, greeted them.

"I am glad to see you paid heed to your vision, Jake." Rowtag's voice was deep, soft, and calming now, unlike the foreboding tone in previous visits.

Jake nodded. "Rowtag, why was a hit man sent here? Who are Mingan and Hurit? Why does the Spirit World continue to show them in our bodies?"

"Are my grandparents in trouble?" Dakota followed quickly.

A small smile crossed Rowtag's face as he raised his hand. "Children, I know you have questions, as many have since the beginning. The answers will soon come clear. Come, follow me."

Rowtag led the couple past the waterfall to the foot of the hot spring Jake and Dakota had bathed in often. "Jake, Dakota, look deep into the bubbling water."

Jake glanced at Dakota, his face flushed hot with embarrassment.

Her eyes widened.

Rowtag chuckled. "Yes, I saw everything that happened in this spring. I led you here. It was a test. I needed to know if lust would weaken each of you, and if the sins of the flesh would deem you not worthy of the journey ahead. Now, relax and stare deeply into the pool."

Jake's and Dakota's eyes glazed as the pool percolated. The hypnotic dance of bubbles calmed as the water cleared. Below the surface, a village appeared. The view zoomed-in on a young brave walking into an ornately decorated teepee. He opened the front flap, and the earthy smell of kinnikinnick hung in the wisps of smoke filling the teepee.

An elderly man stood to greet him. His weathered buckskin matched the years of wisdom on his face. A raven-feathered head dress fell below his waist, and rows of turquoise beads cascaded down his chest. To the left and right of the elder stood two spears anchored into the earth, their shafts adorned with eagle feathers and topped with rattlesnake skulls.

The two men greeted each other in an ancient language, which the Spirit world allowed Jake and Dakota to understand.

"Mingan, please sit," Askuwhetean said.

"Great Grandfather, it is nice to see you. Why do you not come into the sun more?"

"I can not speak with the Spirits out there. My days in the physical world are coming to an end. The Spirit world will soon welcome me."

Mingan's eyes welled. "Great Grandfather, did you call me here to say goodbye?"

"No, Mingan, it is time for you to go on the Journey, as my father and his father did, and their fathers have since the beginning. When your father and grandfather were taken by the Spirits, you became next in line to lead our people, as you know. First, you must add a sacred feather to each of these spears."

"Great Grandfather, eagles fly above our head every day. Their feathers fall to the ground. This task seems simple. I have heard of the Journey since I was young. I expected much more of a test for the leader of our people."

Askuwhetean smiled and shook his head slightly. "You remind me of your father, so confident, quickly jumping to his own conclusions. No, Mingan, the feathers you will retrieve come from sacred eagles that live on the High Mountain, where the Great River splits. You will climb above the clouds to reach a special land, one few return from."

Mingan paused and his brow dropped. "Great Grandfather, if this land is so dangerous, how did you survive? And all the leaders of our people before you? How did my father and grandfather live?"

"My son, you will need to trust in the Spirits and believe *this* is your Destiny. You will face evil that few have seen since the Great Flood. Stay true to our beliefs, and you will return to lead our people."

"This evil, Great Grandfather, will it be in the shape of man or beast? Can I drive my spear though its heart?"

"No, you cannot kill this evil we call the Six. They are of our flesh and bone, but their magic is too strong. They were sent from the Great Spirit to guide humans in the beginning, but they strayed. Their quest for power undermined the Great Spirit. They quickly recognized the flaws of our people and exploited them."

Mingan frowned. "Why did the Great Spirit not kill them? Why did the Great Spirit allow them to gain control of the people? Why did they not die in the Great Flood?"

THE PYRES OF DESTINY

"When the world flooded, the Great Spirit allowed only the top of the High Mountain to remain. The Six retreated to caves there. Instead of killing them, the Great Spirit decided the best punishment would be to imprison them for eternity on the mountaintop, where they could only look down on the flooded land they loved. Eventually, the Great Spirit allowed the waters to return to the skies, and He breathed life into the land once again, creating two great tribes—the People of the Sunrise, our people, and the People of the Sunset. The Six now stand imprisoned for eternity on the apex of the High Mountain, looking down on both tribes. Their thirst to destroy the Great Spirit's creation torments their souls."

"But why did the Great Spirit allow them to poison the first creation? Why do they still exist when they can no longer harm us, other than to live out their punishment?"

"My son, the Journey will answer this."

Mingan took a deep breath, forcefully blew it out, and looked at the ground.

His Great Grandfather smiled, seeing the young brave's frustration.

"Great Grandfather, one last question: why have I never seen the People of the Sunset? Why do both tribes not come together as one great tribe?"

"I do not know that answer. When the Great Spirit created both tribes, he separated them by the Great River and High Mountain. He provided both tribes with land, rich with great hunting and fertile soil, more than either tribe will ever need. Both tribes have prospered for many generations separated from each other. It is as the Great Spirit designed."

The water in the spring began to bubble, blocking Jake and Dakota's view of Mingan's world.

"Rowtag, why did you end this?" Jake said.

"Jake, Dakota, it is time for you to return to the physical world. I will show you more when you visit again."

"Rowtag, what about my grandparents? Are they safe?"

"Yes, child, they are. Your great grandfather has the vision, and he has protected them."

"Protected them from who, Rowtag?" Jake barked. "Did Dibella send a hit man after them also?"

Jake and Dakota's eyes fixed on the fire as the grip of the medicine wore off.

Dakota looked terribly worried. "Jake, what the hell does all this mean?"

Jake shook his head, his eyes fixed on the ground. "I don't know, but I'm sure we'll find out soon enough. We need to meet with your grandfather."

"I agree. Let's head down the mountain at first light."

CHAPTER 3
EYES OF THE NIGHT

The sun dropped behind the mountains, the canyons darkened, and the cool night air rushed in. Sam and Matt struggled to their feet and passed the canteen between them several times as they gathered their senses.

"I'm gonna kill both of those motherfuckers, slowly," Sam hissed.

He ripped a piece of his torn shirt into a long shred. He then bent over and poured a small amount of water into the desert sand to make a thick paste, scooped some up, and packed it to the side of his head where his ear once resided. He held it in place with a makeshift bandana from his torn shirt.

Matt did the same in an attempt to stop the bleeding from his detached hairline, and said, "First we have to find our way out of these canyons before the wolves, grizzlies, and mountain lions start moving around. Our blood will smell like a fucking buffet to them. Those assholes thought they would fuck us up by going a different direction out of here. I guess they thought we couldn't read tire tracks. The ranch is east of here. We traveled for about thirty minutes. I figure we're about ten miles from that Indian's ranch. Let's get moving."

The two paused after several hundred yards, and Matt said, "Don't you think this is a bit too easy? Why didn't they kill us, knowing we'd be back to finish our assignment?"

Sam shook his head. "No idea, brother. Maybe they're up on the cliffs watching us. Gonna let us think we're out, then ambush us just like their ancestors. All I know is, when we reach that ranch, I'm gonna torture that bastard's old lady in front of him, then stick my gun in his ass and blow the top of his head off while his wife begs for mercy."

Matt chuckled. "You have fun with that. I'll take care of Jay. He likes to fucking scalp people. Well, I'll show him how a white man does it. I will flay him, starting at his ankles so he can watch as I peel his skin up his body."

Anger and revenge fueled the two as their pace quickened. The last bit of twilight gave way to the early stars of night, and the desert came alive with the first howls of wolves echoing through the canyons.

Sam looked down at the blood-soaked dressing on his leg. "This walk *is not* allowing the blood to coagulate. I'm leaving drops in our trail. How much longer do you think we have, bro?"

"Maybe four or five miles. Let's repack that leg again and take a break for a few minutes. Let our heartbeat slow the flow of blood to these wounds."

They repacked their perspective injuries and sat quietly, resting their bodies. The starlit wilderness around them bustled with the crunching of brush from small animals on their nightly hunt. The hooting of owls, yelping of coyotes, and occasional howls of wolves filled the canyons with the song of the night.

"It is peaceful out here, isn't it?" Matt said.

"Yep, I can see why people move here and stay. Beats the fuck out of the East Coast. Maybe when we get done with all this shit, I'll move out here."

"Fuck, dude, who you kidding? You're gonna give up chasing whores around the big cities back home? You gonna give up smoking weed and hit the peace pipe with your new Indian friends?"

Sam thought for a second. "Well, as for the whores, if they all look like that Dakota chick, fuck yea."

"Speaking of Dakota, I wonder how Decker is doing taking care of her and that asshole Jake Michaels. He should be off the mountain by now and close to our pickup point in Dubois."

Sam chuckled. "He'll be fucking blowing our phones up if we're not there. One good thing is, he'll contact the man and alert him something is wrong when we're not on time."

"Let's get going. We'll finish our job at the ranch and call him," Matt said.

As they stood, a twig snapped behind them, the crack louder than what they'd been hearing. They looked at each other, realizing something larger was behind them.

Sam raised his hand and signaled for the two to separate, in hopes that whatever lurked in the darkness would become confused.

They nervously moved forward, their eyes focused on the darkness. As if someone had hit a light switch, eye glare lit up the brush.

"We're fucking surrounded," Matt whispered.

Sam nodded. "The eyes are about two feet from the ground, too low for wolves unless they're crouched. My guess is coyotes. Slowly bend down and try to find a decent size rock. We'll stand back to back and work our way forward. We'll yell once we're in position. Hopefully, they'll scatter and let us pass."

The two slowly bent down, avoiding any sudden movement, then rose back up. They stood backs pressed against each other's, armed with baseball-sized rocks.

"You ready?" Sam said.

"Let's do this."

The two screamed at the top of their lungs, and the brush crashed around them as the animals fled.

"Fuck, man, that was close," Matt said. "Let's get the hell out of here before they change their minds."

The two picked up their pace, and soon came to a split in the dirt road.

Matt looked up at the stars and bent down to look for tire tracks. "To the right, Sam."

As Matt stood, a snarl from behind caused the hair on his neck to stand up. Some animal had come close.

Matt and Sam spun, and froze. Dark outlines with red eye glare slowly closed in on them.

They raised their rocks and yelled, but the creatures did not heed. As the pack moved in, their outlines become clearer.

Matt gripped his rock. *"What the fuck?"*

With precision, the creatures launched at the upper bodies of the two men. Claws dug deep into their backs, and razor-sharp teeth tore at the flesh on their faces. The brothers struggled to push the abominations off of them, but another pack closed in from behind and buried their teeth into the achilles of both men, quickly falling them.

Screams echoed through the canyons as the creatures tore at the assassins' flesh. The assault slowed as Matt and Sam's fight to live slowed.

The creatures stood and moved aside. As the two men labored for their final breaths, the pack's eyes widened and they cocked their heads, seemingly amused by the assassins' final moments.

The brush to the left parted, and the apparent leader of what Matt could only think of as cannibal dwarves walked towards he and his brother. The stocky creature had dark skin and a bloated belly. Long black hair framed a weathered face, from which blood-red eyes glowed eerily. He moved between the two dying men, looked to the heavens, raised his arms, and prayed in an ancient tongue.

He hunched slightly to look into Matt's eyes.

Matt's final gasps inhaled the pungent odor of the dwarf's breath.

The dwarf smiled. "Hiihooteet, Nih'o'o'3oo."

The cannibal leader moved his attention to Matt's brother.

Sam stared into the dwarf's crimson eyes, and with his final breath pushed out, "Fuck you... and Dorothy."

Again the dwarf smiled, whispered, "Hiihooteet, Nih"o'o'3oo," then turned and disappeared into the dense brush.

The pack dragged the assassins' lifeless bodies into the darkness.

PART TWO

TAKEN

CHAPTER 4
DELIVERY

"ABQ, this is Four X-Ray Tango, requesting decent to ten thousand feet. Over."

"Four X-Ray Tango, you are clear for decent. Will you be landing at ABQ or ranch? Over."

"ABQ, we will be landing at ranch. Over."

"Four X-Ray Tango, 10-4, you are clear to land at your discretion. There are reported strong crosswinds west to east off the mountains. Over."

"10-4, ABQ, thanks for the warning. Goodnight. Over."

Gibson began his decent towards the Triple Diamond Ranch. He pulled one ear of his head set to the side, and looked back into the cabin of the Gulfstream 200. "Rip, prepare the cargo for landing."

Rip responded with a thumbs-up. He stood and looked into the eyes of the eleven women shackled to their seats, most puffy and red from days of crying, some glazed and distant, and three, noticeably defiant.

"Ladies, welcome to your new life."

He moved from seat to seat adjusting each of their seat belts in preparation for landing.

"Triple Diamond Ranch, I'm ten minutes out. Over."

"10-4, Gibson, taxi to the normal spot. Over."

"Will do, Doc. Over."

Doc walked across the marble foyer to a set of ten-foot-tall mahogany doors, and knocked lightly.

"Come in," an authoritative voice answered.

"Mr. P, Gibson is on approach. He should be on the ground in fifteen minutes."

A small smile crossed the chiseled jawline of the stately man sitting behind the massive oak desk. "Very good, Doc, call me when the cargo is ready for inspection."

"Yes, sir, will do."

The doors closed behind Doc.

Mr. P unlocked a safe beneath his desk, retrieved a cell phone, and sent a group text:

> *Pheasants have arrived. We will hunt on Saturday. Cocktails served at seven on Friday.*

He stood, adjusted his bolo tie, and reached down to grab his black Stetson. He moved to the office powder room, looked in the mirror, adjusted his hat, and combed his grey beard.

He grabbed a putter and dropped a handful of balls on the office putting green to pass the time while awaiting Doc's call.

Gibson taxied the Gulfstream in front of the barn and killed the engines.

Rip exited the plane into the night chill, and walked towards the barn.

Doc met him half-way.

"Damn, Doc, it's cold tonight. Do you want the cargo sent to the guest quarters for prep, or straight to the barn?"

"Take them to their quarters and have them shower. I'd imagine several of them haven't bathed in a few days. Have them put on hospital gowns afterward."

"10-4, Doc." Rip turned back towards the plane.

"Hey, Rip, make it quick. The boss is waiting on my call."

Rip responded with a thumbs-up.

Gibson, who'd emerged from the cockpit to look in on the frightened women, turned as Rip entered.

"Doc wants them sent to quarters to shower and change before the boss comes down."

Gibson nodded. "10-4. Let's get them up." He turned his attention back to the women. "Ladies, we're going to remove your restraints.

When you exit the plane, please do not think about running. First, there is nothing but wilderness for miles. Second, it's twenty degrees out there, so you won't make it till morning dressed as you are. Third and foremost, you can't outrun a bullet." He paused and looked each woman in the eyes. "Nod your heads if you understand."

Sniffles filled the quiet cabin as bloodshot eyes and half-hearted nods responded.

"Good. Rip, please escort our guests to their quarters."

Mina White Eagle stepped from the plane into the cold night air. She turned to grasp the hand of her childhood friend, Kimimela Locklear.

As the two girls walked silently in the group, Mina replayed the events of the day like a waking dream.

> At noon, Kimi and her walked from class at the University of South Dakota to the dining hall. Two good-looking young men pulled up in a Mercedes Benz, rolled the window down, and identified themselves as members of an exclusive off-campus fraternity. The passenger invited them to a party at the frat house.
>
> Kimi instantly agreed, and rhe driver leaned over and asked them to hop in the car.
>
> Mina grabbed Kimi's hand, asking the two young men for a second with her friend. "Kimi, we don't know these boys. You just heard about the three missing girls from Sioux Falls."
>
> "Mina, they were hikers. Hikers go missing every day in the Badlands. Look at that car and those guys. Do they look like kidnappers? That fraternity is loaded with sons of doctors, lawyers, politicians, and very wealthy businessmen. Maybe we just met our way off of that fucking reservation!"
>
> "Kimi, this school is our way off the reservation, not finding rich men."
>
> Kimi smiled and brushed Mina's hair off her right shoulder. "My Mina, you're so beautiful, you will light that room up. C'mon, let's have some fun. That's what collage is all about. Pleasssssse...."

"Girls, we're holding up traffic. Are y'all comin?" the passenger said.

Mina took a deep breath, looked in Kimi's pleading eyes, then at the handsome guys in the car, and said, "Okay, let's do it."

The girls jumped in the back of the car. The smell of new leather and pot filled the cabin.

"Do you boys have any more of that weed?" Kimi said.

The driver looked back in his rearview mirror. "Sure do. Didn't know if girls as hot as you all got high."

Kimi chuckled. "We grew up on a reservation. I'm sure what you boy's have is nothing compared to the smoke we've had."

The passenger passed the girls a bowl, and they took several hits each.

The next thing Mina remembered was waking up in an open, generic room filled with a row of bunks. Her clothes were replaced by hospital scrubs, her hands were cuffed to iron bedposts, and someone had stuffed a gag in her mouth. She looked down the row of bunks and counted ten other women, all dressed and bound as she was.

After several hours, the group was taken from the room and loaded on the plane.

The captives left the tarmac and stepped onto a meticulously landscaped pathway. In the distance stood a large, contemporary house. A warm glow from two-story floor-to-ceiling windows gave the stately home and inviting approach. A lighted water fountain danced in the middle of the circular driveway.

Rip looked back at the group. "Ladies, welcome to your quarters."

Mina looked at Kimi, her brows drawn together.

Kimi shook her head.

The group approached the deep front porch that spanned the length of the house. Hand-carved rocking chairs accompanied by small tables formed intimate groupings scattered across the gleaming wood deck. Thick timber columns soared three stories to the roof line.

A neatly dressed gentleman stepped from the set of ten-foot entrance doors. "Welcome, ladies, please come in."

The group was led to the right of a massive stone fireplace in the middle of the slate foyer.

They entered a stately circular room appointed with two-story windows on its perimeter, through which moonlit, snowcapped mountains in the distance commanded attention. At the center of the room stood an impressive four-sided stone fireplace, and rich, brown leather couches and high-backed chairs were placed around the room.

To the left of the circular room's entrance stood an expansive wood and stone bar with seating for twenty, not counting several neatly placed four-top bistro tables.

The gentleman gestured towards the inviting leather couches. "Ladies, please be seated. I will have some refreshments sent out."

"Mina, what the fuck is this place?" Kimi whispered.

"I don't know."

Two women dressed in evening gowns entered the room carrying large silver serving trays. They said nothing as they stopped in front of each woman, offering bottles of sparkling water and an assortment of hors d'oeuvres. Several of the shaken, scared women shook their heads at the offer.

Shortly after the two servers retreated, a tall, blonde woman entered the room. She carried herself with the poise of a runway model, her black evening gown setting the backdrop for a stunning diamond necklace. Her enchanting good looks commanded the attention of the women.

"Ladies, I see several of you did not eat. I understand. I remember my first night here also. I know you're scared, confused, and wonder where you are and what is happening. I will answer these questions."

Mina gripped Kimi's hand tightly.

"My name is Jill. I came to this ranch ten years ago, the same way each of you did. Please, look around this room. If you haven't noticed, each of you possess a beauty that men, and some women, find alluring. That beauty is *why* you were chosen. Several of you will stay with me on this ranch, while the rest will embark on a journey to lands beyond your wildest imaginations. This journey will be filled with the finest clothes and jewelry, and living conditions only the wealthiest can afford. You will live in houses seen only in magazines, sail on yachts in exotic oceans, and relax on tropical beaches privy to *only* a select few in the world. Your part in this will be simple: satisfy the men and women that afford you this lifestyle."

"*We will be whores*?" a young brunette blurted out.

Jill smiled and took a sip of her champagne before answering.

"I hate that word. You will provide the same comfort to these people as you would your ten-dollar-an-hour husband. Instead of living in a single-wide trailer, sucking his cock, *grateful* for the meager security he provides, you will suck another man's cock while you look up at his hundred-thousand-dollar Rolex. Instead of your old man getting up off the coach when you're done, and offering you a beer from a dingy white refrigerator, your host will offer you a cocktail from his bar while you look over the teak rails of his yacht. So, you see, in a way, aren't we all whores?

"Now, possibly, for a few of you, this journey will be different. You will be called to serve a greater purpose. But, let's not put the cart before the horse, shall we? The next step in your new life will be to meet the gentleman that made all of this happen. I'm going to excuse myself for now. Peter will escort you to your quarters. You will shower, then put on the hospital gowns laying on your beds. This will be the last time you will dress in modest, common clothing. When you return from your meeting, each of your closets will be filled with a wardrobe from the finest designers in the world. Good evening, ladies."

"*The police will find us, you bitch. My father is retired FBI. I will be no one's whore*," the brunette shouted.

Jill paused, turned, smiled, and calmly walked in front of the brunette. Her piercing blue eyes glared at the defiant woman. "I like that fire. It turns me on. Maybe I'll have you sent to my room tonight, and I'll break you like a wild horse."

Jill moved to the center of the group, her eyes narrow and face stern.

"Ladies, let me assure you that *nobody* is coming to your rescue. We have provided our clients with a service for the past twelve years. One of our promises to them is that there will *never* be any threads connecting them to us. How we do that is simple: make sure we are never discovered. Let me put this into perspective."

She pointed at the brunette and two girls to her left.

"These young ladies were hiking in the Badlands. They were reported missing two days ago. An exhaustive search is taking place as we speak. It will produce nothing. A week will go by and their backpacks will be discovered on the Mexican border. Several days later, an anonymous tip from Brazil will send law enforcement on a wild goose chase. Eventually, the search will be abandoned. Several of you are from the Reservations. You have been reported missing by your families. Unfortunately, Native American women go missing every day. Most are never found and quickly presumed dead. Resources are not exhausted on a demographic that has no power or influence in the government's eyes."

Jill focused her attention on Mina and Kimi.

"These two ladies were abducted today from a university. It will be a day or two until they're reported missing by their parents, when cell phone calls are not answered. Their phones, clothes, and an empty liquor bottle will be located by the police at a remote area along the Missouri River. An extensive search will produce nothing. Case closed."

The statuesque blonde moved in front of the fiery brunette, bent down to glare into her tearing eyes, and placed her hand on the girl's trembling knee. "No, little girl, Daddy is not coming for you, or any of you. Accept your destiny. Embrace your new life."

Jill stood. "Peter, please take them to their rooms."

"Yes ma'am. Ladies, please follow me."

The eleven women followed Peter up a set of wide oak stairs to the second floor. He moved down a long hall, depositing each woman in a separate room.

Mina turned the door knob inside the spacious room. As she suspected, it was locked from the outside. She walked to the king-sized bed, lifted the hospital gown placed on the pillows, and threw it across the room. She crumbled face-first onto the bed, her sobs muffled by the thick down comforter. She briefly gathered herself and rolled over, stared at the ceiling for a moment, then panned around the opulent room.

"Ladies, please get in the showers. We will be assembling in twenty minutes," a female voice commanded over a speaker set in the left corner of the room.

Mina assumed there were hidden cameras to compliment the speaker system. She sprang up from the bed, raised both middle fingers, and between sobs yelled, "Fuck you! Fuck you!"

Numb, she shuffled to the bathroom. Gold fixtures adorned the double marble sinks. A smoked glass wall separated the walk-in stone shower from the dressing area.

She surveyed the bath for cameras, and reluctantly, she disrobed, covering herself and quickly slipping into the shower. Multiple heads sprung to life automatically, drenching her with a soft warm rain. She adjusted the digital temperature control six degrees up. For a moment, her world relaxed, as tense muscles released under the pulsation of the water. Her thoughts cleared, and she regained her composure.

"Ladies, ten minutes. Please finish," the speaker announced.

Mina took a deep breath, washed the shampoo from her long onyx hair, and allowed the soothing water to drench her for another minute before reaching for a towel outside the shower. She dried behind the privacy of the smoked glass, and wrapped the towel around her before moving to the well-appointed makeup area. She dried her hair, then looked down at the assortment of expensive makeup, choosing a light plum lipstick. She looked in the mirror to apply the lipstick, and stopped. "No, I'm not making myself look good for you bastards." She threw the lipstick to the table.

"One minute, ladies" the speaker announced. "Please dress in the hospital gowns provided, and assemble in the hall when you hear your doors unlock.

Mina slid her arms into the hospital gown before dropping the towel to the ground. She looked up at the speaker. "*No*, I'm not giving you pricks your cheap thrills."

When the door clicked, Mina exited and moved next to Kimi in the hall, and grasped her friend's hand.

Kimi looked at Mina as tears welled in both women's eyes. "Mina, I am *so* sorry. We should have *never* gone with those boys."

"Kimi, I could have stopped us, but didn't. We're here now. We'll figure this out. Just play along with these bastards for now."

Kimi dried her eyes and nodded.

Jill stepped onto the landing at the end of the hall. "Ladies, there are two limos waiting outside for us."

The captives followed Jill outside, and separated into two groups at the cars.

After a short drive, they arrived at a massive timber barn. The limos drove through the twenty-foot-tall double doors and stopped.

"Ladies, please exit and follow me," Jill directed.

The group walked across the dirt floor, turned left between two stables, and entered a finished area. Polished cement replaced the dirt, and a waist-high elevated stage ran the length of one wall. A full bar and small café tables filled the left side of the room.

Jill escorted the ladies to the stage and directed them to line up in a row.

The lights dimmed in the room as the stage brightened.

A brief silence was broken by the opening of a door. The thud of cowboy boot heels echoed through the room. The stage lights blinded the girls, only allowing them to see outlines of three men.

One of the outlines moved towards the stage, coming into the light.

"Ladies, welcome to your new life. Folks around her call me Doc Beanbag. While you stay with us, *anything* that is bothering you physically, I need to know about. Your health is important to our operation. Now, I'm going to do a quick physical exam. Please remove your hospital gowns."

The group of women paused, looking down the line at each other.

"Fuck you," a blonde-haired captive yelled as she broke ranks, jumping from the stage into the darkened room. She darted for the door the three men had entered from, and quickly disappeared into the darkness of the night.

Doc shook his head, calmly walking from the light of the stage. "Rip, turn on the compound lights and dull the stage lights."

Surrounding the door the blonde had run through was a floor-to-ceiling glass wall. The compound lights illuminated the night and the glass wall framed the outdoors like a movie screen.

The captives watched as the blonde created distance.

Doc slowly walked towards the door and into the compound. He drew a sidearm from under his lab coat, raised the pistol and fired. The large caliber gun echoed in the night as the blonde pulled her shoulders together, lurched forward, and crumbled to the ground.

Doc placed the side arm back into his holster and returned to the room.

Rip walked next to Doc and shook his head. "Damn, Doc, that was over a hundred yards. Gotta be a record."

"Yeah, Rip, she had some wheels. Make sure she's dead. You know what to do afterwards. Kill the compound lights, please."

The room echoed with sobs from the captives, many of which had crumbled to their knees.

Doc walked back on stage as the lights brightened on the girls. "Ladies, an unfortunate event, but I hope we have your attention now. Please, stand up and *drop your fucking hospital gowns!*"

One by one, the women disrobed, each covering themselves as best they could.

"Ladies, drop your arms or I will have them restrained," Doc ordered.

The captives stood fully exposed.

"Now, please turn and face the wall behind you, and bend over."

After thirty seconds in the compromising position, Doc directed the women to stand and face forward.

"Ladies, my name is Mr. P," a voice announced from one of the outlines in the center of the room. "I regret we had to start our business relationship with such a tragic event. By now, I have nearly ten-thousand dollars invested in each of you. Your peer's death cost me one hundred thousand dollars, and maybe much more. I *do not* like business losses. I think you see my patience is non-existent. Each of you has been hand-selected to join my operation. You will live in luxury. Gone is your life in rundown pueblos, college dorms, and meager apartments. The men and ladies you will entertain are the wealthiest one percent in the world. You will grow to love your new life, or... very simply, you will not have a life. Now, forget your preconceived notions of sex slavery and human trafficking. Those end in misery and death. Your life will be of privilege and longevity, should you choose so. Ladies, it's very simple: use the assets you were born with, and live; disappoint your hosts, and... well, you've seen the end results. Thank you, and welcome to your new life. Doc, please continue."

Doc pulled a pair of latex gloves and a tongue depressor from his lab coat. He moved in front of the first captive in line.

"Open wide, please, and say ahhh."

Doc placed both hands on the women's throat, examining her lymph nodes. Next he pressed down on her shoulders, examined her breasts, and listened to her heartbeat.

"Very good, now please place your legs at shoulder width."

Doc looked directly in the woman's eyes, gently inserted his finger between her legs, and moved deeper inside of her.

The woman tightened with his probing.

Doc shook his head and withdrew his finger. "Number One, no.

He changed his gloves and moved to the next captive, repeating the same exam and exclaiming, "Number Two, no."

Exams of the third and fourth women ended with the same, "No."

He stepped in front of Kimi.

She stared forward as he performed the beginning of the exam. When he pulled the latex gloves on and looked her in the eyes, she turned away as he entered her.

Doc paused for a second, withdrew his finger and smiled. "Number Four, yes."

He shuffled over to Mina and performed the initial exam, spending a bit more time on her ample breasts. Mina looked as if she would vomit at his touch.

The snap of the gloves seemed to sicken her further. Kimi kept a close watch, as if to protect her friend, though she knew she couldn't do much. The pupils in Doc's eyes dilated as he pushed his finger past a place where, Kimi knew from private discussions with Mina, no man had been before. Just as had been the case with Kimi.

"Number Five, yes."

Doc moved down the line, reporting all "No," until the last captive. He turned to face the mystery outlines in the room. "Number Ten, yes. That's three out of ten, Mr. P. The Client will be happy."

"Very good, Doc, have one of our new arrivals sent to your room. I will inform the Client. Have a good night, everyone."

Mr. P exited the room. The lights came up as the bright stage lights dimmed.

Jill walked down the line of women handing out tissues.

"Ladies, you can wipe yourselves and get dressed. There will be refreshments at the guest house. Have a good evening."

Jill walked up to Doc, reached through his lab coat, grabbed his semi-hard dick, and chuckled.

"Those exams get you horny, Doc. I remember my first one, then you choose me to relieve you. Which girl do you want?"

"I would love to have that dark-haired one with the big tits, Number Five."

"Doc, you know the rules—no virgins—but I'll tell you what, you take one of the others and I'll join you. How's that?"

Doc smiled. "That works for me. Do you have a preference which girl you want in that pretty mouth of yours?"

Jill looked at the women as they pulled their hospital gowns on.

"Hmmm, that brunette, Number Seven, gave me a little trouble earlier. Let's welcome her to the operation."

"Yeah, she has a nice tight ass. Good choice. See you in an hour?"

"An hour it is."

"Oh, Jill, tell our runner she did great. I loved the little death crawl at the end—nice touch, very convincing. Send her to the island for a long weekend."

"Doc, she's Sergio's favorite, and the only girl that can stomach fucking that fat sweaty pig. He's on the guest list this weekend. Are you sure Mr. P will be all right with that?"

"He'll be fine. Sergio paid for a new toy this weekend. He won't miss her."

CHAPTER 5
WELCOME TO OUR WORLD

Kelly leaned against the stone shower wall as pulsating water cleansed the indignity of the exam she and the other girls had endured. She closed her eyes and tilted her head up into the gentle cascade of the rain shower head. In the darkness, behind closed eyes, she couldn't run from the perverse look in Doc's eyes as he'd entered her. She backed away and crumbled to the shower seat, burying her head in trembling hands. The events of her capture two days ago, and now this perverse place, numbed her from head to toe.

She stepped from the shower and stood naked in front of the steamed mirrors. She wiped an area clean and looked herself in the eyes. *I'll play your sick games for now. I have no choice. But your ends are coming, you bastards."*

After drying, she opened the double doors of the master closet. Inside, double rows of designer clothes hung from three walls. The fourth wall was covered with six tiers of footwear. In the center, a seating area included a head-high, tri-fold mirror. She moved around the closet, pushing clothes aside to admire them. In the lingerie area, she selected a sapphire-colored, thigh-high silk teddy.

She moved to the sitting area in the suite, poured a glass of wine, and searched the channels for a feel-good movie. A light knock on the door broke her first moment of relaxation in several days.

"Who is it?

"It's Jill, are you decent?"

Kelly reached for a robe. "One second. Okay, come in."

Jill wiggled the door knob.

"Kelly, we reversed the locks. You'll need to let me in, please."

Kelly opened the door, and stepped aside as Jill entered.

Jill looked at the glass of wine and the television, and smiled. "I see you're settling in."

"I will *never* settle in here, and be part of your sick operation."

Jill walked up to Kelly and brushed her hair to the side. "Come with me. I want to show you something."

Jill led Kelly down a long hall, across a flying bridge to another wing of the house. She stopped at a window and pointed down at a Porsche convertible.

"That's mine. I get a new one every year. My parents believe I'm a successful business woman in Santa Fe. In a way, I guess I am."

"Your parents? You mean you applied for this job on your own? You can come and go as you please? What kind of woman takes part in this? What kind of soulless bitch are you?"

Jill chuckled. "No, I was brought here just like you. I realized quickly that there is no escape, and accepted my fate. I earned the trust of Mr. P and Doc, and within six months I reconnected with my family. Your circumstances are not as grave as you believe."

"I don't fucking understand. You said our belongings would be found in Brazil, leading to an eventual case closure!"

"And they will, but you and the other girls have several days before we start setting up your deaths. How you conduct yourselves in that timeframe will determine your futures."

Jill turned and continued to a set of double doors. She opened one side and looked back at Kelly. "Please, come in."

Hesitant, Kelly followed Jill through the double doors into an expansive suite three times the size of hers. The décor and layout rivaled the most expensive penthouses in New York City.

Kelly panned the room.

Jill saw the look in her eyes. "Not a bad payment for fulfilling the fantasies of the rich, huh? Like I said earlier, payment for whose cock you suck in life is a choice. I choose to be paid well for my work."

"But you're not giving me a choice. You *fucking* kidnapped me!"

"No, Kelly, you're wrong. Your choices start tonight," a male voice said from behind Kelly.

Startled, she turned to see Doc locking the doors.

Kelly's eyes darted back to Jill.

Jill approached Kelly, saying nothing, and released the bun, letting her blonde hair cascade across her shoulders. She opened the latch on her evening gown, allowing it to fall to the ground.

She noted that Kelly swallowed hard watching Jill's toned, sun-kissed body move gracefully across the room. The piercing gaze of her deep blue eyes forced Kelly to look away momentarily. Jill moved within arms' length, reached out and stroked the young woman's cheek. Her hand slid slowly down to Kelly's left shoulder as she moved behind the trembling captive.

Jill whispered, "Have you ever been with a woman?"

Kelly shook her head no.

Jill moved in front of her, and looked deep in her eyes while untying the terry cloth robe. Kelly stood motionless as Jill slid the robe off her shoulders then to the floor. Jill pulled closer, kissing Kelly softly on the lips while slipping the spaghetti straps of the silk teddy off her shoulders. She stepped back admiring Kelly's nakedness.

Doc approached the two women with a pipe. He lit the glass bowl, drew a deep hit, and passed it to Jill.

She drew a deep hit then exhaled the sweet-smelling smoke before passing on the pipe. "Kelly, this is an ancient mixture of herbs. It will open your mind."

Kelly drew from the pipe, and the smooth concoction warmed her lungs. A feeling of euphoria set in as she exhaled.

Jill led her to the bed, drew her in close, and passionately kissed her. Their breasts met. Jill looked down, grasped her tits and rubbed her hard nipples against Kelly's. A wave of disgust and excitement rushed through Kelly's body.

Doc joined the two women. He moved behind Kelly. His hard dick pressed against her lower back as he kissed the side of her neck.

The seduction repulsed her. She wanted it to stop but had no power over the inebriating smoke. Her inhibitions faded and lust coursed through her body.

"Lay back," Jill said.

Kelly set her head on the soft pillow. Jill straddled her at hip level, and Kelly locked her eyes on Jill's as the seductress slowly grinded pubic bone to pubic bone. Kelly's stomach tightened, she let out a small moan, clenched the sheets and closed her eyes.

The balance between dreams and reality teetered. In a realm void of *all* taboos, Kelly moved fluidly with Jill and Doc in a well-choreographed erotic dance.

Seconds became minutes, minutes became hours. Finally, the unnatural staying power of the drug began to wear off. One by one, each collapsed to the bed panting and exhausted.

Jill gazed into Kelly's eyes again and quickly mounted her. Her piercing deep blue eyes were replaced by dark black pupils, her countenance both demonic and angelic. Kelly, terrified, struggled to move from under Jill, but the entity pinned her arms down with a supernatural grip, as if she had been restrained to the bed.

Kelly closed her eyes as the abomination leaned in, pulled her lower jaw down, and slipped its scorching tongue to the back of Kelly's throat. She jerked her head to the side, gagging.

Jill's and Doc's laughter echoed in Kelly's head.

She opened her eyes. Jill looked normal.

Jill pulled a bed sheet up and wiped sweat from her drenched body. "Welcome to our world, Kelly. You performed well."

The duo crawled next to Kelly, intertwining themselves with her. The effects of the smoke and the intense sex had taken a toll on the three, and they slowly drifted off.

The early morning sun pierced Jill's room. Kelly opened her eyes, hoping last night had been a dream, but reality quickly set in as Jill's breath heated her shoulder. She looked over the human spider web entangling her. She moved Doc's leg and dick off her waist, and Jill's arm from across her chest, and sat up.

"Where are you taking that hot ass of yours?" Jill muttered through a slight smile.

"I need to use the bathroom and take a shower."

"You can use mine if you like. I can have coffee and breakfast sent to us as you shower. Doc and I are going horseback riding today. Care to join us?"

Kelly forced as smile. "No, a lot has happened. I need to process this and check on my friends."

"As you wish. Share with them what we discussed. Let them know they will seal their own fate. We really aren't monsters. Our world is just a bit different. You'll see over the next several days. Last night you made the right choice. You've earned the freedom to move about the ranch at your will. Enjoy its amenities."

"Choice? *What fucking choice did I have*? You two drugged me and raped me."

Jill reached over to grab a remote from her bedside table. A large screen TV facing the bed turned on. "Does this look like rape?"

Last night played back on the screen, resembling a high-quality porn movie. Kelly's stomach twisted, as details clouded by the intoxicating smoke became clearer. As the tape neared its end, anxiety set in as she remembered the demonic morphing of Jill. She watched closely. The final scene of the encounter was Kelly asking if, '*they could fuck in the morning.*' There was no recording of Jill's transformation. She lowered her head for several moments.

Doc was awoken by the movie. "I'm ready if you two are," he said, stroking his hard cock.

Kelly looked at him and turned away repulsed.

Jill said, "No, Doc, she's had enough."

Kelly crawled out of bed, grabbed her teddy, threw her robe on, and left the room.

PART THREE

COMPARING NOTES

CHAPTER 6
MORE QUESTIONS THAN ANSWERS

Honi let out a faint whimper and nudged Jake's elbow.

Jake opened his eyes to find Honi starring at him from three inches away. "What, boy, do you need to go out?"

Dakota stirred under the bear fur blanket, groggily asking, "What time is it?"

"The sun is just starting to come up, probably around six-thirty."

"Ughh," she said, pulling the bedding over her head.

Jake opened the cabin door and followed Honi outside. The Sun crested the mountain tops, turning wispy clouds a brilliant orange against deep blue skies. He took a deep breath of the mountain air before returning inside and starting the coffee.

"Hey, sleepy head, we need to get around and head down to the ranch."

Beneath the fur blanket, Dakota mumbled, "I know. Why don't you crawl back under here with me for a few minutes?"

"Nah, I'll pass. I need some coffee."

"Jake Michaels, you better be kidding and get your ass underneath these blankets."

Jake crept up on her and ripped the blankets down, dangling his semi-hard dick inches from her face.

She reached up and stroked him several times. "Well, I see *he* didn't need coffee."

Jake crawled on top of her and pulled the covers over them.

Dakota positioned his cock and pulled him inside of her.

Jake arched his back in response, burying himself deeper. "Wow, so much for foreplay. I guess the honeymoon is over."

"We don't have time. Now stop talking."

He thrusted deeper, quicker, and harder.

Dakota responded with shallow pants and increasingly louder moans.

Honi raced through the open cabin door and slid sideways across the wood floor, then gained his footing and jumped into the bed.

Jake lay down on Dakota, pulling the blankets over their heads. "Honi, *no,* go away."

The wolf crawled on Jake's back, pressed his cold nose under the blankets and nudged Dakota's cheek.

"Oh my God, his nose is freezing," Dakota blurted out between laughs. "Jake, just finish. I lost my concentration."

Jake tried to raise his hips against the wolf's weight and started laughing. "He's too heavy. I can't move." He rolled to the side, allowing Honi to fall between them.

The wolf rolled on his back and wagged his tail.

"Thanks, Honi, now Daddy is gonna have blue balls all day." He turned to Dakota. "Well, are you ready for some coffee now?"

Dakota rubbed Honi's belly. "Yeah, I guess we have no choice." She played with the wolf for a few minutes, watching Jake's ass move around while he made the coffee. "C'mon, boy, let's get up."

She rolled out of bed, walked up behind Jake, reached around and grabbed his limp dick.

She looked back. "Honi, birds outside."

Honi shot off the bed and darted into the meadow barking.

Dakota raced to the door and shut it behind him, then sat at the table. "Bring him over here. I can't have my man walking around with blue balls."

Jake did as instructed, smiled, and looked down at her. "Special cream for your coffee, Ma'am?"

She looked up, rolled her eyes, and pulled Jake from her mouth. "Do you want me to call Honi back in?"

The two finished their morning tryst and prepared for the trip to the ranch.

Jim walked downstairs to find Jay and Anna sitting at the table having coffee.

"Good morning, old man, sleep well?" Jay said.

"Like a log. You got up early."

"I smelled the coffee and Anna's cinnamon buns baking. I could not resist."

Jim walked past Jay, patting him on the shoulder before kissing Anna on the cheek.

"What do you two have planned today?" Anna said.

"We are going to head to the cabin and see Jake and Dakota. Jay wants to fish."

Anna rolled her eyes. "They have been through a lot. Perhaps they would not appreciate the company."

Jim shrugged. "I have papers Dakota needs to sign regarding her petition to the Bar for exoneration. They are time sensitive."

Anna nodded. "What do you think, Jim? Will they give her a pass?"

"I believe so. I have made some calls."

Jay looked down while stirring his coffee. "I still cannot believe that whole case. Jake Michaels was willing to give up his freedom to keep Dakota's secret. He is a good soldier, and a good man."

Anna said, "He saved our Lomasi and fell in love with her, but I am surprised Jake did not return to his wife and family once the truth was exposed. I am sure Dakota insisted on it, despite her own feelings for him."

Jay paused and looked up at Anna. "I saw things the day we arrested him. There is more to this story. It is not over, Anna."

"Do you think he has more secrets? What did you see?"

Jay shook his head. "No, we have seen Jake Michael's story. It goes beyond him and Dakota, beyond all of us. I saw the Ancients in the forest."

Anna sighed. "Jay Storm Walker, you sound like my father now."

Jim chuckled. "We need to get going. Anna we should be back by nightfall. I love you."

Anna said, "Well, take your time or stay up there tonight. I think I'll go to town and spend a night with Father."

Jim hugged his wife and walked out the door.

Jay stepped in front of Anna. "Thank you for the hospitality. It was nice to spend a few days with Jim and you. It has been a while since we did this."

"Jay, you are always welcome, you know that. You two be careful riding out there."

Jay hugged her and smiled. "I will bring that old man home tonight."

Jake glanced at his watch, then the sky. "Eight o'clock, looks like great weather. We should be at the ranch by noon or so. Are you ready?"

"Let's do it," Dakota said.

Jake threw his leg over the quad, reached out to help Dakota on board, and started the engine.

The back of the quad dipped suddenly. Jake and Dakota looked back to see Honi standing on the trailer.

"I guess we didn't have to ask him," Jake said.

Dakota wrapped her arms around Jake. "Forward, Captain."

The trio moved at a comfortable pace, taking time to admire the flaming fall foliage. Each canyon presented its own unique post card beauty, and every turn dazzled the senses. The aspens had reached their peak, painting the mountains with rushes of brilliant gold beneath the deepest of blue skies.

Dakota snapped picture after picture. "No matter how many falls I've seen out here, they never get old. Each one is unique in its own hues."

Jake nodded and turned his head. "It's my favorite time of the year. Up ahead, we'll pull over and take a pic of Buffalo Canyon. It should be on fire."

He pulled the quad over and killed the engine. The two dismounted slowly, groaning as they moved their tight muscles. They stretched briefly, then made the short walk to the edge of the canyon rim.

Honi froze, his ears perked as he lifted his nose into the west wind.

"What is it, boy?" Jake paused, looking in the same direction. "Do you hear that, Dakota? It sounds like quad engines."

Dakota listened intently. "I do hear that. Let's get back to the quad and grab the rifle."

The three dashed to the quad. Jake knelt behind it, resting the rifle across the seat and steadying the scope on the trail ahead. "Dakota, grab my pistol and take Honi into the brush."

"Do you think Dibella sent more hitmen already?"

"I don't know. I sent a confirmation text, but maybe they were alerted when the last one didn't show up at a pickup point? Doesn't matter, I have a dead bead on the trail ahead. They won't make it far. Tuck in. They're getting closer."

Jake slowed his breathing as the sound of the engines drew closer, clicked the safety off, pulled the gun tight to his shoulder, and looked through the scope. He caught a glimpse of two quads through the trees as they made the last turn before facing him head on.

As the targets became clear, Jake squinted, lowered his gun and stood up. "It's okay, you guys can come out. It's your grandfather and Jay."

Dakota walked to the trail with Honi at her side. "I wonder what they're doing up here. I hope Neiwoo is all right."

Jim pointed to the trio ahead, and Jay nodded his head. They accelerated, closing in on Jake and Dakota.

Dakota walked forward to greet them. "Woo Woo, Jay, is everything all right with Neiwoo?"

They stopped their quads and dismounted. Jim hugged her. "Your grandmother is fine. Why are you heading to the ranch?"

Jake walked up and reached his hand out. "Colonel, Jay, we had some trouble at the cabin. We were heading down to warn you."

Jim glanced at Jay, then back. "We too had a problem, and were coming out to do the same."

Jake said, "Dibella's men?"

"Two of them, well-trained spooks," Jay interjected.

Jake nodded. "He sent one our way. We're closer to the cabin than the ranch, so should we head back there and discuss the details?"

"Woo Woo, what do you think this is about?"

"I do not know, Lomasi. We will compare notes."

"Do you think we should head back to the ranch instead, so Neiwoo isn't by herself?"

Jim shook his head. "I told her we were heading up here. She decided to spend the night in town with Samuel. She will be fine there."

Dakota's face relaxed. "Does she know about anything?"

"No, just that your great grandfather had a vision of trouble heading my way. When I returned without reporting any incidence, she dismissed it, as normal."

"A vision? What kind of vision, Woo Woo?"

"Let's get back to the cabin, and we can discuss all of this," Jake suggested.

The group agreed and mounted their quads.

Jay pulled his quad up to the cabin's hitching post, killed the engine, and looked at Jake and Dakota. "Different circumstances since my last visit out here."

Jake smiled and nodded. "Yeah, maybe one day you can come out just to relax. Last time, you arrested me for killing a Dibella, and now a Dibella is trying to kill me... hell... and you."

Jay shook his head. "They were after Jim. I would have just been collateral damage."

Jake threw his leg over the quad tank, dismounted, and helped Dakota off. "Well, gents, we should compare notes. Let's go inside."

The group assembled around the kitchen table. Jake moved the small radio in the middle of the table.

"Does that work well out here, Jake?"

"Not bad, Colonel. It picks up the local station in town. I use it mainly for weather and news. Speaking of weather, there's a chance for an early fall storm overnight, maybe a few inches up here."

"Winter comes early." Jim looked at his watch. "The weather should be coming up in fifteen minutes. Let's hear what they say."

"Yes sir." Jake switched the radio on and set the volume just loud enough to hear during conversation.

"Would anyone like some coffee?" Dakota said.

Jim removed his hat and settled back in the old wood dining chair. "That would be great, Lomasi, thank you."

"Yes, please," Jay said.

"Dakota, do you want me to do that? I think I have the hang of it now."

"Jake, really...."

Jake laughed. "Be forewarned, gents, we're still trying to master the percolator thing. It's not Starbucks."

"Hell, nothing can be worse than field coffee," Jay joked.

"Some of the worst," Jim agreed. "Jake, do you have a scratch pad?"

"I do, sir. Let me grab it."

Jake set the lined yellow tablet and pen in front of Jim.

Jim drew a vertical line dividing the page in half. He headed one half, '*Ranch,*' the other half, '*Cabin.*'

"Jake, tell me about the one sent here."

Jake retrieved the assassin's rifle from under his cot and laid it across the table. "He was ex- military, Colonel. His vantage point, the way he laid, and his weapon, all points to one of us."

Jay examined the rifle. "SOCOM MK-12 Mod 5, 300 Win Mag. Most likely ex-SEAL."

Jim nodded. "How old would you say he was, Jake? Did he have any service tattoos or distinguishing marks?"

"Maybe mid-thirties. He was in full camo, and honestly, I interrogated and eliminated with extreme prejudice. I couldn't tell you if he had ink or not."

A slight smile on Jim's face accompanied a quick nod. "I understand. Where is the body?"

"In the old mine shaft atop the falls."

"Well, so much for us or anyone ever seeing that body again," Jay added.

"How did you know he was up there?"

Jake glanced at Dakota, then fixed his eyes on Jim. "A vision, Colonel."

Jim looked at Jay, who responded with raised eyebrows.

"What kind of vision?"

"I drifted off to sleep and dreamed Dakota and I were at the falls. A scope glare from atop the rocks warned me, but it was too late. He killed both of us, and Honi too."

"So, you woke and took care of business?" Jay said.

"Yes, and the dream was spot-on about where he laid in wait."

Jim paused for several seconds before scribbling some notes, then looked at Jay and took a deep breath. "We too were alerted by a vision. Samuel called and warned of two white men at the gate that were sent to kill me. Given past events, I paid a bit more attention to him this time. I had planned to head there and pick up some trash. Fortunately, Jay was visiting and joined me."

"Woo Woo," Dakota said, her nerves clearly frayed. "Would they be so brazen to shoot you on the lane in broad daylight? There are too many hikers and fishermen traveling that road right now."

Jim shook his head. "Their intent was not to shoot me. Samuel warned me not to shake their hands. The one assassin insisted I do so." Jim reached into his shirt pocket, pulled out a ring box, and opened the top. He placed it on the table. "Careful, do not touch it. After Jay and I subdued them, we found one of them wearing this. He insisted I shake his hand. Look at the small needle and chamber in it. We assume the liquid inside is poison, most likely to mimic a death by natural causes."

"Professionals, Colonel, just like our guy?"

"Yes, but these guys did not carry themselves like prior military, more so like spooks," Jay said.

"I assume you eliminated the risks?" Jake said.

"We let them go after a *convincing* interrogation. I am confident they are not dumb enough to return, or even to warn Dibella. We got their confirmation message and sent it. Dibella believes we are dead."

Jake stared at the assassin's ring. "If they're loyal, they may report a failed mission to Dibella. This could turn into a war."

"No, Jake," Jay said. "They will never be seen again. The canyons can be a dangerous place at night." His tone was steady and confident.

Dakota huffed in exasperation. "I just don't get why he would attempt this right after the trial. It would be *so* obvious."

Jay nodded. "Your grandfather and I talked about that last night, before knowing of the attempt on your lives. It would appear reckless if all three of you suddenly came up deceased. Jim dying of natural causes would be overlooked. Now, given the attempt on your lives, it seems sloppy — not a move Dibella would make."

The group paused and reflected on Jay's comments.

The silence was broken by a news alert coming from Jake's radio.

"We are saddened to report that the body of District Attorney Joe Ross has been recovered from a remote section of Whiskey Gorge. Ross was reported missing late last night. It appears the DA lost control of his motorcycle and he and the bike were thrown over the guardrails into the deep gorge. More information will be reported as they come available. Again, DA Joe Ross is confirmed dead."

"Oh... my... God! His poor kids. They're young," Dakota said with no small bit of anger.

Jim shook his head. "I did not care much for him, but he did not deserve that. He had a bright future."

"He was a good DA," Jay added. "He just needed to stay focused on Wind River and not his own agenda. I saw a different side of him after the trial, after dealing with that asshole Sellman. I believe he may have seen the ghost of his future, and it woke him up."

Jake starred downward and said nothing. After several seconds, he pounded on the table. "Son of a bitch! That bastard had him offed, also."

Dakota moved from the kitchen to Jake's side. "I don't understand. What are you thinking?"

He looked up. "Think about it. If we turn up dead, all eyes point to Dibella. The D.A. turns up dead at the same time, the attention deflects from him. Jim's death would have been reported as natural causes, most likely due to the stress of the trial. They would have never found our bodies. I'm sure the hitman would have made it appear, here in the cabin, that we simply moved off the grid. The press would spin it as a chain of unfortunate deaths in Indian Country and painted you and I as anti-establishment. Case closed."

Jim nodded. "Joe knew about South America. He was present when I threatened Sellman during the trial. I am sure Dibella was made aware of that. His hitmen said the reason they were sent here was our knowledge of South America. With all of us gone, his secrets below the border would stay hushed."

Jay rocked back in his chair. His eyes tightened. "This is too simple. There is more... *much* more."

"What are you thinking?" Jim asked.

"You have known me a long time." He paused. "Something does not feel right. It has not felt right since I escorted Jake off this mountain."

Dakota placed her hand on his shoulder. "Uncle Jay, what do you mean?"

"Spirits, Dakota, powerful enough to stir the Ancient ones. I saw them in the burial grounds behind the cabin, the day we arrested Jake. I heard their language when Jake drifted into their world at the jail. *You* did also, but you did not realize it."

Silence fell over the group as a haunting blues song filled the cabin. Jake reached over to the radio and turned it off. "Well, what's our next step?"

Jim snapped the ring box shut. "Our ghosts pay a visit to Dibella. We end this."

PART FOUR

THE SEARCH

CHAPTER 7
THE MISSING

Margaret White Eagle woke from a splintered night's sleep. She held up the phone she'd grasped all night, and adjusted her eyes to the morning light. There were no answers to any of her texts or voicemails since yesterday afternoon. It was not like her daughter Mina to ignore her. Texts from Mina's twin sister, Winona, reported no response either, an alarming development as the two sisters had made plans to spend the weekend together.

She rolled over and looked at the picture of her husband Robert on the far nightstand. Tears filled her eyes as she gently rubbed his unwrinkled side of the bed. "Something is wrong with our Mina, my love. I wish you were here. I can't face losing her and you in the same year."

Margaret stared deep into the eyes of her late husband's picture. Visions of his last breath and final words, "*I will watch over you and the girls from above... thank you for sharing your life with me,*" opened a well of tears, quickly soaking her pillow.

Her phone rang. She dried her eyes and drew a deep breath, fighting back sniffles. "Winona, have you heard from her?"

"No, Mom, no answer to calls or texts. I'm on my way over. We need to go see Billy at the Vermillion Police Department."

"Should we not start with our Tribal Police?"

"No, I have a bad feeling. I think we need to eliminate as much red tape as possible right now. Let's talk to Billy, and then we can alert the Tribal police. I'll be there in twenty minutes. Love you."

Margaret rushed a shower and a cup of coffee, knowing Winona would be punctual, a trait she got from her dad. As she finished drying her hair, a knock came at the front door.

"Come in, honey, it's unlocked," she yelled from the bathroom.

"Margaret," a male voice called out.

The unexpected deep voice startled her. She walked from the bathroom and looked through the peephole. "Joseph, you startled me. I was expecting Winona."

"I know. She's at the car talking to Susan. She called us on her way over and asked if we had heard from Kimi. Susan and I didn't give it much thought until Winona called. You know Kimi has always been more a free spirit and independent. We speak with her only a few times a week."

"Joe, something doesn't feel right. Mina *never* loses contact with us. We chat every morning or evening."

"Winona said you were going to Vermillion. Susan and I will join you if that's all right? We can drive my car."

"That sounds good. I'm almost ready. I'll be right out. There's fresh coffee if either of you would like some?"

"Thank you, but we stopped on our way over. I'll see you in the car."

The four-hour drive to Vermillion passed slowly. Anxiety beset the two families as the hours passed with no contact from the girls.

Winona reached for her phone. "We're about ten minutes out. I'm going to let Billy know we're close." She hit redial. "Hey, you, we're ten minutes out. Should we meet at the station?"

Billy said, "Yeah, I'll meet you in the lobby. Text me when you're out front. Have you heard anything?"

Winona's tone changed. "Nothing, Billy, from either Mina or Kimi."

"Okay, we'll talk when you get here."

Margaret shook her head. "This *is not* like her."

Winona placed her hand on her mom's. "Maybe Kimi and her went hiking and they're out of cell range. Don't let your imagination get to you. We *will* find them."

Silence fell on the car for the last several miles of the trip.

As Robert pulled in front of the Vermillion Police Station, Billy stood on the stairs waiting.

Winona jumped ahead of the group, greeting Billy with a familiar hug. She pulled away and looked him in the eyes. "Hey, how have you been?"

Billy's face softened and his sky-blue eyes locked on her. "I've been good, Nona. I've missed you."

She smiled. "I know, Billy, me too."

He broke his gaze and looked over her shoulder. "How is your mom doing?"

"She has her days since Dad passed, and *this* is not what she needs."

He wiped a single tear streaking down her cheek. "We'll find her."

Billy moved around Winona to greet Margaret as she reached the top of the stairs. He opened his arms and hugged her without saying a word.

Margaret held him tight for a second before stepping back. She blotted her eyes and sniffled. "Billy, I can't lose her."

He took a deep breath and fought back a rush of emotions. "We *will* find her, I promise."

Billy looked over her shoulder to see Joe and Susan walking slowly up the stairs. They joined the two on the landing and flanked Margaret.

Joe reached his hand out. "How have you been, son?"

"I'm good, Mr. Locklear."

Billy broke his grip and slid over to hug Susan.

"Billy Kellerman, you look more and more like your dad every day. He was a good man and a fine officer. I trust he taught you everything he knew, and you *will* bring Kimi and Mina home."

"Mrs. Locklear, it's early in the case, not even twenty-four hours since Mina's last text. We will find them." He pulled back from the group. "Let's go inside."

The group followed Billy through the lobby and down a short hall to his office.

He opened the door wide to a small but comfortable room that was laid out efficiently. A dark oak desk sat in front of a double window adorned with southwestern print curtains. To the left sat a small leather couch and a mini refrigerator topped with a Keurig. To the right, a three-tier book case dominated the wall, its shelves filled with books and personal affects, the most prominent being a picture of Billy and Winona set against a mountain backdrop.

"Please, come in and make yourself comfortable. Can I get anyone a bottle of water or cup of coffee?"

He watched Winona's eyes as she entered. They darted to the picture on the bookshelf. She paused her gaze on it, then back to Billy. He smiled lightly and she returned a slow blink and slight nod. "Water would be great," she said.

"Yes, water, thank you," the rest of the group responded.

Billy retrieved five waters as the group settled in. Margaret and Winona pulled two office chairs close to the front of the desk. Mr. and Mrs. Locklear sunk into the leather couch.

Billy situated a legal pad in front of him. Notes from his earlier conversation with Nona filled half the sheet.

"Mr. and Mrs. Locklear, when was the last time you heard from Kimi?"

"She texted both of us Monday night," Joseph replied, "saying her science test went well and she was exhausted. She said she would call us this Friday."

Billy jotted notes. "Okay, so it's going on three days." He paused and said, "Margaret, Nona forwarded me a picture Mina took yesterday around 10 AM of her and Kimi. That was the last thing you received from her, correct?"

"Yes."

He nodded, then concentrated his stare on the note pad. "I took the liberty of running a track on both of the girls' phones. I'm waiting for a report. We should have it shortly. That may give us some idea the direction they traveled after they sent that picture."

Margaret said, "What do you think, Billy? The news of those three hikers that disappeared in the Badlands is all over the news. They've been gone for almost a week now. Could this be related to Mina and Kimi?"

"Honestly, Margaret, I don't know. The one girl's dad is a retired FBI agent, and they have a massive search going on. So far, I've heard they don't have a single clue except the girls' last known campsite. As we all know, the Badlands are vast and dangerous."

Joseph interjected. "I remember your dad doing a search out there for the Reynolds girl twenty years ago. After two weeks, they found her.

"Yeah, she was lucky. Dad was a great tracker."

A knock at the door interrupted the conversation.

Billy looked towards the door. "Come in."

A female officer entered and reached out with a folder towards Billy. "Sergeant, I have the report you requested."

"Thank you, Kelly."

Billy examined the first page of the report, then rifled through the remaining eight pages before setting it on the desk. He fixed his eyes on Nona and, after a brief pause, panned the room. "The report shows both of their phones went dead just outside of town at approximately the same time. They were traveling west."

Margaret shook her head. "I don't understand, Billy. What does that mean?"

Billy hesitated for a moment, knowing his words would be difficult for both families. "One of two things—either catastrophic failure due to damage, or the batteries simply ran out. Based on the time of the last signals being shortly after noon, and within seconds of each other... I would have to believe the phones were destroyed."

"As in destroyed to end their tracks?" Nona spoke in a quiet monotone and fixed her stare on the folder.

Margaret broke down. "*Nooo*, not Mina, *not* Mina."

Nona looked up at Billy and her eyes glassed over. She shook her head and lipped, "*No.*"

Billy stood. "I am ordering a cruiser to the last known position of the phones. I'll join them on scene. Please feel free to stay in here as long as you need. Nona, I'll call you as soon as I know something. Mr. and Mrs. Locklear, I will contact you separately if you're all not still together." He grabbed his sports coat, hurried towards the door, and paused to look back over his shoulder. "I *will* find the girls. I promise."

Detective Blake Roberts stood on a sharply eroded butte towering above the sprawling grasslands of the Badlands National Park. He panned the vastness with his binoculars, dropped them to his chest and shook his head. "Two hundred thousand fucking acres! It's like finding a needle in the haystack, Joe."

Joe Running Horse pulled his binoculars down. "One week, Blake, and not a single trace of those girls. It's like the earth swallowed them up."

Blake took a deep breath and forcefully exhaled, rattling his lips. "Let's head back to base camp. The skies look angry."

The two men traversed the butte and returned to their Jeep. They loaded their gear and paused before jumping in the vehicle.

Blake lit a cigarette. "I don't get it, man. Their hiking partners said the girls prepared packs for a short hike. They alerted us shortly after sunset when the girls didn't return. We had a search party on scene within one hour. The most they could have traveled in this terrain was eight, maybe nine miles. Our search has scrubbed a thirty-mile radius now, and not a single friggin' shred of evidence."

Joe shook his head. "We've worked hundreds of cases out here, and never seen a trail go dry so quickly, especially in such a populated part of the park. It makes no sense."

"Joe, maybe these girls aren't in the park."

"What are you thinking?"

"I don't know, man. Maybe they were yanked from here?"

Joe nodded. "I thought about that, but three girls at one time? It seems like a stretch."

"I know, but hell, we've combed this place for a week, morning, noon, and fucking night. They're... not... here."

"Do you want to call off the search?"

Blake drew a deep drag from his cigarette. "Hell, you know that's not my call. Kelly Johnson's father is running this. He's used every resource his political pull can muster. Hell, we even have the Governor up our ass."

Joe tossed the last of his gear in the Jeep. "Thirty years in the FBI buys you a lot of clout. Perhaps we need to convince him to move his resources in a different direction."

Blake looked west at swirling ominous black clouds. "Let's head back, partner, before that shit gets here."

The two arrived at the search camp to find it abuzz with law enforcement agents from multiple branches of the government. One large tent and three smaller ones formed the command center, while press trucks and a sea of reporters circled the perimeter. The whine of two helicopter engines starting up capped the organized chaos.

Blake maneuvered the Jeep through the press line and parked in front of the main tent. "This place looks like a fucking military base. Jesus."

The two officers entered the main tent and approached a long table covered with topo maps and three men hunched over studying them. Blake said, "Captain."

The three men looked over their shoulders then turned.

"Blake, Joe, give us some good news," Captain Hollis said.

Blake shook his head. "Nothing, sir."

Mike Johnson approached Blake. "Detective, we've decided to move the search to the canyons. We have a hundred National Guard troops on their way."

"Mr. Johnson, we've flown hundreds of hours through those canyons. In all do respect, sir, I think we are wasting our resources."

"*Wasting, Detective?* There is no *fucking wasting* when it comes to my daughter and those two girls." Johnson's elevated voice drew the attention of the tent.

Blake's face blazed hot and he stepped back. "Captain, can I speak with you for a moment, please?"

"Roberts, if you have something to say, you can say it right here," Johnson barked.

Blake snapped back, "Mr. Johnson, I understand you're upset, but let me *fucking* make this clear. This is *my fucking jurisdiction*. Joe and I know the Badlands as well as anyone. Very well, you want to hear what I have to say? Those girls *are not here!*"

A hush fell across the tent as Johnson glared at Blake.

"Blake, what are you saying," Captain Hollis said.

"I'm saying, Captain, these girls have been taken from here."

Johnson's brow crinkled, and his tone softened. "Detective, what proof do you have of this?"

"I have no hard proof other than the fact we have not found one shred of evidence these girls are still here. It's as if they've simply disappeared, and we know that's impossible."

The group of men looked at each other.

"Joe, what are your thoughts?"

"Captain, I'm with Blake. If we would have found *something* in the past week, I would agree to keep searching here. We expanded the search radius by a factor of four, and found not even one trace of *anything*...."

Johnson shook his head. "Gentlemen, we're talking about three very smart, athletic girls. I find it hard to believe, first, that they would put themselves in a position to be abducted. Second, in my experience, abductions are normally singular, maybe a double, but three girls at one time? And let's not forget Cindy was here training for an upcoming mixed martial arts fight. She can handle herself. In fact, all the girls have some self-defense training."

Blake said, "Mr. Johnson, this does not mitigate the fact that they are still twenty-something-year-old females who can make poor choices, and a gun wipes out any self-defense training they have. And to repeat Joe's point: not even one trace of anything."

Johnson's head drooped, and his voice turned stoic. "Where would we begin?"

Blake glanced at the pictures of the three girls pinned to a white board riddled with colored dots, time lines, and search coordinates. "Honestly, a week has passed. These girls could be anywhere. My guess is, given their physical attributes, they were targeted by traffickers, most likely cartel. South America would be my focus."

Johnson turned his attention to Captain Hollis. "What do you think?"

Hollis glanced at Blake. "I believe it would be wise to start looking in another direction."

"Okay, Detective, I'll contact the State Department and have them reach out to our friends in Brazil and Venezuela. But, if no one objects, I would still like to have the Guard sweep the canyons. It will make my wife and the other parents feel better, and maybe the press coverage will lower the guard of the kidnappers."

Blake glanced at Captain Hollis, who nodded in return. "10-4. Joe and I will coordinate the search with the Guard while you talk with Washington. And Mr. Johnson, I want to bring those girls home also, but sometimes we get too close to a situation, and have blinders on."

Johnson sighed but held his tongue.

Billy drove up to the search crew in a wooded area just outside of town. He jumped from his cruiser and was greeted by Sergeant Ray Simmons. "Ray, anything yet?"

"Nothing, Billy, but we just got the dogs on site. We swept the ditch, and now we're heading into the pines. Normally, the ping is pretty tight. We should find something within a few hundred yards."

"10-4, let's hop in there."

The two men moved slowly though the carpet of fallen pine needles.

Ray said, "How is Nona?"

"Shaken up, man, but I worry about her mom. First Nona's dad, and now this... I'm not sure how much she can handle."

"Well, hopefully they turn up soon. One of the favorite swimming and party spots is just through the woods. Maybe they got fucked-up last night, dropped their phones, and are passed out down there. Wouldn't be the first time, as you know. These college kids get away from home and go nuts."

"I know, Ray, but not Mina. She's pretty straight-laced. Now Kimi, that's a different story, but Mina keeps her grounded."

A voice called through the pines. "Hey, Sarge, over here."

Billy and Ray rushed to one of the canine handlers.

"Skip, whatcha got?" Billy said.

Skip pointed to a disrupted pile of pine needles off the nose of the tracking hound. "Two cell phones, Billy."

Billy and Ray carefully removed them from beneath the pine needles.

"Are they the girls', Billy?"

Billy dropped his head. "They match the description. The batteries are gone. Let's get them back to the families for identification. We'll have the lab charge them up to make sure. I don't like this, Ray. Have the search party work their way to the river."

CHAPTER 8
THE INNOCENT

Mina opened her eyes and prayed the past twenty-four hours had been a bad dream. The high noon sun shined through the clerestory above the patio doors. She rolled from bed and shuffled to the patio doors, wiping the sleep from her eyes, then slid the curtains open and walked onto the oversized patio. Breathtaking views of snow-capped mountains whisked her from captivity, albeit for only a few seconds. Giggling snapped her back to reality as her attention was drawn to a resort-sized pool complete with a waterfall and a tiki bar. Several men and women walked about naked, carrying tall umbrella-topped drinks. She stared at the sight, perplexed by their levity.

Are the women captives just like me, or are they workers? Perhaps they're guests and could help me escape?

She looked to a cabana on the far side of the pool. A couple openly had sex on a massage table as pool goers passed by unfazed. Numb and confused by the open carnal activity, she returned to the room.

After a quick shower, she opened the doors to the expansive walk-in wardrobe closet. Brands she'd only seen worn by actresses on red carpet events hung from the hangers. She slid hanger after hanger aside, admiring the clothing, all in her size four. For a split second, she forgot her plight and felt like the rich and famous at a hedonistic resort. A salmon and black floral print sundress caught her attention. After drying her hair and finishing her makeup, she slipped the sundress on. She looked at all angles in the dressing mirror and admired how perfect the dress accented her athletic body.

"I'll play your game for now," she murmured.

She walked across the hall and knocked on Kimi's door.

"Who is it," a faint voice answered.

"It's me, open up."

Kimi greeted her at the door in a towel. "Mina, why are you all dressed up? Fuck these people. I'm gonna look as bad as I can."

"Kimi, listen, you need to see something. Come with me."

She led Kimi by the hand into her room and to the patio. "Look at the people at the pool. Do they look unhappy?"

Kimi's gaze panned the water playground, stopping on a woman giving a blowjob on one of the lounge chairs. "What is this place?"

"I don't know, but we *are* gonna find out. Let's play their game for a bit and gain their trust."

"Mina, we're virgins. It's a promise we made to each other when we were young. Do you remember?"

"Of course, I do."

"Are you saying we turn into whores here? Start *fucking and sucking* strangers?"

"No, all I'm saying is let's play their game until we find a loose link. Hell, we've been cock-teasing boys for years. We know the promise of sex is their weakness. Let's look as hot as possible, then go for their balls and get the hell out of here."

Kimi looked in Mina's eyes. "Where is here? Where do we run to?"

Mina pointed her head to the East. "Look at the base of the mountains. That's cactus and sage. We're somewhere in New Mexico or Colorado. We only flew for a few hours from South Dakota. In those mountains are ski resorts. *They* will be our freedom."

Kimi's expression lightened. She smiled slightly and shook her head. "I'm glad one of us paid attention in geography class. Okay, I got us into this. I trust you to get us out of it. Just like all the other crap I've gotten us into."

"C'mon, let's get back to your room and pick out something that will make their little dicks stand up."

Kimi raised a provocative brow. "Should we really fuck with them and throw on bathing suits?"

Mina shrugged. "Hmm, it appears bathing suits are optional out there."

Kimi pointed. "Well, it would be really easy to find the weak ones. Look over at that guy."

Mina followed Kimi's finger to a guy walking around the pool fully erect.

The two girls giggled.

"Well," Mina said, "I guess their dicks point to the way out. Guys are sooo easy. Let's stick to clothes for now. Heck, I don't even know if we're allowed over there. I say we just meander about the grounds today and learn the lay of the land."

Kimi stepped back into the room. "Okay, let's start finding the weak link. Come help me pick out something."

Kelly pulled the door to Jill's room closed behind her. She slid to the side and braced her back against the wall. Her body trembled as the scenes of last night played over in her mind. She gained her composure and shuffled towards her room with her head hung low. With each step, her blood boiled and anger displaced shame. She raised her head, pulled her shoulders back, and her eyes widened. She paused at a set of windows. The sun gleamed off Jill's Porsche in the cobblestone courtyard below. A group of women jogged past it, each one worthy of a fitness magazine.

Could these women be free to move about, as Jill promised, and chose this lifestyle?

She opened the door to her suite and was greeted by a freshly made bed with a red rose and a small envelope addressed to her. She opened the scented envelope to find five, crisp one-hundred-dollar-bills and a note bearing a lipstick kiss that simply read, '*Last night was just the beginning of your new life.*'

She threw the note and money to the bed, removed her robe and teddy on her way to the bath, and slipped into the shower. She looked upward into the warm stream and brushed her hair back, allowing the water to cascade over her for several minutes. She scrubbed gently at first, then more firmly, trying to wash the memories, scents, and fluids of last night from her body. She stepped from the shower, wrapped a towel around herself, cleared an area on the steamed mirror, and stared into her own eyes. She then filled a cup of water and swished forcefully before spitting the taste of Doc and Jill from her mouth. She repeated this several times, and as their taste diminished, her taste for vengeance increased. A wry grin crossed her face. "Enjoy this now, pricks, your days are coming," she whispered.

She hurried her makeup, dressed quickly and left the room. She knocked gently on the door across the hall. "Beth, it's me. Open up." She slid one door down. "Cindy, open up."

The two girls stepped into the hall, made up and dressed in the designer clothing.

Cindy rushed to Kelly and hugged her. "Oh my God, you're all right. We've been worried sick when you didn't open up last night or this morning."

"I'm fine. I'm glad both of you are dressed. Let's go for a walk outside."

Beth said, "Kelly, I don't think we can just wonder around here. Remember, they shot that poor girl last night."

Kelly reached out and grabbed her hand. "No, *trust* me, we'll be fine." She motioned upwards with her eyes to the cameras, and pointed down the hall with her head.

The girls nodded and followed Kelly down the steps, across the front porch and into the warm sunshine.

"Kelly," a voice called out.

Kelly spun to find Jill leading a jet-black horse. She quickly turned back to Beth and Cindy and whispered, "Game time."

"Jill, good morning. He's beautiful."

"Thank you, I've had him since he was born. Are you sure you don't want to join Doc and I on a ride? We have a stable of horses. Beth and Cindy are more than welcome to join us."

"Thank you, but I'm a bit worn out from yesterday."

Jill smiled coyly. "I understand. Well, enjoy the ranch. If you aren't too bashful, the pool is partying right now. Clothes are optional."

The girls stood silent and watched Jill lead the horse around a turn, past the porch, and disappear.

"What... the fuck... was that all about?" Cindy said.

Kelly turned to her friends. "Let's find a quiet place and I'll fill you in."

The group walked towards the pool. The sounds of reggae and laughter jumped from the privacy hedge-lined area. Glimpses of naked bodies passed behind the openings in the foliage.

"I don't understand this place," Beth said.

"I think I have an idea." Kelly pointed. "Up ahead, let's climb that small outcropping and talk."

The three continued down the dirt road. From a small out building, yards from the outcropping, two cowboys armed with sidearms emerged.

"Ladies, where y'all heading?" the taller cowboy said.

"Down to that outcropping to get a little sun. The pool is a bit crowded today," Cindy replied.

The shorter cowboy stepped forward. "I have some good weed if you three would like some company."

Kelly said, "Thank you, but we just arrived yesterday and are a bit tired. Maybe another time."

"Y'all new workers or came in on the plane?"

Kelly paused. "Came in on the plane."

"Oh really? Well, maybe it be a good idea to head back to the house," the tall cowboy said.

Kelly watched the two slide their hands to their sidearms. The two groups looked at each other without saying a word.

A loud whistle broke the moment. "They're all right, boys, let 'em pass."

The group turned to a trailhead on the right as Doc approached on his horse.

"Yes sir, Doc," the tall cowboy said.

Both men tilted their hats, bidding the women a good day.

Doc looked down from his horse. "Kelly... ladies."

Kelly forced a smile. "Doc."

"Where you girls going?"

Kelly pointed to the outcropping. "Up ahead. We need some alone time. It's been a confusing week."

"I understand. It'll soon make sense. Tomorrow will give you all a better grasp of your future. See you at dinner tonight."

Doc passed and met with Jill near the pool.

Kelly spit on the ground. "Your future is coming too, *cocksucker*."

"Kelly, *what* is going on? Jill and he act like they know you?" Cindy said.

"Let's get to the top of the rocks, and I'll tell you."

The three girls sat for hours atop the rocks, often in silence. They stared at the sun as it dropped behind the highest peak of the mountain.

Kelly said, "I guess we should get back and prepare for dinner, and not draw any more attention to ourselves."

Cindy stood and took a deep breath. "I agree. I think we have our plan in place, as disgusting as it may be."

Beth remained seated and dropped her head between her knees. Her voice crackled. "I just hope I can do this. You girls know I've only been with Jeff. It disgusts me knowing I may have to be with someone else. It would kill him, and maybe me."

Kelly turned and hugged her. "Honey, if we get out of here, we'll all have to bury secrets. But at least we *will have* that choice. Our only chance to survive this is to stay here. If they send us from this ranch, we will be separated from our families forever. Just keep reminding yourself of that, no matter how bad it gets." She pulled away and dabbed a tear from Beth's eyes. "Okay?"

Beth nodded. "Okay."

The women reached the front porch and were greeted by a dapper older gentleman. "Ladies, on the table is the menu for this evening. You will find a wardrobe rack in each of your rooms with a nice selection of evening gowns to choose from. Cocktails will be served at seven sharp."

The women each picked up a menu and headed up the stairs. They stopped in the hall between their rooms.

Kelly said, "Shall we meet in my room at ten of seven? That gives us an hour and a half."

"Sounds good," Cindy and Beth answered in unison.

Mina and Kimi met in the hall at 6:50.

Mina said, "You look beautiful."

Kimi pushed a few strands of Mina's hair off her shoulder. "As do you. Shall we tease a few cocks?"

"Let's do it. The two stoner cowboys we met today at the lake should be at the ranch bar this evening. They should be well liquored by the time we're done with dinner. I believe these backless gowns should grab their attention."

"Yeah, and a little loosening of the straps and some bending over should push them over the edge. Guys love tits."

"Kimi Locklear, you slut."

"If they only knew we're virgins."

The two girls giggled, interlocked their arms, and walked down the hall. They heard the sounds of three doors open behind them and turned to see Kelly, Beth, and Cindy.

"Should we hold up and walk down with them?" Kimi said.

"Sure."

Mina and Kimi walked back to the trio.

"You three look beautiful," Kimi said.

"Thank you, so do both of you," Kelly replied.

"I'm Kimi, and this is Mina. I guess if we're stuck here, we should get to know each other."

"My name is Kelly. This is Cindy and Beth."

"Kelly Johnson?" Mina said.

Kelly tilted her head. "How did you know my last name?"

"Your disappearance is all over the news. Your dad is interviewed nightly."

Kelly paused for a second, silenced by a rush of emotion. "So... when did you two get kidnapped?"

"Yesterday afternoon from the University of South Dakota," Mina answered.

"How did it happen?" Cindy asked.

Kimi interjected. "Two hot guys asked us if we wanted to go to a party at one of the wealthy frat houses off campus. Mina said no, but I insisted."

Kelly said, "Let me guess, they offered you some weed, and the next thing you know you were shackled to a bed?"

Mina nodded. "Yep."

Kelly shook her head. "They have this operation finely tuned. I wonder how many girls these bastards have grabbed."

"I don't know, but Kimi and I *do* know one thing: we're *not* staying here. I don't know if you girls saw the pool, but it looked like the set of a porn movie. This is all about sex, and we plan to use that against them."

Cindy rolled her eyes and raised a dangling finger up to mimic an erection. "Little heads thinking for big heads."

The girls laughed.

"Well, ladies, there is power in numbers. Let's stick together, be smart, and get out of this place," Kelly said.

Mina said, "Has anyone talked with the other girls?"

Beth spoke up. "We haven't, but I saw two of them running around naked at the pool with drinks in their hands. They appeared to be settled in nicely, probably street girls that feel they hit the lottery. Obviously, we don't want to confide in them. One, as we know, was killed. That leaves the two oriental girls and the other Native American girl, none of which I've seen since last night."

"Well, I guess it will be just us working together. Shall we head downstairs?" Mina said.

The group reached the bottom of the stairs, and the dapper man from the front porch directed them to the bar area behind the gathering room. Candles and warm lights illuminated the area. A piano player filled the room with a soft melody. The girls approached the bar and placed their orders.

Jill entered the bar area and sauntered to the piano. She asked the musician to pause.

"Ladies, you all look stunning this evening. I know the last several days have been difficult, but I hope your accommodations and, *for some*, the fringe benefits are making your stay more enjoyable." Jill raised her brow and shot a glance at the two girls that spent the day at the pool.

Both giggled and raised their cocktails in a cheering motion.

Jill turned her attention back to the group. "For those who may not be finding this arrangement appealing, please remember, there is *no* turning back now. Embrace this new life. Tonight is your night. Relax, drink, do whatever you want with *whomever* you want. There will be some gentlemen from the ranch joining us this evening. They were hand-picked by me. I believe you'll find them... delicious. Tomorrow, you will meet the people that make all of this possible. It's why you're here. So again, I will leave you alone for the evening. Have fun and quench your thirsts and desires."

Chapter 9
A Step towards Hell

Jake opened his eyes to the sound of the cabin door, and watched Jim, Jay, and Honi walk out and into the morning sun. He yawned deeply and stretched his arms upward.

"How did you sleep?"

He looked up at Dakota snuggled in her cot. "Not bad, considering Honi fought me for floor space and a draft from under the door hit me in the face all night."

She smiled. "It's only one night."

Jake sat up and motioned towards the front door with a nod of his head. "They were up early. I guess I should make some coffee."

Dakota stretched. "I'll get some breakfast going. Woo Woo wants to head down the mountain early and beat the storm."

Jim and Jay returned to the cabin twenty minutes later.

"That coffee smells good," Jay said.

"Best on the mountain," Jake joked.

Jim walked over to Dakota at the stove and hugged her. "Good morning, Lomasi."

"Good morning, Woo Woo, scrambled with deer sausage okay?"

"Sounds perfect, reminds me of the days hunting up here with your great grandfather."

"I miss those days," Jay said. "They were good times."

"We were young men back then, Jay. Not sure where almost sixty years have gone?"

Jay shook his head. "The three hills have passed quickly."

Jim patted Jay on the shoulder. "I suggest we finalize our plans, so we can spend a few more years on the fourth hill."

Dakota suggested, "Let's eat and get some cowboy coffee in us so we can think straight."

The group sat down to enjoy the hot coffee and breakfast. Jim and Jay reminisced about their younger days on the mountain.

Dakota and Jake listened intently, imagining life in Wind River during simpler times.

Jim ended the lighthearted conversation. "Okay, enough of those days. Let's concentrate on our next move with Dibella."

Jake said, "As we touched on last night, I believe we need to pay a visit to him before he has time to send more of his goons out here. It's only a matter of time before he realizes the first three are missing."

Dakota said, "And we all can't hide out here forever. Woo Woo, Jay and I need to return to work, and Jake has made commitments with the National Alzheimer's Group. The minute we come off this mountain, Dibella will know his guys failed."

Jim nodded, drew a deep breath, and scribbled on his pad.

Jay set his coffee down. "I suggest we travel to Texas and surprise him. I agree with Jake—the silence from his hitmen will start to make him uneasy."

Jim looked at Jay and nodded. "Okay, Jay and I will fly out tonight from Jackson Hole."

"What about me?" Jake barked.

"And me? I would love to see him squirm after everything his sons put me through," Dakota added.

"Jake, you and Lomasi need to protect the ranch and stay with Anna. If we fail to convince Dibella to back off, he will have people mobilized here before we can return."

Jake glanced at Dakota, then fixed his eyes on Jim. "Very well, Colonel."

Anna unloaded the last bag of groceries from that car as the sound of quads in the distance garnered her attention. She fixed her eyes on the grasslands past the pastures, and smiled as the machines came into sight. She rushed the last bag into the house and returned to the porch.

In her normal fashion, Dakota raced ahead to reach the ranch house first. She jumped off the quad and walked to the porch to hug her grandmother. "Neiwoo, I thought you were in town with Great Grandfather?"

"I was, but we needed groceries, and he had a full day planned with the Tribal Elders. I am glad to see Jake and you come down. I wasn't expecting you for another couple days."

As rehearsed, Dakota responded, "I have to go into the office. Woo Woo got a call on his way up yesterday. He has to travel to Texas tonight to meet an old client, and I need to prepare some stuff in a hurry for him."

"Well, that stinks. You and Jake needed a break after this past year."

Dakota sighed. "I know. Oh well, sooner or later we had to get back to reality."

Jim walked onto the porch and hugged Anna.

She leaned back and looked up. "Lomasi said you have to travel to Texas tonight. Would you like me to go with you?"

"Thank you, my dear, but there is no need. In fact, Jay said he would tag along. He has a nephew in Dallas that he has been planning to see."

"When will you be back?"

"If all goes well, tomorrow evening."

She shook her head. "Jim White Feather, with all this technology, you still insist on face-to-face. When will you jump into the twenty-first century?"

"When the twenty-first century welcomes old men like me and our beliefs. Let me get my bags packed."

Anna watched Jim walk into the house, and turned to Dakota. "Now you know where your bullheadedness comes from. It skipped your mom and landed on you."

Jay and Jake joined the women.

"And Jay Storm Walker, you enable him," Anna scolded.

"What did *I* do?"

"I know you use all the latest technology in your searches. When he got that call from his client, why did you not suggest Skype? Instead, you tell him you will tag along?"

Jay chuckled. "Anna, I have known him since high school. Do you think after all these years that stubborn old man is going to change?" He hugged her. "Let me get packed. You know how he likes to be at the airport two hours early, as if Jackson Hole is LaGuardia or JFK."

Jake set his and Dakota's backpacks on the porch. "Mrs. White Feather, nice to see you. I hope you don't mind if Honi and I spend the night?"

"Jake Michaels, how many times have I told you to call me Anna? Now give me a hug, and of course I don't mind."

Honi whined when the two hugged.

Anna laughed and bent down. "Okay, Honi, I will hug you too."

"Honi, you're such a big baby!" Dakota laughed.

"Well, shall we go inside?" Anna said. "I need to finish putting the groceries away and plan dinner. Anyone have any requests?"

"Possum pie and squirrel gravy biscuits," Dakota blurted.

"Darn, Lomasi, I just used up the last of the squirrel gravy. How does pasta sound?"

Dakota rolled her eyes. "Okay... if we have to."

"Jake, she is such a brat. I hope you know what you are getting into."

Jake winked at Dakota. "I'm learning."

"Jake, Jim is leaving, so you can put your stuff in Dakota's room if you like."

Jake's and Dakota's eyes widened.

Anna laughed. "Seriously, you two. I've been to that cabin. There are *not* two bedrooms there."

Jake glanced at Dakota. "Ahhh, thank you, but I'll stay in the spare room. I would feel a bit better. I don't need the colonel on me. In fact, it's gonna be a nice night. Honi and I may sleep in the cave. I love it up there."

Dakota smiled. "Oh, that sounds awesome. I would also, but I need to get the stuff done for Woo Woo. Neiwoo and I will have a glass of wine and get caught up on some TV. But, I'll come and watch the sunset with you. It's so beautiful from up there."

Anna shook her head and mumbled something in Shoshone as she walked away.

"What did she say?" Jake whispered.

Dakota shrugged her shoulders.

The master bedroom door opened and Jim walked into the living room. "Jake, I assume you *will* be staying in the second spare room. You will have to move Anna's treadmill to the side."

Anna, Jake, and Dakota looked at each other, paused for a second, and laughed.

Jim looked at the three. "Did I say something funny?"

"No, Colonel, we just spoke about the sleeping arrangements. I'm staying in the cave, by my own choice."

Jim shook his head and walked with Anna into the kitchen.

Jay closed the spare room door behind him and approached Jake. He lowered his voice just above a whisper. "My AR is under the bed. I know you brought the sniper rifle with you, but... just in case."

"Thank you. I'm staying in the cave tonight. I'll have a view from all angles. Dibella's guys would have no shot at making it to the house."

Jay nodded and patted Jake on the shoulder, then moved into the kitchen next to Jim. "Well, old man, should we head to the airport?"

"Sounds good, Jay."

Jake, Dakota, and Anna pushed away from the table.

"Neiwoo, that was fantastic, as usual. I'm stuffed."

Jake set his fork down. "Me too. One more bite and I won't make it up to the cave."

"Speaking of which," Dakota said, "the sun is gonna set in about forty-five minutes. Let's help clean up, grab an after-dinner drink, and head up there."

Anna stood. "No, you two go ahead. I'll clean up."

"Neiwoo, no, we'll help. It won't take long."

"I insist. You two go. That's an order."

Jake and Dakota gathered their gear, made the climb to the cave, and settled in at the entrance.

Dakota poured two sifters of bourbon and settled back in a camp chair. "Cheers."

Jake tapped her glass. "Cheers."

"What do you think about all this?"

"I think Dibella backs off. I think Jim and Jay make him a deal that puts this to bed."

Dakota pondered for a second. "I wonder what the Spirit world would show us up here? Too bad you didn't bring the medicine."

Jake smiled and pulled a pipe from his denim jacket. "I wondered the same thing, and whether we could walk amongst the Spirits that Samuel communicates with in there."

"Very smart, Jake Michaels. You never cease to amaze me."

The two moved inside the cave and built a small fire. The dancing flames illuminated the ancient meeting place as earthy-colored wall art sprung to life. Dakota pointed at a landscape scene depicting herds of buffalo. "That's my favorite."

Jake snickered. "Well, don't get run over by them in the Spirit World."

She mockingly laughed. "Oh, okay."

Jake lit the pipe and drew a deep hit, then passed it to Dakota. After a second round, the warmth of the medicine crept through their bodies, and they entered the Spirit world on the outskirts of an Indian village.

"Jake, this is not the mountain. Where are we?"

"I don't know. I assume it's Wind River before white men."

A thunderous rumble caught their attention, and they spun to see a cloud of dust billowing above towering stone outcroppings.

"Dakota, duck behind these rocks."

The pounding of horse's hooves drew closer, and hooting and hollering echoed through the canyons.

"War cries," Dakota whispered.

The dust cloud moved closer and the ground thundered.

Jake placed his palm on the dusty soil. "There must be hundreds."

Suddenly, the canyons quieted as a blood red moon eclipsed the sun and bathed the land in a crimson hue. The unnerving silence lasted for minutes... then piercing screams bounced from canyon wall to canyon wall, growing louder and louder, until reaching a deafening roar.

Jake and Dakota covered their ears, but abruptly, as if a light switch had been thrown, calm replaced the dread. In the distance, an orange sky glowed.

"Should we go down there, Jake?"

He stood and stepped from behind the boulder. "I can't believe the Spirits would show us this and want us to ignore it."

The two made their way through the twisting canyon towards the orange sky. After several hundred yards, they paused, and Jake pointed forward. "That should be the last bend. Are you ready?"

Dakota nodded.

As they drew closer to the bend, the smell of smoke danced in the wind. With each step, the odor turned more putrid, and Jake quickly identified the smell. "Dakota, you don't want to see this. Let's turn back. Death is around the corner."

Jake grabbed her arm to spin them but their feet were frozen in place, their attention forced forward. The ground moved towards the orange hue like a conveyer belt, and the steady pounding of a single tribal drum reverberated around the canyon, growing louder as the bend approached. The two struggled to break the grip of the moving earth beneath them.

"Jake, I *don't* like this. We have no control. Where is Rowtag? *What* is this place?"

"I don't know, but whatever is ahead won't be pleasant."

The couple made the turn and the ground released its grip. Ahead, heaps of smoldering embers stood against the darkness as far as the eye could see. Orange cinders swirled in the foul winds.

"Dakota, let's not go any farther."

They spun to retreat, but came face-to-face with a swirling portal that blocked the path.

Jake raised his hand to touch the black abyss. The portal was solid as a brick wall. *"What the fuck?* I guess we have no choice but to move forward." He grasped her hand. "Are you ready?"

"Yes."

Their footsteps were deliberate and their eyes focused as they approached the first smoldering heap.

Jake tugged at her arm. "Dakota, turn away." But his warning was too late.

The pair stared into the glowing, collapsed timbers of a teepee fallen across three smoldering corpses, clearly a woman and two children.

They pressed forward and quickly discovered the carnage did not discriminate against age or sex. Naked, impaled women lined the twisting avenue of a village. Vultures picked at their flesh as wild dogs lapped blood puddles at the base of the stakes. Disemboweled warriors lay strewn about, many holding spears and arrows, unlaunched and unfired. Children and elders, hacked to pieces, lay in bloody heaps.

"Are we in hell?" Dakota murmured.

"I don't know, but whatever hit them, it hit fast and hard. This village never had a chance to fight back."

"What kind of enemy could be so lethal?"

Jake put his arm in front Dakota. "Stop. *There* may be your answer."

In the dull light of the glowing orange hue, through the swirl of embers, five mounted figures appeared. In the darkness on the canyon rim, hidden from Jake and Dakota, a sixth looked down.

The five marched their snow-white horses forward in a slow steady prance. As they approached, their features became clearer. Long onyx hair fell over the chiseled shoulders of the three men. Platinum hair framed the faces of the two women by their sides. Each rider wore buckskin pants. The muscles of their naked torsos rippled with each stride of their horses. Rows of colorful beads cascaded over the women's naked breasts. Each man garnished necklaces of snake skulls and eagle talons.

The five halted their horses, dismounted, and walked forward in unison. Their faces came into the light as they passed a blazing Pyre.

Their piercing blue eyes and striking features caught Dakota's attention. She whispered, "They're not Indian." As they got closer, a faint yellow aura emanating from their skin became visible.

The five circled Jake and Dakota. Their hypnotizing stares froze the two in place. After several moments, the five tilted their head back and sniffed loudly. One of the males broke the circle and approached Dakota. A faint smile softened his chiseled jawline. "Sheer tol-dah ee-sheh."

The walls of the cave came into focus as Jake reentered the physical word. He looked at Dakota.

Her eyes remained glassed. After a few seconds, a quick jerk of her arm signaled she was returning from the Spirit world.

"Hey, you," Jake said.

"Wow! What the fuck did that mean?"

"I don't know. What was that language?"

"I have no idea. It wasn't Arapaho or any native language I recognize."

Jake drew a deep breath, knowing what they had seen was different. "When your grandfather returns, we need to go back to the cabin and talk to Rowtag. Maybe he can tell us what the hell that was all about."

Dakota stared into the fire. "Maybe *hell* is the operative word."

CHAPTER 10
FACE TO FACE

After the plane touched down in Dallas, Jim and Jay picked up their rental car and started the hour drive to Dibella's ranch.

"We've made good time, and should be at Dibella's by seven," Jim said.

Jay nodded. "What do you think?"

"I think he will shit his pants at first. It is not everyday that dead men show up at your door. Then, I believe after we present our ultimatum, life will move on for all of us without complications. How do you feel?"

Jay inhaled deeply. "I believe we will start a war with people more powerful than Dibella."

"Do you believe South America goes past Dibella? I have to think there are not many people in that food chain richer or more powerful."

"This is not about South America, my old friend. This is about something darker and more sinister."

"Jay, please, you are starting to sound like Samuel in your old age."

"I am not talking about Spirits. I am talking about flesh and bone evil."

"Like what and who?"

"I do not know exactly, but this goes past Dibella. He cannot be responsible for every missing girl from our reservations. I am sure you have seen the news about the three white girls missing from the Badlands?"

"Yes, one of their fathers is retired FBI. But, the Badlands claim victims all the time. Do you suspect foul play?"

"One of the officers there, Joe Running Horse, contacted me last week and wanted to know if I would join the search. I declined, but asked him to send me the specifics and a topo map of the area the girls were last seen. He is the best tracker up there. His words to me were, *'It is as if these girls simply vanished.'* We know that is impossible, unless they were abducted by an organized and experienced group."

Jim scoffed. "Could Dibella be so brazen, with all the exposure Jakes's trial created? Would he still be operating a trafficking ring with the Feds and the press up his ass?"

"No, that is what I am saying, Jim. This is above him. He is a power player in this, but not the big fish."

Jim paused. "Do you think we are stirring a hornet's nest by confronting him?"

"Do we have a choice? The minute he suspects Jake, Dakota, and you survived, he will send more. I believe grabbing the bull by the horns before more blood is spilled is our best decision."

Jim nodded. "His exit is ahead. We will soon find out. Oh, and by the way, if that asshole Sellman is called into the meeting, please keep me from beating him to a pulp."

Jay chuckled. "You are asking a lot, my friend. Who will keep *me* from doing it?"

The two men laughed as they turned onto Dibella Ranch Drive. The road meandered between perfectly soldiered pines on both berms. In the pastures behind the pines, herds of horses and cattle dotted the landscape as far as the eye could see.

"Looks like there is a lot of money in the livestock industry," Jay said.

"Three generations worth, and would have been four, had his sons not visited Wind River."

Jay shook his head. "Nih 'o'o' 3oo, their greed has no boundaries."

"That was more than white man greed, Jay. That was about power, lust, and perversion. Those sins have no ethnic boundaries."

Jim pointed to a right turn. "This is it, my friend. Are you ready?"

"Yes, let us introduce Dibella to a ghost."

After a two-mile drive, the men approached a massive, double, wrought-iron gate adorned with the letter "D" on each side. An armed man approached the car from a guard shack the size of a small house.

Jim rolled his window down.

"Gentlemen, can I assist you?" the uniformed man said.

Jim presented his driver's license. Jay flashed his badge and ID. "We are here to see Mr. Dibella."

"Gentlemen, it's a bit late. I don't recall your names on a guest list for today."

"We are not on the list. This is a surprise visit," Jim said.

Jay leaned over to make eye contact with the guard. "I assure you, if you call Mr. Dibella, he will allow us to pass."

"May I have your IDs, please?"

Jim and Jay handed over their licenses.

"I'll be right back, gentlemen."

After a few minutes, the gates to the ranch opened and the guard approached the car. "Mr. Dibella will see you gentlemen. Here are your ID's. If you will, please pull over in the parking area behind the guard shack, turn your car off, and step out the vehicle."

"Of course," Jim said.

Three armed guards approached the car as Jim parked. One guard used a mirror suspended from a long pole to examine the undercarriage of the rental car.

Jim and Jay stepped from the vehicle.

"Gentlemen, are you armed?"

Jim and Jay responded in unison, "No."

"If you don't mind, we need to frisk you."

"No problem," Jim said.

After the quick search, two of the guards jumped into a Jeep labeled with Dibella's branding. They pulled alongside the rental and said, "Gentlemen, please follow us."

Jim and Jay climbed back into their car, and the two vehicles wound along the meticulously landscaped lane. In the distance, Dibella's house dominated the rolling pastures.

Jay looked off the road through a rush of woods. "I think he has a mote."

Jim laughed. "A mote?"

"Yes, you can see it through the woods up ahead."

As the two cars made a sweeping right turn, the pastures gave way to a wooded area. The road straightened, and on the horizon stood a white steel bridge, and behind that, Dibella's mansion.

"Son of a bitch, Jay, you were right."

The two cars approached a small gatehouse to the right of the bridge, and the gate lifted.

Jim looked down both directions of the wide, slow-flowing river as they reached midpoint of the bridge. "This is a great deal of security for a cattleman."

Jay nodded. "Security, or a perverse show of wealth."

The escort car stopped in front of the pillared entrance, and a guard waved Jim forward. "Mr. White Feather, we will park your vehicle. Please follow Rubin into the house."

Jim and Jay walked into the massive foyer.

A young woman in business attire approached. "Gentlemen, Mr. Dibella will be with you shortly. Can I offer you a drink?"

"Bourbon on the rocks, please," Jim said

"I will have the same," Jay followed.

"Very good, please have a seat. I will have your drinks brought out."

Jim and Jay sunk into a high-back, brown leather sofa to the right of the slate foyer.

The young woman returned. "Mr. Dibella is finishing up a call. He will be just a few more minutes."

Jim and Jay sipped on their cocktail as their eyes panned the foyer area.

Jay Said, "Who has a fountain in their foyer and a twelve-foot-wide marble stair? I feel like we are on a movie set."

Jim chuckled. "Tony Montana or Al Capone may enter anytime."

As Jim finished his statement, a pair of mahogany doors opened, and Dibella took a step past the threshold. "Gentlemen, please come in." He turned and walked across the gleaming wood floor to his desk, and stood stoically as Jim and Jay approached.

From a side office, Sellman entered and moved to his right.

"Gentlemen, I believe no introductions are needed. Have a seat," Dibella said.

The four men took their respective chairs and exchanged glares.

Sellman broke the tense silence. "Why are you here?"

"In all do respect, Mr. Sellman," Jim said, "that is something we would like to discuss in private with Mr. Dibella."

"No," Dibella interjected. "Mr. Sellman will remain. I would assume an attorney and a law officer did not travel from Wyoming to exchange niceties. What is the purpose of your visit, gentlemen?"

Jim glanced at Jay, who nodded in return.

"Very well, Mr. Dibella. A few days ago, two men approached Jay and I with intent to carry out a hit. That was, shall I say, unfortunate for them."

"So how is this *my* problem, Mr. White Feather?"

"During a somewhat unorthodox interrogation, they confessed that you hired them."

Dibella chuckled and looked at Sellman. "So, gentlemen, you are here to implicate me in your attempted murders?"

"And the attempt on Dakota's and Jake's lives. They too survived, and withdrew a confession from their assailant, which also implicated you."

Sellman swirled his scotch, took a sip, and placed it on Dibella's desk. "Okay, Chief, I've heard enough of this bullshit. Obviously, the peace pipes have been working overtime on the reservation. Let me get this straight: three trained hitmen were sent to execute you, Deputy Dawg, Pocahontas, and her fucked-up soldier. You subdued, interrogated, and drew a confession from each? Is this correct?"

Jim's eyes narrowed as he gripped the arms of the leather chair. "Mr. Sellman, I warned you during the trial, and now *I am promising you*, refrain from your rhetoric or find your tongue and you separated."

Dibella jumped in. "Gentlemen, *enough*. Mr. White Feather, why would I want you, your granddaughter, and Michaels dead? Please do not say revenge. I saw the tape and what my boys did. It sickened me. Would it not look obvious if you three showed up dead after a much-publicized trial?

Jay interjected, "The D.A. also met an untimely death at the same time our executions were to be carried out. This was not about revenge, Mr. Dibella."

"*Then what is this about?*" Sellman barked.

"South America," Jim said.

Sellman shook his head. "Please, Mr. White Horse, I told you when you approached me with this crap, looking for a deal for Michaels, that it was bullshit. The charges were dropped."

Jim snapped back. "If South America was bullshit, why did the hitmen confess to that being the reason for their contracts?"

Dibella raised his hand. "One second. Mr. White Feather, how did you know about the charges in South America? And please help me understand why I would order a hit on the D.A.? This is starting to sound like a Hollywood movie."

"I had a client who was involved with a company that did business with your South America operations. He came to me with an issue. Unfortunately, he met an *untimely* death while solo hiking, and the case never moved forward. However, in our discovery, Dakota and I were informed of your sons' charges, and involvement with my client's partners in a pornography ring. As for the D.A., he was present when I attempted to use this information as leverage for a plea for Jake Michaels."

Dibella leaned forward on his desk. "So, you believe I ordered your deaths to quill any further investigation over a pornography ring my dead sons were or were not involved in."

"Yes, and we believe it moves past pornography and into a much darker enterprise," Jay said.

Dibella sat back in his chair and crossed his arms, and a smile crept to his face. "Please, I can't wait to hear the continuation of the plot."

Jay leaned forward and glared at Dibella. "You know your sons were involved in a human trafficking ring. The tape made that clear to *everyone* in the courtroom. We believe you are the leader of that ring, and are gathering evidence to indict you. *There* is the continuation of your plot."

Dibella sprung forward and slammed his fist on the desk. Veins throbbed in his forehead. "*I have heard enough!* I found humor in your frivolous hitman stories, but when you walk into *my home* and allude to the fact you intend on soiling *my name* because of indiscretions of my dead boys, I have lost my fucking humor. Now... *why the fuck are you here, and what do you want?*"

Jim and Jay paused, looked at each other, and Jay nodded his head.

Jim relaxed into the leather chair. "We want a truce, before more blood is spilled. We want you to stand down on any further hits, and in return, we will bury South America."

Dibella took a deep breath, trying to calm his trembling hands. "Gentlemen, how can I stop something I did not order?"

Sellman's face flushed. "And besides, how do we know you two are not making this whole thing up to perpetuate more bullshit and extort Mr. Dibella down the line?" He looked at Dibella. "Vincent, I've heard enough from these two ass clowns."

Jay reached into his pocket and withdrew a plastic sandwich bag and a small ring box. He unwrapped the contents of the bag and threw an ear on Dibella's desk. He opened the box and displayed the assassin's ring. "These are the only things left from the two sent to kill Jim. The third man will never be seen again. *I am sure...* you have wondered why they have not checked in."

Silence fell over the room, and the four men glared at each other.

"Again, gentlemen, I do not run a criminal enterprise with hitmen at my disposal. I have nothing to do with the contracts on your life or my dead sons' indiscretions. If you feel you must pursue me and your human trafficking ring bullshit, feel free. Now, I want you off my property, and any further contact will be through my attorney and proper legal lines." Dibella pulled a cigar from his coat pocket, grabbed his Stetson, and walked onto the balcony behind his desk, closing the doors behind him.

Sellman leaned forward in his chair and looked Jim in the eyes. "His sons were pieces of shit. I told you that in Joe Ross's office. He and his wife were sickened by that tape. He is squeaky clean, always has been and always will be. If this hitman mumbo-jumbo is real, you are barking up the wrong tree. One thing is for sure, if there is a contract on your lives, it's only a matter of time before they come back to finish the job. Now, get the fuck off this ranch and forget Vincent Dibella. It appears you have bigger problems in Wyoming."

Sellman sprung up and walked to the patio doors, but paused and looked back. "You know your way out. Security will escort you back to your car."

Howard Sellman walked over and stood beside Vincent Dibella on the edge of the patio, and patted his shoulder.

The billionaire's eyes fixed on the rolling pastures. "What is this all about, Howard?"

"I don't know, sir. If it *is true* an attempt was made on their lives, it would make you a person of interest. Perhaps someone who holds a long grudge against you has found their time to strike."

"Did they leave that ear and ring?"

"Yes."

"Take them to our friends in Dallas. See if DNA can identify the hitman, and if they know of any syndicates that would use a poison ring. Tell them to keep it quiet, though. The last thing we need is some rookie investigator getting ahold of this."

"Yes sir."

"And Howard, send a few men to Wind River to kick up stones. Have them keep an eye on White Feather, his granddaughter, and Michaels. The last fucking thing we need is something happening to them so soon after the trail, and now a visit here. This company can't handle any more bad publicity."

"I'll get on it."

Jim and Jay left the office and started the drive off the ranch.

"What do you think, Jay?"

"I think Dibella is clean and will shake the trees to find out who was behind this, and put an end to it. His empire cannot risk any more bad press."

"So, you believe three men facing their own deaths would lie?"

"I believe they told the truth, or at least what they *thought* was the truth."

CHAPTER 11
THE PARTY

Kelly opened her eyes and struggled to focus. The lingering effects of trying to drink her situation away made her head throb. She rolled out of bed still wearing last night's cocktail dress, fumbled with the zipper, and allowed it to fall to the ground. A knock at the door made her scramble for a robe, nearly tripping over the gown laid at her ankles.

"One second. Who is it?"

"It's Mina, Kimi, and Cindy."

Kelly shuffled across the room to open the door.

"You look like shit," Cindy joked.

"I feel like shit. How many shots did we do?"

"I stopped at four, but you kept going with those the two girls from Lubbock."

"Those Texas girls can party. Where is Beth?"

Cindy rolled her eyes. "She's coming. You know she won't step into public without her makeup and hair done, even in this jail."

"Okay, let's wait till she's here before we go for our hike. Let me grab a quick shower."

The girls watched Kelly shuffle to the bathroom and bounce off the door frame.

"Hike, my ass! She may not make it out of the shower," Mina jested.

The girls chuckled. "No, she'll surprise you. I've seen her bounce back from worse mornings and give me a run for my money on the trails," Cindy said.

A light knock came at the door. "Hey, let me in," Beth said.

Mina opened the door. "You look like you're doing a photo shoot, not going hiking."

Beth said, "Thank you, I'll keep playing their game. Where's Kelly?"

"In the shower," Cindy said.

"How does she feel?"

"Like shit, but she'll be fine. You know how fast she recuperates."

"Do you think we did good last night?"

Cindy and Mina responded with a single finger to their lips, and motioned with their eyes to the intercom.

"I think everyone did good with their drinking last night," Kimi quickly answered.

Beth mouthed, *Oops, sorry.*

Kelly walked from the bathroom with a spring in her step, pulled her wet hair into a ponytail, and finished a bottle of water. "Okay, bitches, let's grab a bite from the kitchen and hit the trails."

Cindy looked at Mina and Kimi. "Told you."

The group left the kitchen and walked off the front porch. They looked up at the morning sun and drew a deep breath of fresh morning air.

"Any other circumstances and I would say what a beautiful morning," Mina said.

"Ladies, you all look like fitness models."

The group turned to see Jill approach from the side courtyard.

"Where are you all venturing this morning?"

"We're going for a hike to clear the cobwebs from last night," Kimi said.

Jill looked at Kelly and smirked. "I heard a few of you enjoyed the open bar."

"Yeah, maybe a bit too much," Kelly joked.

"Well, enjoy your day. Please be back by four, so you can prepare for tonight's party."

The sound of a helicopter in the distance caught the group's attention.

"I see one of guests is arriving early," Jill said.

The girls watched the black corporate helo circle overhead before touching down behind the pool. The doors opened as the rotors came to a stop, and a distinguished-looking middle-aged gentleman stepped to the ground, followed by three dark-suited men with earphones and black glasses.

Jill looked back as she walked away. "Ladies, enjoy your workout."

The girls watched her pace quicken to the helicopter. She greeted the guest with a kiss and a slight backwards leg kick, followed by a caress of his broad shoulders. The gentleman smiled and voiced something. Jill backed up, opened her hoodie, and dropped it to her waist, exposing her naked back.

"What a slut," Cindy growled.

"What's up with the men in black behind him?" Mina said.

"Who knows, maybe he's an alien?" Kimi said.

The girls chuckled.

"Okay, let's get away from all the commotion," Kelly said.

In unison, the group jogged past the pool and the watchful eyes of Jill and the new guest.

"New toys, I assume?" the guest said.

"Yes, the two in the back are off limits. The one leading the group may stay with me. The other two are available. We have six to choose from this evening, plus, of course, our regular party favors. I assume you are here for something fresh?"

"Yes, something a bit *exotic*, shall we say."

Jill grabbed his hand. "I believe we can fill that order."

The girls jogged past the stables and the rock outcroppings they'd stopped at the day before, and approached a split in the trail with a sign pointing right to Mirror Lake. They paused to catch their breaths.

Kelly wiped the sweat from her forehead and took a deep gulp from her water bottle. "Shit, the liquor is flowing from me. I probably smell like a bottle of Fireball. What do you all think? Should we head to the lake?"

"Can you make it another three miles uphill?" Cindy said.

"Yeah, let's slow the pace and take it steady. We have plenty of time to discuss our plans."

After a steady climb and a few breaks, the group reached a dense aspen and pine forest, where the shade offered a welcome break from the high desert sun.

"One second, girls," Mina said. She walked into a thick rush of ponderosa pines and quickly disappeared.

"Where is she going?" Cindy said.

"I'm sure she saw something important. She believes we're in Northern New Mexico," Kimi said.

"Girls, come here," a muffled voice called out from the pines.

The group walked to Mina, who stood on a rock ledge looking over deep canyons.

"That's a beautiful view, Mina. Look at the snowcapped mountains in the distance," Beth said.

"It is pretty, but that's not what I'm looking at. It's the mountains in the distance. That's Colorado, which means ski resorts and our way out of here."

"That's about fifty miles," Kelly said.

"We can make that in three days, easy," Cindy followed.

Mina pointed down at one o'clock. "Look at that ravine. The ranch sits above it. We could slip into it and through the canyons to the base of that mountain." Her finger moved left, directing the girl's attention to the proposed escape route.

"I can't imagine it being that easy," Kimi said. "I'm sure girls have tried in the past. How could we buy enough time before they send search parties out? You guys have seen the security and the dogs. Not to mention, I'm sure they have helicopters. The best we could do is maybe a few hours' head start."

Kelly drew a deep breath and stared across the valley below. "They have a weakness."

Mina said, "What kind of weakness? It appears they have this running like a fine-tuned machine."

"The reason we're here: sex. Let's take a break. I'll share something with Kimi and you."

Kelly retold Jill's own story, reiterating the trust and freedom she'd earned in the organization. She followed with the drug-induced seduction by Jill and Doc.

Mina and Kimi stood speechless for several moments after she finished.

"So, we use sex to gain their trust?" Mina mumbled.

"Yes."

Kimi shook her head. "Mina and I are virgins. We made a promise to each other as little girls that we would save ourselves for the right guy. I'm not fucking these pigs to gain my freedom. There has to be another way out."

"Kimi, if we gain Jill's and Doc's trust, they may allow us to stay on the ranch, versus shipping us out. Once we're gone to who-knows-where, we'll never see our families again. It's our only chance."

"So, we go from virgins to whores, fucking guys *and* girls?" Mina blurted.

Beth sat on a boulder, dropped her head and sobbed.

Cindy knelt in front of her and lifted her chin. "Shhh... we'll be okay, honey. We *will* get out of here."

Beth shook her head and wiped the tears from her eyes, regaining her composure. "*No*, I won't do this to Jeff. We're getting married in eight months. I'm not fucking anyone. I *will* kill them all first."

The group stared at Beth, then at each other.

"Maybe *that's* our way out," Mina muttered.

The girls returned to the ranch and approached the front porch. Jill sat at one of the café tables with a well-dressed, thirty-something, dark-haired woman.

"Kelly, may I see you for a second," Jill said.

Kelly glanced at Jill then back at the girls and winked. "I'll be up in a second. Game on."

She sauntered across the porch followed by the lustful stare of the two women.

"Delicious, isn't she?" Jill whispered.

"Very. Is she for sale?"

"Not yet. I believe I'm keeping her."

"Will you share that sweet pussy?"

Jill giggled. "I think we can work something out, and yes, it *is* sweet."

Kelly saw the two talking as she made the walk across the long porch.

"Kelly, how was your hike?" Jill said.

"It was good."

"Do you have the girls prepared for this evening?"

"I believe I have them calmed a bit."

"Very good. I want you to meet Miss Smith. She's a good friend of the ranch and a big contributor to its success."

Kelly reached her hand out. "My pleasure, Miss Smith."

The raven-haired women looked up, and her turquoise eyes mesmerized Kelly for a second. She reached out and lightly gripped Kelly's outstretched hand. "You can call me Dominique."

The two held the grasp for several moments, their eyes locked.

Jill watched the brief intimate moment between the two women, and fidgeted in her chair as a rush of desire moved between her legs. She cleared her throat, breaking their stare and grip. "Kelly, why don't you get ready? Our guests have all arrived and are anxious to meet you all."

Kelly smiled at Jill and Dominique. "Very well, I assume I *will* see both of you this evening?"

Jill winked. "I guarantee it."

Dominique watched Kelly move towards the door. "I would keep her also. Might I suggest the three of us enjoy a late evening tonight?"

Jill looked towards her car. "Hmmm, my Porsche is two years old now...."

"Pick your color tomorrow and I'll have a check sent."

"Deal. Would you like a man to join us?"

Dominique admired the profile of Kelly as she walked into the house. "No, I don't want a dick to interrupt what I will do with her."

Kelly and Cindy met in Beth's room after they dressed. There was a faint knock on the door.

"Who is it?" Beth said.

"Mina and Kimi."

Cindy opened the door. "You whores look beautiful."

With a wry smile and wink, Mina responded, "Dressed to kill."

"Kelly, what did that bitch Jill and her friend want earlier?" Kimi said.

"They wanted to know how we were all doing. I told them fine, given the circumstances."

Kelly made an eye motion towards the speaker. "Shall we have a drink and walk out on the patio. We can watch the guests arrive from the main house."

The girls mixed their drinks and pulled the patio door closed behind them.

"I flirted with those two bitches. I'm telling you all, lust is their weakness. Play the game tonight with these rich pricks. I'm sure Jill and her friend will have their way with me this evening. If that's what it takes so we can buy time here, so be it. Girls, *we are* in survival mode. We must stay on this ranch for any chances of escaping this hell." Kelly said.

Mina said, "I think we follow Beth's plan. We flirt, get them drunk, and kill them all while their pants are below their knees. Look down, girls. We're only twelve feet from the ground. All we need to do is climb over and hang from the wood beams jetting out on the corners. Now the drop is maybe seven feet into the sandy soil."

Beth walked to the edge of the patio and stared into the distance. "Either way is risky at best." The defeat in her tone was clear, she was losing faith.

Kelly took a deep breath. "Maybe there's another way."

"What are you thinking?" Kimi said.

"The night Doc and Jill had their way with me," Kelly said, "I was drugged. Whatever was in the smoke made all my inhibitions disappear. Maybe I can convince Jill or Doc to give me some to share with you all. I'll tell them it will help you get through your *first time* as it did me."

Mina said. "So, we drug *them* instead?"

"Yes."

Kimi nodded. "I like it. We play along with their little game, and when we're one on one, we convince them how great the sex will be with the drug... then nighty-night."

Kelly said, "Yep, no sex, and no blood on our hands either."

Beth said, "What about you, Kelly?"

"Don't worry about me. I'll keep Jill occupied. The ranch will be in chaos once security realizes you all have escaped. That's when I'll make my move. The drug is strong, so it should give you a couple hours head start before the guests can report anything."

"What about the other girls?" Kimi said.

"Three of them seem to be doing just fine," Kelly said. "I think they all got laid by those cowboys last night. The others are keeping to themselves. Maybe they have a plan. Regardless, once we get out of here, we'll send the authorities back for them."

The guests assembled in Mr. P's office. A server offered each of them their favorite libations.

Jill entered shortly after the cocktails were served. She floated gracefully across the marble floor to the sitting area in the oversized office. "Ladies and gentlemen, good evening. If you would please make your selves comfortable, Mr. P will join us in a few minutes."

The guests settled into the leather furniture.

A maid approached Jill with a silver tray filled with lines of cocaine. She leaned over and filled each nostril. "Thank you, Freda. I'm sure our guests would like to get their night started also."

The maid stepped in front of Sergio Delucca, an obese, olive-skinned man. His long, curly dark hair gleamed with product to match the constant sweat on his forehead. He struggled to lean forward and help himself to the blow, so the maid moved the tray towards him. He snorted four lines and tilted his head back.

"I need to lose some fucking weight," he blurted after sniffing deeply.

James Radford, the pleasant-looking middle-aged man Jill had met earlier at the helicopter laughed. "You've been saying that for five years now. Every time we meet, it looks like you found more, versus losing any."

Sergio laughed deeply and grabbed his quaking belly. "All bought and paid for. The girls in Sicily love it."

Dominique rolled her eyes. "They only love it because they're scared you'll have them killed."

Sergio's attempt to reach around his belly and grab his crotch fell short at mid stomach. "Not true. They love what I have under the roof."

Dominique had leaned forward to sniff a line, and now looked off quickly as she laughed. "Damn, Sergio, you almost made me blow this stuff all over the office."

"We have plenty more," a deep western voice said from behind the group. Mr. P entered from a door on the left side of his office.

Steven and Michelle Cornwell stood. Steven shook Mr. P's hand and patted him on the shoulder. "My dear friend, it has been far too long."

"Three years too long, Steven. You look good, and your lovely wife is as beautiful as ever."

Michelle placed her hands on both of Mr. P's shoulders and leaned in to kiss him on the cheek. "Always the charmer, you are. We've missed you, Joe."

"Well, you've had your hands full over the past several years. I assume the doctors have done their job?"

Michele nodded and looked at her husband. "We're celebrating two years in remission."

Mr. P smiled. "The tabloids had him dead and buried three years ago."

"Only the good die young," Steven said, as he lifted his head from the coke tray. "I trust you have some treats for Michelle and I, something young, perhaps?"

"Is eighteen young enough? And *very* tight, according to Doc's exam," Jill interjected.

Michelle licked her lips. "Mmm... sounds scrumptious."

Mr. P walked in front of the group.

"Ladies and gentlemen, let me introduce you to tonight's menu. Jill, please dim the lights."

A screen lowered from the office ceiling. The exam night played, followed by clips of each girl showering and changing in their rooms, then random shots of each at last night's party. The lights came up and the screen retracted.

Jill stepped next to Mr. P. "Number four, five, and ten, as you saw, are off limits. Kelly, who was number six, will most likely stay here on the ranch, and I'll groom her. She has appeared to be a *very* willing candidate. The other six are available."

"Where's my girl, Sabrina? You used her as the runner? I haven't seen her since I've been here," Sergio said.

Jill nodded. "We sent her on a much-needed vacation to the islands. We figured number seven may be a nice new toy for you. Her name is Beth."

"Huh, well I'll try her out tonight. She'd *better* give a million-dollar blow job, and that ass better be tight. Let me have another line of blow," he grumbled.

Jill took a deep breath. "I'm sure she will be worth your investment. If not, maybe one of the others will be. We will have a new flock at the end of the month, should none of these girls suit you. I'll credit your account should Beth not be worth your investment."

Mr. P looked down at his watch. "Jill, it's time for our guests to meet their hostesses."

Jill looked at the group. "Shall we head to the guest house?"

The girls reached the landing and were greeted with soft piano music from the great room below. At the bottom of the stairs, a formally dressed doorman stood with a silver tray lined with champagne.

"Ladies, good evening. Champagne?" the dapper man offered.

Mina, Kelly, and Cindy obliged.

The doorman looked at Beth and Kimi. "If champagne is not to your taste, perhaps the bartender can mix your favorite libation." He stepped back from the group and nodded his head slightly. "Enjoy your evening. Our esteemed guests will arrive shortly."

The group moved to the great room and paused. Bistro tables topped with lace linen and single candles lent an air of formality beneath the seductive, soft lighting from the black iron and crystal chandeliers. A low dancing flame in the double-sided stone fireplace cast a warm glow on the polished wood floors.

"I would be impressed if not for the sick circumstances," Mina said.

"Fuck these pricks," Beth said, catching the attention of two servers filling cocktail trays on the buffet table.

Kelly squeezed her hand and whispered, "Relax, be calm, and let this play out tonight. We *will* be gone by morning."

A set of headlights through the floor to ceiling windows caught their attention. Their eyes followed the long black limousine as it pulled around the circular drive.

Jill emerged from the front passenger side and opened the rear doors of the limo. One by one, the guests emerged, the last to exit a heavy man.

"Look at that fat piece of shit," Kimi hissed.

"If he picks me, all bets are off on the drug, he'll take his last breath before his little dick starts to get hard," Mina whispered.

Jill led the group into the foyer. "If you all could pause for a second, I am going to assemble your hostesses. Bedford, if you could please take a drink order from our guests."

"Of course, ma'am," the doorman answered.

Jill moved in front of the fireplace, picked up a champagne glass, and tapped it with a spoon. "Ladies, if you would please join me."

The ten women conversed on Jill.

"Ladies, tonight you will meet some of the people that make all of this possible. If chosen, your lives will be more opulent than you can ever imagine. Now, for some, you will merely be *entertainment* for the night. Not all of our guests look for long-term arrangements. But, eventually each of you will be placed. Remember my words when we first met. As you look up from between their legs, ask yourself, *'When I finish, do I want a beer from a white dingy refrigerator or a hundred-dollar glass of champagne from the teak bar on the yacht?'* Please, be your most charming selves and understand there is no escaping this destiny. Embrace it, don't fight it. Mina, Kimi, and Aiyana, please retreat to your rooms. You will find suitcases. Please pack for three days of travel. The rest of you, join our special guests and make their evenings special."

Mina and Kimi looked at Kelly, Beth, and Cindy. The group quickly huddled to the side of the fireplace.

"What... is... happening?" Mina said.

Jill looked back at the women. "*Now*, ladies." Her eyes fixed on Kelly. She motioned two male servers towards them, never breaking her icy stare.

The two men gently nudged Kimi and Mina from the group and escorted them from the great room.

Aiyana obediently followed.

Jill's eyes remained locked on Kelly. A wry grin crossed her face, followed by a mocking laugh as she turned her attention to the guests in the foyer.

CHAPTER 12
INTO THIN AIR

Billy sat alone in his office. He stared at the girl's phones and the corresponding data history reports, shook his head, and took a sip of bourbon.

"Yes," he answered to a faint knock on the door.

Winona opened the door slightly and peeked in.

"There's no one here, Nona. Come in."

She pulled a chair to the front of the desk and looked down at the phones.

Billy pressed back in his chair and exhaled forcefully.

She stared at him for a second and then his glass of bourbon. "Do you have another one of those?"

"I'm sorry, Nona, how rude of me."

Nona smiled. "You're forgiven, Billy Roberts."

He poured her a drink and sat back into his chair. "How's your mom?"

"Not handling this well, as you could imagine."

"I don't get it, Nona. It's like they vanished."

She shook her head. "I find it hard to believe, between the two of them, in broad daylight, neither could send a text or something if they felt they were in danger."

"I don't think they ever felt threatened."

"What are you saying, Billy? Do you believe they were killed instantly?"

He shuffled through a stack of papers, then slid a missing persons flyer of Beth, Kelly, and Cindy across the desk. "No, I feel they are very much alive, for now."

Her eyes narrowed. "I don't get it."

Billy slid two more flyers across the desk. "These two girls were reported missing near Yellowstone ten days ago, Aiyana Begay and Evie White Flower. No attachment to each other. Both stayed in separate hotels in Jackson Hole, both reported by their traveling partners as missing in broad daylight. Aiyana went out for lunch and never returned. Evie went for a run, *in town*, and simply disappeared. Both had their phones."

Nona lined the posters up and examined each one. "All very pretty girls."

Billy leaned forward. "Look at their physical descriptions—all around the same height and weight, all with very athletic builds."

"What are you thinking?"

He swirled his glass, took a sip, and locked his eyes on her. "Traffickers."

Nona shook her head. "You know Mina and Kimi. They're smart girls. How could they be abducted on a busy street in the middle of a campus? Hell, you know how busy Jackson Hole is this time of the year. There is no friggin' way a forced abduction could happen in broad daylight."

"You're right. These girls weren't forced. They were tricked."

"How, and who could be so convincing to trick all these girls?"

Billy shrugged. "I don't know."

Nona turned at the sound of a knock. "Is it okay we have drinks?" she whispered.

"It's fine. I'm off duty." Then, to the door, "Come in."

"Billy, I think we might have something on the missing girls," Officer Chet Wilson exclaimed.

Billy sprung forward in his chair. "What do you have, Chet?"

Chet rushed to the desk holding out a manila envelope. "Pictures."

Billy opened the envelope and laid a group of black and white photos across his desk.

Chet said, "These were shot by security cameras at the Travel Rental Car lot. One of the employees saw the girl's flyer and recognized them. They walk past the lot every day. She remembered that one of her male coworkers, who ogled at the girls daily, commented, '*I have no shot,*' after watching them get into a new Mercedes with, '*Two good-looking rich pricks.*' They're a little fuzzy up close—the lab did the best they could—but there's enough for a positive ID."

Billy examined the pictures, shook his head, and passed them to Nona. "Here's your trick."

She examined the photos, drew a deep breath, and looked up. "Two good-looking rich guys, two single girls...."

"Chet, do we have anything from the street cameras, or other security cameras on that block?"

"Just one, Billy, at the intersection of Main and Ellis showing the car heading south. We ran the plate. It was off a rental car in Florida matching the Mercedes make, model, and color, but that car was never rented."

"That figures. They probably have several plates, all bogus."

Nona interjected, "How many white, hundred-thousand-dollar Mercedes could be running around? Can't we just put an APB or whatever, out across the country?"

"Shit, it doesn't matter. These guys are pros. That car will probably never be seen again. They won't get tripped up with something that simple. Chet, any matches on the passenger's face?"

"Nothing."

"Okay, man, good work. Let me know if anything else pops up."

Chet closed the door behind himself.

Nona and Billy sat silent, looking down at the collage of pictures on the desk.

"What's the next step, Billy?"

"I don't know. I'm gonna reach out to the search team in the Badlands and let them know what we have. The Johnson girl's dad is ex-FBI, as I'm sure you've seen on TV. Maybe he has resources we don't, and these pics can help?"

Blake Roberts leaned back in his chair and examined the white board on his wall. Threads strung between the missing girls' names crisscrossed in a quagmire of colors. He lit a cigarette, took a deep drag, and exhaled, filling his office with a plume of white smoke. A knock broke his concentration. "Come in."

"Has the white board spoken to you yet?" Joe Running Horse said.

Blake shook his head. "Joe, it's like these girls were sucked up by the earth. I don't fucking get it. Every clue is a dead end."

Joe waved the air parting the smoke. "If the Cap walks in, he'll flip. How many times has he told you not to smoke in here?"

Blake chuckled. "I lost count. What's he gonna do, fire me with one year left to retirement?"

"If you make it to retirement."

"If I find out I'm terminal, I'm suing the Indian Nation for introducing tobacco to white men."

"And we will countersue for white man's introduction of booze."

"*Touche'.*"

The phone rang, interrupting the long-time friends' banter.

"Yes, this is Detective Roberts. How can I help you, Sergeant Kellerman? One second, please, I'm gonna put you on speaker. My partner Joe Running Horse is in the room."

He pressed the speaker button and said, "Sergeant, can you repeat that please?"

"Sure, we have two missing girls in Vermillion. There appears to be several uncanny similarities between our cases. We have surveillance photos of *our* girls' last sighting."

Joe glanced at Blake with a raised brow. "What kind of similarities?"

"The physical characteristics between our girls, your girls, and two missing in Jackson Hole are nearly identical—almost same height, weight, and build, all very good looking. More interesting is the fact that our girls and the two in Jackson appeared to vanish into thin air, in broad daylight."

"Yeah," Blake said, "the 'vanish' part has us fucked up here. Our girls were *very* athletic. Hell, one was a mixed martial arts fighter. Each of them had their heads screwed on straight."

"Same here. I personally know both of our girls. We found it hard to believe they would let their guard down or, at least, not put up a struggle. Until we saw the photos. What is your email? I'll forward the file."

Blake gave it to him.

Within seconds, Blake's email alert sounded, and Joe walked around the desk to view the file.

Blake leaned into his computer. "Son of a bitch! Well, there *is* our answer: good-looking guys and hormones. I assume you have no make on the passenger or the car, Sergeant?"

"No, but my resources are limited. I hoped maybe, with the FBI involved in your case, they can get something out of these pics. My theory is these guys are part of a well-tuned trafficking ring, and that car will probably never be seen again."

Blake looked up at Joe. The slow shake of his partner's head and narrowed eyes confirmed the gravity of the situation. He leaned back in his chair and lit another cigarette. "Sergeant Kellerman, thank you for the call and the photos. I'll forward these immediately to the FBI."

"Detective Roberts, let me run a theory past you in line with the trafficking. The case that just ended a few weeks back in Wind River, involving the Dibella boys... what's your thoughts on a connection? The female attorney they tried to abduct fits perfectly in this pattern."

Blake paused. "Are you alone, Sergeant?"

Billy hesitated for only a second before saying, "Yes."

Blake lowered his voice. "We're moving our search from a missing person to a possible abduction. The press knows nothing about it. We'll continue with search crews out here, just as a smoke screen, while the FBI moves behind the scenes on border towns and South America. Your photos have all but sealed the deal on *our* abduction thoughts. Regarding the Dibella case, I didn't even think about that. Not sure how it might be related, since it was shoved down our *fucking* throats by the media for almost six months. But, didn't those boys die almost a year and a half ago?"

"They did. But who knows, maybe they were just foot soldiers, and not the group of '*bored rich kids*' as the press painted them."

"Hell, Sergeant, nowadays, you never know. I'll bring it up to the Feds when I call them. I'm sure they'll be reaching out to you. Is the number on my caller ID your office or cell?"

"It's my office. My cell is 211-555-0180."

Blake jotted the second number down. "Thank you, Sergeant Kellerman. I'm sure we'll talk again."

"You're welcome, Detective, and please, call me Billy. Let's snatch our girls back from the thin air they disappeared into."

"10-4, Billy, and my name is Blake."

Blake hung the phone up and spun his chair towards Joe. "What's your thoughts, partner?"

"I think we are too late."

Blake nodded slightly. "Unless the traffickers slip up, or by the grace of God, I agree."

Billy stared down at the phone, then lifted his eyes to Nona.

"What are you thinking, Billy?"

"I think we need a miracle."

CHAPTER 13
TEARS OF THE INNOCENT

Kelly excused herself from Cindy and Beth and walked through the bar area into the women's powder room. She locked the door and leaned against the wall, taking several deep breaths to calm herself and her trembling hands. Jill's soulless stare had sent shivers through her — the same look she'd seen the night they seduced her. *This time*, it was no hallucination; it was very real, and shook her to the core. She stared in the vanity mirror and blotted a tear from her eye before fixing her mascara. She then primped her hair, pulled her shoulders back, and straightened her posture.

"I won't let you scare me, you bitch," she hissed, and exited.

"Kelly," Jill called from the bar.

Kelly spun and smiled. "Jill, I didn't see you. Let me get Cindy and Beth and we'll join you?"

"No, Dominique and I would like to have a word, please."

"Sure." Kelly stepped to the bar.

The bartender greeted her with, "May I get you a drink?"

"Yes, Jack and Coke please."

"Please, dear, so blue collar," Dominique interrupted. "Blanton's and Coke for her."

"Yes ma'am," the bartender answered.

"Shall we have a seat?" Jill said.

The three women moved to a lone bistro table in the corner of the room.

Jill stirred her drink and looked into Kelly's eyes. "You looked a bit shocked when I broke up your little gaggle."

"Not shocked, just a bit surprised. I thought Mina, Kimi, and Aiyana would be big hits... given their *unique* situation."

"Mmmm, how I would love to taste that pure nectar," Dominique said. She licked her lips and sighed.

Jill chuckled. "Wouldn't we all."

Kelly wrinkled her brow. "I don't get it. Why can't you? It appears there is nothing off limits here."

"There is only *one* thing off limits here... virgins," Jill answered.

Domonique scoffed. "Yes, *all* my money and I can't order one."

Kelly bit her tongue as her eyes darted towards Dominique.

Jill, seeing the discontent on her face, patted Kelly's hand. "Yes, Dominique, but you must admit, we do provide some very *inexperienced* young ladies for you."

Dominique rolled her eyes and swirled her King Louis. "Hmmm, I guess, but a fresh pussy would be nice. Speaking of which, Kelly, Jill tells me your nectar is quite sweet."

Kelly paused and searched for words other than, *Fuck you, bitch!* With a coy smile, she said, "Well, perhaps this evening you will find out."

Jill half smiled and cocked one brow as she glanced at Dominique.

Dominique paused, reached into her purse, and retrieved a small crystal vial and a silver coke spoon. She filled each nostril with a heaping bump of the white powder and tilted her head back. "Perhaps, or I may want a hard cock tonight. Or both." She offered the vial to Kelly.

"No thank you, but, Jill, I would like to have some of that smoke Doc and you gave me, especially for Beth and Cindy. They're having a rough time with all of this. I know it helped me the other night."

Jill smiled. "Yes, it certainly *did* help you. If they're chosen tonight, I will make sure they are provided with some."

Kelly leaned in, her eyes flirting and voice lowered. "Well, in the event we carry this party on tonight, I would *definitely* like more. It made my orgasms almost... supernatural."

Dominique stood up and moved behind Kelly, and caressed her bare shoulders. She gently slid her hands beneath the loose silk cocktail dress and cupped Kelly's tits before running her fingers across rock hard nipples.

Kelly squirmed in her seat.

Jill sipped her drink while looking up, not to miss a moment of the impromptu seduction.

Dominique stopped abruptly, retrieved her purse and drink, and looked down at Kelly. "I don't think you need the help of any drugs. Maybe, or maybe not, we finish this tonight."

The two remaining women watched Dominique exit the bar and enter the main room.

Kelly, flushed, took a sip of her drink, adjusted her dress and stood up. "I'll be right back. I need some fresh air."

Jill chuckled. "And that was just your tits. She is amazing in bed. Just wait."

Kelly stepped onto a small deck off the bar area and looked to the stars. Her stomach churned with the thought of a tryst with Jill and Domonique.

How long can I keep this up? Will our plan work?

She rejoined Jill after freshening herself.

"Shall we join the others?" Jill said.

"Yes, I'm sure Cindy and Beth are missing me. By the way, where are Mina, Kimi, and the other girl going?"

"In time, Kelly... in time. Tonight, I want you to learn the basics of this operation, and... have some fun."

Mina sat on the edge of the bed and stared at the empty suitcase. Anxiety gripped her as she imagined the hell that lay ahead. The group's plan to escape the ranch had been squashed in a moment.

A knock broke the dread that raced through her mind. "Who is it?"

"It's me."

She unlocked the door to allow Kimi in. "I see you're packed."

Kimi set her suitcase down and looked over Mina's shoulder at the empty suitcase. "Having a hard time picking your wardrobe?"

Mina rolled her eyes. "How can you make jokes at a time like this?" She grabbed Kimi's hand and led her to the patio, shut the door behind her, and said in a harsh whisper, "Do you realize these fucking pricks just crushed any chance we had at escaping? We needed the other girls, especially Kelly."

"No, Mina, our chances just improved."

"What do you mean? *How* is that possible? We have no idea where we're going, or if we can even trust the other girl. She's kept to herself since we've been here. Hell, for all we know, she could be a plant."

Kimi grabbed her hand. "Think about this, Mina. I assume we're heading to a buyer. I'm sure he or she will not have this amount of security personnel around twenty-four/seven. We find his or her weakness, exploit it, and bail. As for the other girl, Aiyana, we have no choice but to assume she's real. We just don't confide in her until we know for sure."

Mina stared squarely in Kimi's eyes as she processed her words. "Okay, it's not like we have much choice, do we?"

"Not unless we switch into running gear and make a break now."

"I thought about that, but look around. There are friggin' armed guards everywhere. We wouldn't make it past the pool."

A loud knock at the door halted their conversation.

Mina moved to the door. "Who is it?"

"It's Doc. Open up, please."

Mina shot a wide-eyed glance at Kimi, took a deep breath, and opened the door.

Doc brushed past her and moved to the bed, where he set down a medical bag. "Ladies, good, I'm glad you're both here."

"Why, you gonna finger both of us again?" Kimi hissed.

Doc chuckled. "I wish, but sorry to disappoint you. I need you both to pull up your dresses and drop your panties, if you're wearing any." He turned away, opened the bag, produced two syringes and two small ampoules, then turned back to the girls and smirked. "Ladies, we can do this one of two ways: you can bare those cute asses to me *only*, or I can have a couple men come in and help. Trust me, you don't want to choose the latter. Now, *pull up your fucking dresses!*"

Doc drew the liquid from both ampoules as he watched the girl's underwear drop to the floor.

"What are you giving us?" Mina asked.

"It's a typhoid vaccination. You'll be spending a few days in South America."

Doc moved behind the girls and paused for a second, no doubt ogling their naked asses, then administered the doses. "You can drop your dresses. We've had a change in plans. Your flight has been moved to first light. Jill asked that you return to the party and entertain our guests." He repacked his medical back and exited.

"That fucking guy creeps me out," Mina hissed. "He's probably gonna go jerk off now. Poor Kelly... she had to fuck that scumbag."

"Yeah, when he was using the alcohol pad on me, I could feel his breath on my ass. He must have been inches away. Fucking perv." Kimi exaggerated a whole-body shiver.

Mina plopped down on the bed. "Well, now we know where we're going. South America is a big continent with several countries. We *will* disappear forever."

"He said a few days, if we can believe him. I wonder if we're coming back after that."

Mina shook her head. "Who knows, but let's get down stairs and pass this to Kelly. Maybe when she's working Jill, she can get more info."

The two women made the turn towards the landing and caught Jill's attention from below.

She noticed them, and then they exchanged nonchalant eye contact with Kelly and nodded slightly before making their way to the entrance foyer.

Jill turned from chatting with some man and walked towards them. "Ladies, sorry for the change in plans. The weather is a bit challenging over the mountains this evening. So please, relax and enjoy. Remember, you are spoken for. If *anyone*, including our guests, insist on your company, let me know." She returned to the man, and the two chuckled and glanced back at Mina and Kimi.

"God, I fucking hate her," Kimi whispered.

"She *will* get her day, trust me," Mina responded.

Mina glanced across the great room and made eye contact with Kelly and Cindy.

Kelly made a drinking motion and pointed her head to the bar area.

Mina touched Kimi's elbow. "Kelly just signaled us to the bar. Let's get a drink."

The four girls bellied-up to the brass rail in front of the bartender, who said, "Ladies, what will it be this round?"

"Four shots of tequila," Cindy said.

Kelly waited for the bartender to turn away, and whispered to Mina, "I thought you all were gone already."

Mina watched the bartender pour the first shot. "The flight got delayed. We're heading to South America, or at least that's what that scumbag Doc said when he gave us a vaccination."

Kelly said, "Damn, we needed a few days to figure this out."

The bartender poured the third shot.

Mina nodded. "I know, but he said we were only going for a few days."

"I wonder what that means?"

"I don't know, but here comes the bartender."

Mina grabbed her shot, stepped back from the bar, put on her best game face, and raised her glass. "Saludes, you sluts."

"Saludes," the three responded before downing the tequila.

Kimi made a sour face. "God, I hate that stuff. Where is our other slut?"

Cindy pointed past the fireplace in the main room. "That fat fuck over there took a liking to her. He requested she change into a more formal gown, drop her hair, and put on red lipstick. God, he's gross. I pray he doesn't choose Beth. She's not strong enough."

Jill walked up to said fat fuck, bent over, and said something that made him smile. He slid his obese body forward, slowly stood up, downed his drink, and waddled past the stairs towards the kitchen area.

Jill strolled over to the girls. "Well, ladies, it would appear Beth may have a new home, providing she remembers what I said. I'm told Mr. Amore has a dick as wide as a beer can. I hope she can handle him." She let out a mocking laugh and walked away. She took several steps and looked back. "Cindy, grab your drink. Mr. Distinguished would like to speak with you. Follow me, please."

Cindy glanced at Kelly, her eyes looking for reassurance.

Kelly whispered, "Remember the plan. Use the smoke if he takes you upstairs."

The girls watched Cindy meet with Mr. Distinguished, and after several minutes, he bent his arm to escort her towards the stairs.

She looked back at Kelly as she placed her foot on the first step. Her eyes welled as she lipped, *'Why?'*

Kelly dropped her head. "I need another shot."

Beth finished changing into a black strapless gown. She dropped her shoulder-length hair and added a medium red lipstick, as requested, and walked into the hall.

One of the security staff greeted her. "Ma'am, please follow me."

The man led her down the hall in the opposite direction of the stairs. After a left turn then a quick right, they came to set of double doors. He unlocked the doors and swung them open to another wing. He relocked the double doors, positioned himself in front of them, and pointed down the hall. "The third door on the left is open. Please go in."

Beth followed his finger down the red-carpeted hall. Ornate woodworking and aged oil paintings adorned the walls. Soft classical music flowed from the intercom. With each step, her heart pounded. Thoughts of her life raced before her. To her knowledge, she was the only girl in the group selected at this time.

Can the plan work if I'm the only one chosen? Will the other girls be punished if I escape? Is the timing off?

Soon, she would have to make a decision with dire consequences should it go wrong.

She reached the third door, which sat directly across from an elevator, opened it slowly and entered an opulent sweet. After two steps, she was met by overpowering cologne and shook her head, "*No,*" then raced back to the door and rattled the locked handle feverishly. Defeated she leaned against the wall as the reality of the situation sent tremors through her body. The thought of satisfying anyone but her beloved fiancé made her dry heave. She took several deep breaths, refocused on the plan, then moved to the center of the room and surveyed it. On the bar, a bag of weed and a pipe sat on a silver serving tray.

Good! Kelly was successful.

Next, her eyes were quickly drawn to a set of french doors and a long fur coat that lay across a chair beside them. She swung open one side and walked out on the patio. The room sat on the opposite side of the mansion. The drop to the sloped landscaped beds was a bit higher than her room, but would allow for a natural tuck and roll. The grounds where dark and gave way to a wooded area a football field's length away. Unlike at the front of the house, no army of security guards moved about. At the edge of the woods, the glow of one elevated guard shack and the outlines of two men drew her attention. She smiled and nodded before reentering the bedroom.

The chime of the elevator was soon followed by the sound of the electric lock at the door. Mr. Amore opened the door, walked forward a few steps to the bar, and paused. "You look beautiful, Beth. My name is Sergio. Would you like a drink?"

She swallowed hard. "Red wine, please."

Sergio looked down at the weed and pipe sitting on the bar next to the wine and scoffed. "They know I have fucking asthma."

Beth watched as he threw the girl's plans into the trash, and felt the blood draw from her face.

He poured both drinks and met her in the middle of the room.

"This is one of the most expensive wines in Italy. I have it flown in by the case. I know this *arrangement* may not be ideal, but expensive wine is only the start of a life of luxury, *if* you embrace it."

"I don't get it. With all your money, why would you need to resort to human slavery for your women."

Sergio chuckled. "Human slavery? My dear, this is the furthest from slavery. You will be paid more money than you'll ever earn. In fact, every woman that I have contracted with this ranch has chosen to stay in my employment after their contract was up."

Beth shook her head. "I don't understand. What contract? I didn't sign any fucking contract with these people or you."

"No, you didn't, but I did. Depending on how this evening goes, I will offer you a job for one year. My offer will range from five hundred thousand to one million dollars, either of which would allow you to leave my employment at the end. And both allow you to contact your family immediately."

"How do you know I won't contact them and turn you and *this* operation in?"

"Because you love them. The tentacles of this operation reach deep into the pockets of some of the most powerful people in the world. It is much bigger than you can imagine. What you see here is nothing compared to the real purpose of this enterprise. Do you not think other girls have tried to expose this? It is ironic that, once they tried, their loved ones met untimely deaths." He downed his glass of wine and let out a mocking laugh that sent shivers through her body. "Must be a curse or something. Now... enough talk. Let's see what your contract will be worth. Take off your dress."

Beth's hands trembled as she slipped the spaghetti straps off her shoulders and allowed the dress to fall in a heap at her feet.

Sergio backed up and ogled her. "Drop your panties. I want to see what I'm paying for. Leave the heels on."

Her eyes welled. His stare tore at every fiber in her body as she allowed the thong to drop to her ankles.

He nodded and stepped forward, and ran his meaty hands across her breasts. He pulled her nipples forward and rubbed them between his sausage fingers. "Very nice, Beth." He slid behind her and kissed the back of her neck while cupping both ass cheeks. His hot breath, reeking of booze and garlic, sickened her. "Have a seat on the chair."

He removed his sports coat and sweat-soaked white dress shirt. Long black body hair covered his large man boobs and rolls of glistening fat. He dropped his pants and his stomach fell past his pubic area. He walked towards her, lifted his stomach, and exposed a large but flaccid cock.

"This is where you earn your contract." He forced his dick to her lips. His sweat-soaked stomach pressed against her forehead.

All she could think of was her family, her fiancé, and the escape route from the patio. Tears streamed down her cheeks as she took him in her mouth. He thrust forcefully, causing her to gag several times.

He pulled from her mouth and stepped back. "Damn liquor is running through me," he grumbled. "Go doggy style on the end of the bed. I'll be right back."

She watched him waddle across the suite into the bath. *No, I'm not letting him touch me one more time.*

Quickly, she grabbed a bottle of water and the belt from his pants, slipped on a pair of sneakers lying at the foot of his bed, and snatched the fur coat on her way out the patio doors. She donned the oversized jacket and tied the belt around her waist. For a large man, his feet were surprisingly small, and the fit of the sneakers built confidence she could run unencumbered. She threw both legs over the iron railing and perched on the thin ledge of the cement deck. Unlike her side of the house, there were no wood joists to hang from and drop to the ground. She looked back to see Sergio exit from the bath and quickly discover she was gone.

His eyes met hers. "*Stop, you cunt,*" he bellowed, lumbering towards the patio.

She looked down, took a deep breath, and dropped. Her legs crumbled with the impact. She rolled as planned, allowing the slope to aid her fall.

Then a dull thud followed. A single tear rolled down her cheek as she stared blankly to the stars, and the faces of people she loved faded into darkness.

Jill was chatting with Michelle Cornwell when a member of security interrupted.

"Ma'am, can I speak with you for a second?"

Jill recognized the urgency in his eyes. "Excuse me, Michelle." The two stepped from earshot of the guests. "What is it, James?"

"There's been an accident in Mr. Delucca's room."

CHAPTER 14
A WOMAN'S INTUITION

Jake and Dakota walked down from the cave and paused on the back deck. He looked up at the early night sky and breathed deeply. "The smells of fall are fading quickly. Should we sit out here and have a cocktail?"

Dakota smiled. "Jake Michaels, you read my mind. Let me grab my phone in case Woo Woo calls or texts. I fucking dread turning it back on. I'm sure it has blown up over the past three days."

"Yeah, I should Skype with the kids while I'm down here. Soon the snows will fly and I won't be able to talk with them on a regular basis."

"Well, I was thinking about that. Let me grab a couple beers and my phone. I'll be right back."

Jake settled into the patio chair, leaned his head back and looked at the first stars of the night. The dark, violent visions Dakota and he had just experienced rattled him, but the screen door opening snapped him out of it.

"Were you falling asleep? Don't tell me the old man in you is coming out?" Dakota laughed and handed him a beer.

He chuckled and exaggerated his head movement, looking her over from head to toe. "An old man can't handle you. No, I was thinking about the Spirit World we just visited. It had no connection to the world Rowtag shows us. I don't get it."

"Maybe we should talk to Great Grandfather in the morning."

He nodded. "I think that's a great idea. Now, what were you thinking regarding the coming winter?"

She placed her beer on the table, leaned over, and placed her hands on his. Her eyes sparkled. "Well, I think you should stay down here for the winter."

"On the ranch?"

"Hell no! We would never be able to spend any time with each other. I think you should get a place off the mountain."

"Like in town? No fucking way. I don't want to deal with people all day, and Honi needs open space. Plus, where would I get the money to rent?"

"Don't think I thought about all that?" Dakota pulled a letter from her back pocket and slid it across the glass table. "This was in my mail. It's an offer from MBO for the exclusive rights to tell your story. It's mid six figures plus 2% of any residual profits."

Jake looked at the envelope's post mark. "Damn, it's dated the day after the trial ended. When did you get this?"

"The morning I left for the cabin. I didn't open it until we got back this afternoon. I figured we could talk about it tonight."

Jake lips rattled as he blew out forcefully and stared down at the envelope. "I don't know, Dakota. Do you want all that attention? Hell, it's as much your story as mine. Do you want to relive that nightmare? Plus, Alexi and the kids will be in the spotlight. If Dibella gets word of this, he'll have a legal team assembled so damn fast our heads will spin. Production would never get off the ground. Sounds like a fucking nightmare."

"I also thought about all that. We don't have to make any decisions right now. As for having you down here with me for the winter, while we figure out the money stuff, I do have another idea."

"I'm sure you do. What is it?"

"Well... over on a part of the ranch I haven't taken you to, is what's left of an old homestead. Originally, my grandparents were gonna use the well there and build their home, but Neiwoo wanted to be able to look over the ranch, so they built up here. I'm sure Woo Woo would allow you to build a small home there. I have money for that. It wouldn't be fancy, but would be ours."

The look in her eyes made him realize that, one way or the other, he would be spending the winter off the mountain. "Okay, let's take a few days and figure all this out. Obviously, we need your grandfather's blessing. Have you heard from him?"

Dakota looked at her phone. "No, not yet. I'm sure his meeting with Dibella will be lengthy. Let me text him."

Shortly after her text, the phone rang.

"Woo Woo, how did it go?"

"Dakota, it's Jay. Your grandfather is driving. Hold on while I put you on speaker."

"Hey, Lomasi, how is everything on the ranch?"

"It's fine, Woo Woo. Have you met with Dibella yet?"

"Yes, it was very short. Of course, he and that ass Sellman deny everything. However, I believe we shook the tree enough. We will talk more when I get home."

"Did you expect anything but? When will you be home?"

"We are taking an early morning flight. I will be in Jackson by 9 AM."

"Okay, see you in the late morning. I love you."

"I love you too. Tell your grandmother I will call her as soon as I get to the hotel."

"I will. She went into town for pancake mix. She should be back soon."

"Pancake mix? At eight o'clock?"

"Yeah, she decided to go and get Great Grandfather early tomorrow morning. You know the store doesn't open till nine on Saturdays. He insisted on sausage and pancakes. He claims the home won't feed him good breakfasts."

Jim laughed. "Yes, just like they starve him at lunch and dinner, yet he has gained twenty pounds since moving there. Okay, I will call her in a bit. Goodnight."

"Goodnight, Woo Woo."

"That comes as no surprise with Dibella," Jake said.

"Nope. Do you want another beer?"

Jake stood up and grabbed the empties. "Yeah, I'll get them. I need to use the bathroom anyway."

She looked down at her phone and the ninety unread emails, waved her hand *bye bye* at them, and stood up to stretch. As she turned and looked up at the old cave, a feeling of dread sent a shiver through her.

Ancestors, what are you trying to show us?

The screen door startled her. "Damn! You scared the crap out of me."

Jake laughed. "Did you forget I'd be right back?"

"No." She turned and nodded back at the cave. "I have a bad feeling about what my ancestors are trying to show us."

Alexi sat in Jake's office, rifling through the endless pile of mail that had arrived every day since the trial. One by one, she shredded solicitation after solicitation from attorneys across the country, but an official letter from the State of North Carolina Vital Records caught her attention. It was a recision of Jake's Death Certificate, along with paperwork for him or his attorney to sign. A second paper addressed the absolution of their marriage and the legal ramifications of Jake's living status. A rush of emotions froze her as she looked blankly at the paperwork.

Several seconds passed before a text from Danielle drew her back to reality.

> *Hey, Mom, just spoke with Dad on Skype. He's off the mountain and at Dakota's ranch. He's calling the boys. You should Skype him.*

She starred at the text for a moment, then responded.

> *Cool, maybe I will. Out and about right now. Luv you.*

She looked down at the State paperwork again, then scrolled through her contacts to find Dakota's number, and sent a text.

> *Dakota, it's Alex Michaels. I have paperwork from N.C. Dept of Vitals I need to forward.*

Dakota looked at the text, stood up from the kitchen table, removed her sweat jacket, and walked into her grandfather's office where Jake sat on the computer.

Jake looked up as she entered. "Damn, you fill out a bra top and workout shorts. I thought you were cold?"

"I was until the heat kicked on. How are the kids doing?"

"They're good. They didn't expect me to Skype them so soon after the trial. So, it was a nice surprise."

"I just got a text from Alex. She said some paperwork showed up we need to know about. Do you want to Skype her?"

He paused for a second and stared blankly past her.

"Jake, what's wrong?"

"I can't remember her Skype account."

She exaggerated her *'what the fuck'* expression as she pressed her phone forward and wiggled it. "Duh! I can text her back for it. Are you okay? That's *if* you want to talk right now."

He chuckled and took a deep breath. "Wow, maybe the smoke is killing my brain cells instead of healing them. Yeah, I know she's gonna get flooded with shit and will need our help till it blows over."

Dakota texted her.

Hey, Alex, nice to hear from you. What is your Skype account?

The text came back with the account.

Okay, thanks. Jake is calling.

Alexi answered the video call, her face taking up the full screen.

"Hey you," Jake said.

"Hey yourself. Can you back up a bit? I can see your nose hairs."

He chuckled and repositioned. "Is that better?"

Alexi seemed to quickly pan the room behind him. "Much better. Nice office."

"It's Jim's. Yeah, makes my old office back home look like a broom closet."

"Well, this 'broom closet' afforded us a nice lifestyle for many years."

A fond smile crossed his face as he nodded. "Yes, it did. How are you?"

"I'm good, just trying to wade through this sea of mail that arrives everyday since the trial ended. It appears you and your adventure are in great demand from every media outlet known to man. How are you handling your newfound fame?"

"I'm not. I went to the cabin to escape it all."

Dakota listened to the friendly conversation from just off to the side, and sighed inaudibly. She pushed her hair off her shoulders, walked behind Jake, and looked down at the screen.

Alex's eyes darted past him, quickly noticing the skimpy spandex shorts, bra top, and two beers in her hands.

She refocused on Jake, her expression hardened. "Yeah, it appears escape is your MO."

Jake was taken by surprise in her sudden change of tone. "Hey, that was unfair. But... I guess I deserve it."

She paused, took a deep breath, and looked down. "No, you didn't, and I didn't reach out to argue with you."

Dakota listened to the banter, smirked, put her sweat jacket on, and walked behind Jake. She bent over to fit in the screen. "Hello, Alex, how are you?"

The two women looked into each other's eyes and, after a brief pause, Alex forced a slight smile and quick raise of her brow. "I'm good, Dakota. How are you handling all this attention since the trial?"

"I turned my phone off and stayed out of town. I know I'll have a lot of work to do bringing this guy back from the grave. I just needed a break."

Alex watched as Dakota touched Jake's shoulder. "Yeah, I'm sure you'll have your hands full. That's the reason I called." She held the form from North Carolina to the screen. "Do you recognize this?"

Dakota examined the letter. "No, but it appears generic. Can you scan it to me, and I'll have Jake sign it and return for your signature if needed?"

"Sure. I also have several other important documents. Jake, how long will you be off the mountain for?"

"I don't know yet."

Dakota flicked his thigh below the screen view.

Alexi raised her brow. "Oh, are you planning on staying on the ranch for a while?"

"No, I came down to sign some paperwork for the DA's office, then head back up. Unfortunately, he was killed in a motorcycle accident, and I don't know how that will affect things on Monday."

"Alex," Dakota interrupted, "please forward any documents you get that appear to be legal in nature. You won't overwhelm me. Also, just an FYI... MBO wants to purchase the rights to Jake's story. Obviously, it will impact all of us. Their initial offer is generous and could easily help all of us recover any wages we lost though this."

Alex glared into the screen. "Wages.... *Fuck the wages!* I buried my husband. My kids lost their father. Our lives were turned upside down. On several occasions, I didn't want to live anymore. Then, Jake resurrects in the middle of a sensational trial as a knight in *shining fucking armor* rescuing the beautiful damsel in distress. *No!* I don't want a fucking penny from any of this. *I want* the life I had a year and a half ago. *I want* to wake up next the man I loved for over thirty years, *the man* that I started every day with on a walk through our neighborhood, *the man* whose leather chair I'm in right now, which hugs me every day because *he* won't. *I want the man* whose shoulder you just touched, and which I can't." Tears streamed down her cheeks and her lips quivered. "That is worth more *fucking money* than they could ever offer. *No!* I won't watch Hollywood retell our story. I have to go."

The call ended.

Jake and Dakota stared at the computer, and Jake lowered his head.

Dakota stood up, walked to her grandfather's bar, and poured a glass of bourbon. She looked back at Jake, whose head remained bowed, and raised the glass to her mouth.

Well played, Alex Michaels. Well played.

Alex wiped the tears from her eyes and threw the tissue on Jake's desk. The suspicions she'd had towards the end of the trial had been confirmed. Jake and Dakota were much too familiar with each other. She shook her head and smirked.

You are young and beautiful, Dakota, but you didn't see the look in his

CHAPTER 15
NOT TONIGHT

"What type of accident, James? Is Sergio okay?" Jill asked

"It's not him, it's the girl. She fell."

"Fell from where?"

James panned the room. "Follow me outside, please. Let's use the kitchen entrance. I called Doc. He's on the way."

Jill and James ran into Dominique and Kelly on their way towards the rear patio.

Dominique ran her eyes across James's broad chest, past his thin waist, and stopped at his crotch. She licked the rim of her glass. "Jill, he's yummy. You can't wait till later? Maybe the three of us could share him."

Jill smiled. "He is, but I need to tend to some business with the staff. I'll be right back."

Dominique looked at Kelly and mimicked a blow job. "I bet she *does* have *business* with his '*staff*.' What a slut."

Kelly forced a smile and looked back at the pace Jill and the security guard walked down the hall. "She *is* in a hurry, isn't she?"

Dominique locked her arm arounds Kelly's. "Oh well. Come, darling, let's do a shot."

Jill exited the patio doors and turned left. A small crowd gathered in the dim light at the end of the house. She quickened her steps and approached the circle of security personal. They parted, allowing her to view Beth's body laid face up in the manicured beds.

Doc knelt next to her. He pulled his hand from her carotid, looked up and shook his head.

Jill's gaze darted towards Sergio's balcony.

Sergio stood there in a robe, smoking a cigar and casually looking over the group.

Jill walked beneath him and barked, "What the fuck happened?"

He swirled his glass of wine. "I went to the bathroom, came out, and saw her standing on the ledge in my fur coat. She looked back and jumped. I guess she landed wrong and cracked her skull. Dumb bitch."

Jill glared at him for a couple seconds, took a deep breath, and stepped back to Beth's body. "Looks like she was trying to make a run for it, Doc."

"Yep, I assume the sneakers belong to the fat man. She had a bottle of water in the fur jacket. Not sure where she thought she was going. She would have never made it past the sentry lasers."

Jill shook her head. "I guess our fake shooting wasn't good enough for her. Maybe now the other girls will realize there *is no* escaping us. Untie that belt and open the fur up. What's she wearing?"

Doc laid the coat open. "Not a thing."

Jill looked down. "Good. I'll be right back. Leave it open."

"Hey, I paid for her," Sergio yelled.

Jill stopped dead in her tracks. "I know. I'll talk with Mr. P and will be up to discuss this unforeseen event shortly."

She calmly walked back into the party through the front door. Cindy and Mina stood to the right of the entrance.

"Cindy, find Kelly and have her gather the rest of the girls. Meet me on the front porch. I have something to show you all."

A few minutes later, Kelly, Cindy, Mina, Kimi, Aiyana, and Wendy joined Jill on the front porch.

Jill glanced at the group. "Kelly, where are the others?"

"Beth is with Mr. Amore, the two girls from California went upstairs with the couple, and I saw the young Zuni girl and Wendy go upstairs with the older gentleman."

Jill nodded. "Very well, follow me."

The group walked off the front porch and made their way to the rear of the right wing. In the moonlight light, they saw several figures gathered in a circle. Muffled chatter and laughter broke the night silence as they got closer.

Kelly whispered to Cindy, "I don't like this. Something feels bad."

Jill approached ahead of the girls. "Step aside, boys."

Kelly adjusted her eyes to the shape on the ground, and broke into a run. "*No, Beth, No!*"

Cindy, Mina, and Kimi raced forward.

Cindy collapsed to her knees next to Kelly, who cradled Beth's blood-matted head. She closed the fur coat around her naked friend and looked up at the men surrounding her. "*Get away from her, you bastards!*"

Kimi and Mina held each other and sobbed.

Aiyana looked towards the stars and prayed.

Jill walked slowly towards Beth's feet.

Kelly glared up at her. "You promised she would be safe." She looked back at the balcony. "He killed her."

"And I will *fucking* kill him," Cindy hissed.

Jill half-smiled and shook her head. "Ladies, look at what she's dressed in. Look in the coat. There's water. She tried to escape and bashed her pretty head on the rock. He paid a half a million dollars for her ass and probably never got it. So *no*, he didn't kill her."

Cindy launched at Jill, catching her across the face with an elbow and snapping her head sideways. She followed with a left hook.

Jill caught the swing in mid-air, and her piercing blue eyes locked onto Cindy's. They widened as her grip grew stronger, dropping the girl to her knees.

Jill's strength clearly shocked Cindy, who looked up as if what stared back terrified her. She jerked violently to break the grip, and the sound of grinding bones was followed by screams of writhing pain. Jill smiled and let go, and Cindy crumbled onto her side.

Jill kept her eyes on the ground for several seconds as she spit blood from her torn lower lip. "Take her to the stable," she commanded the security staff.

Three men pulled Cindy to her knees and dragged her away.

"Kelly, you and the rest of the girls go to your rooms and freshen up. Our guests have needs."

Jill waited until the girls were out of earshot, then pointed with her head to Beth's body. "Doc, take her and wait for my call. Maybe one of our guests has a fetish for necrophilia. Maybe we can still make a few bucks off her."

"Hey, what about my money, Jill?" Sergio grumbled from the balcony.

"I'm heading to Mr. P's right now."

"And the bitch left me with blue balls."

Jill rolled her eyes. "Take your pick and I'll send them up to relieve you."

"Send me the one who punched you in the face. She can taste her friend's spit on my dick." Sergio belly-laughed.

"I don't believe you'll want her after she's punished. I'll send someone up shortly."

Jill entered the main house and stepped into the powder room outside of Mr. P's office. She looked into the mirror at her mangled lowered lip, then closed her eyes and whispered, "A-do-nai ra-pha sa-phap." As a tingle ran threw her body, she opened her eyes, watched the injury heal, smiled, applied her lipstick, and exited into the foyer towards Mr. P's office.

"Come in, Jill."

She closed the office doors behind her and sauntered to the globe bar. "Can I get you a drink?"

"No, I'm fine. I assume you're her regarding the unfortunate business loss we just suffered."

She finished her pour and turned. "I am. Doc is looking at our guest's profiles to see if, perhaps, one may have a fancy for some *dead play*. Maybe we can recoup some of our investment."

Mr. P nodded and pulled a cigar from his desktop humidor. "I'm sure Sergio wants a refund?"

"He does, but maybe I can persuade him into another girl or a credit."

"In a more pressing issue, I received a call from Washington. The FBI is going to use a search in the Badlands as a cover. They believe Beth and her friends are victims of sex trafficking."

"And why the sudden shift?"

Mr. P slid two profile folders across the desk. "Two of our pickers got sloppy. A street camera picked them and their car up while they were grabbing Mina and Kimi. A witness is working with a sketch artist as we speak."

Jill sat and opened the folders. "Hmm, they're two of our best assets in the field. It's not like them to be sloppy."

"Unfortunately, they slipped up. The Feds will allocate endless resources to find these guys. The Dibella debacle made our investors squeamish. Once they find out about the Feds, they will close their wallets."

Jill sipped her bourbon, rolled her eyes and sighed. "Well, the Feds can have fun with that. Our operation is too smooth. Even if they find these two, they'll never tie them back to us. You know that. Our operation has way too many layers."

Mr. P leaned back in his chair, took a deep puff of his cigar, and blew a plume of smoke over his desk. "Let's make sure. Have Doc leave a clue on Beth, then dump her body outside of Seattle."

Jill leaned forward in her chair with a coy smile. "A clue? You *have* piqued my interest. What sort of clue? What are you thinking?"

He chuckled. "Quite the morbid bitch, aren't you? You and Doc use your imaginations. Let's send the FBI in a different direction. Poor Beth was possibly the victim of the two serial killers they have on film in South Dakota."

She swirled her sifter. "Hmm, well that will require more than one body, in a reasonable amount of time."

"I'm sure you can arrange that. We seem to suffer an extraordinary number of casualties in our line of work. As for those two liabilities, make sure they're eliminated."

"Yes, sir, the FBI will chase ghosts." She stood up and walked towards the door.

"And Jill...."

She paused with her hands on the double brass handles. "Yes."

"Make sure that fat fuck didn't leave any DNA on, or in, her."

She glanced back over her shoulder. "Of course."

Jill walked into Doc's darkened exam room, where he was examining Beth's body with a light wand.

"Did Sergio leave any evidence on or in her, Doc."

"Doesn't appear so. Only fluid showing up looks like her own blood."

"Any takers on some Necrophilia?"

"Nope, not with this group."

"Okay, just as well. Mr. P has a unique project for us, and she's the first victim discovered."

Doc turned the exam room lights up. "Victim? And what sort of project?"

"She's the victim of a new serial killer or killers. Maybe a cult? I'll leave that up to you. He wants to send the FBI on a wild goose chase. He wants the body dumped outside Seattle."

Doc beamed. "Finally, I can use my creative talents."

Jill patted him on the shoulder. "I knew you'd like that."

"What's the reason?"

"It appears the FBI may be getting smarter. They have reason to believe this last group of girls are victims of sex traffickers."

Doc scoffed. "Well, I did voice my opinion that we should lay low till the smoke cleared from the Dibella trial. The press drove the whole trafficking thing into everyone's fucking head."

Jill approached the exam table and looked down at Beth's naked body. "It's a shame. She was beautiful. Oh well, I'll let you get to work. I have to attend to a table filming."

"I would not mind *at all* being part of that one."

"I don't think you would, Doc. She's going for ten rounds. It will get sloppy. But, since our *little issue* in Wind River, we owe our Special Clients more *bang for their bucks*, if you would."

He nodded. "The Dibella boys were the best. Our operation will miss them."

"Yeah, they had a flair for the camera. It'll take a while to replace them, but we will. A stiff dick and greed will always prevail. See you later. Have fun."

Doc looked down at Beth. "Jill, pick a number between 1 and 10."

Jill thought for a second. "Six."

He rolled Beth over and smiled. "I know exactly what I'm gonna do."

Jill walked through the stables into the entrance of a large pasture. "Bobbie Joe, you have your boys ready?"

"Yes ma'am, ten cowboys and one Indian."

"Well, she's not an Indian but she'll do. Bring her out."

Two men held Cindy's bound arms tightly as she thrashed around. They pulled her under the stable spotlight.

Jill approached, looked her in the eyes and smiled. "I like the Indian maiden outfit, Bobbie Joe. Take off her gag. I see she's still full of fight. That's good. She'll need it."

Cindy spit in Jill's face. "Fuck you, bitch."

Jill calmly wiped her forehead and right cheek, and pointed her head towards the dark pasture. "Out there is the freedom poor Beth wanted soooo desperately. I'm going to cut you lose and give you a three-minute head start. Then, a group of very horny men are gonna come after you. If you elude them, over that mountain is freedom. If they catch you, you will be a star." Without turning away from Cindy, she said to Bobbie Joe, "Cut her loose."

Cindy rubbed her injured hand and looked Jill in the eyes. "I'll kill each of the men you send after me. Then I will come back for you."

Jill rolled her eyes. "Do you know how many times I've heard that? Time is ticking, so you better get movin'. Oh, and by the way, my men know your skills in the ring. They're not too shabby of fighters either."

Cindy glared at her, then turned towards the ten cowboys leaned against a horse fence and dashed into the darkness of the pasture.

"Bobbie Joe, tell your men to be careful. I need all of them ready for the table. Hit her with a dart once you catch her, but keep that off film. She's about a hundred and ten pounds. Use enough to slow her, but we still want to make her resistance look real."

"Yes ma'am."

Jill glanced at her watch. "Give her another minute and start this party."

"Will do, ma'am."

Jill walked from the pasture into a raised area overlooking a round room. In the middle stood a knee-high, eight-foot, round table covered in white padding. Four shackles where anchored into each quadrant, and video cameras lined the circumference of the room. She walked over to a wall of night surveillance screens and watched the cowboys give chase through the dark pasture.

Cindy raced across the open fields heading for the outline of the mountains visible in the bright moonlight. The ruts in the plowed field slowed her pace, and she paused for a second to look back. A group of grey figures closed in on her. She estimated they were six hundred yards out. She dashed forward, focused on the silhouette of a wood line against the starlit sky. Suddenly, a low familiar roar caught her ear. She crested a small knoll and sunk to her knees.

"No, you fucking bitch! No!" she screamed.

Below her, the moon illuminated a rushing river, full of swirling eddies and rapids. She climbed down the river bank, bent over and felt the frigid water. She had no chance of surviving the high desert night soaking wet... *if* she even made it across.

"Okay, you pieces of shit, you're not taking me this easy." She climbed back to the knoll and waited for the approaching group.

Bobbie Joe pointed. "There she is, boys. I knew she wouldn't be dumb enough to cross the river at night. Get the cameras ready."

The group slowed their pace as they approached their quarry, forming a half circle.

Cindy put her left foot forward and moved into a fighting posture.

Bobbie Joe said, "Now, Miss Cindy, we don't need to make this rough. Why don't you just come along peacefully? We don't want that pretty body of yours all welted up for the camera."

"Fuck you," she hissed.

One of the cowboy's blurted out, "Yes, you will be, and the rest of us."

The group's laughter intensified her anger. "I'll bet you dickless fucks can't even get it up. Who wants to try first?"

A stocky, dark-haired cowboy stepped forward. "Well, I don't want sloppy seconds, boys. If I tie her up, she's mine first on the table." He moved forward with a set of zip ties in his hand.

Cindy moved towards him and, with lightning speed, caught his left temple with a roundhouse kick. The cowboy fell in a heap and lay motionless on the ground.

"Get up, Wesley," Bobbie Joe yelled.

The cowboy did not budge.

Cindy spat on the fallen cowboy. "Well, I guess he won't be first to have me." She looked at the group and growled, "Who's next?"

Bobbie Joe took a step forward and shook his head. "No, little girl, this is *not* how we play this game. Turn off the cameras, boys." He pulled a pistol from his belt and fired a muffled shot at Cindy.

She recoiled her left leg, and looked down to see a dart in her thigh. Slowly, she felt the earth spin. When the group approached her, she threw slow-motion punches and stumbled as she attempted to kick. Their laughter echoed in her ears as two men grabbed her arms and tied them behind her back. A third man ripped her maiden garb off, leaving only a turquoise neckless on her naked body.

They escorted her back to the stable, with two men staying in front to film her. The tranquilizer began to wear off as the light of the stable grew closer, and she struggled to free her arms from the ropes around her waist. Tears fell down her cheeks as grim reality set in.

Jill walked from the stable and met the group. She approached Cindy and circled her. "Good job, boys, not a mark on her. Take her to the table."

Cindy looked back. "*I will kill you, bitch!* You hear me? I'll kill you."

Jill smiled and mumbled, "I'm glad to see you have some fight left in you, little girl. Let's see how you are in an hour or so."

The men forced Cindy down on the round table. They restrained her ankles in two shackles, and moved to cut the ropes from her wrists."

"Be careful, boys. That rattle snake can still bite," Bobbie Joe said.

The men's strength was too much for Cindy. One at a time, they shackled her wrists.

Jill entered the room and stood at the feet of Cindy's spread legs. She crawled forward on the table and buried her tongue between Cindy's legs.

Cindy squirmed, "No, you bitch!"

Jill kneeled up and backed off the table. "That's sweet-tasting, boys, if a bit dry. Have fun with her. And remember, save yourselves for the rapture."

The lights dimmed in the room, and a spotlight fell on Cindy's face as circus music played.

Bobbie Joe grabbed the edge of the table and gave it a spin. "Let's see who's first."

When the table came to rest, Cindy looked up at the crotch of tall, dark-haired cowboy.

"Dwayne, you lucky bastard! That's two in a row, "Bobbie Joe said.

Jill paused the music and announced over the speakers, "Okay, Cowboys, show our captured Indian what you all got for her."

The cowboys removed their clothes and took turns spinning Cindy in front of them, smacking their half-hard dicks off her face to the beat of the circus tune.

"Let the bidding war begin," Jill's voice rang over the intercom. "Round two, boys... you know the drill."

The lights softened and traditional porn music replaced the frivolity of the circus tune. Tears poured down Cindy's face as the first man crawled on top of her. She thrashed about, but to no avail. One by one, the cowboys spun her in front of them and took what was not theirs. With each assault, her fight weakened. She laid her head to the side and prayed for them to finish.

The lights brightened, the music lowered, and Jill walked into the room. "Looking good on film, boys. The bids are rolling in. Take a break, get yourselves something to drink." She approached Cindy, firmly grabbed her forehead and turned her head straight. "Yes, I said a break. *Now*, maybe next time you'll think twice about defying me. I believe you'll like the last half of this game. It's always a favorite of our bidders. Have fun, and oh... relax. As you have felt, these boys are quite large."

Jill exited the room.

The cowboys all donned dark glasses. Then, one shackle at a time, they released Cindy's wrists and ankles, placed her face down, and propped a wedge-shaped pillow under her stomach.

She offered no resistance, and sunk deeper into a far away place as the lights dimmed. Retro music pulsated over the speakers and strobes flashed in synchronicity. One by one, the cowboys entered Cindy's forbidden zone. The burning pain and relentless hammering inside her drove her to the brink of collapse. The rhythmic pounding of the music and flashing lights took her to the edge of sanity.

When the last man finished, the music and strobes stopped.

Jill announced, "Time for the rapture, boys." She glanced down at her laptop as the bids rushed in at a frenzied pace. She killed the live stream and smiled. "Sorry, money shots aren't free."

The lights rose to a calming dim, and one of the men adjusted three cameras to focus on Cindy's thousand-yard stare. He positioned two bolsters on either side of her head, forcing her gaze into the cameras. A symphonic march began to play, and the beat quickened, along with the operatic chanting. One by one, each of the cowboys stepped up and released their load on Cindy's face. As the music climaxed, so did the last cowboy.

The main lights snapped on and the room silenced. Cindy stared forward into the camera, dripping with the cowboy's deposits, all emotion and glimmers of life faded.

A slow clap sounded behind her. Then Jill walked up, bent down, and looked into her eyes. "Beth and your spirits were strong, but not tonight."

CHAPTER 16
MINGAN AND HURIT: THE JOURNEY

Jake woke in the spare room, after the visions in the cave had rattled him enough to elect not to sleep there. He tossed and turned all night thinking about how upset Alexi was on the video call. He took a deep breath and stared at the ceiling. He heard the muffled voices of Samuel and Anna from the kitchen as the first light of sunrise above the mountains shined through the sheer curtains. He rubbed his eyes, yawned, and threw his legs off the side of the bed.

Honi looked up and jumped to the floor, wagging his tail.

Dakota woke to the voices of Great Grandfather and Neiwoo. She smiled, pulled the old down comforter under her chin and snuggled, then rolled onto her side and gazed at the hill behind her. As the early morning sun shined into the mouth of the cave, snapshots of the vision raced before her eyes. The cave no longer represented a whimsical snapshot of her ancestors, but rather a portal into a nightmarish world. She struggled to recall the foreign language the Spirits spoke in. The word 'ee-sheh' was the only one she remembered clearly.

Jake's voice from the kitchen broke her concentration and prompted her to get up.

As she opened her door, Neiwoo looked up from the kitchen and said, "Good morning, Lomasi."

Dakota started down the stairs. "Good morning, you three are up early."

Samuel said, "I have already hunted the early dawn plains and prepared my kill for dinner."

She smiled and hugged him. "Great Grandfather, what did you kill?"

"A buffalo."

"Well then, you are a great hunter, since they have not roamed here for over a hundred years."

Samuel shook his head. "Yes, Lomasi, do not remind me, but an old man can dream."

She moved to Anna, hugged her, then to Jake. Her eyes sparkled as she leaned in to hug him. "Good morning."

He pulled away, smiled, and rubbed her shoulders. "Are these pajamas thick enough?"

She kicked her leg forward and looked down. "Yep, and footies too."

He chuckled and pulled a chair out for her at the table.

"Coffee, Lomasi?

"Yes, Neiwoo, that would be great. Thanks."

Samuel glanced across the table. "Jake, I thought you would have spent the night in the cave."

"It was a bit cold last night, sir."

"Aagh, great warriors do not fear the elements, Jake."

"Well, sir, this warrior had a choice between a soft bed or the hard ground. It was not the elements I feared, but my back."

Samuel chuckled. "Very well, I will give you a pass. I have not been up there in years. Perhaps you and Lomasi could help me up there today?"

Jake darted a glance over his shoulder at Dakota, who stood at the refrigerator. Her eyebrows raised. "Great Grandfather, that would be cool. We would love to take you to the cave. Maybe you can tell us stories like you did when I was young."

Samuel nodded. "Very good, we will go after I do my morning prayer."

"Lomasi, are Jake and you heading back to the cabin today?" Neiwoo said.

"Yes, we're gonna wait for Woo Woo and Jay to return. I need to talk with them. Then we'll leave." She focused on Samuel. "Great Grandfather, you should come up with us before the winter hits. It's been years since you've been there."

Samuel stood up. "I will think about that. First, let me thank the Spirits for another sunrise."

The group watched Samuel leave through the patio doors.

"Lomasi," her grandmother said, "he is too old for that trip. Your Grandfather has been trying to take him out there for years to visit his father's and brother's graves. He always makes an excuse."

"I know Neiwoo, but I know he would enjoy it."

Honi whined at the patio door as he watched Samuel pray.

Jake laughed. "No, Honi, he's not playing. Let him finish."

Honi glanced at Jake, then back out the patio doors, and his head tilted up as his whines became more urgent.

Dakota said, "Jake, he's looking up the bluff. He must have seen an animal, maybe another wolf or coyote."

"No, that's not his normal whine when another animal is around. He growls. As soon as Samuel is done, I'll let him out."

Samuel heard Honi. He looked back at the wolf and followed his gaze to the top of the hill.

He finished his prayer and walked to the patio door. "Jake, can I let him out?"

"Yeah, he see's something on the hill, probably a tumbleweed or something."

Honi bolted through the door and shot up the hill towards the mouth of the cave. He hunched down and growled, pacing slowly back and forth in front of the entrance.

Jake and Dakota walked onto the patio with Samuel.

"I guess I better go up there and see what that big baby sees or smells in there. Let me grab my gun," Jake said.

Samuel grabbed Jakes's arm. "A gun will not help you with what he fears." He reached down and pulled a small sage plant from the rocky soil. He lit in on fire, quickly extinguished the flame, and waved the smoking plant in the air. "Take this, and place it at the entrance of the cave. Fan the smoke into it. We will go up there after Lomasi and you dress."

Jake glanced at Dakota, then grabbed the smoldering bush.

He climbed the rocky hill and reached Honi. The agitated wolf quickly placed his body between Jake and the cave.

"It's okay, boy, there's nothing in there."

Honi continued to snarl as sunlight filled the cave, allowing Jake to survey every inch. He shook his head and moved Honi to the side. "There's nothing there, boy."

He bent down and waved the slow burning sage, and light winds carried wisps of smoke inside. The smoke moved to the center of the cave and swirled. Jake squinted, then recoiled as a shadow figure appeared in the smoky vortex.

A disembodied growl filled the cave, and Honi launched forward at the entity. The dark opaque figure vanished as soon as the wolf met it in mid-air.

Jake sat back, stunned.

Honi circled the cave, his demeanor calmed and tail wagging. He walked out to Jake and licked his face.

"What was that, boy?"

Jake stood up and looked down at Dakota and Samuel. His face said enough.

Samuel said to Dakota, "We will go up and close what Jake and you opened. I will prepare." He turned and left for the house.

Dakota moved towards Jake and Honi as they reached the bottom of the hill. "Jake, what happened up there? I heard a growl, but it didn't sound like Honi. What did he leap at?"

"I don't know, Dakota. It was a shadow figure. The growl came from the cave. It shook me to my core. It was pure evil. What the fuck did we awaken in there?"

Dakota looked up and shook her head. "No idea, but Great Grandfather said he was going to prepare, so he can 'close what we opened.'"

"All right, let's get changed. So... he knew we visited the Spirit world. How does he know these things?"

"I don't know. Maybe he'll tell us when we're in the cave. I'll meet you back here in fifteen minutes."

Jake, Dakota, and Samuel met at the base of the hill.

"Are you ready, Great Grandfather. You can hold my arm as we climb."

"I will be fine, Lomasi. I just need to climb a bit slower."

"Great Grandfather, what is happening now in the cave?"

"Do not talk about it until I have prepared. We do not want to invite it out."

Dakota shrugged her shoulders at Jake, and they continued the short but tricky climb in silence.

Upon arrival, the group stood for a moment at the entrance.

Samuel donned a simple lapis beaded neckless with a single silver talisman resembling an eight-pointed sun. He handed Jake and Dakota each a piece of raw blue stone. "Do not, under any circumstance, allow this stone to drop from your hands." He retrieved a long bone pipe from his pack and drew several puffs, blowing the smoke into the cave. "Kookou'un heneeteniihoot." He stepped into the cave, held his hands up, and paused. He looked back. "Do not cross the threshold until I say so." He circled the cave and sprinkled a fine powder around the perimeter. "You can come in now."

"Great Grandfather, what is this all about?"

"The Spirit Jake saw in the smoke was a trespasser from the underworld. Honi's essence frightened it away. When Jake and you entered the Spirit World here, you opened a portal. For now, those spirits can not leave this cave and cross the surrounding land I have blessed, but my magic will die when I do. We will need to go back into the Spirit World and seal the gate. They cannot harm us there, or in the physical world, while we hold the sacred blue stone."

The group sat in a circle around the makings of a small fire.

"How will we seal it?" Jake said.

"I will make a deal with them."

"Great Grandfather, the Spirits we saw spoke a different language. It was not ours, or any Native American dialect I have heard."

Samuel's brow furrowed. "Lomasi, do you remember those words."

"Not all of them, just one or two. One was 'ee-shah' or something like that."

Samuel lowered his head. "Ee-sheh."

"That's it. Great Grandfather, what language is that?"

"It is a language older than ours. It is ancient Hebrew. Some Christians believe it was the language of Adam and Eve. Others believe it to be the language of angels."

"Samuel," Jake said, "why would Native American Spirits speak old Hebrew?"

Samuel held his hand out. "Help me up, please. There is nothing my magic can do. Jake, you and Lomasi did not see the Spirits of my people. You need to go to the cabin for answers, where you will be protected by sacred ground."

"Great Grandfather, what about the evil spirits coming through the portal and harming us on the ranch, or people in town."

"Lomasi, Jake and you did not open a portal. I was mistaken. Jake saw a shadow person. They are harmless to those with any type of faith. They have walked the land as long as mankind. Some believe they are actually here to protect us. I have no idea why one chose to manifest itself up here. I will look for answers in the Spirit world." He reached into a buckskin satchel and handed Jake a pouch. "This is stronger than what both of you have had. It will keep you in the Spirit World longer. You both need to find answers."

The group stood.

Samuel's eyes panned the cave walls, and he smiled. "I remember as a little boy, sitting here and listening to my grandfather tell stories of these hunts. His great grandfather painted some of these walls. It is nice to see them again."

Jake leaned back in the rocker on the front porch and gazed at the browning grasslands of the ranch. He lifted his gaze to the golden aspens dotting the distant mountains, took a deep breath of contentment, and closed his eyes.

When the screen door opened, he half turned his head and opened a single eye.

Dakota set a sandwich on the table and sat down next to him. "Did I wake you?"

He smiled. "No, just enjoying a peaceful fall moment."

She looked towards the mountains. "It's so beautiful." She paused for several moments. "So, what do you think about everything that happened up at the cave?"

"I don't know. Hopefully, we can get some answers from Rowtag. As soon as your grandfather get's back, we'll head to the cabin."

She looked at her cell phone. "It's almost noon. The plane landed at ten. He should be here soon. Do you want to talk with him about putting a place up for the winter before we leave? Give him some time to think about it?"

"Let's wait till we come back down next week. I'm sure he's tired from the trip and dealing with Dibella and that asshole Sellman."

She nodded. "Good point."

Anna leaned through the screen door. "Your grandfather just texted. Jay and he are coming through town now."

"Cool, thanks, Neiwoo. I'll be right back, Jake. Let me finish packing so we can leave as soon as we're done talking with him. I don't want to ride at night."

"Sounds good. I'm packed up."

Jake leaned back to relax for a few more minutes before Jim arrived. His quiet time ended with the sound of Jim's truck coming up the stone drive. He stood up and peered back through the screen door. "They're here."

Dakota and Anna stepped on the front porch as Jim parked, and the three walked out to greet the men.

Anna and Dakota hugged Jim and Jay.

Jake shook their hands and bent down to grab their luggage. "I'll get these. You both look exhausted."

"Thank you, Jake," Jim said.

Neiwoo said, "Honey, are you and Jay hungry? I have stew on the stove."

Jim looked at his watch. "You cooked an early dinner, Anna?"

She rolled her eyes. "Father claims the home only feeds him canned soup and sandwiches for lunch."

Jim chuckled. "Does he not realize we pay for his food?"

Anna smiled. "I think he just likes to have his family around the table. It will be ready in twenty minutes."

"Okay, that gives me time to fill Dakota in on our client. Jake, I need to see you also, regarding an email I received from Sulphur Springs."

"Yes sir."

Jim, Jay, Dakota, and Jake walked into Jim's office.

"Jake, leave the door open, please. Anna will get suspicious. We will talk low. There's not much to share."

"What did they say, Woo Woo?"

"Of course, they denied everything. Jay is inclined to believe them. I am not so sure."

"Jay, why do think they're innocent?" Jake said.

"My gut tells me, Jake, that Dibella is not that careless or stupid. I believe he was not aware of all his sons' illegal activity. Sellman protects the Dibella name well."

Dakota snapped, "I find it hard to believe that arrogant bastard cares about anyone but himself."

"So, who ordered the hit on us?" Jake said.

Jim shook his head. "I do not know, but I believe we rattled Dibella enough that he will use his tentacles and find out."

Jay said, "Think about it for a second. If any of you end up murdered, Dibella would be suspect number one. He has enough damage control to do with what came out during the trial."

Jake took a deep breath and stared at the floor. "Is it possible that an enemy of Dibella could have seen a perfect opportunity to settle an old score?"

Dakota's eyes narrowed. "What do you mean, Jake? Like someone was framing him?"

"Yep."

Jay glanced at Jim. "Funny you say that, Jake. Jim and I talked about that possibility on the way home. Someone looking to frame him could not ask for a better scenario, or timing."

"Well, if that's the case, we're not safe. Whoever *is* behind this won't stop," Dakota said.

Jay said, "I believe Dibella and Sellman will fish out whoever is responsible. They have too much to lose. In the meantime, I will arrange a unit to be at the ranch gate twenty-four/seven."

"But Jay, we can't be prisoners here. Grandfather and I have the practice. Jake has a life to reclaim."

"I understand. I suggest we give it one week. Let Dibella use his resources to call off the dogs."

Dakota paused and quickly analyzed the conversation. "Jake and I are heading back to the cabin. I trust in the Spirits. Maybe they will give us some answers."

Jay looked at Jim and shrugged. "They warned them once."

Jim rubbed his eyes. "Maybe we trust in them also, Jay. How would I explain to Anna a police unit is at our gate around the clock, without worrying her?"

Jay leaned back and thought for a moment. "Well, old friend, we have planned a hunting vacation for years. I guess this would be a good week to do it."

Jim nodded. "It would not alert Anna, and I would feel better with you here with me, just in case we are wrong and Dibella *does* send more goons. Maybe we convince Samuel to stay also?"

"Can he still shoot?"

"I'm sure, but I was not thinking about asking him to stay for his gun skills. He would make a good watchdog. His visions warned us once."

The four agreed they had a plan in place.

Jake and Dakota reached the cabin as the sun dipped behind the mountain peaks.

Jake unlocked the door. "Let's eat, then see if Rowtag can answer some questions."

Dakota pulled her pack from the quad. "Sounds good."

A little less than an hour later, Jake pushed his plate aside and opened the new batch of herbs Samuel had given them. A pungent pine smell caught him off guard. "Damn, this smells like a moldy Christmas tree."

Dakota fanned her nose. "Whew, I can smell it across the table."

He pulled a clump of shredded unknowns from the pouch and filled the pipe. "Are you ready?"

She chuckled. "You take the first hit."

They moved in front of the fire, where Jake lit the pipe and inhaled lightly. "It's actually very smooth." He took a deeper drag and passed the pipe to Dakota.

She drew a deep hit and exhaled forcefully towards the fire. The heavy smoke hung in the cabin, creating a haze in front of the dancing flames.

Jake felt his head lighten, and his body tingled. He entered the Spirit World in front of the waterfall. The world was lucid and void of the dreamscape he was accustomed to. He looked around for Dakota.

"Jake, over here."

He joined her to the right of the waterfall. "Where's Rowtag?"

"I don't know. What should we do?"

A sparkling orb appeared before them. It floated at eye level then retreated into the brush tunnel towards the hot spring.

Jake held her hand. "I guess we follow it."

The orb hovered above the bubbling water, then disappeared. The pool glassed over, and movements beneath the surface drew their attention. As before, they looked down upon Mingan's village.

Mingan stood at the end of his village, his trusted wolf by his side, and looked back at his people. He raised his spear and turned to begin his journey to the High Mountain.

Several days passed. His journey took him beyond the farthest point of the world he knew. The lush green forests were replaced by rocky outcroppings, sparse vegetation and cactus. The Great River widened and shallowed, and the Great Mountain dominated the horizon.

He looked at the setting sun and decided to make camp in a shallow cave.

"Wahya, we will sleep in here tonight. Tomorrow, we will reach the foot of the Great Mountain."

The young wolf cocked his head and settled at the master's feet, his eyes focused on the night world beyond the cave.

The chirping of birds announced a new day. Mingan sat up, stretched and walked into the morning light. He panned the high desert landscape for signs of game, then switched his focus to the Great River. "Well, Wahya, it appears we eat fish again today."

The two made their way downstream looking for still water to allow Mingan to spear his quarry. In the distance, the river narrowed and the sound of crashing water caught his ear. He smiled, knowing a waterfall would have a pool at the bottom. They approached the top of the falls.

Wahya stopped abruptly, and his tail dropped. His slow growl alerted Mingan.

He readied his spear and crouched, until the sound of splashing and female laughter baffled him. *There are no people beyond my village.* He crept closer to the edge and peered into the pool below.

A young maiden frolicked in the clear waters below. She swam forward then turned to float on her back. The early morning sun glistened off her bronzed body. Her beauty both captivated and confused Mingan. Her features were more delicate than the girls in his village, and her breasts more ample. Her hair was dark, like theirs, but glistened with a blue hue.

Wahya snarled.

"Shhh, you will scare her." Mingan fixed his eyes back on her as she stood up in the waist-high pool and sauntered to the shore. Her body moved with a grace and fluidity, unlike the deliberate walk of the girls in his village.

Is she a spirit sent to tempt me, as Great Grandfather warned?"

Wahya stood and growled, his eyes focused to the right of the pool.

Mingan followed his gaze and sprang to his feet. He ran to the lip of the waterfall and plunged into the turbulent water at the base of the falls. He surfaced and yelled, "*Shashtsoh.*"

The startled maiden positioned her arms, doing the best to cover her nakedness, but Mingan raced from the pool and stood between her and a large brown bear.

The beast stood on his hind legs, towering over Mingan. Its roar shook his insides.

Mingan raised his spear over his head and yelled, but a second beast, to the right of the bear, drew his attention. Visions of his and the maiden's death flashed before his eyes.

How can I fend off a bear and a wolf?

Wahya dashed at the bruin's legs, nipped at its left calf and retreated, barking constantly. The bear took his eyes off of Mingan and focused on Wahya, and Mingan reared back and threw his spear deep into the exposed chest of the beast. The bear howled in pain and dropped to all fours. It lumbered towards the brush before crumbling in a heap.

Mingan approached the fallen bear. He circled it from a distance to ensure it was dead, then retrieved his spear. Wahya moved to his master's side.

The maiden stood frozen by the event she'd witnessed. When Mingan looked towards her, she quickly realized she still stood naked, and she dashed behind a group of sage bushes.

Mingan waded through the pool and stepped on the sandy shore several yards from her. Their eyes fixed on each other. After several moments, she signaled him to look away. He turned to face the Great Mountain.

Why is she here? Who is she? Is she from the People of the Sunset?

He could hear as she scurried up a small rocky incline to a group of flat stones, where she had placed her clothes. He turned to see that she had dressed, and now readied her bow and stared at him.

"Hotousihi'," she yelled.

Mingan raised his brow, surprised she spoke his language, and faced her full on. "Mingan, nenee'eeshih'inoo?"

She lowered her bow. "Hurit."

He paused. "How do you speak my language?"

"It is the language of my people. Where do you travel from Mingan?"

"From the Land of the Sunrise."

She squinted and cocked her head. "The people of the Sunrise have the skin of a rattlesnake and speak with a strange tongue."

"And who told you this?"

"My people, the people of the Sunset."

He laughed. "I was told your people had the snout of a boar and were covered in course hair."

She lowered her bow and took several steps forward. "You spied on me like a young boy, and saw that is not true."

"*No*, it is not, and if I had not heard you splashing and laughing like a young girl, you would be half eaten by now."

She glanced at Wahya. "How do you control the wolf's spirit?"

"I do not control his spirit."

She raised her bow. "*Only demons* can speak to animals."

"More lies of your people. If I was a demon, I would have let the bear kill you and devoured your flesh with him. I was warned by my Great Grandfather that I would be tested on my journey. How do I know you are not a witch sent by the Evil Ones to tempt me?"

"Tempt you? What would I tempt you with?"

"Your beauty."

A sparkle rose in Hurit's eye, and she looked away for a second, perhaps to regain her composure. "You have a smooth tongue like a demon. What journey do you speak of?"

"I am going to the top of the great mountain to fetch a sacred feather and prove my worth. I will lead my people, just as my father and my grandfather, and the fathers that came before them."

"So, *demon*... you are the son of the Chief of the People of the Sunrise?"

"Great Grandson. My father and grandfather are with the Great Spirit. Tell me, *witch*... why are you in the middle of the wilderness by yourself?"

"I too am on a journey to prove myself to my people. As eldest daughter of our Chief, I must gather sacred berries from the Great Mountain. I then will choose a husband to lead my people alongside me."

"Why does your brother not lead your people?"

"I have no brother, only sisters."

She set her bow on the ground and approached him. "Thank you for saving my life."

The sparkle in her eye froze him. She turned, smiled, and took several steps before looking back. "Perhaps, two future leaders of their people should make their journey together."

The hot spring bubbled, erasing Jake's and Dakota's view of Mingan and Hurit.

Jake looked up. "Sounds like a familiar story. Seems like I've been saving you since the beginning of time."

Dakota chuckled. "And again, I thank you, my brave warrior, but this tells us nothing."

"Children," a familiar voice called from behind.

They turned, and Jake said, "Rowtag, we feared you would not show. We have questions."

"I will not tell you of Mingan and Hurit's journey. You will learn that soon enough."

Jake shook his head. "No, Rowtag, it's not about them. Dakota and I visited the Spirit World on her grandfather's ranch. We had a vision... a dark, violent vision."

Rowtag took several steps forward. "What was this vision of, Jake?"

"You cannot see everything we see?" Dakota chimed.

"No, Dakota. Any land not on these sacred grounds, I am blind to."

"I don't understand," Jake said. "You told us you have been feared by Gods and mortals since the beginning."

"And I was, Jake. You will come to understand as both of your journeys continue. Please, tell me what you saw."

"We saw a hellish landscape, a village decimated, its streets lined with women impaled on stakes, children and old people hacked to pieces, the men of the village all dead, their weapons never drawn. The cries of misery and the smell of burnt flesh filled the air. At the end of the village, we were approached by five Spirits, or demons, on horseback, three men and two women. They spoke in a tongue we later identified as Ancient Hebrew."

"Please describe them."

"The men had long dark hair," Dakota said. "Their features were chiseled and perfect. The women's hair was blond, almost platinum, and they too had perfect features. All had piercing blue eyes."

Rowtag's eyes narrowed, and his voice hardened. "You must never visit the Spirit World again when not on these sacred grounds. You are not ready to face that evil."

"*Who* are they, Rowtag?" Jake commanded.

"The Six."

Jake said, "There were only five."

Dakota interjected. "Are they behind the men who tried to kill us and my great grandfather?"

"No, Dakota. Mortals gave those orders. The Six, like me, cannot pass into the physical world. That portal was sealed after the last cleansing."

"Why would they appear to us? What do they want? One of the men looked at me as if he knew me. He spoke with a pleasing tone."

"I cannot answer that. They only appear to those easily persuaded by their empty promises."

"You call them the Six, but there were five," Jake repeated.

"As I said, I am blind beyond these sacred grounds and have been for many millenniums. I do not know where the sixth was, perhaps perished. It is time for you to return to your world. Travel the footsteps of the men behind the night your paths crossed. You will find those who wish to do you harm."

Rowtag began to fade. "What is the cleansing?" Jake yelled.

Rowtag pointed at the hot spring.

The flames of the fireplace became clearer, and the warm glow of the cabin's log walls came into focus. Jake widened his eyes and shook his head to clear the last bit of the intoxicating herbs. He watched Dakota as she drifted back into the physical world.

"How long where we gone?" she said.

"Almost forty minutes. What do you think?"

She took a deep breath. "I think our original thoughts about Dibella were correct, and we need to see if Mingan and Hurit's story leads us to the truth of the Six. Maybe, the Six—or Five—and Dibella are connected somehow, and Rowtag can't see it."

"Jay and your grandfather believe Dibella isn't involved."

"Maybe he isn't directly, but like Rowtag said, travel the footsteps of those asshole sons of his that attacked me that night."

Jake chuckled. "I don't believe *asshole* is in his vocabulary."

Dakota quickly straddled Jake and pushed him back into the bear skin. "Neither is what I am about to do with you."

Chapter 17
Choices

Kelly sat on the edge of her bed staring blankly into space. Beth's death had brought the reality of her situation full circle. Jill's unnatural overpowering of Cindy and heartless disregard for Beth's death terrified her. Her mind could not erase Jill's soulless eyes the night she was seduced. It had become evident that a deeper evil resided on this ranch than she'd realized. Her time, and the time of the other girls, was running out.

Where was Cindy taken? Will I see her again?

She needed answers quickly. She needed to find the weak link in this operation, *regardless* of the sacrifices.

She freshened up and prepared to return to the party.

Kelly reached the landing above the foyer as Jill walk through the front door. Their eyes locked in an icy gaze. Jill raised on eyebrow and half smiled. Kelly, staying true to her plan, softened her brow and smiled.

Steven and Michelle Cornwell met Jill at the door. "Jill, is everything all right with Sergio?" Steven said.

"Yes, he's fine but there's been an unfortunate accident with one the girls."

Michelle said, "Accident? What sort of accident?"

"It appears she attempted to flee and landed awkwardly on her drop from the balcony."

Steven said, "That's too bad. Which girl was it?"

"Beth."

Michelle stirred her drink. "That's a shame. Sergio bid a king's ransom for her. She was a fine piece of ass."

Steven said, "Yes, we bid quite high also. I looked forward to getting *in that ass.*"

Michelle slowly licked the rim of her glass. "Mmmm, I looked forward to watching you, my love."

Kelly reached the foyer, overheard the end of the nonchalant conversation, and took a deep breath, fighting back her desires to pounce on Michelle Cornwell. She shot a cross glance at Jill, and then turned towards the great room to join Kimi and Mina at the fireplace.

"Kelly", Jill called out, "please join us for a second."

Kelly stopped in her tracks, forced a smile, and turned towards Jill and the Cornwells.

"Kelly, I believe you have met our guests," Jill said.

"Yes, we briefly spoke."

Jill turned to the Cornwells. "Kelly and Beth were best friends."

Kelly's blood boiled, knowing Jill had seen the look on her face when she overheard the Cornwells discuss Beth.

Michelle sipped her drink. "It's a shame, dear. Sorry for your loss. I don't understand *why* she would want to escape from the life she was offered here."

Kelly's eyes narrowed and nostrils flared. "And what life is that?"

Jill interrupted. "A good life, if you make the right choice, unlike your other friend." She pointed out the door towards the front courtyard.

"Mina, Kimi, hurry," Kelly cried out as she burst through the double doors into the moonlit courtyard.

Cindy shuffled across the circular drive towards the front porch, her head lowered and body naked.

Kelly ran forward and wrapped her arms around her trembling friend. Her cheek met with Cindy's wet, matted hair, and she pulled back. In the light cast by the courtyard fountain, a clear picture unfolded of what her friend had endured.

"Kelly, she... is... evil, she... is... evil. Look at her lip," Cindy whispered. "I wish... they would have... killed me." She gently pushed Kelly away and shuffled towards the front porch.

Kelly stood motionless watching her friend walk away.

Cindy's shuffle was deliberate and labored. When she reached the front porch and the brighter lights, blood streaks running down the back of her right leg became visible.

Kelly dropped her head as Cindy's ordeal finished playing out in her mind.

Mina yanked a blanket from one of the couches and rushed to Cindy, covering her from the gawkers inside. Kimi joined her, holding Cindy's waist as the two girls helped Cindy up the porch stairs. They ushered her past Jill and the Cornwells in the foyer.

James Radford joined the group in the foyer as the girls reached the first landing of the main stairs. "Jill, an added surprise — the Table... very nice. Is the tape for sale or is it spoken for?"

"No, this one sold in record time. It shattered the previous record by almost a hundred K."

Radford looked up the stairs, focusing on the blood streaks. "How many?"

Jill looked up and swirled her martini. "Ten."

Radford nodded. "Well, she must have really pissed you off."

Jill looked up as the girls crested the top landing. "Yes, but I think I've tamed her now."

Dominique joined the onlookers in the foyer. "Well, there's two off the menu for the night. Jill, our choices are becoming limited. Perhaps your little pet, Kelly, will have to be passed around?"

Jill turned to the guests. "There are still four beautiful girls available. I'm sure Mr. P will make some financial concessions. I'll be right back."

Jill stepped from the front porch and moved through the courtyard. Her eyes locked onto Kelly's 'if looks could kill' stare. The two women met at arm's length.

After a tense moment of silence, Kelly hissed, "What kind of monster are you?"

Jill smiled. "I'm not. I'm a business woman charged with providing a service to some of the most powerful people in the world. If I fail, they will exterminate me like a common bug. I don't fail, and those who stand in my way are merely collateral damage."

Kelly squinted and shook her head. "Collateral damage, Jill? My best friend is dead and my other best friend may as well be. *I fucking trusted you and you fucking lied to me.*"

"And where did I lie, Kelly? Beth fell to her death. It was an accident. Cindy attacked me. I could have had her killed, but I didn't. She'll recover from a few dicks inside of her. So... tell me... where did I lie to you?"

Kelly glanced at Jill's lip, then looked into her eyes. "Who dies next, Jill. Is it me? Kimi? Mina? Or maybe, you discard Cindy as damaged goods?"

"*Nobody* dies, Kelly. We're not in the death business. We're in the pleasure business, as you were all told in the beginning. *If* someone dies, it's by their choice. It is in my company's financial best interest to keep each one of you healthy."

Jill took a step closer, reached out and gently placed her hand on Kelly's shoulder. "Now, you *must* make a choice. I have offered you a life beyond your wildest imagination, a chance to earn your freedom and be part of your family's life again. Join me, or be bid on and sent away, with *no* choice of who you sleep with."

"Of all the girls that have passed through here, why me, Jill?"

"Because, you are me years ago."

Jill walked towards the house, but paused, looked over her shoulder, and smiled provocatively. "Domonique and I will meet you in the bar. It's getting late. Perhaps, my hot tub would do us all a bit

CHAPTER 18
A NEW DIRECTION

The roar of a jet engine snapped Kelly from a deep sleep. She focused her eyes to the early morning light shining through the open patio doors.

Jill walked in from the patio. "Good morning, Sunshine."

Dominique growled and rolled over, pulling the blanket off of Kelly.

Kelly pulled the sheet from the opposite side of the bed to cover her nude body.

Jill smiled and approached the bed. "Why so bashful? You weren't last night."

Kelly, half awake, grumbled, "What was that noise?"

"That was Mina, Kimi, and Aiyana leaving for their new life. Would you like some coffee?"

Kelly sat up and shook her head. "No, I need to go see how Cindy is doing."

"Cindy will be fine. We hit her with a dart containing an amnesia drug before her punishment. She'll remember little to nothing of last night. If she asks, tell her security tranquilized her after she attacked me."

"How many guys raped her last night? Two, three, four? She's gonna know something happened. How do I explain that?"

"The number of men is not important. Tell her we had a guest that enjoys sex with unconscious girls and leave it at that, if she asks."

"You have all the fucking answers, don't you, Jill?"

"As you will also, my dear, in time."

"What are you going to do with Beth's body. Discard it like a piece of trash?"

"No, she will be found, and returned to her family for a proper burial. Despite what you think, we are not 'monsters,' as you say."

"Can I see her one last time?"

"I'm sorry, but she left the ranch last night."

Kelly bent over and retrieved her clothes from the floor. "So, what's next for the rest of us?"

"Well, the other girls have been chosen. They'll leave the ranch today. You made the right choice last night and will stay here. As for Cindy, I'm undecided."

"Can't she stay here? I'll work with her."

"No. Like any business, we need to turn a profit. Her staying will give us little return."

Kelly stood, locked her eyes on Jill, and slowly approached her. She untied Jill's silk robe, dropped to her knees, and buried her tongue inside Jill.

Jill pulled Kelly's head tight and arched her back, and her body trembled.

Kelly pulled away and looked up. "Is there any room for negotiation?"

Jill caught her breath and smiled. "You little whore. You're learning quickly. Now finish what you started, and I'll think about it."

"Then I would have nothing to negotiate with." Kelly stood, turned, and headed towards the door. She grabbed a robe from the bedpost, looked over her shoulder, and licked her lips. "You know where to find me."

She walked with confidence down the hall towards her room. Once inside, she crumbled in a heap on her bed, buried her face in a pillow, and sobbed uncontrollably. Her body convulsed as the events of the past twelve hours raced through her mind.

Can I keep this up? Can I keep it together long enough to get Cindy and I out of this hell?"

After a quick shower, she hurried to Cindy's room.

Cindy, still groggy from the sedative, shuffled to answer the knock on her door. "Who is it?"

"It's me, open up."

Cindy unlocked the door to let Kelly in, walked slowly back to her bed, and fell face forward. "I feel like shit. What the hell happened last night? I don't remember anything after trying to kill that bitch Jill."

"They hit you with a tranquilizer after you attacked her."

"I woke up nude this morning. Who brought me to bed?"

"Mina and I did."

Cindy sat up and forced her eyes wide open. "What are they doing with Beth's body?"

"Jill said they were going to drop her in a place she will be discovered and returned to her family."

"Do you believe that cunt, Kelly? I do remember one thing, her eyes... they changed when I attacked her."

"Changed, like how?"

Cindy squinted and looked away, shaking her head. "They went from soulless black to demonic looking to ocean blue, like there were several people looking at me. She's evil. I wouldn't trust a word she says."

Kelly took a deep breath. "Cindy, we have to play her game right now. The longer we can stay here, the better chance we have of getting home. The rest of the girls are gone. It's just you and me left."

"How, Kelly? How do we stay here?"

"She's a nympho. It's her weakness."

Cindy bounced to her feet. "*What are you saying*? *We fuck her and her friends*?"

Kelly grabbed her hand. "What choice do we have? If we don't, we'll be sent on a plane to bum-fucked Egypt, forced to sleep with disgusting pigs like that fat prick who bought Beth."

Cindy's eyes narrowed. "Is that what you've been doing, Kelly? Have you been *fucking* her?"

Kelly dropped her head and paused. Her eyes welled as she looked up. "I'm doing whatever I can to get us home."

Cindy winced and put her hand above her pubic bone.

Kelly said, "What's wrong?"

"I don't know. I guess my period is coming. I feel like I was fucking all night. Who knows? Maybe I was? I can see these sick bastards coming in here when I was drugged and having their way with me. Are all those rich pricks gone?"

"Yes."

"Good. Okay, I'm gonna take a shower, have something to eat, and lie back down. I need to wrap my head around all this. And hey, I'm sorry I snapped. I guess if I had to make a choice between her, or those gross, old, fat pigs, to save our lives, she would win. At least she's young and beautiful."

Kelly smiled. "No need to apologize. Get some rest. I'll come back around one. Maybe we'll go for a walk?"

The two women hugged and parted ways.

Detective Blake Roberts stepped onto his deck and took a sip of coffee. He looked up at the early morning South Dakota sun, closed his eyes and inhaled deeply, then slid a chair out from his bistro set, plopped a thick file on the glass table and sat down.

"Daddy, Daddy, look at the puppy."

Blake looked up to see his young daughter racing across the yard with their new retriever pup in tow.

His wife, busy in their garden, looked back at him. "They're gonna be best friends."

The distant crack of a hunting rifle snapped him back to reality. He looked at the yard and garden, long since reclaimed by the grasslands, and dropped his head, retrieved a thin silver flask from his breast pocket, and livened up his morning coffee.

After lighting a cigarette and taking a deep drag, he looked up and exhaled forcefully, then opened the file and turned his attention to a map of the Dakotas. From one end of both states to the other, colored dots representing missing women jumped off the page. The highest concentration lay on the reservations and big cities. He shook his head, took another deep hit of his cigarette, and leaned back.

His glanced down at his phone vibrating the glass table, and grabbed it. "What's up, Cap?"

"Blake, we just received a call from a small police department on the outskirts of Seattle. They may have found Beth Gray?"

Blake sprung forward, stumped his cigarette out and grabbed his pen. "Alive?"

"No."

"Have they made a positive ID?"

"All but a family member. She was wearing what she was last seen in. The body is being flown to Rapid City. It will arrive around noon."

"10- 4, Captain. I'll be in. What kind of shape is she in?"

"Other than a single head wound, nothing remarkable. The local coroner on scene said it appears time of death was in the past ten hours. We'll do an autopsy in Rapid City once ID is made."

"Okay, thanks."

Blake dialed Joe Running Horse. "Good morning, did the Captain call you yet?"

Joe sounded as if catching his breath. "I don't know, man, I just walked in the house from my run and heard your call. What's up?"

"They found Beth Gray outside of Seattle. She didn't make it."

Joe paused for a second. "Damn. The Pacific Northwest is off our radar. Why would traffickers head in *that* direction and not south over the border?"

"I don't know, Joe. The body will be here at noon. Maybe the autopsy gives us some clues. I'm heading over there in about a half hour."

"10-4, partner. I'll meet you there. Let me get the kids off to school. Gennie had to go in early today."

Blake chuckled. "The kids are in high school. When I was—"

"I know, I know... you walked five miles one way, in snow, up to a tall Indian's ass."

Blake laughed. "Not five miles, four. Okay, see you there. Tell Joe Jr. I plan on being at the game next week, and hug Mari for me."

"I will. See you as soon as I can."

Blake placed his phone on the table and lit another cigarette. He stood, walked to the deck rail, and looked over the seemingly endless prairie. "Well, looks like you hold another secret."

Blake pressed through the chaotic Park Service Headquarters making his way to Captain Hollis's office.

Hollis stood at the whiteboard, stringing a yellow yarn from the girls' campsite to the location of Beth's body. Mike Johnson stared blankly at the pictures of his daughter Kelly and her best friends, laid out on the conference table.

Hollis turned. "Blake, where's Joe?"

"He'll be here shortly, Cap."

Blake walked over to the table and placed a hand on Mike's shoulder. "Mike."

Mike's eyes remained locked on the photos. "Throughout my career, I wondered what parents felt in this situation. I... I tried to put myself in their position, but until you're there, you can't understand it."

Blake shot a glance at Captain Hollis while searching for the words to console the grieving father. "Mike, as you know, Beth's death *does not* mean Kelly isn't alive. We have a trail now to follow."

Mike nodded and sniffled. "I know. I'm searching for the strength to continue, for the strength to face Beth's parents, Cindy's parents, and my family. I'll be fine. This just came as a shock."

Blake patted Mike on the back and joined Hollis at the board. "Captain, who's making positive ID in Rapid City?"

Hollis handed over a manilla file folder. "Her brother. Her parents are not good right now. I'd like Joe and you to meet with the coroner and stay until the autopsy is done. Given the urgency, they'll perform it as soon as identification is confirmed."

Blake looked at his watch. "Okay, Joe should be here any minute. We'll get on the road ASAP."

Mike looked up. "Blake, there will be an old friend of mine there. His name is Webb Sadler. He's a good forensics guy. I'll let him know you're coming."

"10-4, Mike."

Blake exited and walked to the employee parking lot behind the station. He lit a cigarette and called Joe. "Hey, how far out are you?"

"Right around the corner."

"Don't park. Meet me at the back door. We're heading to Rapid City."

"Roger, see you in a second."

Blake finished his smoke as Joe pulled up, and hopped in the passenger seat. "Do you want me to drive?"

"Nah, it's too early for that."

Blake chuckled. "Wise ass. Okay, let's go."

"What do you think, man? Seattle throws me for a loop."

"Honestly, Joe, I have no fucking clue." Blake thumbed through the folder Hollis gave him. "It says she was found at dawn, in a small ravine by a couple joggers, just off a main road."

"Sounds like she was dumped."

"I agree."

Joe shook his head. "Why would traffickers drive that far just to dump her? It makes no sense."

"I don't know, maybe they weren't abducted by traffickers. Or, maybe they were. Maybe she gave some resistance and they killed her. Hopefully, the autopsy gives us some clues."

The two bounced scenarios off each other for the remainder of the ride, and pulled into the parking lot of Rapid City General Hospital just past noon.

Blake stepped from the car, stretched, and lit a cigarette. "You ready, partner?"

Joe snickered unhappily. "Are you *ever* ready for an ID and an autopsy?"

The duo entered the hospital, took the elevator to the basement, and followed the signs to the morgue. Two uniformed officers escorted a visibly shaken young man past them. Blake looked at Joe. "That never gets any easier."

Joe shook his head. "It never will."

Two well-dressed men and a frumpy older man stood near the viewing window at the morgue.

One of the well-dressed men stepped forward and held out his hand. "Federal Agent Steve Harris. This is my partner, Fred Allen, and our forensic consultant, Mr. Webb Sadler."

Blake shook his hand. "Agent, Detective Blake Roberts and my partner, Detective Joe Running Horse."

With formal introductions out of the way, Blake looked towards the viewing window. "Agent Harris, I assume that was Beth Gray's brother that passed us?"

Harris nodded. "Yes, he made positive ID."

Joe said, "What time are they starting the autopsy?"

Webb Sadler looked up from a file in his hand. "In ten minutes, Detective."

Blake said, "I assume, Mr. Sadler, you'll be in there?"

"Yes. Hopefully she gives us some clues. I've known Kelly Johnson since she was a baby. Her daddy and I worked many cases together. It will kill him if we don't find her alive." Webb turned, hit a button on the wall, and entered the morgue.

The officers watched through the viewing glass as Webb approached Beth's body. He looked up, slowly nodded, and the viewing window curtain drew closed.

Blake took a deep breath and pointed towards a group of chairs in the hall. "Well, gents, shall we have a seat and share some notes? It's gonna be a while."

The Chief Medical Examiner of Rapid City approached Webb, slipped a latex glove off, and extended his hand. "Mr. Sadler, Doctor Jason Garcia. It's a pleasure to meet you."

"Doctor Garcia, likewise."

A young, attractive, dark-haired female joined the men carrying a set of scrubs, a smock, and a face shield. "Mr. Sadler, I believe you've met my associate, Doctor Abey Morning Star."

Sadler politely dipped his head and smiled. "Yes, we met earlier."

Dr. Morning Star extended the autopsy gear. "Mr. Sadler, as soon as you are prepped, we can begin."

"Thank you, Doctor."

The two coroners wheeled Beth's body through of set of swinging doors. Webb stepped into the prep room, scrubbed, dressed and joined them.

They pulled the sheet from Beth's body and carefully slid her from the gurney to a stainless-steel table.

"Mr. Sadler, is there anything specific you need to examine before we remove her clothing?" Doctor Garcia said.

Sadler panned Beth's body. "No, Doc, we'll analyze the clothing later."

The doctors carefully cut off the clothing and laid it out on another table.

Sadler surveyed Beth's body for any obvious injuries. He noted bruises on her left knee, left hip, left elbow, and left shoulder. Her hair was matted with dried blood, predominately on the left side. "It appears she fell, judging by the sequence of bruises on her left side."

Doctor Garcia said, "I agree. The bruising is consistent with a fall."

Doctor Morning Star felt the bones around each bruise. "The bruising is minimal. Her fall was not from great heights. It appears nothing is broken."

Sadler's brow wrinkled. "I find it strange her clothing has no damage to correspond with those bruises."

Doctor Garcia raised a brow. "Good catch, Mr. Sadler. That is peculiar."

Doctor Morning Star said, "Perhaps she wasn't in those clothes at the time of the injuries."

Sadler's brow wrinkled. "Hmm, why would someone redress her? Based on the amount of blood on her flannel shirt, they did it quickly."

Doctor Garcia glanced at the clothing and nodded. "Let's get her cleaned up and see what we find."

As Doctor Morning Star gently rinsed the matted blood from Beth's hair, she paused, leaned in closer to the head wound, and reached for a set of forceps. She carefully separated Beth's hair and pulled back a flap of skin around the wound. She retrieved a small green object, half the size of a penny.

"What do you have, Abey?" Doctor Garcia said.

She lifted the small object and held it out. "Pediocactus Knowltonii, commonly called Knowlton's miniature cactus."

"Cactus, in Seattle?" Sadler said.

Doctor Morning Star shook her head. "No, this is a *very* unique cactus from my home state of New Mexico. In fact, it's only found in one county in Northern New Mexico. Given how deeply imbedded it was in her scalp, I would say it was there at the time of the injury."

Sadler examined the small plant in the forceps. "Hmmm, that could be a huge break in this case. Are you sure, Doctor, that these grow nowhere else?"

"I'm positive, Mr. Sadler. I'm a cactus lover. Other than in someone's private collection, they are rare. In fact, they're endangered."

Sadler stepped from the table. "Doctors, please excuse me. I need to pass this information to the investigators outside. Continue with the autopsy. I'll be back shortly."

Sadler entered the hall. His look of urgency must have alerted the four investigators, prompting them to spring up and rush to him.

"Webb, I've seen that look before. What is it?" Agent Harris said.

"They found a small cactus imbedded in her head wound, a very unique specimen found only in one county in northern New Mexico."

Blake darted a glance at Joe and then back to Sadler. "New Mexico? Why the fuck would her abductors travel that far south to travel north again, then west?"

Agent Allen said, "Yeah, that would be a hell of a lot of road exposure given how publicized this case is. Shit, those girls photos are on every news station across the country daily."

"I agree," Agent Harris said.

Joe took a step forward. "Perhaps they weren't on the road. Think about it. These girls, the girls from the University, and the two from Yellowstone, disappeared into thin air. I believe *air* is the operative word."

The five men exchanged eye contact as they considered Joe's theory, and slowly, each one nodded.

"Grab a victim, move them quickly to a pick-up point, and fly them out," Blake said.

Agent Harris said, "That would take a great deal of planning and money. I would have to assume they'd need a private jet. It sounds like a big investment for a trafficking operation."

Blake said, "I spoke with the investigating officer working the University case. He called my attention to the fact that all these girls had striking good looks, common height and weights, and all athletic. These girls are being handpicked, gentlemen. I don't believe we have an ordinary trafficking ring."

Sadler cut back in. "Men, I'll let you all discuss this. Let me get back to the autopsy and see what other secrets Ms. Gray may give up." He turned and buzzed himself into the morgue.

"Doctors, sorry, I felt it important to share the cactus information. Have I missed anything?"

"No, Mr. Sadler. Doctor Garcia and I decided to pause."

"Thank you, doctors."

Doctor Morning Star shaved a swath of hair to expose a short wide gash, and measured the wound. "Five-point-eight centimeters long by five centimeters wide, nearly circular, with a depth of one-point-nine centimeters. Fairly deep, indicative of blunt force trauma. Mr. Sadler's theory of a fall holds weight. It's possible her head struck a rounded rock, but rounded rocks in the desert are rare... unless around creek beds."

Webb said, "Or private gardens."

Doctor Morning Star looked at the tiny cactus. "Good point, Mr. Sadler."

Doctor Garcia nodded. "Let's do a rape kit, then open her up. Maybe we find more surprises."

Doctor Morning Star swabbed Beth's mouth and vagina. She rolled Beth on her side, spread her buttocks and paused. "Gentlemen, look at this."

The trio stared at a one-inch patch of raised, burnt skin at the entrance to her anus.

Doctor Garcia wrinkled his brow and moved close to the wound. "That looks like a fresh brand."

"It looks ancient, like Sanskrit or something," Doctor Morning Star added.

Sadler retrieved his camera from the prep room. "Doctors, let me photograph that so I can have it analyzed immediately."

Sadler shot several photos and forwarded them to his forensic team in D.C. He took a deep breath and looked at the puzzled medical examiners. "This complicates our fall theory. I doubt that brand was voluntary."

Doctor Garcia looked at his assistant. "Let's open her up."

"Doctors, I am going to excuse myself and regroup with the investigating team. Please call me when you're finished. Thank you both for putting a rush on this autopsy."

Sadler rejoined the four men in the hall.

"Are they done, Webb?"

"No, Steve, we found another clue, this one more baffling. There appears to be a fresh brand at the entrance to her anus."

"*A brand,*" Blake interjected. "What kind of fucking brand?"

Sadler pulled his camera out and showed the group the pictures of the strange symbols. "I'm waiting for my people in Washington to identify it."

Blake shook his head. "Cactuses... brands... I need a smoke."

Joe chuckled as he watched his partner head for an exit door. "This case already has him half crazy. Buy stock in Marlboro, gentlemen."

Sadler said, "Go grab yourselves something to eat, or drink. It will be a while before they're done in there."

The men sat patiently in the lobby. They passed time examining their own files and making small talk.

Sadler's phone chimed. He looked down at the text message then up at the group. "The symbol is ancient Hebrew. It means the number six."

The group exchanged looks with each other. The door to the morgue opened, snapping them from deep concentration.

Doctor Morning Star approached. "Gentlemen, her stomach is completely empty and her bowels have very little contents. Oddly, she shows no sign of dehydration or malnutrition."

"What does that mean, Doc?" Agent Allen said.

"Her stomach was pumped. Whoever had her, wanted to make sure food did not hint where she had been held captive. They've gone to great lengths to cover their tracks, except for this little guy." She held up the specimen bag containing the tiny cactus.

Sadler said, "And the rape kit, Doctor?"

"Clean, Mr. Sadler."

Blake walked towards the group after a bathroom break just as Doctor Morning Star buzzed back into the morgue. "Did she have any more clues?"

Joe said, "The symbols mean the number six... and her stomach was pumped."

Sadler looked at the group. "Gentlemen, I believe we *may* have this all wrong. This *is not* a trafficking ring. I believe we could have a ritual killer on our hands. I hope I'm wrong, or we will be learning how to count in Ancient Hebrew."

CHAPTER 19
A LITTLE VOICE

Blake and Joe rushed from the morgue. Blake dialed his phone as soon as he hit the parking lot.

Captain Hollis answered. "Yeah, Blake."

"Captain, we have a strong lead."

"Mike's phone just rang before you called. He's talking with Sadler. What's happening?"

"They found a small cactus tangled in Beth's hair. It only grows in one county in Northern New Mexico. It appears that's where she died. We need to quickly switch gears and concentrate all our efforts there. Also, Cap... she was branded."

"Blake, did you say *branded*?"

"Yes. This may be more than a trafficking ring. I'm sure Mike will fill you in. Joe and I are heading back. We'll see you in an hour or less."

"All right, Blake."

Blake hung the phone up as they reached their car, and looked across the roof at Joe. "Well, partner, let's see how fast we can get home. Hit the lights and make some noise."

Mike Johnson hung the phone up and bounced to his feet. "Captain, can you please pull up a map of New Mexico on the computer?"

Hollis looked over his monitor and motioned Johnson to his desk. "Already on it. Blake said something about a fucking cactus and Northern New Mexico."

"Yeah, Webb said it only grows in San Juan County."

The two men zoomed in and panned the map.

Johnson banged his fist on the desk. "*Fuck!* Where the hell do we begin? That's a lot of open country."

Hollis shook his head. "I don't know, Mike. My boys are inbound. What did Sadler and his guys think?"

"That's all I got right now. We'll put our heads together as soon as they all get here. Do you know anyone that knows that area?"

"I don't, but I'll reach out to the Park Services in New Mexico." Hollis pulled his eyes from the map and looked at Johnson. "I assume Sadler told you about the branding?"

Johnson dropped his head. "Yes."

Hollis squeezed the frazzled father's shoulder. "Mike, we'll bring her home."

Kimi listened in to the radio chatter.

"JAC, this is 4 X-ray Tango, requesting decent to 13,000 feet and clearance to Elk Horn Ranch. Over."

"4 X-ray Tango, you are cleared to 13,000 feet. Maintain flight path to Elk Horn Ranch. Have a safe landing. Over."

The plane banked right after crossing over the Tetons and began the steady descent to Elk Horn Ranch.

Rip stood up. "Ladies, please make sure you're buckled up, and prepare for landing."

Mina squeezed Kimi's hand, while Aiyana's gaze stayed fixed on the cabin wall in front of her.

The pilot brought the Gulfstream to a stop after a short taxi to a pole barn hanger, and exited the cockpit. "Ladies, please remain in the plane until Rip tells you."

Mina and Kimi watched the pilot, the one they called Gibson, meet with two long-bearded men dressed in full camo. He spoke with them briefly, shook their hands, and returned to the plane. "Rip, hand them off. We'll leave as soon as I refuel."

Rip said, "Ladies, follow me."

He escorted them from the pole barn along an ornately landscaped path. They crossed over an arched wooden bridge that sat above a gently rambling creek. The snowcapped Teton range dominated the sky above the lush pine canopy.

Mina whispered to Kimi and Aiyana, "We're at the base of the Tetons. Jackson Hole is not far from here."

The two girls nodded.

Rip looked over his shoulder and smirked, obviously having heard. "You all can talk freely. Don't matter. Hell, you can even try to run."

The three girls looked at each other, and Kimi mimicked him behind his back.

Mina said, "*It's obvious* where we are. The Tetons are unmistakable. These mountains crawl with hikers, climbers, and hunters year-round. What makes you think we can't escape your sick little fucking world?"

Rip chuckled. "Up around the bend, you'll get your answer."

The group made a right turn on the path into a small opening. Two Native American women dressed in camo stood next to a jeep.

"Wait here, ladies," Rip said. He walked forward to greet the two women as they moved towards the group.

Kimi noticed their fluid movement and striking good looks as they got closer. "They move like runway models."

Mina nodded. "Yeah, and I don't see any guns. They look too prissy to be guards. I think we can outrun them and that load of shit, Rip."

Aiyana broke her silence. "We can't. They are Deer women."

Kimi said, "Aiyana, that's an old myth. You don't believe that crap, do you?"

Aiyana locked her eyes on Kimi and Mina. "We are surrounded by dark forces, and have been since we were captured. I haven't said much to any of you because I didn't know who I can trust. We have been separated from the others for a reason."

Mina interrupted. "Yeah, because we're virgins and some rich fucks want to pop our cherries."

Aiyana shook her head. "No, Mina, there's more to it. You'll see."

One of the women in camo handed Rip a black satchel, and he walked back to the girls. "Ladies, enjoy your stay. Don't fuck too hard." He laughed and departed the opening.

The two women approached the girls. They slowly circled their captives in opposite directions, then met in front of the trio, took a deep breath simultaneously, and smiled.

"My name is Helena, this is Mirana. Please, follow us," the taller of the two women said.

The five women stepped up into the jeep and pulled from the clearing. The road winded through dense alpine forests while maintaining a steady climb. Breaks in the trees provided glimpses of the shrinking valley below. The road leveled as they crested the mountaintop. After a short distance, the forest opened to an alpine meadow. In the distance stood a palatial stone mansion built into the side of a granite mountain face.

Helena looked back at the three girls. "Welcome to your Destiny."

Billy sat at his desk staring at a stack of files he had read through a dozen times, when his office phone snapped him from deep thought.

He pressed the speaker button. "Sergeant Kellerman."

"Billy, this is Blake Roberts."

"Blake, do you have any updates on your end?"

"Are you alone?"

"I am. What's up?"

"Billy, we found one of our girls, Beth Gray, early this morning outside of Seattle. Unfortunately, she didn't make it."

"*Fuck!* What happened to her?"

"A head injury. We rushed an autopsy, and are still waiting on final results. I'm about forty-five minutes out from my station. Sit tight and I'll call you from a secured line. For right now, keep this between us."

"10-4, I'll sit tight."

Billy hung up the phone and shuffled through the missing photos on his desk until he reached Beth. He stared at for a second and shook his head. A light knock drew his attention from the picture.

"Come in."

Nona entered with two bottles of water and a bag from a local burger shop.

He smiled, looked down at his watch, leaned his head back and ran his hands through his hair. "Damn, it's lunchtime already?"

"Actually, past lunch. You look like hell. Did you get any sleep last night?"

He pointed his head to the office couch. "Not much."

"Billy, you can't push like this, or soon you won't be thinking straight."

"I know, Nona. I'm starting to run on empty. How's your Mom and the Locklears doing?"

"I convinced them to go home today."

He nodded. "It's best. I'll stay in constant contact with you."

Nona shook her head. "I'm staying, Billy."

The two locked eyes.

He gave a slight nod and smiled. "Okay."

She held her gaze. "Now, officer, let's get some food in you."

After the two finished lunch, he leaned back in his chair. "Detective Roberts called me before you came in. They found one of the girls from the Badlands this morning outside Seattle. She didn't make it."

Nona's eyes welled and her head drooped. "How?"

"I don't know any facts right now. He was on the road and will call as soon as he reaches his office. It should be soon."

Nona looked up. "If something happens to Mina, it will kill my mom."

"Hey, remember it's only a theory that Mina and Kimi are connected to these girls' abductions. If they are, maybe this girl had an accident and they dumped the body. It wouldn't make sense for traffickers to kill her. There's no profit in a dead girl."

Billy's phone rang. He looked at Nona and put his finger to his lip.

"Sergeant Kellerman."

"Sergeant, Blake Roberts. Can we speak?"

"Yes sir, Detective."

"All right... we found Beth Gray in Seattle with an apparent head wound. The autopsy confirmed cause of death was indeed blunt force trauma. It appears she may have fallen and hit her head. During the autopsy, the Medical Examiners found a very rare tiny cactus embedded in her wound. It's so rare, it only grows in one county of New Mexico."

Billy's eyes widened as he looked at Nona. He signaled to her to write notes. "Detective, let me interrupt for a second. I'm confused on the geography of all this. Why would traffickers abduct girls in South Dakota and Wyoming, travel to New Mexico, to travel back to Seattle? That is a fuck-ton of exposure and risk. Plus, why Seattle and not south below the border?"

"Billy, we had the same questions. Then, a more heinous clue surfaced that muddied the trafficking angle. It appears she was branded inside her buttocks with the ancient Hebrew symbol for the number six."

Billy squinted his eyes. *"Branded? Like a fucking cow?"*

Nona put her hands over her mouth and shook her head as tears puffed her eyes.

"Yes, it was very small, an inch in length."

"Detective, why would traffickers brand their abductees, especially in a place that would be visible during sex. It makes no sense."

"We're starting to believe that maybe this isn't your common trafficking ring — maybe something darker."

"Like a cult?"

"Maybe, Billy. What we don't know is: is the number six a marking for some other purpose, or to place the victim in numerical order? Regardless, time is of the essence. We're formulating a search plan and have called in local talent from New Mexico. You're more than welcome to join us here."

"Why aren't you setting up shop in New Mexico?"

"That part of New Mexico is sparsely populated. If those girls were there, or still are, we don't want a bunch of strangers milling around and warning these cocksuckers."

"But her body was found outside Seattle, Blake. Why not search there?"

"The local boys and the FBI are there. Let them do their thing and draw attention from New Mexico. My partner Joe has a theory they dumped the body there as a decoy to draw us off track. One other thing, a rape kit came back negative and her stomach and intestines were empty, but she wasn't dehydrated. It appears they pumped her insides to make sure no diet clues were left behind that could hint at regional foods. They were very careful, but missed the most damning evidence."

Billy glanced at his watch. "Okay, Blake, it's almost two. I'll be there a bit before seven. Call me on my cell if anything pops up." He hung up the phone and looked at Nona, and his voice softened. "Go be with your Mom at home. I'll keep you in the loop every step of the way. Don't say anything until the FBI goes public."

Her voice crackled. "Okay."

Billy pulled into the Badlands Park Service Headquarters a few minutes before seven. He rushed past a heard of reporters that swarmed on him as soon as they noticed the Vermillion markings on his police car. He declined comment and entered the building, stopping at the front desk and flashing his badge. "Sergeant William Kellerman here to see Detective Roberts."

The receptionist looked at his badge and nodded. "Yes, Sergeant, they're expecting you. I'll let them know you're here." She pointed to a large glassed office with the shades drawn. "They're in the conference room."

He smiled and tipped his hat. "Thank you."

Billy entered the room to find seven men hunched over a conference table looking at a large topo map.

A man with an unlit cigarette dangling from his lips looked up and rushed over with his hand extended. "Billy, Blake Roberts. Nice to meet you. Let me introduce you and fill you in."

Blake introduced Billy to Captain Hollis, Mike Johnson, Joe Running Horse, Agent Harris, Agent Allen, and Webb Sadler.

"Billy, here's what we have." Blake pointed to an enlarged topo map of San Juan County. "The largest population of these plants are found here—" He stabbed his finger into the map. "—near the Colorado border. Now, there's a great deal of private land owned by tech billionaire, Joseph Percovelli."

Billy's brow furrowed. "Do you think he's involved?"

Captain Hollis said, "Not at first, but then we thought about the airplane angle. It appears Mr. Percovelli owns a Gulfstream that flight records show traveled from a private landing strip north of Westover the day your girls were reported missing. The plane landed at his ranch in the circled area on the map."

Agent Harris said, "Our records show a hunting outfitter, owned by Percovelli, owns the private landing strip in Westover."

Billy shook his head. "Why would someone that rich be involved in a trafficking operation? And what about this fucking brand?"

Agent Allen said, "Why would the Dibella boys be involved in one? It's about more than money to them. Flight records also showed several private jets and helicopters arriving and departing from the ranch over the past several days, all owned by very wealthy, powerful people. As for the brand, we only have theories."

Webb Sadler stepped forward. "*Now*, it's not uncommon for Percovelli to entertain the rich and famous. Flight records show private jets from around the world land at his ranch throughout the year. That makes a search warrant a bit tricky." He paused for a beat. "Until this little guy." He held up the evidence bag with the tiny bloody cactus.

Blake said, "Gentleman, let's retrace for a second. Agent Allen mentioned the Dibella case. Does the FBI think this is all connected? Could Vincent Dibella and Percovelli be the money behind this?"

Agent Allen glanced at Agent Hollis, who nodded. "Detective, Vincent Dibella has been on our radar for years. While he has some gray area business deals around the world, he's a pretty straight guy, at least we thought. It appears Percovelli's jet was busy today. It flew from New Mexico to Jackson Hole area, continued to Dibella's ranch in Abilene, and appears to be heading back to New Mexico right now."

Captain Hollis said, "We have specialized swat units securing the perimeter of Percovelli's ranch as we speak. We'll move in at first light."

Billy said, "What about Dibella's ranch?"

Web Sadler interjected. "It would be tough getting a warrant based on a flight between two billionaires' properties. If we turn something up at Percovelli's place, maybe we'll have probable cause."

Jill lay panting and staring at the ceiling. She sat up and scooted her way off the end of the bed, sauntered to the patio doors, and swung them open to let the New Mexico night breeze cool her sweat-drenched body. She looked back towards the bed and lit a joint. "Boys and girls, that was amazing."

A text alert drew her from the balcony doors to her desk. She picked up her phone and glanced at it, and a wry smile crossed her face. She walked onto the balcony, looked towards the snow-capped mountains, and took a deep hit of the joint. Then she looked up and slowly exhaled a cloud of smoke towards the moon.

On her way back to the room, she ran her hands through the bubbling water of a hot tub. "Anyone up for an early morning water adventure?"

Chapter 20
Doubts

Vincent Dibella sat at his desk staring at the portraits of his three sons that adorned the far wall of his office. He took a sip of scotch and dropped his head. When his wife entered from the foyer carrying a plate of food, he looked up, and his sunken, bloodshot eyes met hers.

A compassionate smile crossed her face. "You need to eat something." She walked to the front of his desk, placed the plate in front of him, and slid a chair up. "I had Josephine make your favorite."

He forced a smile. "Thank you, I'll eat in a bit.... Margaret, where did we go wrong raising them?"

"We didn't, Vincent. Their vices and demons were more powerful than our love."

"I can't get the visions of what they did to that poor girl out of my head. If Jake Michaels had not stopped them, who knows what they would have done. Where did that evil come from?"

Vincent's gaunt appearance and broken spirit seemed to crush Margaret, who dabbed her eyes with a tissue.

She knows any words she speaks could not heal me, her once steadfast husband. I have to work through this myself, as does she.

"I don't know," she said.

Sellman walked up to the open double office doors and paused when he saw Margaret.

Vincent looked over his wife's shoulder and motioned him in.

Margaret glanced back and stood up. "Come to bed early. You need to rest."

She passed Sellman and looked back, and her eyes welled as she slowly shook her head.

Sellman took a deep breath and continued to Vincent's desk. He looked down at the plate of food. "You need to eat."

Vincent nodded. "I know, I will. Have you heard anything from our guys in Dallas?"

"Yeah, I just spoke with them. There was no DNA match to the ear. He was a ghost. The ring produced no clues. It's actually pretty common in the assassination world. If it was a plot against you, it's been kept quiet. There's no chatter."

"So, right now, if something happens to any of them, I remain a likely suspect."

Sellman nodded. "Unfortunately, yes. I think we need to dig a bit deeper into South America and see what your boys were really involved in. I'll head south at first light. Try to get some sleep."

Vincent swirled his scotch and water and finished it. "Howard, spare *no* expense down there to find answers, and beef up our security in Wind River until this is over. I don't want a hair harmed on that girl's head or her family's.

"Yes sir."

Jim and Jay sat on the front porch rockers. Jay finished his drink, picked up the bottle of bourbon on the table between them, and emptied the remaining liquor into each of their glasses.

Jim looked to the night skies and smiled. "Jay, remember the old days, when we sat out here in our tents? No worries, no cares... just planning our hunt in the morning."

Jay chuckled. "That was a lifetime ago, my old friend. Times I think about often. Times my mind would escape to, when hell raged around us in Nam."

Jim took a sip of his bourbon. "It appears Hell found us again."

"Nah, Hell did not come looking for us. We just happen to be in its path."

Anna opened the front door. "Jim, Jay, come look at the news."

"Anna, it is almost midnight. What are you doing up?"

Anna motioned them. "Come, hurry."

The two men followed Anna into the house and in front of the TV. A reporter stood in front a large building engulfed in flames. The caption in red on the bottom of the screen read, '*Massive explosion at Dibella Ranch.*'

"Are there fatalities?" Jim said.

Anna said, "The reporter said the firefighters have not been able to enter the house, but there are no reports of anyone fleeing the fire."

Jay looked at Jim. "Like I said, we just happened to be in its path."

Captain Hollis fumbled for his ringing phone in the dark. The time read 3:45 AM. "Hollis."

"Captain, it's Webb, sorry for waking you."

"No, it's fine, Webb, I was getting up in forty- five minutes anyway. What's up?"

"Vincent Dibella is dead, along with his wife and several of his house staff."

Hollis forced his eyes open. "Dead? What happened?"

"It appears a massive gas explosion at his home. We're moving on Percovelli before sunrise. In case there *is* a connection, we don't want to give him any time to start cleaning things up. He'll know Dibella's place, or what's left of it, will be crawling with investigators."

Hollis paused. "Well, that closes that possible loop. Okay, I'll meet you at the station in a half hour."

"No, we don't want to alert the press outside the station, just in case there's a plant passing information to whoever's behind all this. We have a safe house outside of town. It's at 546 Mill Creek Road. Meet us there."

"All right, Webb, I'll contact my guys."

Hollis called Blake and Joe and informed them of the fire and new plans.

Webb looked down at his watch and up at the group of anxious law enforcement professionals. "Are we ready?"

Each man exchanged glances and nodded.

Mike Johnson said, "Let's bring my daughter and the other girls home, if they're in there."

Webb patted him on the shoulder, and nodded to Agent Harris.

Harris picked up a mic. "Tango One, this is Alpha One. Over."

"Alpha One, loud and clear. Over."

"Tango One, put the eyes in the sky and move at your discretion. Over."

"10- 4, Alpha One. Please confirm when you get drone feed on your end. Over."

Agent Allen fine-tuned the monitor and gave a thumbs-up as the drone lifted above the ground.

"Tango One, we have a visual. Over."

The group gathered around the monitor as the drone made its way over the tree tops and descended from the mountains towards the ranch. The night vision camera captured the details of the ground below with crisp resolution. In the distance, the lights from the ranch shined in a bright green on the screen. As the drone moved closer to the ranch, the operator adjusted the camera to compensate for lighting.

"Alpha One, we have heat signatures on the east side of the smaller house. Can you see that? Over."

The men strained their eyes on the remote monitor. "Barely, Tango One. Over."

"Roger, Alpha One, we'll zoom in as we get closer. We have five distinct signatures on the second floor of the building. They're gathered around a square heat signature, possibly a hot tub. Over."

Blake looked at his watch. "It's five o'clock in the fucking morning. A hot tub?"

Hollis raised his finger to quiet Blake.

"Alpha One, we are switching camera to day vision. There's enough light from the building. Stand by. Over."

The monitor screen went dark for several seconds, then lit with a clear black and white screen. As the drone flew closer, five persons were visible. The drone zoomed in, capturing three females and two males in a hot tub. The two males stood up in front of the two seated females. The third female walked to the opposite end of the large tub, lifted a bottle, and looked towards the drone.

"Looks like we interrupted a party," Agent Harris said.

The camera zoomed in. After a minute, the two females stood and leaned over the edge of the hot tub as the males moved behind them. The cameras focused on their faces.

"*Turn away, Mike!*" Webb yelled. He put a folder across the screen.

Mike Johnson stared at the blocked screen, his eyes emotionless, his face stoic. He dropped his head, wobbled across the room, and collapsed into a couch. A transmission echoed in his head. "Alpha One, we have positive identification. Over."

"Roger, Tango One, stand down. Wait for further orders. Over."

Mike's sniffles broke the awkward silence in the room.

Webb walked over and helped him up. "Come on, Mike, let's get you out of here."

Mike shuffled from the room, his eyes glued to the floor.

Hollis looked at the shocked group. Their downward stares and shaking heads confirmed his own thoughts. "Our case just fell apart, didn't it?"

Agent Harris said, "It will be damn near impossible to justify any probable cause and storm the ranch."

"What about Beth Gray and the cactus?" Blake said.

"And Kimi and Mina?" Billy interjected.

Harris drew his hands slowly down his face, pulling his chin down, and shook his head. "I don't know. The autopsy showed no sign of struggle or any conclusive evidence that she was murdered. All indication was she fell."

"*She was fucking branded!*" Blake snapped.

Harris drew a deep, exaggerated breath. "I know, Blake, but that definitely wasn't fatal. Hell, after what we just saw, who knows what these girls are into? Shit, the other two may have the same brand. It was pretty fucking obvious they were enjoying themselves. Did you see the look on Cindy Fowler's face? Hell, she looked like she was shooting a porn flick."

Webb walked through the door.

"How is he?" Hollis said.

"He's trying to gather himself and call his wife to let her know Kelly and Cindy have been found alive."

Agent Allen said, "What's our next move, Webb?"

Webb threw his hands up. "I don't know. I'm waiting for word from Washington. Percovelli has a group of attorneys that will eat us up if we don't dot our i's and cross our t's. I've requested twenty-four-hour surveillance on the ranch while HQ figures out the next move."

Hollis stepped forward. "Do we make a statement to the press and end this circus?"

Webb said, "No, not yet. Let them believe we're still searching until we can confirm the locations of the other girls. I'm not sure what we saw in that video tells the whole story. I've seen enough cases of Stockholm Syndrome to have my doubts."

CHAPTER 21
MINGAN AND HURIT: THE CLIMB

Jake opened his eyes to the sounds of morning songbirds, and looked at Dakota sleeping peacefully. In his past life with Alexi, he would contemplate how to playfully annoy her, but not in this life. That was Jake and Alexi's morning, and it would remain that way for as long as he could hold those memories.

He sat up and quietly made his way from under the comforter and into the kitchen. Honi sprung to his feet and raced to the front door for Jake to let him out.

"Shhh," Jake said to the excited wolf.

"He's fine, I'm awake," Dakota said from bed.

"Sorry, I was trying to let you sleep in."

Dakota rolled from the bunk and stood up. She reached for the ceiling and stretched side to side. As Jake eyed her naked body from head to toe, she looked down at his growing dick. "Are you sure you're not twenty years old?"

"If I was, you wouldn't be able to handle me."

She rolled her eyes and reached for a robe draped over a kitchen chair. "I've been taking it easy on you." She walked over, kissed him, grabbed his dick and stroked it several times. She stood back, looked down at his full erection, and playfully raised her eyebrows. "Maybe later. Let's go for a run."

He opened her robe, ran his hands over her hard nipples, gently slid his finger between her legs and stepped back. "Your loss this morning. One day he may stop working."

She pulled her robe shut and chuckled. "I doubt that. Now, make me some coffee. If it meets my standards, perhaps I'll take this robe back off."

He shook his head and walked to the sink. "Nope, not interested anymore."

She dug through a pile of clothes, said, "Hey, brat, put that thing away... for now," and tossed him a pair of running shorts.

He turned back to the sink and started the coffee.

"Jake, where are my running shorts?"

He turned to see she had removed her robe and was bent over a pile of clothes. She wiggled her ass at him. "I can't find them."

"That's it, you little tease."

She heard him coming, laughed and ran in a circle, jumped over a coffee table and out the door.

Jake gave chase through the field, and yelled, "Hey, it's fucking cold out here!"

Honi saw the two from across the field and gave chase. Just as Jake caught Dakota, gently pulled her to the tall grass and moved on top of her, Honi caught up to them and started licking both their faces.

Dakota covered her face, and Jake turned away.

"Oh my God! What was he eating?" Dakota said under her hands.

Jake laughed and jumped up. "I don't know but it was definitely dead. That's fucking disgusting."

Honi continued trying to lick Dakota's face.

She laughed, trying to push him away with one hand while covering her mouth and nose with the other. She struggled to sit up, but the young wolf was enjoying play time too much and blocked her. The more she laughed, the more excited Honi got. "Jake, call him."

"Nope, that's what you get for being a cock tease."

"Jake Michaels, if you ever want to get inside me again, you better help."

Dakota managed to roll on her belly and bury her face in her hands. "*Jake*," she commanded between giggles.

"Honi, come, playtime's over," Jake said.

Honi turned and ran to Jake's side.

Dakota sat up, ran the back of her hand across her mouth, and made a sour face. "That was friggin' gross."

Jake looked down at her. "A just punishment for a wench like you." He reached out and helped her to her feet. "Let's go down to the hot spring and get cleaned up. I'll go grab some towels and our robes."

"And I'll grab us some coffee."

The two sat in the bubbling spring enjoying their morning coffee.

Dakota broke the silence. "Jake, I was thinking about our last visit to the Spirit world and the Six. Do you think we somehow woke a long dead evil, or opened a portal for them down at the ranch?"

"I don't know. I thought about that also. It's like we tilted the balance of something. But, Rowtag said the Six can't pass into our world."

Dakota paused. "He also said to follow the footsteps of the Dibella boys, that it would lead to answers. I wonder if some how they were influenced by the Six, or even controlled by them?"

Jake sipped on his coffee and raised an eyebrow. "You mean, like possessed?"

Dakota shrugged. "Maybe, or, if not possessed by them, then possessed by their promises."

"I guess anything's possible, but those kids had everything. What could they be offered that would be *so powerful*, it led them to trafficking and rape and who knows what else?"

Dakota shook her head. "I don't know. Maybe Mingan and Hurit's story will answer this, if the Spirit world continues to show us their journey. They were punished for something heinous."

"What's your take on the missing member of the Six? Could it be Rowtag? Can we trust him?"

Dakota's eyes narrowed as she thought for a second. "He *did* answer quickly who that group was. His words, '*men and Gods feared him*' still plays heavy on me. As for trusting him, do we have much choice right now?"

"Good point." Jake looked up. "The skies are growing angry. Should we head back to the cabin and pay him a visit?"

Dakota stood up, sauntered across the spring and straddled Jake. "First, you have some business to finish."

He chuckled. "*I* have business to finish? You're the one that was prancing around naked, stretching, and shaking your ass at me. I think *you* have business to finish."

She reached below the water. "Okay, you win."

Jake stoked the fire and joined Dakota on the bear skin rug. He loaded the pipe and started their journey to the other realm.

On the far side of the field, Rowtag stood in front of a roaring fire. A pungent smoke filled the air. He stirred the embers with his spear, looked to the heavens, and raised his arms from his sides. "Heneeteniihe3en beteenbiito'owu." As his words echoed loudly through the Spirit world, he dropped his head and arms, waved his spear above the fire, and extinguished it.

Jake and Dakota approached him.

Jake said, "Rowtag, what were you doing?"

"Protecting this Sacred land from evil that surrounds it."

Dakota said, "Did Jake and I do something to bring evil to Wind River? Did we open a portal or something for the Six?"

Rowtag smiled and pointed his spear towards the waterfall. "Children, continue with Mingan and Hurit's journey. Learn the answers along their path." On the last word, he vanished.

Jake shook his head. "Can't he just fuckin' answer a simple question?"

A loud clap of thunder shook the ground.

Jake looked at Dakota and grimaced, then looked to the skies. "Sorry."

The two made their way to the edge of the pool and looked into the waterfall. The cascading water turned a brilliant purple, then slowed to a trickle. The rocks, normally hidden behind the falls, sparkled in brilliant yellow for several seconds, then calmed. Mingan and Hurit's world appeared.

Mingan, Hurit, and Wahya stood at the base of the High Mountain.

Mingan fixed his focus upwards. "The top is in the clouds. My people talk of great furred beasts that still roam there, long gone from our land."

Hurit's eyes followed the ascent of the mountain. "My people speak of winged serpents so large that they block the sun when they fly overhead, and of a tribe with large bony features, their bodies covered in thick hair. They eat human flesh and leave footprints twice the size of the largest man."

Mingan chuckled. "Look what our people said of each of *our* tribe's appearances. These are just ancient stories told around night fires. Let us begin our climb and retrieve our quarry, then take our place amongst our people."

The three spent the first day of travel steadily climbing from the barren high desert and scorching sun to cooler, shaded, green alpine forests. They reached a small stream flowing from a fissure in a granite rock face.

Mingan looked towards the low sun on the horizon, panned the area, and nodded. "We will spend the night here. I will fish."

Hurit looked at the forest floor. "And I will gather pine branches to build a shelter and start a fire."

The two went about their tasks and regrouped as dusk settled in.

Mingan laid four fat trout next to a knee-high campfire, then shook the roof of a chest-high lean-to. "You build a good fire, and a sturdy shelter."

Hurit, making her final adjustments to the shelter, glanced at the fish. "And you fish well."

Hurit had positioned the pine-thatched shelter several feet from a large granite boulder. She'd placed the fire ring halfway between the shelter's opening and the stone's flat face to reflect the heat back on them.

Mingan skewered the fish and settled across from Hurit. After several minutes, he removed his buckskin top and wiped the sweat from his brow. His gaze fell down her body. "Are you not hot?"

Her eyes narrowed. "I hope you do not expect me to remove my top. You have seen enough for one day."

Mingan, defeated in his inuendo, looked back at the flame.

Hurit dropped her head, hiding a smile. "Mingan, do your people speak of an ancient evil that lives on the mountaintop?"

"Yes, my great grandfather called them the Six. They have great powers. It is said they lay with men and women, and when they are done, they eat them... uncooked. Do your people have a name for them?"

"Yes, we call them soul stealers. My people believe they tempt you with all your wishes, and in return will take your soul. It is said there are seven, one for each sin that destroyed the old tribes."

The two stared silently into the campfire. A rustling in the brush, past the flame's light, caught their attention. Mingan raised a single finger to his lips, his eyes wide, and whispered. "We spoke of them, and now they come." He reached for his spear and quietly rose to one knee. As the noise from the brush crackled in the dead silence, Mingan turned back to Hurit, his face panic-stricken. He rose to both feet and paused, his spear readied for battle as the noise drew closer.

He spun towards Hurit. *"Boo!"*

She jumped.

He fell to his knees, laughing uncontrollably. "Like I said earlier, stories for the campfire."

Hurit leaned across the flame and punched him in the leg. *"You are an ass.* I hope you come face to face with them. I bet you run like a child."

"Yes, like I ran when you were about to be eaten."

"The only reason you stayed there was to watch me naked. I bet you played with that little thing between your legs. I would have slain that beast without you."

He mocked her splashing motions. "I am sure. You could have splashed him to death."

Her eyes squinted and cheeks grew hot as he continued with his mocking splashing motions and girly yells. She thought for a second, calmed, and started to laugh. "You are dumb. I am going to sleep." She crawled into the shelter and tucked under her blanket.

Mingan stood up, stretched his arms to the night sky and prayed.

Hurit watched the muscles in his back flex and swallowed hard. She closed her eyes and drifted into the dream world.

The early morning sun shined through the pine branches of the lean-to. Wahya paced in front of the shelter and whined.

Mingan sat up and scooted forward. He hugged his wolf, stood and stretched, letting out an excessively loud yawn.

Hurit opened one eye. "Are you always so obnoxious?"

Mingan looked back and chuckled. "What kind of leader will you be if you are not the first to rise and greet the new sun before your people?"

"Ughh." Hurit pulled her blanket over her head.

"Come, Hurit, we must reach the top before the sun sets."

The two gathered their belongings and started the day's climb. After several hours, they reached the snowpack and stopped.

"The temperature will drop quickly," Mingan said. "We should change into our furs."

Hurit looked up at the towering snow-covered cliffs and sheer rock faces before her. A thick cloud layer stood between them and the mountain's summit. "How high must you go for your feathers?"

"Until I see the Sacred Eagles soaring. The land looks barren and frozen up there. How will you find your sacred plants?"

Hurit panned the cliffs. "I am told they grow in the crevices of the rocks."

The two climbed slowly, their breathing taxed by the thinner air. When they reached the cloud layer, the warmth of the sun disappeared and biting, wet winds stung their faces. As the pitch became steeper, the two climbers changed the angle of their ascent.

After several arduous hours, the thick clouds dissipated and the high mountain sun warmed their faces. They reached a small rock plateau and stopped to catch their breath in the thin air.

Mingan panned the cliffs above and raised his hand. He turned to Hurit and raised a finger to his lips. He looked up and to his left and pointed. She followed his finger to two large eagles gliding in the currents.

She sidled up to him and whispered, "There should be feathers on that large ledge below them."

He nodded and traced an imaginary path to the ledge with his spear head. "Perhaps you will find your sacred bushes tucked behind those ledges."

The trio made their way from the plateau to the entrance of a narrow slot canyon dividing two towering granite faces. The passage, at times no wider than shoulder width, twisted and turned for hundreds of yards thru a labyrinth of smooth, rounded rock faces.

Mingan looked up and pointed forward. "The sky widens ahead. We should be in the open soon."

"Mingan, look—to the right of your finger, on that ledge, the bush with sacred berries...."

Mingan nodded. "It is not very high. We can get up there."

The two climbed up until they were right below the rounded ledge.

"Hurit, this rounded rock gives us no hand holds to climb. I will stand against it. Climb up my back." He braced himself. After several clumsy attempts and some belly laughs, she climbed onto the small ledge.

She peeked over the ledge and beamed. "There is more than I expected. I can fill my entire sack." After several minutes, she shimmied to the edge and repeated the same climbing action in reverse. "Now, let's find your feathers and get back to our people."

As Mingan had figured, the narrow canyon soon emptied onto a small rock plateau that, only a hundred yards long, narrowed into a ledge that wrapped around a sheer cliff face. The cry of a sacred eagle, hidden from sight, pierced the thin air.

Mingan looked at Hurit. "I must go along that ledge. The winds will be strong. It is best you stay here with Wahya."

She shook her head. "No, I have climbed this far. I will help you retrieve your feathers."

The determination in her eyes impressed him. He nodded and smiled, then bent down and stroked his wolf's head. "Wahya, stay."

They reached the ledge and paused. The dizzying drop forced both of them to press against the cliff face as the winds swirled in all directions. "Are you sure?" he yelled over the howling gusts.

She nodded.

He reached his hand out. "Keep your belly against the wall and don't look down. Grab my hand."

The two joined hands and slowly shuffled along the ledge. Inch by inch, they moved forward. The winds, constantly changing directions, made it difficult to brace themselves. Ahead, a blind corner gripped them with anxiety.

Mingan looked at her. "Are you sure?"

She leaned her head against the rock face, closed her eyes for a moment, and drew in a deep breath. When she looked at him, the confidence in her eyes reassured him. "Yes."

Mingan reached one leg around the blind corner searching for the ledge. His foot found nothing but air. He retracted it, took a deep breath, and shimmied closer to the corner. He peeked around the rock face, let go of her hand, and jumped around the corner.

"*Mingan.*"

He peeked up from around the corner and laughed. "Look down."

She looked past his shoulder to find a much broader ledge, which flowed into a large, flat plateau riddled with sparse rushes of grass and bushes. She jumped down to join him, and her eyes caught something in the distance. "Look at the cave."

The fire came back into focus for Jake. He rubbed his eyes and waited for Dakota to rejoin the physical world.

A couple seconds passed, and she opened her eyes.

"God," she said, "it's like watching a TV series. I wish Rowtag would just tell us what all this means and quit the fucking drama."

Jake stood up to stretch. "I guess he has his reasons."

CHAPTER 22
THE MORNING

Jill stepped from the shower, wrapped a towel around her head, and poured a cup of coffee. She looked at Kelly and Cindy sprawled naked across the silk sheets of her bed. She walked over and placed a comforter across them.

Cindy stirred and opened her eyes halfway. "What time is it?"

Jill smiled. "It's early. Go back to bed."

Cindy's eyes dropped shut. The intoxicating mixture of booze and ancient smoke had not worn off her yet.

Jill walked onto the patio, wearing nothing but the towel on her head, and faced the mountain where the surveillance units were tucked away. She patted the towel several times and dropped it to the ground. She primped her hair in a teasing manner, allowing it to fall over her sun-kissed shoulders.

Halfway up the mountain, the reflection of a rifle scope caught her attention. She smiled, stretched her hands over her head, and bent side to side several times.

"Alpha One, are you getting this? Over."

Hollis, Blake, Billy, and Joe looked at each other and smiled. "Roger, Tango Two, maintain visual for as long as possible. We're still waiting on word from Washington."

Webb, Agent Harris, and Agent Allen entered the room.

Webb said, "Anything, men?"

Hollis pointed his head towards the monitor. "Just this."

Webb raised his brow. "The perks of being wealthy. I assume she's the same woman we saw late last night with our girls?"

Webb clicked on the mic. "Tango Two, zoom in as close as possible to her face. Let's get it into our database. Over"

"10-4, Alpha One. Over."

The woman on screen dropped her arms, tilted her head back, and stretched her lower back, pushing her chest out. She then turned, bent over to retrieve her towel, and sauntered back to her room.

Webb said, "Tango Two, did she give you enough time for pics?"

"Roger, Alpha One. Forwarding them to HQ now. Over."

Webb glanced at his crew and nodded. "Good work, Tango Two. Over."

Blake pulled out a cigarette. "How long before we get results?"

Agent Harris said, "If she's in the US database, maybe twenty minutes or so. If we have to look internationally, maybe an hour."

Twenty minutes passed.

"Alpha One, this is Tango Two. We have visual on the blonde female entering main house. Over."

"Roger, Tango Two, keep an eye on her. Over."

A text alert pulled Webb's attention from the monitor. He looked down and shook his head. "Gentleman, our blonde is a ghost. There are no matches in any domestic database. HQ is running an international search."

Jill entered the main house, walked across the marble foyer and opened the double doors to Mr. P's office.

He looked up and smiled. "You look spry this morning. Did you have a *good* night?

Jill took a deep breath and raised her brows. "It was delicious."

Mr. P leaned back in his chair. "What brings you around so early? I assume you heard about Vincent."

"Yes, he was one of the few good men that visited here for honest business. It's a shame he went to his grave knowing his sons were total fuck-ups. They served us well, but their times had come. It's partially why I'm here. More urgent, it appears the police are on to us. They're in the mountains surrounding the ranch. It's time to shut down this operation."

"Jill, this isn't the first time the police or Feds have snooped around here. You know my lawyers will squash anything. Move the remaining two girls into the bunker, and let the Feds come poke around."

Jill smiled. "It's not the cops. The Client has given the order. I'm freeing the girls."

Mr. P leaned forward and glared at Jill. "*Who the fuck* do you think you are? That is *not your decision*, and *it's not* the Client's decision. I have fed the twisted, perverted hunger of the Client, and the most powerful people in the world, for the past decade. You *are not* going to free those girls. I will have them killed before I let them talk. Do you realize the implications if they reach the police? They'll identify our last guests, who will sing like song birds to save their own pitiful asses. The domino effect will be felt around the world, and our secret society will be exposed. *No, Jill,* you will not free those girls. In fact, get out of my office before I have security come in and make you disappear with those other two cunts."

Jill sighed, rolled her eyes and chuckled. "*Secret society...* you know nothing about secret societies." She unzipped her hooded sweatshirt, removed her tank top, stepped out of her shorts, and slinked around Mr. P's desk.

"You can use that pussy on our guests. It has no power over me."

She glared at him. "Take the gun from your desk, put it to your mouth, and end your miserable life."

Her icy stare pierced his soul. "Fuck you! If I pull that gun, it won't be for me."

Her eyes closed, then sprang open void of any color, only large black pupils. Her body tensed and her head flung back. First, the veins in her throat flared, followed by the veins cascading down her body. Her muscles twitched violently, and dark, coarse hair sprang from her skin.

Mr. P trembled, paralyzed with fear.

She leaned into him, her once delicate features now replaced by a receding forehead, protruding brow line, and wide nose. Her hot breath smelled of rotten meat. "*Do it!*" she growled.

His hand trembled as he fumbled for the desk drawer, retrieved the small caliber revolver, and lifted it to his mouth. His eyes widened as hers narrowed.

"*Do it.*"

He cocked the hammer. A muffled shot followed.

She watched his eyes turn bloodshot and his body slump over the desk. She then ran her thick finger through the blood on the headrest of his chair, brought it to her mouth, and sucked it clean. She stepped back, raised her hands to her sides and mumbled, "Sha-ma a-do-nai."

Quickly, her body transformed back to its goddess form. She dressed, opened the safe, and retrieved a file labeled 'South America.' She placed it on Mr. P's desk and walked from the office, closing the double office doors behind her.

Mr. P's secretary greeted her as she walked onto the front porch. "Good Morning, Jill, you are moving around early."

Jill smiled. "Mr. P and I had an urgent meeting regarding Vincent Dibella. If you would, Nancy, please do not disturb him until ten o'clock. He's on a conference call with his attorneys."

Nancy's eyes softened. "Yes, what a shame with Mr. Dibella. He was always so nice when he came here."

Jill smiled. "Yes, he was a gentleman. Have a nice day, Nancy."

"You also, Jill."

"Alpha One, this is Tango Two. The blonde just left the main house. She spoke with another woman dressed in business attire, and is heading back to the guest house. Over."

"Roger, Tango Two. Over."

Jill made her way to her room, walked through the door, sat on the bed next to the two sleeping women, and nudged both of them. "Ladies, rise and shine."

They both grabbed their heads and lazily opened their eyes.

"What was in that powder last night? My head feels like it's ready to explode," Kelly grumbled.

Cindy said, "My fucking brain hurts."

Jill chuckled. "Drink some coffee. Caffeine will neutralize the lingering effects. Now, ladies, as I told you... if you make the right choices, as you did... you will one day see your families again. I told you I was not a monster. I just have a much higher power to serve. Today, you can leave here. As we speak, there are police officers surrounding the property. I have arranged a wire for a million dollars into each of your accounts. It is legitimate and listed as payment for professional services. Now, get dressed and take a morning jog through the pasture towards the river. The police will rush to you."

Jill retrieved two contracts from her desk drawer and handed them to Cindy and Kelly. "Please review these. I'll be right back." She stepped into the bathroom.

Cindy and Kelly paged through the contracts.

Cindy shook her head and whispered, "She's lying. This is a set-up, probably some kind of sick game for one or their perverted clients. Why would she be so calm? She'll fry for her involvement, not to mention all the people we can bring down."

Jill walked from the bathroom. "I would have thought you two would be in the middle of the pasture by now."

Cindy said, "Jill, why would you let us leave here knowing we can tumble this enterprise and implicate very rich powerful people, not to mention you?"

Jill smiled and walked to the bed. She leaned forward and kissed Cindy on the lips. "That will be your choice, my dear. Just remember, those powerful people have tentacles that reach across the world and into a darkness beyond your most terrifying nightmares. Would you want to see something happen to you or your family members, now that you're free, and... not to mention... wealthy?

Jill straightened and half shrugged. "If it was me, I would say I accepted a job offer with Percovelli International and signed a non-disclosure agreement. Unfortunately, Mr. Percovelli committed suicide this morning. You'll find the contracts were dated and executed two days ago. Oh, by the way, did I mention that Beth's family will also receive her million dollars? As for me, I have business to attend to that can't be interrupted. So, as long as both of you make the right choice, everyone will move on with their lives, including Mina, Kimi, and Aiyana. It's your decision, ladies. I'm not sure you want blood on your hands. Trust me... it stains."

Jill walked to the bedroom door, paused, and glanced over her shoulder. "Oh, and look shocked when the police swoop in on you in the field. Remember, this is a workday and continuation of contract obligations with Percovelli International, should you choose the terms and conditions of our employment." She closed the door behind her.

Kelly looked at Cindy. "Do we really have a choice? Let's have a cup of coffee and get some fresh air."

━━⟨ ☙ ⟩━━

"Alpha One, this is Tango Two. Over."

"Go, Tango Two."

"Alpha One, our targets have walked onto the deck drinking what appears to be coffee. We also have visual on the blonde. She is getting into a black Porsche. Over."

Hollis shook his head and looked at Webb.

Webb threw his hands up. "Tango Two, maintain visual on the two girls. Over."

"Roger, Alpha One."

Blake looked at Webb and the two FBI agents. "What's our play, gents?"

Agent Harris said, "Until we get some indication these girls are in harm's way, there's nothing we can do. HQ is working on a search warrant based on the cactus, but without some indication from those two girls that they're in trouble, or a reason to come onto the property, we're in a fucking holding pattern."

Webb stared blankly at the monitor as Kelly and Cindy enjoyed their morning coffee then retreated into the room. A text broke his pondering. He sprung to his feet. "Gentlemen, we have our way in. A 9-1-1 call was just received from the ranch. It appears Percovelli has been found by his secretary with a gunshot wound to his head."

"Alpha One, Tango Two. Over."

"Go, Tango Two. Over."

"Our girls have left the house and are jogging towards the pasture. Over."

"Tango One, a 9-1-1 call was just received by local dispatch. Have the local units move in with first responders. Over."

━━⟨ ☙ ⟩━━

Cindy and Kelly moved at a slow pace towards the river. When the sudden eruption of multiple sirens wailed through the canyons, the girls paused.

Kelly looked at Cindy. "Holy shit, she wasn't lying. They sound like they're heading this way. Let's get back to the house. Are we sure on our story?"

Cindy breathed deeply and nodded.

Mina, Kimi, and Aiyana walked through the kitchen of the mountainside mansion. A member of the staff offered them coffee and fresh baked pastry. They obliged and moved to the patio with their breakfast.

A strikingly handsome dark-haired gentleman with piercing blue eyes approached them from the far side of the expansive patio. "Good morning, ladies. I trust you slept well?"

Despite her disdain for the enterprise she had been forced into, Mina found something intriguing about the man. He had an air about him that was different from those at the Percovelli ranch. "Yes, we slept well, thank you."

"My name is Dorian. Welcome to my home. I understand your circumstances may seem dire, as your journey to this point would lead you to believe that. However, it is not. Tomorrow this time, you will be free to leave here, and you will be compensated well for your time. Please, enjoy your day. My staff and the facilities are at your beck and call."

Kimi barked, "*Why* would you release us and risk bringing down this sick fucking world we've been forced into?"

Dorian locked his gaze on hers and approached. He brushed her face with the back of his hand and smiled.

A warm sensation rushed through her body. It startled her, but at the same time calmed her.

He took a few steps back. "Come, follow me, please."

The girls looked at each other and, after some hesitation, stood and followed him to the kitchen.

He picked up a remote and turned on a wall mounted TV.

The girls froze in their tracks, their jaws slack. Headlines streamed across the bottom of the screen as cameras panned the Percovelli Ranch.

'Two missing women found at Percovelli Ranch in northern New Mexico. Kelly Johnson and Cindy Fowler are

alive and well. Joseph Percovelli found dead with a single gunshot wound to the head. Suicide is suspected. More details to follow.'

Dorian clicked off the TV and smiled. "Your Destiny is not as dire as you believed." He walked from the kitchen, leaving the stunned girls.

After several seconds, the girls recovered from their shock, and a rush of emotions flooded them. Tears flowed down their cheeks, and sobs of happiness echoed through the kitchen as they drew in close to hug each other. Days of fear, anxiety, and dread had been quelled in a brief moment.

Mina wiped her eyes and drew back a sniffle. "They did it. Kelly and Cindy did it."

Kimi laughed between her crying and hugged Mina again. "I promise, no more rides with good-looking strangers."

Aiyana looked at the two girls and forced a smile.

Kimi and Mina, still in a half hug, turned to her.

Kimi said, "Aiyana, you don't look happy. What's wrong?"

Aiyana shook her head and smiled. "Nothing. I guess I just don't believe it's over."

Mina opened her free arm. "Come over here. It's over."

Aiyana joined in a group hug.

"Ladies," a deep voice came from behind them.

The group turned to find a broodingly handsome, dark-haired, blue-eyed man and a sensuous, blonde-haired woman standing in the entrance of the kitchen. They approached the girls, each carrying paperwork.

Mina whispered to Kimi, "Are we at a model shoot?"

"My name is Josef, and this is Jordana. If you will, please have a seat at the table."

The group sat down, and Jordana handed each of the girls a three-page document. Her piercing blue eyes moved from girl to girl. "In your hands is a contract. This evening, you will take part in a documentary. You will each be paid the sum of one million dollars, and as Dorian promised, granted your freedom tomorrow morning. The terms are very simple. You participate, agree to adhere to the *strictest* non-disclosure, and return to your lives very wealthy young women."

Mina glanced at the first page and looked up. "What sort of documentary?"

Josef said, "It is a study of ancient Native American mythology."

Kimi said, "Why us and not professional actresses? And why so much money?"

Jordana said, "Actresses are scripted. We want to capture reality."

Aiyana said, "And what if we choose not to sign this contract?"

Jordana glanced at Josef and nodded.

Josef locked his glare on her. "You will look over your shoulder for the rest of your life. In the dark, you will find terror, and in the shadows, unholy whispers. If you like, you are free to leave this mountain now... and start your journey into an abyss of endless dread."

Josef's soulless eyes and prophetic tone clearly shook Aiyana to the core. Her face drew pale and her hands trembled.

The *tick-tock* of a wall clock echoed in the silence, as Josef and Jordana stared at each girl in turn.

Suddenly, Jordana broke into laughter, and Josef followed.

The terrified girls stared blankly at them.

Jordana said, "*That's why* we do not want scripted actresses. We want real emotion."

Josef stood up. "Ladies, it's a beautiful day. Please, go enjoy the grounds. Dinner will be served at five. We will film at seven, and be done by ten."

Jordana leaned in. "Relax and have fun with this. Tomorrow this time, you will be on your way home." She placed a cell phone on the table. "Call your folks." She smiled and followed Josef from the room.

Jim and Jay returned a bit past noon from a morning hunt on the Ranch, and approached the front porch.

Anna sprung from the house. "You both need to see the news."

Jim said, "More Dibella coverage?"

"And then some. Another billionaire is dead, Joseph Percovelli. They also found two of the missing girls from the badlands on his ranch. Both are alive and seem to be fine. The FBI are on scene and will be holding a press conference at 12:45 PM regarding new developments in the case."

Jay and Jim leaned their guns on the porch rail and removed their muddy boots.

Anna said, "Are you two hungry? We have twenty minutes or so before the news conference."

Jay nodded. "A sandwich and some of that sweet tea would be great."

Jim said, "Yes, thank you, love."

Samuel joined the two hunters outside. He looked around, stepped from the porch, and looked in the back of the old farm pickup. "Hmmm," he vocalized loudly and shook his head.

Jay looked at Jim and nodded his head towards Samuel. "Here it comes."

Samuel walked to the foot of the porch steps. "I see no deer in the truck. Have they gone south for the winter like the geese?"

Jim chuckled. "No, we did not see anything this morning. The woods were still."

Samuel raised his eyebrows and twisted his mouth. "I guess the deer were much dumber when I hunted—same woods... same weather... same time of the year. Perhaps I need to go next time, so I can taste venison one last time before the Spirits take me." He walked past them, shaking his head the whole time, and disappeared into the house.

Jay laughed. "Man, he likes to bust our balls, has for as long as I have known him. Remember when we hunted with him at the cabin and we would get skunked? He always came back to camp with game."

Jim smiled. "He cheated. I know he had bait or something. Remember, he would never tell us where he was hunting that day. Just *'over the ridge,"* or *'past the stream,'* or *'in the canyon.'* And, he was always on the mountain or here on the ranch a few days before us."

Jay chuckled. "They were good times, my old friend. Shall we go see what the FBI has to say?"

The two joined Anna and Samuel in the living room.

An FBI spokesman stepped in front of the camera.

"First, we are happy to report that Kelly Johnson and Cindy Fowler, two of the three girls missing for the past two

weeks, are safe. We regret that the third girl, Beth Gray, suffered an unfortunate accident and was killed in a fall. There is no foul play suspected, as this has been corroborated by witnesses. The three women, originally thought to be kidnapped, had been recruited by Percovelli International, a private security force, and accepted employment voluntarily. They have indicated that several other missing women, including Mina White Eagle, Kimimela Locklear, Aiyana Begay, and four others yet to be identified, were present on the Percovelli ranch. Their whereabouts are unknown at this time, but it is believed they are also under the employment of Percovelli International.

"Joseph Percovelli was found dead of a single, self-inflicted gunshot wound to the head. Mr. Percovelli has been the subject of an ongoing investigation by an international task force. Based on evidence found on scene, we can now confirm Mr. Percovelli, along with Richard Brett Dibella, Marcus John Dibella, and Shane Rogers, were the masterminds of a South American enterprise that facilitated human trafficking, sex slavery, and pornography. There is no indication that Vincent Dibella, who was killed in a tragic explosion yesterday, was connected. An investigation is still ongoing into his death. We will provide further statements as more facts become available. At this time, we will not answer any questions. Thank you."

The press erupted with a volley of questions as the FBI spokesman walked from the microphone.

Jim turned the volume down and looked at Jay. "I guess that closes the circle."

Jay nodded. "I am sure there will be a lot more fallout from this."

Anna said, "They all got what they deserved."

After several moments of silence, Samuel spoke, his tone steady and prophetic. "The white men were only pawns."

Nona and her Mom stood speechless in front of the TV. Billy had texted her thirty minutes prior telling her he could not talk, but that they should tune in to the news conference. The two women broke into tears and hugged each other.

"She's alive, Nona. She's alive. Mina will come back to us," Margaret forced out between sobs.

Nona held her mom tightly and looked over her shoulder, staring at the wall. Her eyes narrowed as she analyzed the report.

For now, I will support my mom's optimism, but Billy and I need to talk.

Mina dialed her Mom's house phone.

Sniffles on the other end gave way to a familiar voice, as Nona answered, "Hello... hello."

"Nona, it's me."

"Mina! Oh my God, where are you?"

"Mina!." Margaret cried out.

Nona switched to speaker.

"It's me, Momma. Kimi and I are coming home tomorrow."

"Where are you?" Nona said.

"I'll explain everything. I love both of you. Please call Kimi's mom and dad and let them know we'll call shortly. I'm gonna....."

The phone clicked and dead air filled the receiver.

"Nona, can you hear me? Mom?" Mina frantically redialed several times. *"Fuck!"* She slammed the phone on the counter. "We have no signal, but at least they know we're alive."

CHAPTER 23
THE NIGHT

Kimi, Mina, and Aiyana stepped from their rooms dressed in sheer but tasteful white gowns provided by their hosts. They ascended the spiral marble staircase to the grand foyer.

Dorian, with a glass of wine in his hand, walked from the living room and greeted the women. "Ladies, you look beautiful. I trust having the opportunity to speak with your family proved our good intention?"

Mina glanced at Kimi and Aiyana, and each nodded. "Yes, thank you. That was very kind of you."

Jordana joined the group, offering a serving tray with three glasses of wine. "We are waiting for three more of our associates. They will arrive shortly. Please, enjoy this enchanting blend from our own vineyards in Bordeaux."

The three women graciously accepted and sipped the aromatic, robust Malbec.

Kimi raised her brow. "I'm a wine drinker, and this is delicious. Is it a private collection or do you sell it?"

Jordana smiled. "We reserve it for special guests and friends only. Sorry."

Dorian half turned from the group and looked over his shoulder. "Ladies, if you would, please follow me."

He led the women to the rear wing of the mansion, down a long corridor lined with fine art, ending with a set of dark mahogany doors. The group passed through the doors and down a flight of stairs to an iron gate akin to those of medieval castles.

Kimi finished her wine and, a bit giddy, said, "I hope that's the entrance to your wine cellar."

Dorian chuckled. "Yes, in fact it is. I assume by looking at each of your glasses that you approved of our 2008 vintage?"

Aiyana, normally reserved, finished her glass and eyed Dorian from head to toe. "I would certainly like another glass, and maybe I'll lose this gown."

Kimi laughed. "Aiyana, you little slut."

Dorian smiled. "That blend does tend to lower one's inhibitions."

Dorian led the women through a torch-lit stone labyrinth ending at a wood balcony. Below, a large, dimly lit cavern lined with rows of wooden wine racks stretched from wall to wall.

Kimi said, "Are we inside the mountain?"

"Yes, be careful. The steps are steep."

The group traversed the combination of stairs and landings, winding along rock walls to the wine cellar below. They walked between two rows of wooden racks filled head-high with bottles, which stretched for what appeared to be a football field long.

At the end of the row, Kimi paused and looked in both directions, to the end caps of each row. "How many bottles are in this collection?"

Dorian pointed to the left and then the right. "We have nearly a half million bottles, the oldest being from the fourth century."

Aiyana, now feeling the full effects of the wine, joked. "I bet that's a panty dropper."

The two girls and Dorian chuckled.

Dorian said, "I am *sure* it is," and held his finger up. "Since each of you enjoyed our 2008, let me introduce you to a prize vintage of ours. I will be right back." He walked left, turned down a row, and quickly reappeared with a gawdy bottle. "This is one of *our* vineyard's oldest bounties. It is from 1918." He uncorked the bottle, allowed it to breathe for a few seconds, then poured a small amount into four fresh glasses hanging from the end cap. "I suggest you swirl this a few times. Cheers."

The women returned the cheer and sipped the light red, earthy blend.

Kimi said, "Oh my God, this is better than the last."

Aiyana and Mina both nodded.

Dorian pointed to a torch-lit entrance to the left of the wine cellar. "Ladies, let's shoot our documentary."

The group passed through a winding torch-lit tunnel, its walls aglow with bioluminescence. They stepped from the stone passage and were greeted by a magnificent crystal cavern. Hundreds of torches cast rainbow prisms through the quartz adorning the cave's walls. The roof dripped with stalactites of all colors, mirrored in the clear subterranean lake below. Before the lake, an arched, gilded bridge crossed a small stream. The girls ogled at the splendor surrounding them.

Dorian smiled. "Beautiful, isn't it?"

Kimi, buzzed by the wine and slack-jawed, said, "I feel like I'm in a dream."

Dorian walked forward. "Please, follow me."

As the group crested the bridge, the water below sparkled with flashes of light from silver-scaled cave fish darting beneath their feet. They stepped from the bridge onto a fine white sand floor.

Aiyana bent down and sieved the crystals though her fingers. "That is the softest sand I have ever felt."

Dorian bent down and joined her. He scooped a handful. "It's pulverized quartz, the finest sand in the world."

"Formed millions of years ago," a familiar voice called from the darkness beyond Dorian.

The girls looked past his shoulder, and a sudden brilliant blaze of three large pyres lit the cavern. The girls looked at each other, fear replacing the calming buzz of the wine.

Jill, dressed in a flowing, sheer, white robe, sauntered towards them. In her hand was a smoldering bouquet of sage. "No, ladies, those are not your funeral pyres, nor is this your Destiny." She moved in front of the women and waved the aromatic smoke under their chins. "Bo-sem, na-saq, sha-khahh."

The three women responded the same, and Kimi felt her head lighten and body relax, all inhibitions and fears erased.

Jill looked deeply into each of their eyes and whispered, "Prepare yourselves. Cleanse your bodies in the sacred lake."

One by one, the girls dropped their gowns to the sand and stepped into the cool waters to chest-high. In front of them, a bright light rose from the lake bottom.

The oracle broke the surface and dimmed, and a beautiful Native American woman stood on the water. Her long dark hair framed delicate features and enchanting emerald green eyes. She smiled and nodded. "Beebeihit."

A soft chorus of voices responded from the shore. "Be-tu-lah."

The Spirt of the Water slowly sunk below the surface without a single ripple.

The girls turned to the shoreline to find it crowded with small figures, their faces hidden beneath black-hooded robes. Above them, on a stone altar, stood Dorian, Jill, Josef, Jordana, a broodingly handsome man they called David, and a striking woman named Adah. All wore silken white gowns adorned with gold inlay.

On the altar lay three raised stone tables the size of single beds. The head and sides of each table were adorned with 111 white candles. At each base was a simple gold chalice.

Dorian stepped forward. "Kimi, Mina, and Aiyana, step from the lake, and each of you stand in front of one of the tables."

The girls stepped from the water and across the sand.

The hooded figures split into two groups as the girls approached. Whispers, in strange tongues, echoed in the crystal chamber as the girls made their way past the waist-high congregation. As the three took a position at the foot of their respective stone table, Jill, Jordana, and Adah each moved behind a girl and placed their hands on their shoulders. They gently turned the girls to face the hooded onlookers, and moved them back against the stone tables.

"Lie back," Jill directed. Once the girls reclined on the stone tables, Jill, Jordana, and Adah moved to the side of each girl.

Dorian, Josef, and David moved to the front of the altar.

Dorian stepped forward. "*Tonight*, the blood of the pure will feed us. In a vision, I have seen the end of our exile. *We will* walk freely, as in the beginning. *We will* cleanse the earth. Our offspring will *no longer* bear the curse." A loud chorus of ancient tongues filled the chamber, until Dorian held his hand up to silence the crowd. "Soon, we will hold the power, and take back what was ours. *We will break the shackles of the Father.*"

A loud eruption of, "Na-Va, Na-Va," shook the cavern.

Dorian turned to his siblings on the altar and smiled. He raised his hand again, and the cavern silenced. "That is correct. Na-Va, the prophecy, will soon be filled. Tonight, we will feed on the nectar of the enslaved for the final time."

Dorian, Josef, and David pulled their robes over their heads. Each took a position at the foot of a stone table.

Jill, Jordana, and Adah dropped their gowns to the altar, and moved as a group in front of the three men. They split apart and sauntered provocatively towards each man. One by one, the women moved the men's freakishly large dicks to full arousal.

The three men crawled upon the tables and stood on their knees before the three girls.

Each girl looked down and smiled. They spread their legs, laid their heads back, and closed their eyes.

Dorian raised his arms to the sides, lifted his head and prayed aloud. "Zeh be-tu-lah dam ra-ah kol. This virgin blood will nourish us."

Each man mounted the woman beneath him, and the echoes of moans danced off the walls of the crystal cavern as Kimi, Mina, and Aiyana writhed from the pain and pleasure of the flesh, which none of them had ever felt before.

The men paused, withdrew their blood-covered members, and retrieved the gold chalices at the base of the stone tables. They carefully slid the blood from the base of their dicks to the tips, allowing it to drip into the gold chalices. Jill, Jordana, and Adah then filled the chalices with wine and passed them to the hooded audience.

Dorian commanded, "Drink, my brothers and sisters, of the pure nectar of humans."

Jill, Jordana, and Adah moved to the side of each table. They leaned over and buried their heads between the girl's legs, nourishing themselves before the men tarnished the nectar with their seed.

The men remounted the three girls, and the girls' breathing grew jagged and irregular with each thrust as the men, drenched in sweat, drilled deeper and harder. The girl's panting and moans moved to a fever pitch, and one by one, each man tensed and arched back, and a supernatural grunt echoed through the cavern.

Then silence came, and the men dismounted.

The girls lay exhausted, their breathing labored.

The hooded figures moved from the sand into the darkness. Josef, Jordana, Adah, and David retreated to the mansion.

Jill helped each of the exhausted girls to their feet and walked them to the cool, healing waters of the lake.

Dorian darkened the pyres on the altar and redressed. He walked to the edge of the sand. "Lilith, the sage will soon wear off. Please bring them from the water while I prepare the powder."

Jill looked back. "Yes, Shemyaza."

When Dorian approached the three women, Aiyana, whom he'd laid, dropped to her knees and aggressively reached for his dick. Dorian glanced at Jill and chuckled. "And the Council thought they could be cleansed of their vices."

Jill rolled her eyes and lifted Aiyana to her feet. "Okay, little girl, you'll have plenty of those in your day. Time to get back to reality."

Dorian blew a fine powder in each of the girls faces, and said, "Sha-khahh."

Jill said to the girls, "You will forget tonight, and leave this mountain carrying the Seed of Enlightenment in each of your wombs. Ancient blood will soon mix with yours, and course through your bodies. I will see through your eyes, as if they are my own. You will feed the hunger of the flesh, growing stronger with each lover, and passing onto them the Blessing. There is no magic, no medicine, no prayer that can release you. Only I can. You leave as employees of Percovelli International. The last recollection of your visit here will be drinking too much wine. Sleep now, and wake to your Destiny."

As night fell over the Percovelli Ranch, the chaos of the day's events hushed with the darkness. The ocean of press crews withdrew like an outgoing tide, and one by one, local and federal law enforcement units exited the ranch. Several CSI units, two marked cars, and a black Suburban remained.

Cindy and Kelly had spent the majority of the day and early evening behind closed doors with the FBI agents, detailing the events of the past several days in exhausting detail.

Agent Harris, Agent Allen, and Webb Sadler now closed their briefcases.

Sadler removed his glasses, rubbed his tired, no-doubt-bloodshot eyes, and turned his tape recorder off. He looked at the two girls steadfastly in the eyes. "Cindy, Kelly, the statements you made are damning. Some very powerful people will fall. We'll make all attempts to use evidence found on scene as the basis of our investigations and charges, and keep you distanced from the shitstorm to follow, but... you *may* eventually have to testify in person. Are you sure you're prepared to do that?"

Cindy, without hesitation, said, "Mr. Sadler, our friend is dead because of those people. I'm sure."

Kelly said, "We endured humiliation that has scarred us for life. They thought a million dollars would buy our silence. They were wrong. I want to look into the eyes of that bitch Jill, or whatever her name is, when the judge puts her away for life. Their sick little world is over. *Yes, I am sure.*"

Sadler nodded. "Okay, as discussed, as far as anyone knows, you were employed by Percovelli International. Now, I'm sure you are both ready to get off this ranch. There are two cruisers and an unmarked vehicle waiting outside. They will take you to a safe house for the night, where your families are waiting. In the morning, you'll head home. Thank you both for your bravery. Agent Harris will escort you to the vehicle."

The girls stood up from the table, gathered their bags and exited.

Sadler watched them leave, rocked back in his chair, and looked at Agent Allen. "This is going to get dirty, Fred. I'm not sure how far up the food chain this will reach."

Fred smiled and shook his head. "Come on, Webb, deals will be made, the power players will sacrifice a few disposables, and it will be over as soon as the press runs out of dirty laundry."

Webb's phone rang, and he put it on speaker. "Yeah, Blake, what is it?"

"Webb, Jackson Hole police just received an anonymous tip that three girls matching the descriptions of Mina, Kimi, and Aiyana were spotted at an old cabin near where Percovelli's plane landed yesterday morning. Wyoming State Police are waiting for our orders. Should we move in tonight?"

Webb looked at Fred.

Fred spoke up. "Blake, I'll coordinate with Wyoming State Police."

Webb said, "Blake, it's almost eight. I'll have a plane pick us up here. It's about a two-hour flight or so into Jackson. You and Billy pack your bags. I have a bag in my room. Please grab it. We'll move in at first light. Agents Harris and Allen, Captain Hollis, and Officer Running Horse can handle the Ranch Investigation."

"10-4, Webb, we'll be there in twenty minutes or so."

Webb hung up the phone, leaned back in his chair again, and exhaled forcefully, rattling his lips.

Fred raised his eyebrows. "What a day, huh?"

Webb stared at the ceiling. "It's too easy, Fred—too convenient."

CHAPTER 24
MINGAN AND HURIT: SINS

Jake opened his eyes to Honi's whines. He sat up in the bunk and placed his feet on the floor. "I need to build you a doggie door," he grumbled as he made his way to the door. The chill of the early morning rushed through the cabin.

Dakota pulled the blanket over her head. "What time is it?"

"According to Honi, it's time to get up. In our time, a little before six. I'll start the coffee."

He shuffled into the kitchen, started the morning brew, and turned on the radio for the day's weather report and news. The AM station announced, *"Breaking news, please stay tuned for a live report."* Jake turned the radio up.

"As first reported late yesterday, WDUB can now confirm that Kelly Johnson and Cindy Fowler have left the Percovelli Ranch. The FBI also confirms that Joseph Percovelli's cause of death has been ruled a suicide. At this time, the FBI has released no motive for the business tycoon's death. In another developing story, the deadly explosion that claimed the life of billionaire cattleman Vincent Dibella, his wife, and five of his staff, has claimed its eighth victim. Spokesman for Dibella Industries, Howard Sellman, has confirmed that Jose Garcia, the head of Dibella's security, has died of injuries sustained in the blast. WDUB will continue to update these stories as facts become available. In local news...."

Jake shut the radio off and looked at Dakota. Their mutually stunned eyes met in a moment of silence.

"Jake, does this mean it's over? No more hitmen, no more looking over our shoulders?"

He took a deep breath, exhaled and smiled. "Rowtag said follow the footsteps of those who brought us together that night. The last of those footsteps is dead, so... yes, I believe it's over."

Dakota sprang from the bunk, raced to Jake and jumped into his arms, wrapping her legs around his waist. "We're finally free to move about our lives."

He hugged her tightly, kissed her, and let her slide down to the floor. "Yes, we are. Now, all we have to do is figure out the Spirit World stuff so Mingan and Hurit can be free. 'Cause honestly, I'm good without some hitchhiking souls in us. How about you?"

She smiled, grabbed Jake's hand, and coaxed him towards the bunk. "Well, while they're with us, let's give them some pleasure."

Dakota stepped from the bed after their early morning tryst, dressed in her running gear, and looked back at Jake. "Okay, Mister, time to work out."

Jake sighed. "We just did. God, you're gonna kill me."

She smiled and threw a pair of sweats at him. "You need to keep up your stamina."

They walked into the cool morning air, and Jake looked to the northern sky. "Those look like snow clouds. The White Owl will soon take over the mountain."

Dakota nodded. "I think we need to prepare the cabin for winter and call this our last visit. It's time to head to the ranch, and back to reality."

He took a deep breath and blew it out. "I know. You have to get back to work, and I need to make decisions on the MBO offer, and if I want to capitalize on all this craziness. I need to talk to Alexi and the kids. Hell, after my last conversation with her, I'm not sure if she'll want to deal with any of this shit anymore."

Dakota grabbed his hand. "I've been thinking about that. Maybe I could reach out to her with a business proposal and present the best offer we have. I'll make sure she and the kids are compensated well for their time."

He stared into the distance. "Dakota, you heard her on the Skype call. She could care less about the money. I thought she had moved on. I thought after seeing my decline during the trial, she accepted everything. She hasn't. I saw it in her eyes. She wants her life back."

Dakota paused, knowing if she pressed Jake, it could backfire. She'd seen his eyes after the Skype call, and knew Alex Michaels still had a small hold on him. "Okay, let's give her more time. I'm sure when she got home after the trial and had time to herself, a rush of emotions crippled her. For the past year and a half, her life was a roller coaster ride. Every corner of your house is filled with memories. Every daily habit you two shared had to be reworked. Then, all of a sudden, all the healing she did was mute. I was shocked how well she hid her emotions during the trial. Hell, what she has gone through is every bit as gut-wrenching as what I went through, possibly more so. I have to erase an hour from my life. She had to close a thirty-plus-year chapter, only to have it reopened. MBO can wait. Let's make sure her and the kids come to terms with the reality of all this."

He turned and looked at the compassion in her eyes, smiled, and squeezed her hand. "Thank you. Let's go for a run."

They set off on their normal course past the waterfall towards the back canyon. Dakota glanced towards the hot spring as they passed it. "Let's make some time tonight for one last glass of wine in there before the snow falls."

Jake chuckled. "Always trying to get me naked, aren't you?"

She rolled her eyes. "Ahhh... no, that was *your* MO in the beginning. You were so cute and bashful the first couple times we got in there. Now, you just walk around with that thing swinging everywhere."

"Well, I don't hear you complaining."

Dakota raced forward and looked back. "I'm just being polite."

The two made a loop through the canyon and finished their run on the east side of the cabin. They slowed to a walk and caught their breath.

Jake said, "Let's get the cabin winterized, have dinner, and visit Rowtag. We need to ask him to show us the rest of Mingan and Hurit's story tonight. I can't wait till spring."

"Yeah, we don't need any cliffhangers over the winter."

After several hours of work and an early dinner, the two settled in front of the fireplace. Jake packed the pipe, and they made their way into the Spirit World.

The night sky was ablaze with the ghosts of the ancestors of the land. Jake and Dakota marveled at the spectral lights as they walked towards the waterfall.

Rowtag emerged from the dark forest to the left of the falls. "Children, come."

Jake and Dakota followed closely as Rowtag meandered along a small stream. He stopped at a still pool, raised his spear to the sky, and murmured something, then lowered the tip to the water. The dark pool glistened with gold sparkles. "Drink."

Jake and Dakota squatted down and cupped a handful of water.

As they lifted it to their mouth, Rowtag said, "Tonight you will understand the sins of Mingan and Hurit. This sacred water will help you remember details. You will need them. Our journey together is over. Tonight, you will see the path of their Destiny. Learn from them."

With his final word, Rowtag moved into the darkness of the night.

The glittering pool darkened as Jake and Dakota swallowed the sweet, effervescent water. They looked deep below the surface, and Mingan and Hurit's world became visible.

Mingan walked towards the cave perched high in the clouds. Wahya lagged behind, his cautious steps and hunched posture caught Hurit's eye.

"Mingan, your wolf is sensing something."

Hurit looked back and shook his head. "Wahya, come."

The wolf stopped dead in his tracks, looking past his master. His eyes narrowed as his upper lip snarled. His shoulders hunched and the hair stood up on his back. A deep steady growl garnered Mingan's attention.

Mingan and Hurit followed the wolf's eyes to the entrance of the cave. They stared into the dark opening then moved their gaze at each other.

Hurit said, "Let's leave this place. Wahya warns us."

Mingan paused, looked down at his wolf and back into the cave. A movement in the dim light at the entrance caught his attention. He took a few steps forward, focused his eyes, raised his spear and darted towards the cave, yelling.

"*Mingan no, stop.*"

He ignored Hurit's plead and disappeared into the darkness of the cave. Hurit pulled her bow and readied and arrow. After several seconds of dead silence, two skunks scurried from the cave with Mingan behind him. At the sight of the small creatures Wahya let out several whelps and ran in the opposite direction.

Mingan's belly laughs echoed in the still mountain air.

Hurit watched the terrified wolf retreat and raised her hands in Mingan's direction as he walked towards her. "He will fight a bear, but ran from a skunk?"

"When he was young, he tangled with one and was sprayed. The very scent of them, terrifies him."

Mingan walked over to the shaking wolf, bent down and hugged him. "It is all right, Wahya, the stinkies are gone. Come."

Cautiously, the wolf followed his master back to Hurit.

"Well, Hurit, should we go into the cave and prove the ancient myths wrong?"

"We have what we came for, Mingan. Why doubt our ancestors?"

He smiled and placed his hand on her shoulder. "Let us come down from this mountain and return to our people with truths of today. Let us put the old myths behind us. Look what our people said of our tribes. You are as beautiful as the morning sunrise, not the hairy creature they would have me believe. I would have believed, too, for the rest of my life, had the Great Spirit not crossed our paths."

She looked past his chiseled features into his soft eyes and dropped her head to hide her blushing. She looked back at him and nodded. "You are right. It is time to move our people forward." She looked over his shoulder. "It is dark in there. How will we see?"

Mingan panned the high mountain plateau. "I will be right back."

He gathered various tall grasses and sage from the steep rocky hills surrounding the landing. He then rejoined Hurit, bent down and laid the collection on the ground. He quickly bunched the dried vegetation and wound several long strands of fresh green grass around the base, working his way up to a few inches from the top of the makeshift torch, and looked up. "This will burn for several hours."

She raised her eyebrows and brushed her hair off her shoulder. "I am impressed. There is more to you than strong muscles and good looks."

He looked back to the ground to hide *his* blushing this time, and grabbed two rocks. He struck them together several times, letting sparks fall on the loose ends of the torch, until the dried grasses caught fire. He stood with burning torch in hand. "Let us start the future of our people."

The trio, with Wahya right on their heels, entered the cave. Within thirty feet, the torch-lit walls sprang to life with drawings of ancient peoples, who'd been lost in time to the great flood.

Mingan said, "They hunted like we do."

Hurit nodded and moved to the opposite wall. "And did battle with great beasts and tribes of hairy men. Some of the ancient myths are true."

He joined her and raised the flame closer to the wall. "And great winged creatures did fill the skies. The Great Spirt cleansed the land of these beasts. We will tell our peoples that the myths were true. Now, those creatures and tribes are lost to time, even on The Sacred Mountain. Let us move deeper and try to find something from the ancient ones to share with our people."

The cave meandered slowly downward, the smooth walls filled with drawings slowly replaced by irregular ones highlighted by luminescence.

Mingan paused and waved the torch. "The walls sparkle like the night sky."

Hurit's eyes widened. "It is like a dream, a gift from the Great Spirit."

The two pressed on. Mingan paused, and dropped the torch below his waist.

"What is it, Mingan?"

He pointed. "Ahead, I can see light. Let our eyes adjust for a second."

She followed his finger and squinted. "I see it. Did we come to the other side of the mountain? Is this *all* of the cave our ancestors said was the home of great evil?"

He raised the torch back up. "We will soon find out."

The passage narrowed for the next several hundred yards, and the light in the distance became brighter. The trio stepped from the narrow hall into a grotto. The sun shined through a natural skylight, bathing the limestone room. The colors of the rainbow danced in hundreds of crystal stalagmites adorning the ceiling. Water dripped from above into a deep clear pool, creating a peaceful harmony in the chamber. The two stood slack-jawed and wide-eyed.

"Mingan, this cave is a gift from the Great Spirit, not the home of evil. Why would our people create such myths?"

He took several steps forward and shook his head. "I do not know."

They made their way to the soft sand surrounding the small subterranean lake. Mingan bent down and cupped a handful of water. "It has a sweetness, Hurit. Try it."

She bent down and tasted the cool water, paused, and looked up. The beam of the high mountain sun warmed her face. "We should swim in this beautiful water."

He chuckled. "You do like to swim, don't you? It is freezing. I will stick to drinking it."

She stood up, took her pack and bow off, and pulled her deerskin top off.

Mingan turned away quickly.

She laughed. "Oh please, it is not like you have not seen me naked already." She stepped from her pants and dove into the still water. The echo of her splash danced around the cavern. She returned to the surface and looked back at him. "It is not as cold as you think. The sun warms it nicely. You do not have to worry about that little thing getting any smaller."

Mingan's eyes narrowed. Challenged by her jab, he stood up, pulled his shirt off, and allowed his buckskin pants to drop to the ground. "I guess the men from the land of the sunset are small, but not from my land."

Hurit's eyes widened. "It appears I was wrong about you, again."

He said, "If I catch you, you will feel how wrong you were."

He dove in with a splash. Hurit swam towards the middle of the pool, and Mingan gave chase. He soon caught her and the two embraced.

As Hurit looked into his eyes, the cool waters tingled between her legs in a manner she'd never felt before. Her arousal grew as his dick hardened against her stomach. An intoxicating rush dizzied her, and she drew away. "I feel a little strange. It must be the height of the mountain. Let me get to the shore."

He treaded water and watched her swim away. "You are an evil temptress. You just wanted to see me naked."

Once on shore, she gathered her senses and looked back. "Are you coming?"

He swam to shore as she dressed. She turned to watch him step from the pool, and took a deep breath, again becoming unnaturally aroused.

Must be the water or the thin mountain air....

He looked down at himself. "Are you going to stare at it?"

She rolled her eyes. "Don't flatter yourself. I've seen bigger."

"Maybe on a horse," he shot back. He pulled his buckskin pants on and looked up. "The sun will set soon. We will camp her tonight."

Hurit pointed to an opening on the opposite side of the cave. "It goes deeper. Should we continue on a bit more?"

He snickered. "Yes, maybe we will find the 'evil' the elders speak of."

Her eyes traced the splendor of the grotto. "The only evil in this beautiful cave is the fact that our people have been deprived of it by old myths."

Mingan stoked the torch, and the trio waked toward the opening, but stopped dead in their tracks. On both sides of the passage entrance hung stone bowls cradled by and anchored to the walls with a material foreign to both of them. Mingan tapped on the strange material, and a metallic ring echoed in the tunnel.

He looked at Hurit. "It is hard like rock and shines like the yellow stones in the river."

"Mingan, I think we should turn back."

"No, the Great Spirit has brought us here. Let us see what is on the other side. Perhaps we can return to our people with knowledge beyond that of our ancestors — knowledge lost to the waters of the great flood."

When he moved his torch closer to the odd ornaments to examine them, a small blaze jumped from the bowl, setting both of them back on their heels. The tunnel glowed with a yellow hue. "It burns like animal fat, but does not smell of flesh."

Hurit looked down the tunnel. "It is lined with them."

One by one, Mingan ignited the bowls as they made their way down the long passage, until he lit the last set of bowls hanging several yards from the passage end. The flames reflected off the edge of a much larger pool of water, its center hidden in the darkness. The trio turned right on the bank and continued along the wall, lighting bowl after bowl. With each flame, the cavern grew and the lake widened. Quartz walls danced with the colors of a thousand sunsets. Stalactites of all shapes and colors dripped from the ceiling. The two stood motionless in the splendor that surrounded them.

Hurit pointed to the opposite shore at a bridge made of the same gold material as the bowl holders. "Mingan, look. Who could have made that?"

Mingan, searching for answers, remained silent.

"I did," a warm voice called out from the darkness beyond the bridge.

Mingan drew his spear, Hurit her bow.

Wahya's shoulder's lifted, and his hair stood up as his growls echoed in the cavern.

From the darkness crept an elderly man, his shoulders rounded, his back hunched. Long gray hair fell about his shoulders. His gait, hobbled by age, showed little agility.

Mingan lowered his spear, but Hurit kept her bow aimed.

Mingan called out, "Who are you?"

"My name is Mastema. Welcome to my home. Please come closer. My eyes and ears are old."

"No, Mingan," Hurit whispered.

"Look at him, Hurit. He is an elder. He cannot harm us."

"*He* may not, but his magic can."

"Have we not seen *enough*, woman, to show you there *is no* magic? There are *no great beasts* or evil spirits on this mountain—only in the old stories. Let us speak with him and learn who he is."

Cautiously, the trio walked towards the elder.

His appearance became less threatening with each step closer. His thin muscles sagged in a bag of pale wrinkled skin. As they crossed the gold bridge, the elder lifted his head and made eye contact.

Mingan and Hurit paused.

The elder's lips moved inward over his gums as he smiled. "I know, you have never seen a man with eyes like the sky. Do not be afraid. What are your names?

Mingan took a step forward. "My name is Mingan. I am from the People of the Sunrise. This is Hurit. She is from the People of the Sunset."

Mastema nodded. "Mingan, son of Kitchi, grandson of Etchemin, great grandson of Askuwhetean and the fathers before him. Hurit, daughter of Alsoomse, granddaughter of Kanti, great granddaughter of Nadie and the mothers before her. Future leaders of your people."

Mingan and Hurit looked at each other, their eyes wide. After several seconds, Mingan said, "How do you know this, old man?"

Mastema said, "Since the Great Flood, your ancestors have visited the mountain in search of knowledge. They share this knowledge with no one, and keep it hidden in tales of great evil and beasts long gone from the land."

Hurit said, "Why would they hide this knowledge?"

Mastema's voice softened. "To protect the future of your people. To prevent punishment from the Great Spirit."

Mingan said, "I do not understand."

Mastema turned. "Come, follow me."

Hurit darted a glance at Mingan, and he nodded.

The elder led them from the cavern into a tunnel. After a short walk, they entered a great room lit by ornate chandeliers, its marble walls lined on all sides with gold statues of men and women adorned in flowing white robes. Their features were soft, and their hair flowed in curls.

The two stood slack-jawed, until Hurit moved to one of the statues and ran her hand over the soft material.

Mastema smiled. "It is called silk. These men and women were leaders of the great tribes before the flood."

Hurit looked back at him. "How many tribes were there?"

"They riddled the land as far as the eye could see, from the highest mountain and beyond."

Mingan and Hurit stood motionless as their gazes panned the faces of the past and the architecture of the room.

Mastema motioned them to follow as he moved to the entrance of another room.

Mingan and Hurit followed slowly, pausing several times to look back at the gallery of statues.

They entered a dimly lit room, where Mastema moved to a side wall and lit several torches.

When the room filled with light, Mingan and Hurit recoiled at what the light exposed. Behind a sheer crystal wall sat six naked people on thrones made of gold and bone: three men with chiseled features and blue eyes framed by long dark hair, and three women with delicate features and blue eyes framed with platinum blonde hair.

Mingan raised his spear. *"The Six, the evil my Great Grandfather warned of."*

Hurit drew her bow.

Wahya, alerted by his master's fear, moved to attack stance.

Mastema raised his hand. "Do not be afraid. They have been still since the Great Flood. I have guarded over them since the waters receded. It is my Destiny to make sure they never walk the land again. Now, you know the truth. Ahead, you will learn what you have been sent here for."

Mingan and Hurit passed in front the crystal tombs, and paused to look into the fixed, icy stares of the sky-colored eyes of the Six.

Hurit stepped closer to the tomb of one of the females. Her eyes moved from the top of the ancient one's platinum hair, past her blue eyes, and down a perfectly sculpted body. "She is beautiful."

"And evil," Mingan snapped.

Mastema looked back. "Mingan, Hurit, come, please."

They followed Mastema through a torch-lit, narrow, winding hall. Ahead, an opening framed the night sky. The group walked out to a cliff edge perched thousands of feet above the valley floor.

Mastema pointed to the east. "Mingan, those are the night fires of your people." He pointed to the west. "Hurit, those are the fires of your people."

Mingan said, "My great grandfather said the Six were punished with the view of our people, but never allowed to walk amongst us again."

Mastema smiled. "The old myths of your people have some truth. As you have seen, The Six, as you call them, have never seen your people. They were entombed before the Great Spirit allowed your tribes to walk this land again."

Hurit said, "This is what we are here for? To see the night fires of our people?"

The elder shook his head. "No, Hurit, follow me."

Mastema guided the trio to the left side of the cliffs and struggled up a set of stone stairs. He pointed to the north and then the south. "Look at the night fires, not of your people."

Mingan's eyes narrowed as Hurit looked up at him. The two stood silent for several moments, each trying to comprehend the truth.

Mingan's voice dropped as his eyes panned the new world before him. "Mastema, why have our people never spoken of these other tribes?"

Mastema smiled and nodded. "They do not know of them. The Great Spirit breathed life into each of your tribes after the flood, and separated your peoples. It was his desire that, until the day a male and female from the east and west met on this mountain, I could not share the truth. Thousands of summers have passed. Hurit and you are the first to meet here. This is the start of your Destiny, and the end of mine."

Hurit said, "What of the people in the north and the south? What is their Destiny? Why did the Great Spirit not choose them to meet on this mountain?"

Mingan said, "Who are the Six entombed here? You said they never saw our people after we walked the land *again*? What do you mean by *'again,'* Mastema? I grow impatient with these riddles."

Mastema smiled. "You remind me of your father. He too had many questions. The Six, as you call them, and two hundred companions, known as Guardians, came from the stars. They were trusted by the Great Spirit, whom they called the Father, to teach and protect the First Ones."

"Protect them from who, Mastema? The great beasts?"

Mastema paused, knowing the truth would be too complicated. "Yes, the beasts whose great skeletons you find in the earth."

He took a deep breath and sighed. "Once here, the Guardians found the land beautiful and the air intoxicating. They developed an insatiable lust for the First Ones, and discovered the Father had made one flaw with his creation: the First Ones had free will. Over the millennia, half of the Guardians banned together, behind the back of the Father and their peers. They decided to remain on this land and rule over the First Ones.

"As you have seen, the Guardians were perfect creations. They used their looks and powers to seduce the First Ones, and turn them from the ways of the Father. A battle between the rebellious Guardians and ones loyal to the Father ensued. The Father, saddened and angered, called home what was left of his loyal Guardians.

"Eighteen of the most rebellious Guardians remained here. The Six, as you call them, stayed here to rule the East and West. A second group of six, four men and two women, left to rule the North, and a third group of six, three men and three women, left for the South.

"The people of the East and West developed into great thinkers and fell to the Six's false promises of enlightenment. They shunned the doctrines of the Great Spirit.

"The people of the North and South, fueled by the lies of the Guardians, believed the tribes to the East and West were determined to take their land. They became great warriors.

"The Guardians knew one day they would have to do battle against the Father, but the tribes would stand no chance against the legions the Father would send. They knew they must pass their powers to the tribes and began breeding with them.

"The Father watched in sadness as the Guardians took the last step to defile his creation. His most trusted elders, known as the Council, called for the death of the fallen Guardians. The Father ruled death was too easy. As punishment, he would take from them what they loved most. He struck their offspring with a curse. The male Guardians' children were born perfect. As they grew, so did the Father's curse. Their shoulders rounded and their spines twisted, causing them to hunch. Their bodies became covered in coarse, putrid-smelling hair, their brows grew pronounced and their bones thick, and their speech was made simple, as was their minds. The offspring of the female Watchers dropped dead from their wombs, grotesquely deformed with skin like scales of a lizard.

"The Guardians, unknowing of the curse, were convinced they would find the right bloodline within the tribes and continue to mate, but did so unsuccessfully. The males moved their attention to virgins only, and the females stopped breeding. When the last pure women of the four tribes died, so did any hope the Guardians had at ruling the land with people of their own image."

Hurit said, "Mastema, are the people of the North and South still under the curse? Are they hideous creatures? What became of the other twelve Guardians? How does all of this create our Destiny?"

"No, Hurit, the Great Flood cleansed the land of the curse. They look as you and Mingan do. The Father damned the twelve Guardians to walk the land for eternity, some as grotesque small people, some as half beast, half human creatures, and others as hideous waif-like monsters, consumed by their own hunger for flesh. Your Destinies are to unite all the tribes and rule side-by-side over them."

She paused, then snapped back, "I barely know him! Why would I want him as my husband? Why would I trust the words of an old man inside a mountain?"

Mastema nodded and smiled, then stepped forward and off the cliff.

"*Mastema, no!*" Mingan tried to grab the elder's shoulder.

Mastema walked several hundred feet into the night sky and raised his arms. A lightning bolt lit the clouds around him and a clasp of thunder shook the mountain.

Mingan and Hurit shielded their eyes and braced against the shaking ground.

The crippled old man made his way back towards the cliff. With each step, Mingan's and Hurit's eyes widened. Mastema's hunched posture straightened with every step, and his sagging muscles grew taught and powerful. His walking stick morphed into a feathered spear Even as a headdress grew from his long gray hair. A tall Faceless Indian that was Mastema stood in front of Mingan and Hurit.

Mingan clenched his spear in hand, but paused, clearly understanding he stood no chance against the sky walker.

"My name is Rowtag," a deep voice came from the dark abyss beneath the flowing headdress. "What I have told you is the wish of the Great Spirit. Your future, the future of this land and its people, depends on it. Do not question your Fate. Hurit, bathe in the Sacred Lake tonight. Mingan, drink from the gold bowl laid on the rock table on the sand. You will be tested tonight. Do not tempt your Destiny. Stay true to your beliefs. Learn from the fall of the First One's."

Mingan said, "How will we be tested?"

The Faceless Indian raised his hand, turned, and disappeared into the night sky.

In Mingan's village, the earth shook with the clasp of thunder on the mountain. People ran from their tents and looked towards the sky. Askuwhetean emerged from his tent. He smiled and nodded, knowing Mingan had completed his task, and that Rowtag had shown him his Destiny, as he had for generations, since the beginning.

He raised the sacred feathered spears and crossed them over his head. "Soon, child, you will lead our people."

In Hurits village, Alsoome, Hurit's mother, and Annawan, Hurit's Father and Chief of her people, looked towards the mountain.

Annawan placed his hand on Alsoome's shoulder. "Our child will come from the mountain with the path of her Destiny. She will take a husband and lead our people."

Mingan led the way as he, Hurit, and Wahya walked from the cliff's edge, through the tunnel, past the tombs of the Six and the great room of gold statues. They reached the lake and dropped to the soft sand, exhausted.

"Mingan, are we being fooled by an evil spirit? No myths of my people speak of Rowtag or this cave. Why would the elders not know of other tribes after all this time?"

Mingan stared into the lake, and slowly shook his head. "I do not know if this Rowtag is an evil spirit or not. Perhaps, if we follow his directions, the truth will become clear."

Hurit scooted in front of him and looked into his eyes. "My future is to come from this mountain, and choose a husband based on love. Not the plan of the Great Spirit, or Father, as Mastema called him. You are a brave, strong man. I believe you will make a great leader and husband. If you were of my people, given time, it is possible I would grow to love you and our Destiny would be as Rowtag speaks."

He reached out and stroked her face. "When I saw you at the bottom of the waterfall, I knew my eyes had fallen on the most beautiful woman I will ever see. I do not need more time to know the Great Spirit has delivered you to me, to stand by my side as our life travels the four hills."

Hurit swallowed hard, and her eyes swelled. She leaned forward and kissed him softly on the lips. "Let us leave this mountain, tell our people the truths we have discovered, and ask the blessings of our elders to continue our courtship." She pulled back and smiled. "Now, turn your back. I will bathe in the Sacred Lake, and you need to drink from the bowl."

Mingan chuckled. "Woman, I have seen what is beneath your clothes. Why so bashful now?"

"And it is the last time you will, unless I choose you to share my wedding bed."

He stood and walked to the edge of the sand near the gold bridge. On a small stone table sat a gold bowl filled with a red liquid. He lifted the bowl to his nose and raised his eyebrows at the fruity smell. He dipped his finger in it, cautiously placed a drop on his tongue, and nodded. A splash from the lake caught his attention, and he turned.

"What did I say?" Hurit yelled from the lake.

He smiled, turned his back, and drank the elixir. His face flushed hot as a warm tingling sensation flowed from head to toe. A feeling of euphoria rushed over him. The crystal walls and quarts stalactites sparkled in dazzling colors. A vision of Hurit and him standing in ceremonial dress in front of both their tribes flashed before his eyes.

His senses cleared and he nodded.

Hurit swam in the Sacred Lake. The cool water warmed around her as a sense of extreme calm relaxed her to a near state of sleep. She made her way to the shore and lay on the soft sand, looked to the ceiling, and closed her eyes. A vision of Mingan and her in ceremonial dress in front of both their tribes flashed before her. She opened her eyes and smiled as the intoxicating bath released its grip on her.

She gathered her clothes and walked towards Mingan at the gold bridge.

"You can turn now," she said.

"How was your swim?"

"It was good. I had a vision of the future."

He smiled. "I know. I was there."

She reached out and grabbed both his hands. "Let's make camp for the last night on this mountain and start our journey in the morning."

Hurit and Wahya lay peacefully on blankets atop the soft sand as Mingan prepared a fire for night. He scooted from the glowing embers and rocked back onto his blanket. After several moments of silence, he said, "Look as the ceiling catches the light of the embers. It is as if the night sky is with us."

Hurit smiled. "It is like a dream."

The slow steady drops of water hitting the lake echoed softly through the cavern, and soon the trio drifted into a peaceful slumber.

In the dark of the cave, six figures moved about. Wahya woke from a light sleep and sprung to his feet. He crept a few steps past Mingan's head and let out a low, slow growl.

Mingan opened his eyes and sat up, clutching his spear.

Hurit stirred from a deep sleep and rolled onto her side. "What is wrong, Mingan?"

Mingan moved to his wolf's side and followed Wahya's stare past the gold bridge into the darkness. "Wahya saw something."

Hurit reached for her bow and moved to a kneeling position.

Mingan took several steps forward.

Wahya dashed across the sand, over the gilded bridge, and into the darkness.

"*Wahya.*" The booming sound of Mingan's voice echoed through the cavern.

The thunder of thousands of wings filled the air, and Wahya darted towards the camp, his tail between his legs, whimpering.

Mingan watched as bats circled and moved though a small hole in the cave ceiling into the night sky, and let out a hardy belly laugh at the sight of the scared wolf.

Hurit hugged the shaking wolf. "It is fine, Wahya. Look at him, Mingan, he is terrified."

Mingan walked back to camp shaking his head. "My wolf will battle a bear, but a tiny bat cripples him and a skunk terrifies him."

He sat down to calm Wahya, running his hand over the wolf's coarse fur, and brushed the backside of Hurit's hand.

She rolled her hand over and gently rubbed his, and their eyes met. "Your hands are strong." She ran her hand up his forearm, past his tight upper arm and over his broad shoulder. She knelt and faced him.

He moved to his knees, and coaxed Wahya from between them. He drew her close, kissed her softly and pulled back. Their eyes remained locked until she pulled him in tight and kissed him with passion. When he moved his lips to the side of her neck, she tensed and let out a shallow gasp. He wrapped his arm around her lower back, bracing her as he guided her backwards and lay atop of her, supporting some of his weight with both elbows.

They devoured each other with kisses, and their breathing quickened as he reached beneath her shirt and ran his hands over her hard nipples. She moved her head to the side and moaned, and he gently pulled the bottom of her shirt up.

She lifted her back, allowing the buckskin to be pulled over her head, and when he grew against her, she opened her legs. He reached down and slid her pants past her thighs. She squirmed as she pulled one leg free from her bottoms, then grabbed the waist of his buckskins and forced them down. The hardness of his cock on and between her legs brought urgency to them both.

He positioned himself for entry.

"Wait, Mingan," she forced through heavy breathing.

Mingan paused, his body trembling. "What is it?"

"We cannot do this. I must save myself for my wedding night. It is the way of my people. I can give myself only to my husband. If not, I will bring disgrace to myself and the Great Spirit will curse me with infertility."

"Hurit, it is also the way of my people, but we have seen our future. I *will be* your husband."

"Children," a soft female voice called from the lake.

Mingan pulled his pants up quickly as Hurit grabbed a blanket to hide her nakedness. Wahya sprung to his feet as they looked towards the water.

A beautiful Indian maiden, aglow with a white aura, walked across the still water towards them. Long dark hair fell about her naked body.

Mingan grabbed his spear and jumped to his feet. "Who are you, Spirit?"

"I am the bearer of truth and things to come. Do not be afraid. Look at your wolf—the beast is calm."

"We have seen the future. Rowtag has shown us," Mingan barked.

As the maiden walked onto the sand, her enchanting beauty and graceful stride paralyzed Mingan for a moment. As she moved past him, a rush of desire like he had never felt before coursed through his body. He lightened his grip on the spear and swallowed hard, finding it difficult to speak.

The maiden moved to Hurit. "Stand, my child, do not be ashamed of your nakedness."

Hurit starred into the emerald green eyes of the maiden, and all inhibitions left her. She set the blanket aside, stood up, and stepped from the one leg of her buckskins still draped around her ankle. The maiden reached out and gently took her hand, and a warm energy flowed from her touch as the maiden led her to Mingan's side.

The maiden moved in front of Mingan. "Stand naked, my child, with your future bride."

Mingan allowed his pants to drop, and his hard dick sprang from the constraints of the buckskins.

Hurit felt herself become drenched at the sight of Mingan standing naked before her. Feelings she'd never experienced made her insides quiver. *Can he feel my attraction? Can he see me trembling for him?*

The maiden smiled. "Rowtag told you of your Destiny. I will show you it. Come and look into the Sacred Lake."

The two followed the maiden to the water's edge. She bent down and waved her hand through the water. Beneath the surface, Mingan and Hurit stood before masses of people on a brilliant white granite veranda, flanked by gold figures of their ancestors. To their sides, four small children stood. The crowds below looked up with love and admiration.

The maiden stood. "This is your Destiny, very much as Rowtag spoke of. You will unite all the tribes. They will love you and you will lead them to their future, as will your children and their children. Tonight, on the shores of the Sacred Lake, you will consummate the union of your people and start your reign. The Great Spirit will not punish you."

Hurit looked at Mingan. "Rowtag warned we would be tested." She turned her eyes to the maiden. "How do we know you are not here to alter our Destiny with lies?"

The maiden smiled. "You were tested, child, by the desires of the flesh, and you stopped before you gave him your special gift. It was a test both of you passed. Now, spend the night enjoying each other. Take him inside you knowing your loins will bear much fruit." The maiden walked onto the lake, turned to look towards the shore, and lifted her hands. Brilliant sparkles filled the cavern as she dropped below the surface.

Hurit turned to Mingan, her loins ablaze with passion. She turned her back to him, reached down and pulled his hands to her tits as she pressed her ass against his hard cock.

As a storm moved over the Sacred Mountain, lightning danced from cloud to cloud, illuminating the night sky. The storm grew closer, and lightning pierced the land below. The earth shook violently with each clasp of thunder and, as the bolts became faster and faster, the ground shook harder and harder. Lightning exploded from the clouds, lighting the night sky like day. Then... calm descended.

The people of the Sunrise and the people of the Sunset emerged from their shelters and looked to the Sacred Mountain. Rain fell upon them, its sweet smell replaced by a putrid odor.

In the land of the Sunrise, Mingan's great grandfather looked to the mountain, and a tear fell from his eye.

In the land of the Sunset, Hurit's father looked to the mountain, lowered his head, and his hands trembled.

Jake and Dakota stared into the flicker of the flames. Their heads cleared as the powerful smoke wore off.

Jake looked down at his watch. "We've been gone for almost two hours."

Dakota took a deep breath. "I still don't fully understand why they were punished?"

Jake shook his head. "The only thing I can assume is they were fooled by the maiden into having sex, and failed to heed Rowtag's warnings. I guess they should have stuck by the beliefs of their people and waited for their wedding night."

"Jake, I find it hard to believe they would be punished for tens of thousands of years because they banged."

"Yeah, it does seem a bit harsh. Maybe it was because they brought together two tribes that were meant to be apart. We may never know the entire story, since Rowtag said we won't see him again — him and his fucking riddles."

"Well, I guess it doesn't really matter much now. After hearing about Dibella, and now seeing all Rowtag wants us to see about Mingan and Hurit, we can resume our lives. We'll just ponder the rest of their story."

CHAPTER 25
THE SIX

Dorian and Jill opened a set of arched wooden doors and entered a banquet room, which seemed pulled from the times of knights and dragons. Minstrel music and jovial laughter filled the hall. They joined the four members of the Six seated at a gaudy marble and gold-clad head table. Before them, the hoard of hooded figures, drunken by wine and human nectar, danced between and atop rows of long rectangular rough-hewn wood tables, ten deep.

Jill panned the festive group and leaned into Dorian and Adah. "Will we share the plan with them tonight?"

Dorian smiled. "No, let them enjoy the evening. When they wake tomorrow, and the reality of their exile sets back in, I will assemble them and break the news. They will question us, and some will vehemently disagree, casting doubts based on previous failures. Tonight, let them lay their heads on their pillows, drunken and without worries."

Adah said, "I have heard grumblings amongst them. They grow restless. They have seen thousands of our new moons rise and fall, only to watch the Keeper of Prophecy streak by in the heavens. How long will they blindly follow that tale? We quench their thirsts and desires with a fresh supply of virgins, but how will they feel when they don't have their way with the three girls we freed this evening?"

Josef, overhearing the conversation, said, "The wine they drink tonight kills their desires." He nodded to a group of naked women, dancing provocatively amongst the hoard. "Look, they pay no attention to them."

Dorian said, "I will give them something tonight, a small peek into the very near future." He moved in front of the head table and raised his arm. The revelry quieted. "My brothers and sisters, a few words.... *Soon*, this world will be ours again. The Omnificent Son will walk this land. *He will cleanse the curse and this planet. We will follow our prophecy, build our army, and free the one the Father still cries over."* He lifted his chalice in the air. *"Grigori."*

The group, roused by Dorian's call to arms, lifted their chalices and replied in unison, *"Grigori."*

Jill finished the cheer, stood up from the table, and strolled to the double doors.

Jordana spoke over the festive crowd. "What's wrong, Jill, do you not like drinking with us anymore?"

Jill looked back, smiled, and returned to Jordana. She bent over and kissed her cheek. "I love drinking with you, sister, but I need to take care of business. Soon, we will drink and fuck and feast on nectar for eternity." She looked over the room. "Along with the rest of our brothers and sisters."

She walked from the mansion to a secluded stone garden bathed in bright moonlight, dropped her dress to the ground, and sauntered through the garden to a marble pool bubbling with waters from the hot springs deep below the surface.

She eased herself in to shoulder depth, looked to the stars, closed her eyes, and said softly, "Ma-al hha-ron."

Two unmarked cars and a black SUV carrying Cindy, Kelly, and two heavily-armed federal agents, left the Percovelli ranch en route to the safe house. The girls stared blankly through their side windows into the darkness as the SUV curved through a high mountain pass.

Cindy looked over at Kelly. "What are you thinking?"

Kelly shook her head gently. "I'm thinking about Beth. The agents said a small cactus found in her hair led them to the ranch. She saved our lives."

Cindy nodded and wiped a tear from the corner of her eye. "I know, and now we'll help put these pricks behind bars. Her death will save hundreds more."

Kelly felt the SUV slow and looked forward to see brake lights from the lead cars. "Why are we stopping?"

The agent in the front passenger seat turned as he held his earpiece. "A herd of elk on the road."

The girls nodded and settled back into their seats.

Suddenly, several flashes lit the darkness as shots rang out.

Kelly lurched forward. *"What, are they shooting the fucking things?"*

The agent in the passenger seat turned. "Both of you drop to the floor. *Alpha One, we have shots fired. Repeat: we have shots fired. Send backup."* Only dead silence answered back. *"Tango One, come in. Tango Two, come in."* Again, dead silence from the radio. The agent looked at the driver. "Let's get these girls out of here."

The driver put the car in reverse, and the SUV lurched backwards but stalled. Repeated attempts to start the vehicle failed.

A movement between the SUV's headlights and brake lights of the two cruisers ahead caught everyone's attention.

"What the fuck?" the driver said. "Who is that?"

The second agent jumped from the SUV and drew his gun. *"Stop!"*

A hysterical voice cried out, "Help me officer, *please!* They will kill all of us."

The driver turned the SUV's spotlight on. "For God's sake, Joe, she's naked. Cover me. Girls, do not unlock these doors."

The distressed woman dropped to her knees, and her pleas echoed off the canyon walls. *"Officer, please help me, I'm shot."*

Kelly and Cindy remained tucked on the floorboards. The girl's pleas were too much for them to ignore, so they peeked over the front seats as both officers walked cautiously towards the woman, guns drawn.

Kelly swung her door open and screamed, *"No, don't! It's a trap."*

The officers turned for a split second.

The woman launched from her knees like a lion and ripped the throat out of the driver. The other agent aimed his sidearm and squeezed off a round, but the women turned the driver into the bullet, then launched him into the second agent, knocking him off his feet.

His head hit the road with a sickening *thud*.

The woman walked to the semi-conscious agent, reached down, disarmed him, and turned him over. She drew her fist overhead and drove it into the small of his back. The crack of bones and a moan of agony cut through the still of the night. A smile crossed her face as she approached the SUV.

Kelly and Cindy held each other as they trembled uncontrollably. Paralyzing fear froze them as the woman sauntered towards the front of the truck, and her mocking laugh echoed in Kelly's ears.

Jill shielded her eyes from the bright spotlight. "Come out, ladies, and face your Destiny."

"*Fuck you, Jill. Fuck you!*" Cindy cried out, between sobs.

Jill chuckled. "I'm afraid, girls, that your fucking days are over. *Now come out or I will drag you out.*"

Kelly looked at the shotgun mounted between the two front seats. She nudged Cindy and whispered, "Let her come to us." Knowing the spotlight hindered Jill's view of them, she slowly reached out and grabbed the gun.

"*Backup is coming, you cunt! Your days are over,*" Cindy barked.

Jill took a deep breath, rolled her eyes, and shook her head. Then, with one leap, she landed on the hood of the SUV and pressed her nose to the front window. Her eyes glowed yellow.

Kelly pulled the trigger and glass exploded outward, blowing Jill off the hood. A dead silence followed.

Kelly whispered, "Look at all the blood on the hood. I think we got her."

Cindy nodded and crawled into the front seat to look on the road. "Jill is laying in a large puddle of blood, and her guts are tumbling from a gaping hole in her back." She smiled. "You got her. You got that bitch." She crawled back to the rear seat and sat next to Kelly. "Backup will be coming soon."

The two girls exhaled and leaned back. Minutes ticked in slow motion on the dark road.

Cindy said, "I can't believe we haven't seen anyone on this road."

Kelly shrugged. "Well, it's almost three o'clock in the morning in bum-fucked Egypt."

Cindy laughed. "Good point."

The side door Kelly leaned against exploded from its hinges. She caught herself from falling out and reached for the shotgun.

Jill grabbed her by the hair and yanked her from the truck, and the gun flew from her grip as she crashed to the road. Jill kicked it into the darkness.

Cindy fumbled for the opposite door to little avail. With a violent jerk, she was pulled from the truck and thrown next to her friend.

Dazed, Kelly looked up at Jill to see her body showed no injury. "What are you?" she mumbled.

Jill snarled, "Some call me an angel. Some call me a demon. I am neither."

Cindy mumbled, "What do you want with us?"

"I want nothing from either of you. I gave you an opportunity to walk away from this, but you choose otherwise."

Kelly sat up. "We didn't say anything."

Jill shook her head. "Kelly, did I not tell you when we first met, but our tentacles are everywhere. Now, you will pay your penance. Both of you, *stand up!*"

The two girls struggled to their feet.

"Remove your clothes."

Cindy said, "Sex? You're gonna have sex with us again? That's our punishment?"

Jill's brow furrowed. "*Remove... your... clothes.*"

The two girls stood naked, trembling in the night chill.

Jill turned. "Follow me."

The girls followed her to the fallen agents.

She bent down and tore a piece of flesh from the mangled throat of the dead agent, stood up, and faced the girls. "No, we are not having sex. You are naked so you can watch your own transformation."

Cindy snapped, "What, are you turning us into one of your kind?"

Jill bit down on the strip of flesh and ripped it into two pieces.

The girls turned away in disgust.

"*Look at me,*" Jill commanded.

The girls turned back to find two outstretched hands.

"Eat."

Cindy growled, "Fuck you, you sick bitch."

In the blink of an eye, Jill grabbed her by the face, forced her mouth open, and shoved the flesh to the back of her throat.

Cindy gagged and spit the bloody mass to the ground.

Jill turned to Kelly. "*Eat.*"

Kelly shook her head and dropped to her knees. "Jill, please, I'll do anything you want."

Jill looked down, grabbed her hair, yanked her head back, and shoved the flesh into her mouth.

Kelly heaved, spitting the chunk of meat to the ground.

Jill stepped back, looked towards the night sky, and mumbled several words in an ancient tongue. She then re-fixed her gaze on the two women. "You will walk this Earth for eternity with an insatiable hunger. As the night falls, you will lurk in the shadows and in the darkest nightmares of mankind."

Kelly felt a rush of intense pain course through her body, and she rolled into a fetal position. Her shrieks of agony pierced the still darkness of the canyon as her body jerked violently. Then... she stiffened and fell quiet, her breathing ran shallow, and her eyes fell shut.

Cindy dropped to her friend's side and cradled her stiff body. "*Stop, you bitch!* You're killing her!"

Jill smiled. "No, I *did* kill her."

Cindy sprang from her knees and lurched at Jill.

Jill grabbed her by the throat, spun her, and wrapped her arms around Cindy in an unnaturally strong bear hug. "Watch your Destiny."

Kelly's eyes opened, and she sprang forward at the waist, then slowly stood. Her complexion turned ashen white, and her skin tightened to her skeleton as all fat and muscle disappeared. Her arms and legs elongated, and sharp nails grew from her twisted fingers. Her back hunched, her neck lengthened, and her eyes sunk deep in their sockets as her facial features decomposed.

Kelly, or what had been Kelly, looked at Cindy with her jaws opened wide, exposing two rows of black canine teeth, and pushed out a blood-curdling, guttural scream.

A moan across the road caught the women's attention.

The creature that had been Kelly lifted its nose to the wind, and turned its wraith-like body in the direction of the fallen agent. Its gangly body moved with a forced, unsteady motion, liking that of a child taking its first steps. The creature hovered over the moaning agent, tilted its head, and paused, as if enjoying the look of dread in the agent's eyes. It slowly dropped to its boney knees, drew up a gangly arm, and thrust it into the agent's midsection. The agent let out a scream with his final breath, after which the creature dug deep and withdrew a handful of entrails.

Cindy cried out, "*Kelly!*"

The creature turned towards her and opened its lipless mouth, producing an evil smile.

In the distant canyons, the whoops of multiple sirens echoed through the night.

Jill commanded, "*Wendigo, change.*"

The creature stood up and, within seconds, Kelly returned. She looked at Cindy, and a tear fell down her cheek before she crumbled lifelessly to the ground.

Jill whispered to Cindy, "Now you see how you will walk this world for eternity."

With a sharp twist of Cindy's neck, the girl dropped to the ground.

Jill gathered the girls' clothes, quickly dressed Cindy, and moved her attention to Kelly. She looked down at the stretch marks her transformation had rendered on the girl's skin. She ran her hand over Kelly's shoulders, upper arms, and elbow joint, erasing the red lines and moving the dislocated joints back to normal. She moved to Kelly's upper back, paused, and smiled.

No, let the medical examiner have fun with this.

She dressed Kelly and returned the girls' bodies, and those of the two agents, to the SUV. She started the truck, placed one of the agent's feet on the accelerator, turned the wheel, and slammed the vehicle into drive.

It accelerated through a guardrail and careened into the deep ravine below.

Next, she moved to the two escort cruisers, where four officers sat in a trance-like state. She pulled one officer from the cruiser and stood him in front of the cars. Then she retrieved a mounted assault rifle from his vehicle, placed the gun in his hands, and showered the cars and three police officers with a hail of bullets. She allowed the rifle to fall to the ground, guided his hand to his service revolver, placed it to his head, and squeezed the trigger.

She stepped back, raised her eyebrows, smiled and said, "A perfect crime scene, if I may say so. Have fun solving this one, gentlemen."

With a few steps she vanished into the night.

Blake's cell phone vibrated the bedside table. He opened one eye to see the time was 1:15 AM. The call was from Joe Running Horse.

"Joe, what's up?"

"Blake, we have problems. I'm standing at a massacre ten miles outside the Percovelli Ranch."

Blake forced both of his eyes open and sat up. "What are you talking about, partner. Please tell me it's not the girls?" He lit a cigarette and turned on the bedside lamp.

"It is. The FEDS are trying to reach Sadler. He's not answering his phone. Can you wake him?"

"Sure, Joe... what the fuck happened?"

"It appears to be a setup. It looks like Percovelli had an insider on the local police. He used an issued AR, killed three of his own and himself. It appears the Agents tried to avoid the trap and lost control of their vehicle. It went off the road and plummeted a couple hundred feet into a ravine. The girls and the Agents are presumed dead. Climbers are heading over the edge as we speak."

"Joe, how the hell could one guy take out three armed officers and force two crack agents to make an evasive maneuver that caused their death? Five, highly trained armed men? Something *is not right*, man."

"I know. As I look at the scene up here, things don't add up. There is a dirt turnoff twenty feet behind where the SUV went over the edge. They could have backed up, turned, and retreated if necessary, not move *towards* the shooter."

Blake lit another cigarette off the tip of his existing one. "*Fuck, fuck, fuck!* What *the hell* did those girls know that was so damning?"

Joe took a deep breath. "I don't think what, but *who*, Blake."

"Okay, Joe, let me get Sadler and Billy."

"Blake, be careful in the morning out there. It could be a trap. I can't believe whoever is *now* running Percovelli's operation will allow those three girls to live."

"If they're even here, Joe. Let me fill Webb in. We'll be back as soon as we can."

The early dawn sun rose over the snow-capped Teton Mountains. Mina, Kimi, and Aiyana were roused from a deep sleep by the wop-wop of helicopter blades. They adjusted their eyes.

Mina exclaimed, "Where are we?"

Kimi paused for a second and looked around the small log cabin. "What the fuck?"

A voice barked over the helicopter speaker, "This is Wyoming State Police, come out with your hands up."

The girls looked around the one-room cabin and realized they were alone.

Aiyana said, "I don't understand. Where is the mansion? Did they drug us?"

Mina jumped to her feet and raced to the door. She held her hands up and walked into the dim light of dawn. "We are alone," she screamed over the sound of the copter blades.

Within seconds, SWAT members raced from the wood line to her side.

"Are you okay, ma'am?" a SWAT officer asked.

Mina nodded. "Yes, we are fine."

Kimi and Aiyana moved into the clearing, joining Mina and a growing group of officers.

A black SUV pulled into the field. Two other men and Billy Kellerman stepped from the vehicle.

"Billy," Mina yelled. She and Kimi raced towards the group. Mina jumped into his arms and sobbed uncontrollably.

Billy held her tight. "It's okay, Mina. You and Kimi are safe now. It's okay. It's time to go home."

"All clear, sir," a SWAT member yelled as he exited the small cabin.

Webb turned to the group. "Before we leave, I'd like to ask the girls a few questions. Let's move to the cabin where we can talk."

The three men and the girls moved to the quiet of the small cabin.

Blake ran his finger through thick dust on a small table to the left of the door as he panned the cabin. "It looks like this place has been vacant for some time."

Webb turned to the women. "Ladies, can you tell us anything about the people that held you here?"

Aiyana shook her head. "We weren't held here. We woke up in this cabin."

Webb's brow wrinkled. His bloodshot eyes darted a glance at Blake and Billy. "Where were you held, Aiyana?"

"In the mansion up in the mountains," Kimi said.

Webb turned and said, "Blake, can you have Sergeant Reed come in, please."

Billy pulled his cell phone out. "Webb, can I call back to my station and let Kimi's and Mina's families know they are alive and safe?"

Mina cocked her head, squinted, looked at Kimi and back at Billy. "Billy, I talked to my Mom and Nona yesterday. They know we're alive and were coming home. Did they not call you?"

Billy and Webb looked at each other. "No, Mina, they never said anything."

Kimi said, "How did you know we were here?"

Webb said, "We received an anonymous tip last night. By the way, where did you call from? I don't see a phone in the cabin."

"From the mansion," Mina said.

Blake and Sergeant Reed reentered, and Webb turned. "Sergeant Reed, you know this area well. Do you know of any mansions in the mountains around here?"

Reed thought for a few seconds and shook his head. "Nope. I've been flying around these mountains my whole life. Only mansion, if you want to call it that, is the old broken-down Bellow's Oil retreat on the north side of the mountains, 'bout three miles from here, but that's been abandoned since the early twenties. Ain't much left of it now but a heap of wood and stone."

Kimi said, "Is it up the mountain from where the plane landed at the hunting lodge?"

Reed nodded. "Yep, about five miles up an old logging road."

The girls looked at each other, and their eyes narrowed as if their minds were racing together.

Aiyana half-smiled and shook her head. "Their magic is strong."

CHAPTER 26
NEXT STEPS

Dakota leaned back in her chair and let out a sigh. She looked at piles of casework strewn across her desk in organized chaos, and shook her head. *How the hell does such a small town generate so many cases?*

She glanced at the time, shut her computer down, and pushed away from the desk. She grabbed her gym bag, left her office, and paused at the front desk. "Sally, I'm heading to lunch. What time is my next appointment?"

Sally looked down at her schedule. "One o'clock."

Dakota nodded. "Okay, thanks, I need a workout. If you need me, call me."

Sally smiled. "Will do."

Dakota opened the front door to a cold, biting wind, then zipped her jacket and looked at the grey skies overhead.

"Won't be long before the White Owl returns," a familiar voice said.

She turned and smiled. "Jay, what brings you into town?"

"Your grandfather called me. He wants to go over to Jackson and look at a new rifle."

Dakota rolled her eyes. "How many rifles does he need? I don't think he has ever fired half of them."

Jay chuckled. "When your grandfather and I were young, he would look down at his old rusty Savage and say, *'one day I will have a gun for every day of hunting season.'* He has held true to his word, but perhaps he lost count of how many days there are."

Dakota leaned in and gave him a kiss on the cheek. "Well, you guys have fun. It looks like snow up on the pass. Be careful."

Jay nodded. "If we get stranded, at least we will have a gun to hunt with." He winked. "Maybe two."

Dakota smiled and shook her head. "Let me get going. My lunch will be over before I know it. Are you staying at the Ranch tonight?"

"I may. It depends on how long he negotiates with the seller. You know how much he loves to dicker."

She rolled her eyes. "That's a yes. See you tonight."

Kat walked from her office pointing at her watch as Dakota walked through the gym doors. "Let's go, girl. You're late."

Dakota smiled. "Some of us don't own gyms and have to work for a living."

After a short stretch, the two women set up a bench to do presses. Kat stood behind Dakota as she pulled the weight from its rack and started her reps. She looked across the crowded gym and eyed a woman approaching the front desk. "Well, *hello* there," she mumbled.

Dakota pushed her last rep up, set the weights on the rack, sat up and looked across the gym to the statuesque blonde that caught Kat's attention. "Ahhh... thank God I didn't need a spot."

Kat chuckled. "It's your first set. You're fine. What do you think brings *her* to town?"

Dakota raised her brow. "I don't know, but I'm sure you're gonna find out."

"Yes... I... am. I'll be right back."

Dakota whispered in a joking manner, "You're such a slut."

Kat looked back and winked before pushing her hair off her shoulder and sauntering towards the blonde stranger.

The blonde finished filling out a sign-in log, placed the pen down, and looked around the gym.

Kat approached her with an outstretched hand. "Hello, my name is Kathy Graziano. Welcome to the Pump House."

The blonde reached her hand out. "Hello, Kathy, Jill Boissonnette."

Kat's eyes sparkled. "Hi, Jill. Please, call me Kat. Do you need a day pass?"

"Okay... Kat. Yes, a day pass would be great, but I may be in town for a bit. Do you offer monthly rates?"

"I do. Can I show you around the gym?"

Jill smiled. "That would be awesome, as long as I'm not interrupting you."

"Not at all. Follow me."

Dakota looked across the gym, and shook her head. *Kat is on the prowl.*

The women circled the gym as Kat pointed out each piece of equipment, and eventually made their way towards Dakota.

"Dakota," Kat said, "I would like you to meet Jill. She may be in town for a bit. Jill, this is my dearest friend, Dakota."

Jill extended her hand. "Nice to meet you, Dakota."

Dakota removed her lifting glove and shook. "Welcome to town, Jill." She shot a glance at Kat standing slightly behind Jill.

Kats' eyes widened as she lipped, *'Wow.'*

Dakota looked back at Jill. "This is a great gym. I'm sure you'll like it. I'd love to chat, but I'm on a time limit."

Jill shook her head. "No, I completely understand. Have a good workout."

Kat said, "Jill, let me show you the sauna and locker area."

Kat gave Dakota a quick peck on the cheek. "I'll call you later."

Dakota nodded. "Okay, after five. My day is crazy."

Jill passed by Dakota, tilted her head slightly upward, took a deep, silent breath through her nose, and smiled.

Jay walked into Jim's office. "Are you ready, old man?"

Jim smiled. "I believe you have me by six months. Yes, let me call and let Sally know to tell Dakota I am leaving for the day."

"I just saw her on my way in, and told her we were heading to Jackson."

"Okay, but before we leave, have a seat. The Feds are holding a news conference in two minutes."

Jay pulled up a chair as Jim switched the TV on.

A spokesman for the FBI stepped in front of the camera.

> *"Late last night, after a successful raid on the Percovelli ranch, Kelly Johnson and Cindy Fowler, two of the missing girls from the Badlands, four members of the local Sheriff's Department, and two Federal Agents were involved in what appears to have been an ambush several miles from the ranch.*

At this time, emergency crews and members of a joint task force are on scene. Sadly, there are no survivors. Initial investigation leads us to believe this was the work of a member of the Percovelli criminal enterprise.

"*Regarding an ongoing investigation into an alleged human trafficking ring masterminded by Joseph Percovelli, evidence has been recovered from his ranch that ties his criminal enterprise directly to the late sons and nephew of deceased billionaire Vincent Dibella. At this time, it does not appear Vincent Dibella or his organization are connected to Percovelli in any way. The death of Joseph Percovelli is a major blow to a human trafficking ring that is believed to have been in operation for years. As our investigation continues, we expect more arrests in this country and abroad.*

"*On a positive note, we are happy to report that, early this morning in the Jackson, Wyoming area, we successfully rescued three women known to be held captive at the Percovelli Ranch. Mina White Eagle, Kimimela Locklear, and Aiyana Begay are safe and in our protective custody. As our investigation continues, we hope to bring many more women home. At this time, we will not field any questions. Thank you.*"

Jim switched the TV off and looked over at Jay. "I guess this is over, my friend."

Jay leaned back and paused for a second. "Do you think Percovelli was behind the attempted hits on us? Maybe revenge for the Dibella boys? Perhaps we were barking up the wrong tree with Vincent."

Jim nodded. "It is *very* possible. Word got back to him that Dakota and I were poking around in South America. We knew members of our client's company were doing business with an international branch of Dibella Industries, run by Dibella's two sons. At that time, we did not know what they were involved in, or their connection to Percovelli, but now we do. I believe we scared him. I think Percovelli saw a perfect opportunity to take us out after the trial. We show up dead and who is suspect number one? Vincent Dibella. Why, he may have wanted to frame Vincent. Who knows? We may never know. Dead men tell no tales."

Jay nodded. "Do you not find it a bit odd the FBI is releasing facts as they happen during an ongoing investigation? Anyone involved will be heading for rabbit holes. It is almost as if they are sending up warnings."

Jim raised his brow. "I thought the same thing, but they *have* been under great pressure since the missing girls from the Badlands hit the national news. Perhaps they are trying to flush those 'rabbits' from their holes. I have no doubt there are some heavy hitters that have visited that ranch. They will be looking for deals to save their own hides."

"Good point. Well, at least we can breathe a bit easier now. Let's go buy that rifle."

Sellman clicked the remote off at the end of the news conference. "Fucking amateurs," he muttered. "Come in," he answered to the knock on his office door.

A serious-looking, athletically-built, bald-headed man entered the room. "Mr. Sellman," he said, with a slight eastern European accent.

Sellman stood up and extended his hand. "Mr. Smith, thank you for coming."

Mr. Smith smirked. "Well, when three of my top men don't return after being in your employment, my interest is piqued."

Sellman looked into his eyes. "As it should be. Scotch, correct?"

Mr. Smith nodded. "A double, please."

Sellman walked to the small bar in the corner of his office, poured two drinks, and returned to his desk. He handed Mr. Smith his drink and motioned with an open hand towards a high-back leather chair. "Have a seat, please."

Mr. Smith took a sip of the scotch, rolled it in his mouth, and nodded. "Very nice — Glenfiddich aged single malt."

Sellman raised his glass. "I'm glad you approve. Now, shall we discuss the reason for this meeting?"

"Please do."

Sellman set his glass down, placed his elbows on the table and leaned forward. "I paid you a very handsome sum of money to eliminate a female lawyer, a half-baked war vet, and an old fucking man. I received confirmation messages from each of your men, yet all three targets are still very much fucking alive. And, your men have gone dark, with *my* fucking money. Can you please tell me how you plan on rectifying this little issue?"

Mr. Smith swirled his scotch, took a sip, and leaned back in his chair. "Yes, I find it a bit peculiar my men failed in what appeared to be an easy mission, and have dropped off the face of the Earth. Perhaps we underestimated our targets. I must ask, with what appears to be an end to the Percovelli trafficking operations and all the Dibellas dead, why do you still want your targets eliminated? I can't see how they're a threat anymore."

Sellman paused, drew a deep breath, took a sip of his scotch and placed it back on the desk. His eyes narrowed. "Mr. Smith, a man in your profession knows better than to ask what your client's fucking motives are."

Mr. Smith stood and placed his half-drank glass on the desk. "Forgive me for asking. I will finish this assignment myself... by next week. Good day."

Jake made the final electrical connection to the small guest cabin on the ranch, stepped inside, and flipped the light switch. The ceiling mounted track lights cast a warm glow off the dark wood flooring in the combination living/dining area. He walked around a half wall to the small galley kitchen, turned the overhead light on, and nodded in approval at the dark cabinets Dakota insisted he hang. With a slight smile, he hit start on his coffeemaker and stepped back.

No more cowboy coffee.

He made his way to each receptacle and light switch to assure the electrical system was operating everywhere. His final check was at a small desk in the bedroom, where he started his laptop and connected to WIFI. After a few seconds, the internet sprang to life, and he opened a new email account, pulled a piece of paper from the desk drawer, and sent an email to all people on the paper. Robert, Johnny, Danielle, and Dakota quickly responded. He answered them with a short response promising more conversation later, as he had more work to do before the sun set.

He stared at one last email address, remembering the last Skype conversation he had with Alexi. His finger hovered over "Send."

How will she look at this? Does she need or want an open line of communication with me? Would it give her false hope? Her words from the skype call echoed in his head. *'I want the life I had a year and a half ago. I want to wake up next the man I loved for over thirty years....'* He looked up as his eyes welled. He swallowed hard to clear the lump in his throat, and retracted his finger. *If I don't send an email, the kids will surely tell her they got one from me... if they haven't already. But, they don't know the hurt she still carries and the feeling still very much alive inside her. I could make things worse, but she will be more hurt if I don't send one.*

"What a fucked-up situation, but hey... don't feel sorry for yourself, Jake old boy. This is the bed you made."

He hit send and stared at the computer. Seconds passed, then minutes.... No response. He lowered his head, nodded, and pushed away from the desk. On his way to the kitchen, a ding stopped him. He raced back to the computer, looked down, and smiled. A simple response of, *'Got it. Busy now.'* eased his mind.

CHAPTER 27
CIRCLES

Joe Running Horse stood at the guardrail as the first gurney was hoisted from the ravine below. He glanced at his watch, downed the final sip of his third cup of coffee, and took a deep breath. His gaze moved to the roadblock set at the edge of the crime scene, where a black SUV parked.

Webb and Blake exited the truck and walked towards him.

"Blake, Webb, you made good time."

Blake held out a fresh cup of coffee. "I figured you could use this."

"Yeah, it's been a long night."

Webb looked at the gurney containing a black body bag as three officers lifted it over the mangled guardrails and set it on the ground. "What number is that?"

Joe shook his head. "It's the first one—took almost six hours to locate the bodies. They were all ejected from the SUV at different points. The climbers said the bodies are pretty beat up. We believe this is Cindy Fowler."

The three men walked to the gurney. Blake bent down and unzipped the bag, took a deep breath, and dropped his head. "It's her."

Webb stared into the dead girl's face. His brow wrinkled.

Blake started to zip the bag up.

"Wait," Webb said.

Blake looked up at him. "What do you see, Webb?"

"Gentlemen, look at her expression."

Joe said, "She looks terrified. We've seen that on victims before."

Webb nodded. "Exactly, Joe... it's a death stare, present when one realizes the end is imminent. She was dead before she went over the cliff. You can close the bag."

Blake stood up. "What are you thinking, Webb?"

Webb panned the area and nodded towards the two bullet-ridden police cruisers. "Let me look at the other bodies."

Joe and Blake followed as he walked towards a covered body laid in front of the two cruisers. He bent down and pulled the sheet from the suspected shooter's face, snapped on a pair of latex gloves, and tilted the dead man's head from side to side.

"Powder burns on left temple," Webb said. "Clean exit wound on right side above the ear. Nothing out of line here." He pulled the sheet back over the corpse and stood up. He looked at the ground making a quick note of spent shell casings. "Looks like a full clip."

He then approached the bullet-riddled cruiser directly in front of the shooter. He moved to the passenger side, leaned in next to the slain officer slumped forward, and gently pushed the body back for a second, then allowed it to fall back into position.

He peered over the cruiser roof at Blake and Joe. "He never drew his sidearm."

Blake glanced at Joe And mumbled, "What the fuck?"

The two men turned to the second cruiser and peered inside as Webb approached.

Joe said, "Same here, Webb. How the hell could three trained officers be under attack and never—not one of them—reach for their weapons?"

Webb looked back at the shooter. "He's at least ten yards from the cars, which would have given them plenty of time to react, unless... unless they were dead already. We'll see what the autopsy reports show. Maybe they'll recover bullets from another gun. Who knows?"

Blake looked back at the guardrail as another gurney was being hoisted over. He lit a cigarette and shook his head. "They have the next body. Let's get back over there."

Joe said, "It should be Kelly Johnson. She was the next closest to the road."

Blake leaned over and unzipped the body bag. "Fuck." He looked back at Webb and Joe.

The three stared for a second at the back of Kelly's head and grotesquely dislocated neck.

Joe said, "What could have twisted her head completely around? I've seen my share of auto accidents, but never a neck injury this exaggerated."

Webb nodded slightly. "It happens, Joe. Blake, slowly turn her so we can see her face."

As Blake turned the body, Kelly's head continued in the opposite direction. "It's like there's no fucking neck bones." Blake supported her limp head and slowly turned it.

Webb leaned in and looked into her lifeless eyes. Absent was the look of fear, as on Cindy's face. He felt around the base of her skull and the twisted purple bag of skin that was her neck. "It feels like her cervical spine was pulverized. I can't feel any bone structure."

Webb stood, took a deep breath, and pushed the air past his lips, making them rattle. "Let's get the two agents up. Joe, have the next of kin been notified yet?"

Joe lowered his eyes and nodded. "We contacted them as soon as the climbers reached the bodies."

Blake lit another cigarette and shook his head. "These poor families. What a fucking rollercoaster ride they've been on. And they say there's a fucking God." He walked away.

Webb squinted at Joe.

Joe sighed and dropped his head for a moment, then looked back at Webb. "His wife and twenty-year-old daughter were killed in a car accident five years ago. His soul is hollow. Give him a few minutes. He'll be fine."

Webb nodded. "Okay, why don't you take him out of here and you two get some rest. I'm going to finish up, head back to the ranch to get an update from Agent Allen, and then I'm gonna to do the same. I'll request an autopsy for late this afternoon. I'll see both of you later."

Joe walked over to Blake and put his arm around his shoulder. Blake nodded, and the two made their way to their car.

Webb dialed his cell phone. "Fred, how are things going with the questioning on the ranch?"

"Nothing earth-shattering yet, Webb. No one is talking."

"Do we have anything on the female they called Jill?"

"We need to discuss that in person. How much longer will you be on the mountain?"

"A few more minutes. I'll be back at the ranch in about a half hour."

"10-4, see you then."

Webb walked into living room of the ranch's guest house where Agent Allen was conducting his interrogations.

Fred greeted him in the foyer. "You look like hell."

Webb half smiled. "I just walked through it on that mountain. Nasty scene."

"Yeah, man, those poor families. I don't know how Mike Johnson will recover from this."

Webb shook his head. "He never will, Fred. The years will pass and the shock will fade, but never the pain. What do you have so far?"

"Not much. Come over to the desk."

Fred handed a notebook to Webb. "I've talked to twenty-two employees, not a single fucking one of which has provided anything of substance. They all indicated the woman they've seen over the years on the ranch appeared to enjoy '*the party*,' as several called it. We've run backgrounds on all of them, and financials, but they're all clean, a couple petty-ass misdemeanors before they were employed by Percovelli. Afterwards, they were model citizens. Bank statements show they well compensated for their work. Many of them were earning close to six figures."

Webb tossed the notebook on the table. "That's a lot of money for ranch hands. Their silence was well compensated. What about the blonde, Jill? Do we have anything on her?"

"That's where it gets interesting. The video the drone shot of her on the porch yesterday has become scrambled."

Webb's eyes narrowed. "Scrambled?"

"Yeah, our IT guys have no explanation. Our sketch artist worked with a dozen workers. Look at these." Fred handed a sketch pad to Webb.

Webb paged through each rendering, shook his head, and handed the sketch pad back. "Twelve drawings, Fred, and *all* twelve are slightly different? We can't even produce a composite from these."

Fred nodded. "I know, and the two girls we could have counted on are dead. Our only hope is the girls we just rescued in Wyoming."

Webb exhaled forcefully. "Well, I'm not sure they'll be much help. All three of them talked about a palatial mansion on the mountainside close to where we found them. The State Police pilot said the only mansion he knows that *ever* existed there is long gone. It's just a pile of timber now. They obviously were drugged or something. The one girl, Aiyana, said '*their magic is strong*' after the pilot commented on the lack of a mansion."

Fred tossed the sketch pad on the desk. "Speaking of pilots, we tracked the Percovelli plane to a private landing strip near Miami. By the time our local boys got a search warrant, they were too late. Witnesses reported two men got off the plane and were picked up and driven away in a white Mercedes. We have no plate, and given how many white Mercedes there are in Miami, we have nothing."

Webb looked around the room. "What about video? I have to believe there's cameras hidden everywhere."

"There are, but they were rigged to erase. Our guys are working on recovery, but it appears unlikely. Percovelli's office had an independent system. It's encrypted, but our techies believe they can break the pass codes."

Webb nodded. "All right, I'm gonna get some sleep. I got approval to start the autopsies tonight on the two girls and our agents. Let me know if anything earth-shattering pops up. I suggest you get some rest also. Where is Harris at?"

"He's getting some shut-eye. He'll be here to relieve me in about an hour."

"Okay, good. Have him keep digging around here. I want you two alternating shifts around the clock until the forensic units are done. Also, I'm having the dash cam films from the two cruisers delivered here. You and Harris work on them. Maybe they'll give us something to stop this circle we seem to be spinning in."

"10-4, Webb, go get some shut-eye."

CHAPTER 28
NEXT ACT

Blake butted his cigarette in an overfilled ashtray and took the last sip of cold coffee. He looked down at his watch and up at the setting sun behind the snow-capped peaks, until a knock at his hotel door prompted him to move from the hotel balcony. *"It's open."*

Joe walked into the disheveled room, and looked at piles of papers strewn about the desk and clothes thrown over top of the couch and bed. Days of take-out food bags and empty wrappers flowed over the rim of the garbage can. He smiled and shook his head. "Are the housekeepers on strike on your floor?"

Blake panned the room and chuckled. "Yeah, I guess I should take the 'Do Not Disturb' sign off the door. Did you get any sleep?"

"I dozed off and on. How 'bout you?"

"Nah, Joe, this case has my brains fuckin' scrambled."

Joe nodded. "Yep, things just don't feel right."

Blakes eyes narrowed. "It's all too orchestrated, like some dark, twisted play, and now we move to the next act. I can only imagine what twists the autopsies will provide."

"I know, partner. I saw Webb in the lobby. He's waiting on us at the bistro."

Blake grabbed two packs of cigarettes and his wallet. "Yeah, we might as well grab a bite and more coffee. It's gonna be a long night."

The two made their way downstairs to Webb, where Blake walked up and tapped him on the back.

Webb turned, smiled, and looked down at his watch. "We have about an hour. Are you two eating?"

Blake and Joe nodded.

Webb stood and nodded towards a high-back, three-quarter-circle booth. "Let's order, then go over there to have a little privacy."

The three placed their order and moved to the table.

Webb pulled his laptop out and placed it so Blake and Joe could see it. "This is the footage from the dash cam in the shooter's car. I have the volume down while we're in here. There wasn't much on it." He hit play.

Blake and Joe watched the video. Their expressions remained focused, occasionally broken by movement of their brows and slight cocking of their heads. The short video ended, and both looked up at Webb.

Webb closed the laptop. "What did both of you see?"

Blake spoke up first. "From the herd of elk up to the shooting, the video is black. What the hell happened?"

Webb said, "We don't know. The computer in the car shows the engine was never turned off. The first crews on scene killed the engines in both cruisers."

Joe said, "The gait of the shooter looks odd, as if he is being assisted to the front of the car. His mechanics look unnatural."

Blake said, "Webb, can you play that back again and fast forward to where he shoots himself. Joe has a good point."

Webb opened the computer and spun it back around at the part Blake requested.

Blake leaned into the small screen and stared intently at it. As it finished, he leaned back and paused for a second. "Webb, what hand was the shooter?"

Webb rifled through a file, then looked up with eyes narrowed. "Left-handed."

Blake and Joe glanced at each other, then back at Webb.

Blake lowered his voice and leaned forward. "Why the fuck is he shooting right-handed, *and* killed himself right-handed?"

Webb dropped his arms to the table and slouched back. "I have no idea."

Joe said, "I imagine there's no dash cam on the SUVs, correct?"

Webb nodded, "Correct, this is all we have."

Blake said, "It looks like about twelve minutes passed from the time the elk crossed to the shootings. Was there any communication from the cruisers or SUV during that time?"

Webb said, "Not a peep. The one officer radioed in that they were stopped by the elk herd, and dead silence after that."

Joe looked up. "Here comes our order. Hold that thought."

The server placed the order on the table. "Can I get you gentlemen anything else?"

Webb nodded politely. "Thank you, that will be it. Please place this order on my room."

Blake watched the server leave and lowered his voice. "Webb, why the hell would their dispatch not alert someone immediately if there was no contact after several minutes?"

"I asked the same thing. I guess it's not abnormal to be stopped in that part of the canyon for elk movement. It didn't raise any red flags."

Blake leaned back and rubbed his eyes. "Okay, let's eat up and get over to the autopsies. I'm sure they will provide more '*what the fuck*' moments."

Webb, with Blake and Joe as passengers, pulled into the side parking lot of the hospital, and all stepped from their vehicle into the blustery New Mexico night.

Joe looked up. "A ring around the moon... snow is coming."

Webb said, "Yeah, they're calling for an inch or so overnight in the higher elevations."

The three quickened their steps as the cold winds lashed their skin.

"Fuck, didn't winter just get over?" Blake growled.

As the three reached the door, Webb's phone rang. "Yeah, Steve."

"Webb, we got into the cameras in Percovelli's office. What time do you anticipate the autopsies will be over?"

"Probably around eleven. Why, is there something urgent?"

"Urgent, no... interesting, yes."

"All right, I'll be back to the ranch as soon as I can."

"Roger, out."

Blake and Joe turned to Webb, and Blake said, "What's up?"

Webb lowered his voice. "They got into the camera system in Percovelli's office. Maybe we'll catch a break."

Blake said, "We sure as hell could use one."

The men walked through the quiet hospital corridors to the elevator.

Blake hit the B button. "Why do morgues always have to be in the basement?"

Webb chuckled. "If they weren't, what would Hollywood do?"

The three let out a nervous laugh as the door opened. An officer greeted them as they stepped from the elevator.

Webb said, "Officer, good evening." Blake, Joe, and he flashed their badges.

"Good evening, sir. The M.E. is expecting you."

Webb paused at the entrance to the morgue. "Okay, boys, I'll get prepped."

Joe nodded towards a second door. "We'll head up to the observation room. Let's hope we find some answers."

Webb entered the morgue's prep room and was greeted by a tall silver-haired man with an outstretched hand. "Mr. Sadler, my name is Dr. Hernandez."

Webb extended his hand. "Nice to meet you, Doctor."

Dr. Hernandez said, "Let's wash up and get busy. My assistant, Dr. Connors, has prepped the bodies."

"Sounds good. Who are you examining first?"

"The young woman, Cindy Fowler."

"Okay."

The two men donned their scrubs, washed their hands, and walked into the brightly lit, sterile white room. Seven stainless steel gurneys sat lined-up beneath the glass observation windows. An eighth gurney sat empty a few feet from the examination table where Cindy laid covered by a white sheet from the neck down.

Webb glanced up at Blake and Joe seated behind the glass, and nodded.

The assistant medical examiner walked up to Webb as he and Dr. Hernandez approached. "Mr. Sadler, Dr. Connors... nice to meet you."

Webb nodded. "Likewise, Dr. Connors."

The three moved to the examination table and paused briefly as they looked down at Cindy. Her frozen expression of dread stared back at them.

Webb said, "Her face muscles have not relaxed."

Dr. Hernandez said, "Whatever she saw prior to death terrified her. Rare, but I've seen this before. Shall we begin?"

Dr. Connors removed the sheet.

Webb's eyes panned slowly down Cindy's battered and broken body.

Dr. Hernandez lifted a scalpel from the surgical tray and made the first incision.

Webb hung his scrubs up in the prep room and exited the morgue.

His two colleagues met him in the hall, and Blake handed him a fresh cup of hot coffee. "You look exhausted."

Webb glanced at his watch then rubbed his bloodshot eyes. "Four thirty in the morning, four autopsies, and nothing out of the ordinary for a car accident. I'm sure the autopsies of the shooting victims will be equally unproductive."

Joe said, "Looking at the shape the bodies are in, it doesn't surprise me. Maybe the labs will give us something."

Blake said, "It just makes no fucking sense how that SUV ended up at the bottom of a ravine, and one officer could take out three others, with not so much as a shot fired in self- defense. *None* of this adds up."

Webb snickered. "Does anything in this whole case add up? Abducted girls seen on video appearing to enjoy their captivity. Percovelli connected to the Dibella boys... all dead. Vincent Dibella, his wife, and half their staff perish in a freak gas explosion. Mountaintop mansions that don't exist. A blonde female that appears differently to people, whose image is erased from our video. No, gentleman, 'nothing adds up' *is an understatement.* Let's get to the ranch and see what Percovelli's cameras reveal, and then get some much-needed sleep."

The three headed towards the elevator.

"Mr. Sadler," a voice called from behind them.

The trio spun. "Dr. Connors, what is it?"

Connors approached the men. "Gentlemen, Dr. Hernandez would like the three of you to move to the observation room for a second. He will explain."

Connors reentered the morgue as the three men moved to the glass in the observation room.

Hernandez spoke into the overhead microphone above the exam table. "Gentlemen, can you hear me?"

Webb pressed a green button mounted on the wall below the glass. "Yes, Doctor, loud and clear."

Dr. Hernandez pulled the sheet down on Kelly Johnson's body and rolled the corpse over. "Gentlemen, when Dr. Connors was prepping the bodies for release, he noticed a slight irregularity on the dermis of Ms. Johnson's thoracic area. We didn't see this during the autopsy due to livor mortis. Let me pull the camera in closer."

The three men looked closely at the monitor in the observation room.

Hernandez pointed to a group of faint, irregular, purplish lines running vertically along Kelly's upper spine for approximately six inches. "When Dr. Connors rolled the body over and the pooled blood moved forward to the abdominal area, these lines became visible. Also note, as I move the camera downwards, the same lines appear on the dermis from the base of the buttocks and outer hips to the upper hamstring, and the back of the knees."

Webb leaned forward and pressed the green button. "They look like stretch marks."

Dr. Hernandez nodded. "Exactly, Mr. Sadler. Now watch this." He nodded to Dr. Connors standing at the head of the stainless-steel table.

Connors grasped Kelly's head with his fingers under the jaw bone. "If you remember during the autopsy, we all commented on the flaccidity of her neck." He pulled the head towards him, grossly elongating the neck.

"What the fuck?" Blake muttered.

Webb hit the green button. "That type of elongation is something we see in a hanging victim, not a car accident."

Hernandez nodded. "We are having a digital X-ray machine brought down, if you can stay for a few more minutes."

Webb hit the button. "Of course, Doc."

A technician wheeled the machine into the examination room and followed Dr. Connors' direction where to place it on Kelly's neck. She turned the machine on, and the digital image filled the screen. Slowly, she scanned the elongated cervical area.

Dr. Hernandez and Dr. Connor leaned closer to the screen, then abruptly stood back, shot a glance at each other, and then glanced up to the observation area.

Webb's eyes narrowed as he stared at the monitor.

Blake must have noticed the look on his face. "Webb, what are we looking at?"

Webb looked down at the two doctors and back up at the monitor. "Every single vertebra has been pulled from each other, as if stretched like an accordion."

Joe said, "What does that mean?"

Webb shook his head. "I don't know, Joe." He hit the green button. "Doctors, any ideas?"

Hernandez said, "None. We're gonna look at the areas of the stretch marks."

The X-Ray technician moved the machine over the stretch marks in the thoracic area of the spine. Again, each vertebra was separated. The machine moved to the base of the hip and buttocks area, and found a clear separation of the femoral head from the hip socket. Hernandez glanced up at Webb, who stood glued to the monitor, as the technician moved the machine to the knee area. Both legs showed gross separation of the femur, tibia, and patella.

Webb rocked backwards, paused, and sat down.

"Webb, explain what we're looking at," Blake said.

Webb shook his head slowly. "It appears that she was stretched, but there are no breaks. I've never seen anything like this."

He leaned forward and hit the green button. "Dr. Hernandez, do you have any idea what could cause these injuries? It's like she was stretched on a rack. The substantial bruising indicates gross soft tissue damage, which we thought was caused by the crash, but.... Is it possible this occurred before death?"

Hernandez looked up and said, "Mr. Sadler, I have no opinion at this time. If we can, I would like to have more tests run on her tomorrow."

Webb hit the button. "Of course, Doctor, take all the time you need. Please update me. I know you have four more autopsies. If that's all you need from us, we'll let you get back to work."

Hernandez nodded and said, "Thank you, we'll update you as tests results come in, and I'll have my full report to you in forty-eight hours. Go get some sleep."

Webb hit the button. "Thank you, Doctor." He stood, stretched his head side to side, and turned to Joe and Blake. "Shall we head to the ranch for the next act in this bizarre play?"

Web drove the three of them, and as they approached the entrance to Percovelli's ranch, a group of heavily armed guards stopped them. They wore black body armor and stood behind four-foot-high concrete barricades. Webb flashed his badge and was passed through.

Blake said, "Jesus, I feel like I'm coming onto a military compound."

They drove to the main house and parked, and Agents Harris and Allen greeted the three men on the front porch.

Harris said, "You boys look like hell."

Webb half smiled. "It's been a long night, Steve. Let's see what you have on the film."

Harris escorted them to a small room in the rear of Percovelli's office, where two IT guys hovered over a computer screen and keyboard.

Webb stepped behind the duo and placed a hand on each of their shoulders. "Good job, boys, on getting into his system. Show us what you have."

Blake and Joe moved to Webb's side and leaned in to see the screen.

Harrison Reyes, the senior computer forensic expert, said, "Webb, we were able to retrieve only the last couple hours on the tape. Everything before that has been erased."

Blake said, "Is there any way to recover that video?"

Harrison shook his head. "No, sir, the system was configured with a powerful bulk eraser. I would assume the administrator, most likely Percovelli, downloaded the video to a storage device, then erased the tapes."

Webb said, "Okay, let's see what's left."

Steve snickered. "If this case hasn't been fucked-up, watch this."

Webb glanced up and returned his attention to the video. "Hit play, please."

The group stood silent as they watched the last minutes of Joseph Percovelli's life.

Harrison said, "I'm fast forwarding, as there's nothing on the tape except his hunched body until the secretary discovers him fifty-nine minutes later." He hits play, and the group watches the secretary discover the body and dial 911. He hits stop. "From there, the tape runs until we were able to shut it off. There's nothing on it except the forensic teams doing their work."

Blake said, "Who the fuck was he talking to? The tape shows the whole room. There's no one there. And who the hell *is this* Jill he's having an imaginary conversation with? What kind of drugs were they doing on this ranch?"

Webb pulled a chair from against the wall and plopped down. He rubbed his hands over his face and breathed deeply. "We believe Jill was the blonde we saw on the deck. Cindy and Kelly told us she was second in charge of the operation, behind Percovelli. We can't identify her. She's a ghost—it appears, after watching this, maybe in the literal term."

Joe said, "Didn't the fear on Percovelli's face before he pulled the gun to his mouth look familiar?"

Webb nodded and, in a flat tone, said, "Just like on Cindy's face."

Blake pulled a cigarette from his pocket. "And what's this shit Percovelli was saying about secret societies and *'the client'*?"

Harris said, "The girls identified some powerful, rich people that were on the Ranch with them. They claim these people were part of an exclusive sex trafficking ring. I assume that is the secret society. As for *'the client,'* we have no idea."

Joe said, "Well, perhaps the girls didn't die in vain. I'm sure, once we start questioning the ones the girls identified, they'll turn on each other in a hurry."

Webb looked up and shook his head. "Joe, we have no case. Our witnesses are dead. Their lawyers will contend their clients were here on business or 'guilty' pleasure. They will push for any evidence we have, including surveillance tapes, and the only tape we have is Cindy and Kelly having sex on the deck. You've seen the video. Did they look like they were in distress? Every worker we've interviewed claim they never saw any women here that didn't appear to be enjoying their stay. Most believed the girls brought here were high-priced escorts. We have nothing."

Joe said, "We have Mina, Kimi, and Aiyana."

Blake snickered. "You mean the three that were in a mansion that existed sixty years ago. Their brains are scrambled. The lawyers would have a field day with them. I need a smoke."

Joe watched Blake leave and looked back at Webb. "He's right. What's our next step?"

Webb stood up. "Let the CSI and forensic teams scrub this ranch from top to bottom. Maybe we get *something* to implicate *someone* that's *still alive*. Or, if we're lucky, find something to allow us to identify and rescue more women this sick bastard kidnapped. For now, it appears Joseph Percovelli ran a trafficking ring. With his death, the ring was destroyed. That's how we'll spin it to the press."

Blake walked back in. "Well, Webb, where do you want Joe and I to concentrate our efforts?"

Webb walked forward and extended his hand. "Blake, Joe and you have been a big help, but go back to the Badlands. I'll keep both of you informed as we continue our investigation. There's nothing more either of you can do here. We're spinning in circles."

Blake paused and nodded, then reached out and shook Webb's hand. "Are you sure?"

Webb smiled. "Yes, go home."

Agent Harris moved to the group. Blake and Joe exchanged handshakes and parting niceties with the Feds, and started from the room.

Joe stopped and turned. "Let us know how the autopsies finish up. Those girls, and Percovelli... something *is not* natural."

CHAPTER 29
QUESTIONS

When the alarm rang in Jake's new cabin, Honi sprang up and raced to the door.

Dakota sighed and lazily reached over to hit snooze, and grumbled, "Thank God it's Friday."

Jake rolled out of bed and shuffled to the door to let Honi out, then he walked into the kitchen and started the coffee pot.

Dakota watched him move about. "Hey, why don't you bring yourself back to bed?" She looked between his legs. "It looks like he slept well and is *wide* awake. Let's christen your new home."

He smiled and looked down. "Well, waking up next to you, he would get hard on an iceberg. Are you sure you have time?"

She threw the cover off and kneeled up in bed. "I'll make this fast. You won't last long. Lie back down."

"Confident, aren't you?"

The two crumbled to the bed panting and drenched from the short but intense tryst. After a few moments of silence, Dakota sat up, looked at him, and with a coy smile said, "I told you, you wouldn't last long."

He chuckled. "That was unfair. That's a secret weapon. *No* man could have lasted long."

She threw her legs over the edge of the bed and stood. She looked back. "I've always wanted to do that, but... don't get used to it. That's for special occasions only." She walked into the bathroom.

"Like every Friday?" Jake yelled.

She poked her head from the bathroom door. "Yeah, every Friday during leap year."

Jake chuckled and stared at the ceiling for a moment. When the shower started, knowing Dakota would be in a hurry, he strolled into the kitchen, poured her a cup of coffee, and started a pan of scrambled eggs.

He walked into the steamed bathroom and placed a cup of coffee on the sink. "I brought you in a cup of coffee, and eggs are cooking, my little sex machine."

"Thank you," she said over the noise of the shower. "What time is it?"

"About 7:30, so you have time."

The shower shut off and Dakota pulled the shower curtain open. "Since you're here, can you hand me my towel."

Jake paused and purposely ran his eyes from her head to toes. "Your whole body is a secret weapon."

She rolled her eyes. "Towel, please."

The noise of a haunting whistle caught their attention.

She said, "Someone is emailing you early."

Jake knew who it was but deflected. "Must be one of the kids, or the folks from the production company. They really want an answer on the documentary. Let me go check on the eggs and see who it was."

Dakota took a sip of her coffee and wrapped the towel around her. "I'll check the eggs. You check the email. I need more sugar anyway."

The two exited the bath. Jake went to the computer and Dakota went to the stove.

She grabbed her phone, tapped something onto it, and a sexy moan came from his computer. "Really, Jake?"

He looked back and laughed. She walked towards him as he finished a quick email and hit send. "Who was it?"

"Alexi."

Dakota raised an eyebrow. "*Oh?* Kind of early, isn't it? What did she say?"

Jake stood up and turned from the computer. "Nothing much, just that she was forwarding paperwork from the Social Security folks."

Dakota looked at him, her voice lowered. "So... she gets a beautiful melody as an alert, probably something from your past, and I get a sex moan? Is that what *I am* to you, Jake? Just a sex toy?"

"Of course not." He walked towards her with his arms open.

She spun and stormed towards the bathroom. "Leave me alone. I have to go to work."

Jake lowered his head and mumbled, "Fuck." He looked up and walked after her. "Dakota, please—"

She slammed the door in his face.

He moved into the kitchen, dished her eggs onto a plate, and set them on the table. He then threw on a pair of sweats and a hoodie, walked into the crisp Wyoming morning, looked up to the clear blue sky, and drew a deep breath. He panned the ranch as he collected his thoughts, and walked back into the cabin as Dakota stepped from the bathroom.

"Your eggs are getting cold," he said.

"I'm not hungry," she said in a melancholy tone.

Jake watched in silence as she rushed to get dressed. He walked towards her as she slipped into her sneakers, reached out and touched her shoulder.

She recoiled. "Jake, I have to change and go to work. *Someone needs to* in this relationship. I'll see you tonight." She sprang up and marched from the cabin.

Jake walked towards the door and watched her make charge through the waving yellow grass of the meadow between the ranch home and the cabin. He watched Samuel greet her a few steps from the porch. They spoke briefly and she entered the house.

Samuel looked towards the cabin and started walking into the meadow.

"Shit, just what I need now, a medicine man up my ass," Jake grumbled.

He went into the cabin, poured a cup of coffee, and walked out onto the small porch to greet Samuel as he stepped from the knee-high meadow. "Good morning, sir."

Samuel paused, looked to the sky, and nodded. "Every morning is a good morning on the last hill of one's life."

Jake chuckled. "Would you like some coffee? It's fresh."

"Yes, that would be nice." Samuel walked in and panned the cabin. "The old place looks good, Jake. You and Lomasi added some life to it in short time."

Jake looked around and nodded. "Fortunately, it didn't need much, just a few days of old fashioned elbow grease." He smiled. "How would you like your coffee?"

"Black is fine. Let us sit on the porch. It is a beautiful morning."

The two men pulled a couple old wood chairs up to a small wood table and sat.

Samuel took a sip from his coffee. "I do not know why white men have ruined coffee with all those fancy creamers. Coffee is meant to be enjoyed as is."

Jake lifted his black coffee into the air with a toasting motion. "I agree."

After a pause, Samuel said, "Lomasi seemed a bit occupied this morning."

Jake took a sip and shook his head. "Samuel, when she and I spent time on the mountain, our lives where peaceful. The outside world could not touch us. Then the trial came and the outside world invaded our world. Now, my past is part of our lives. I know it's tough for her. And, honestly, it's confusing for me."

Samuel set his coffee down and took a deep breath. "During the days ice covered the land, food was very difficult to harvest. My people followed the herds of great woolly beasts. One day, a blinding snowstorm befell a hunting party, and a brave became separated from his group. The snow and blowing drifts quickly covered his tracks, and howling winds silenced his yells. Darkness began to fall. The brave knew he must find shelter or he would surely perish. Slowly, the storm subsided and the night sky cleared. The brave could see the outline of a rock outcropping in the distance. He trudged through waist-high snow and reached the rocks. Under the light of the moon, he saw a cave halfway up the outcropping. However, fresh footprints of a large cat traversed the boulders between him and shelter. The brave knew it would be impossible to make the climb without the cat knowing he was approaching. He looked to the stars and asked the Great Spirit for protection from the beast. The night sky became aglow with the spirits of his ancestors dancing across them. A feeling of warmth fell over him. He looked back at the cave and saw a young maiden standing at the entrance. The maiden motioned him to make the climb. When the brave neared the cave entrance, the maiden walked into it. Beneath his feet were only the tracks of the large cat. He looked at the dancing lights across the heavens, readied his spear, and entered the cave. The heavy breathing of the cat echoed thru the dark cave. He questioned the Great Spirit, and wondered why he would be led to a battle he could not win. A warm glow filled the cave. The brave watched the maiden move to the large sabertooth cat lying on its side, feeding her three cubs. She smiled as she ran her hand over the head of the great cat, then stood and motioned him to follow her. The maiden made her way to the rear of the cave and into a narrow passage. The passage opened into another small chamber. The brave looked past the maiden and could see the night sky in an opening.

"'What is your name?' the brave asked.

"The maiden smiled, extended her arm, and waved her hand side to side. The sound of sliding rocks behind the brave garnered his attention. He spun to see the passage between him and the cat and her cubs was sealed. The brave turned back to the maiden, only to find she had disappeared. The brave walked to the opening of the cave. In the far distance, he could see the glow of fires in his village."

Samuel stood and placed his hand on Jake's shoulder. "Trust the path the Spirits have set Lomasi and you on." He set down the coffee and stepped from the porch. After a few strides, he looked back. "As for whatever disagreement Lomasi and you had, I cannot help with that. The Great Spirit gave us women to keep us guessing." He winked and turned for the ranch house.

Dakota finished with her last morning client and headed for the gym.

She entered and walked past the front desk and into the locker room, where Kat was changing into her workout gear.

"Kat, what are you doing in street clothes?"

Kat rolled her eyes. "Fucking county double-charged me for my electric bill, *again*."

"Ugh, so *you* had a bad morning *also*...."

"Ladies," Jill said, as she entered the locker room and interrupted their conversation.

Kat and Dakota turned.

With a big smile, Kat said, "Hey Jill."

Dakota followed. "Hi Jill."

Jill sauntered towards the two women. "What are both of you working on today?"

"Anything tough," Dakota said. I" need to blow off some stress."

Kat added quickly, "That makes two of us."

Jill moved to a locker next to Dakota. "Well, if you two angry ladies would allow me to join in, that would be great. Fortunately, my morning appears to be better than both of yours, but I'm always up for a challenge."

Kat said, "Sure, the more the merrier. How about a good, old fashioned lower body circuit?"

Jill took a deep silent breath as she candidly admired Dakota's and Kat's varying levels of nakedness. "Lower body sounds good."

Dakota glanced at Kat, who positively blushed.

After the three women finished the last set of their exhaustive workout, they stood together panting and catching their breath.

Kat looked up at the clock. "I have forty-five minutes before I have to train my first afternoon client. Do you girls have time for the sauna?"

Jill, between breaths, said, "Sounds good. My afternoon is free."

Dakota took a deep swig of her water and caught her breath. "That sounds good. My next client comes in at two."

The three went to the locker room, undressed, and wrapped towels around themselves for the walk to the sauna. Kat set the timer on the outside, and the three entered the steam-filled oval wood room. They sat on the bench and dropped their towels.

Jill said, "Well, girls, I hope whatever was bothering you before *that* workout is gone."

Dakota glanced over at her and noticed a gold eight-pointed cross that fell at the top of her cleavage. "It helped. That's a unique cross, Jill. Is it Templer?"

Kat leaned over to see what Dakota commented on. Her eyes first caught Jill's large firm breasts, then the cross.

Jill said, "It has passed from mother to daughter in my family for generations. I'm told it's ancient Egyptian. My great-great-grandmother purchased it when she was over there. I'm not really sure what its true meaning is. I just wear it 'cause that's what all the women in my family have done. They say it brings fertility and will lead a good man into my life."

Kat chuckled. "How's it working?" She lifted her gaze up from Jill's chest and looked down at it.

"I think it stopped working with my mom."

Dakota said, "Maybe I need to borrow it."

"Uh oh, trouble in paradise?" Kat said.

Dakota clenched her fists briefly. "I could have killed Jake this morning. We got done fooling around and his email alert went off, and it was a hauntingly pretty whistle melody. He said it was one of the kids. So, I sent him an email, and what does my alert sound like? A fucking porn star moaning. Come to find out the whistling one was his ex-wife."

Kat chuckled. "Well, girlfriend, you must be rocking his world, you little slut."

Jill said, "They're all the same."

Kat said, "That's why I jumped to the other side. But Jill, that's between us. This town is still a bit behind times."

Jill leaned over, looked past Dakota, and winked. "Your secret is safe. I like the company of a man, but the soft touch of a woman is nice from time to time."

Dakota scoffed. "After this morning, I might jump the fence too."

Kat placed her hand on Dakota's knee. "Jake's a good guy. You guys were meant to be together after all you two have been through. Men are just dumbasses sometimes."

Dakota smiled. "I know, and I probably overreacted."

Jill arched back, drew a deep breath, and stretched her arms over her head. "See, a good workout always calms the nerves. Now we should go have a good lunch and some drinks."

Dakota looked at Kat. "I'm done after my two o'clock client."

Kat shrugged. "Three thirty at The Nickel for pre-happy hour?"

Jill said, "Just tell me where The Nickel is and we have a date."

Kat said, "It's one block down from the gym and make a right. You can't miss it."

Dakota stood and wrapped her towel around herself. "Maybe I'll have Jake meet us around five-thirty. Give us some girl time, and then we can all party?"

With a sly smile, Kat said, "Why don't we just do girl time and let him really think about this morning."

"No, I'm sure he felt like shit all day. I've been really short with my responses to his text. It's time to let him off the hook. I'll see you girls at three-thirty."

Kat and Jill watched Dakota leave.

Jill slid closer to Kat. "So... Miss Gym Owner, does that door lock?"

"Ladies and Gentlemen," the pilot announced, "the weather in Rapid City is clear skies with a temperature of 51 degrees. I hope your flight was enjoyable. On behalf of Delta Airlines and your crew, thank you for flying with us. Flight attendants, please prepare the cabin for landing."

The announcement startled Blake from a deep sleep. "Fuck, that scared me," he grumbled.

Joe chuckled. "I have no idea how you sleep so sound on a plane."

Blake widened his eyes and stretched his neck. "Always could, ever since my days on C-130s in the Air Force." He glanced down at a sketch on Joe's lap tray. "What the hell you doing, partner, drawing creatures for Disney or something?"

Joe picked up his pen and pointed to an elongated and hunched back of the creature. "I wish, Blake. Look at the elongation of the back, and the legs. Does it look familiar?"

Blake's eyes narrowed. "Yeah, it looks like a Wendigo. Where are you going with this?"

"Think of Kelly Johnson's unexplainable stretch marks and bone injuries...."

"Come on, man. I've never known you to put much faith in those old myths."

Joe folded the sketch and put in his pocket. "And I've also never seen disappearing mountaintop mansions or a suspect who has no unique characteristics to numerous people that worked with her every day."

Blake nodded. "Well, partner, you do have a point. I need a cigarette and a drink."

CHAPTER 30
SKELETONS IN THE CLOSET

Jill walked from the gym into the mid-afternoon sunshine, looked up at the deep blue skies, took a deep breath, and smiled. She ran her tongue across her lips and savored the lingering taste of Kat.

She stopped a few doors down from the gym at a local coffee shop. After ordering, she sat at a dainty, black iron bistro table in the small street-side courtyard. Her gaze panned up and down the main street of town, and she thought back to the last time she visited this area — before towns and reservations, when buffalo and elk roamed the land and Yellowstone was merely part of the landscape. She recalled the smell of burnt corpses and cries of agony, and the skies black with vultures waiting to drop on the human carrion she and the rest of the Six had riddled the village with. She sipped her coffee and smirked.

A resilient race, these humans are.

She glanced down at her hotel sitting across the street from Dakota's law office. Two older men stepped from a vehicle parked in front of the law office. She watched Dakota come out and hug both of them. One man reached back into the car and withdrew a rifle. He handed it to Dakota.

Dakota admired it, drew the gun up to her shoulder, nodded, smiled, and handed it back to the taller of the two men.

A bright glint caught Jill's eye from the last room to the left on the top floor of her hotel. She focused on it. After a couple seconds, the glint disappeared. Her gaze darted back to Dakota, her view partially blocked by a group of people walking up the sidewalk.

She sprang up. "No, no, no, not while I'm this close." She stepped to the street, watched Dakota and the two men enter the law offices, and walked quickly towards the hotel.

The front desk clerk jumped up as Jill entered the lobby. "Good afternoon, ma'am."

"Good afternoon, James," Jill replied, as she walked briskly towards the elevator.

She exited on the top floor, then hustled to her room and hastily changed from workout gear into a business suit. She removed the eight-pointed cross from around her neck and gasped deeply as her body wrenched slightly. She moved to the bathroom mirror, let her hair down, and refreshed her makeup.

She left her room and walked down the left wing of the hotel, stopping at the door of the room that corresponded with the glare she'd seen from the coffee shop below.

A knock at the door drew Mr. Smith's attention from Dakota's office across the street. He looked towards the door and lowered his scope.

"Management, sir," a woman's said.

Smith drew a frustrated breath and shook his head. "One second, please." He calmly walked towards the door, stopping at a closet to place his rifle out of sight. He peeked through the peep hole, raised a brow, and opened the door.

"Yes, may I help you?"

The woman smiled. "Sorry for bothering you, sir, but we have reports from guests that our phone system is not working properly. May I check yours? It will only take a second."

Smith nodded. "Of course, please come in."

Jill entered and walked towards the phone, taking quick notice of a guest sheet on the bedside table. "Mr. Smith, have you had any issues contacting the front desk or room service?"

He walked towards her. "Honestly, I haven't tried using the phone."

Jill picked up the phone and cocked her head as she placed it to her ear. "It appears you have no connection either. We should have this fixed shortly." She placed the phone on the hook and turned. "Sorry for the inconvenience, Mr. Smith."

Smith, though clearly annoyed with the disruption, smiled. "No problem, I appreciate the hotel's attention to this. I was getting ready to step out for a bit, so no inconvenience."

Jill launched at him and delivered a crushing right hand to his jaw.

Smith staggered backwards and crumbled onto the bed unconscious.

She quickly picked up a pillow, removed its cover, tied it across his mouth, and then rolled him over and wrapped a second pillowcase around his wrists. Next, she lifted him from the bed and dragged him effortlessly to a desk chair. She rolled a sheet into a makeshift rope and wrapped it across his chest and the chair back. She tore another pillowcase in half and secured his ankles to the chair's legs. She then filled a glass with ice water, splashed his face, and took a step back.

Smith slowly regained his senses. His bloodshot eyes seemed to gain focus as he gazed about the room. He struggled to move, but quickly realized it was to no avail. His eyes widened and his brow furrowed, his face turned red, and his temples flared.

Jill poured herself a glass of wine from the suite's bar and sauntered over to him. She slid a chair directly in front of him, casually took a sip, and sat. "Now, Mr. Smith, *if* that is your real name, we're going to have a chat. But first, I want to make sure you tell me the truth."

Jill reached down, unbuckled his pants, and slid them and his underwear past his thighs. She raised her eyebrows. "Nice package, Mr. Smith. I'm sure you're proud of it." She finished the wine, tapped the rim of the glass off the wood arm of the chair, and lifted the jagged crystal flute into the air. She then grabbed his member and placed the half-shattered stemware against the base of it. "This is simple: answer my questions and you keep your dick. Simple, huh?"

Smith grumbled, his eyes narrowed.

Jill withdrew the jagged glass from his package and sat back in the chair. "First, where is the gun?"

Smith shook his head. "No gun," he forced past the tight gag across his mouth.

Jill rolled her eyes and again grabbed his dick, pressing the jagged glass into the underside of it.

Smith winced as a sharp pain shot through his body, and he let out a muffled whimper.

Jill lifted the glass, dripping with blood. "Mr. Smith, that was your first and last chance. The next time I lift this glass, your cock will be in it. Now... *where is the gun?*"

Smith's eyes looked past Jill. He pointed his head towards the closet, then looked down at his bleeding member.

Jill walked to the closet, opened the door, and retrieved the silenced sniper rifle. She examined it, then set it back down and returned to her chair.

She smiled. "I guess you're wondering how I knew about that, Mr. Smith. Well, sir, by the looks of that rifle, you are a professional. You should have paid attention to the sun. I picked up your scope glint from down the street. It appears you were looking at a mutual target, Dakota Reynolds. Is that true?"

Jill was met with a defiant stare and silence. She took a deep breath and blew it out, slowly shaking her head and rolling her eyes. She moved the glass towards his bleeding dick.

"Yes," he barked through the linen gag.

Jill retracted the glass. "Very good. One last question and we're done. Who sent you?"

Smith dropped his head and paused. Behind his back, he had freed his right hand from the pillowcase.

"Mr. Smith, look at me. I will give you one more chance. Now, *answer the fucking question* before I turn you into a eunuch."

Smith looked up as the woman waved the jagged glass in front of his face. He grabbed her wrist and forced the jagged edge into her throat. Blood squirted across his face as she recoiled backwards. He threw a wild roundhouse at her with his left hand and connected solidly to her jaw. She slumped into her chair grabbing her throat with both hands as blood gushed between her fingers, turning her silk shirt crimson. He watched as her eyes glazed and her body convulsed. Her legs jerked violently, then she fell limp.

He bent over and untied his legs, stood up with the chair still attached to him, and retrieved the broken glass to cut the sheets around his torso and free himself from the chair.

He hovered over her motionless body and snarled. "Fucking dumb bitch."

He grabbed the first aid kit from his backpack and moved to the bathroom to stop the bleeding from his dick. After cleaning it and applying two butterfly stitches, he returned to the room to gather the woman's body. He dragged her into the bathroom and placed her in the soaking tub.

He then placed the 'Do Not Disturb' sign on the door, poured himself a drink, and sat on the edge of the bed gathering his thoughts.

Who was she? Why was Dakota her target also? Can I buy enough time, keeping room service out of here, till I finish my job, or should I abort?

He poured a second glass of scotch and stared at the blood stains on the rug.

Did the scuffle alert someone below? Has security or the police been notified?

A noise from the bathroom jolted him from his thoughts. He looked up, and the breath left his lungs involuntarily.

The woman stood naked in the doorway, absent of the bloody wound to her throat. An amused smile greeted his growing fear. "What's wrong, Mr. Smith? You look like you've seen a ghost!" She walked slowly towards him, chuckling as she watched him tremble.

He reached for his bedside table and retrieved a handgun.

Jill raised her right hand and pointed at the drawn pistol. She made an upright motion with her index finger, and the gun flew from his hand. She motioned upward with both hands, and Smith's arms jerked violently over his head. She looked towards the ceiling, and Smith rose from the bed, his feet levitating off the floor, until his hands met an exposed wood ceiling timber. Jill made a hammering motion, nailing his hands fast to the support beam.

He thrashed and kicked and let out an agonizing scream.

Jill chuckled and levitated until face-to-face with him, mocking his scream. "Yell all you want, Mr. Smith, no one will hear you." She returned to the ground and looked up at him. "Hmmm, I have always enjoyed this part. I find it so amusing, the looks on a human's face when they see me rise from the dead. The sudden shock is priceless when they realize their efforts where futile. Now, let's have some fun, shall we?"

Jill made a parting motion and Smith's dress shirt tore from his body. A downward motion ripped his lower garments down. She raised her eyebrow. "Mr. Smith, your package is even more impressive dangling. It's a shame were not here to fuck. I believe I may have enjoyed it. I *am* going to ask you a simple question. How you chose to answer will dictate how much pain you avoid. First, let me give you a little taste to motivate you."

She raised her right index finger. Her nail grew long and pointed. She walked to him, pressed it into his right side, and made a slow horizontal incision.

Smith wiggled like a fish on a hook as he let out an agonizing scream.

Jill looked up, her nail still imbedded in his side. "Oh, that's just the beginning." She made a quick downward slice, grabbed the flap of flesh, and tore it sideways across his abdomen.

Smith screamed in agony.

Jill stepped back and made a mocking *come on* motion with her blood-covered hand. "Get it out, Mr. Smith, and when you're done, I'll ask you a question."

Smith breathed deeply as sweat glistened on his body and tears dripped from his jaw. "What do you want?" he forced out.

"Who ordered the hit?"

"I don't know."

"That's not the answer I wanted." Jill took a step forward, grabbed his dick, and with a quick slice of her finger, fell the member to the floor.

Smith's bloodcurdling screams bounced off the walls as he jerked violently. An audible *pop* shot through the room, and one side of his body sloped lower than the other as his left shoulder morbidly dislocated. Slowly, his screams faded as he began to lose consciousness.

Jill walked to the bar, filled a glass with ice water, and returned to Smith. "No, no, not so fast." She threw it in his face.

He slowly lifted his head.

"Now, so you can see I'm not a monster, just as I can tear you apart, I can heal you." She bent down and grabbed his dismembered dick, placed it to the bloody root, and whispered in an ancient tongue.

Smith looked down and watched as his dick healed.

"Now, answer my question and I'll leave you in one piece and let you move on."

Smith nodded. "It was Howard Sellman, Vincent Dibella's attorney."

Jill nodded and smiled. "Thank you. See how easy that was?" She lifted both hands to his torn flesh across his stomach, again whispered in an ancient tongue, and healed the wound. She then made a downward motion, and Smith lowered gently to the floor.

His knees buckled and he crumbled to the floor. He moved into a fetal position.

"Thank you, Mr. Smith. As promised, I will let you leave here. First, before you do, I want you to meet a few people."

Smith looked up at her, his body shaking, his eyes wide. He watched Jill wave her hand around the room, cleansing it of any sign of blood or struggle. She retrieved her clothes from the bathroom, dressed, and returned to him as he struggled into a sitting position.

"What are you?" he forced out past trembling lips.

"It's not important. Just know that atonement is real."

Jill turned and walked towards the door, but she looked back. "Time for you to move on, Mr. Smith."

Smith watched the door close. He rocked forward and back, his mind numb.

Suddenly, the room darkened as a black mist blocked the midday sun shining through the windows. The smell of rotting funeral flowers filled the air, and whispers, coming from all directions, echoed in the room. His gaze darted from one disembodied voice to the next as dark figures stepped from all four walls. He shook his head violently. "*No, no.*"

One by one, the spirits of the men, women, and children, all bearing the wounds from his bullets and bombs, closed in around him.

He buried his head in his hands and cried, "*Leave me alone!*"

The entities mocked him, their hallowed laughter piercing his mind in a maddening chorus. A sharp pain tore across his chest, and his breathing labored. He dropped his hands to grab his chest, keeping his eyes closed so as not to look his victims in the eyes a second time. He fell to the floor, his face twisted in horror, his mouth wide as his last breath pushed over his lips.

As Jill strolled towards her room, a smile crossed her face and she shook her head.

After two hundred thousand years of evolution, and several reboots, their minds are still so easily manipulated.

Dakota finished with her first afternoon client. She looked at the picture of Jake and her on the edge of the desk and smiled. "Okay, Jake, time to let you off."

Jake answered his phone. "Hey there."

"Hey... about this morning... I overreacted. I'm sorry."

"No, I should have thought a bit more about your ring tone. You know the old saying: boys will be boys. I've changed it."

"Jake, I love your playfulness. I know I mean more to you than a sex toy. Let's just forget about it. I'm meeting Kat and a new girl from the gym for drinks at 3:30. Come and join us."

He looked around the cabin and nodded. "Okay, I've finished what I wanted around here. I'll meet you at the office around 3:15?"

Dakota smiled. "3:15 is perfect. Luv you."

"Luv you too."

Kat and Jill walked into to The Buffalo Nickle. The bar buzzed with people ushering in the weekend early.

Jill said, "Damn, Kat, does this town work on Fridays? I wonder if we can get a table?"

"Don't worry, I know the owner. We have a table reserved in the side room next to the fireplace. Follow me."

The ladies made their way through the hectic main bar and through an open set of rustic double doors. They stepped into a timber-walled room dominated by a large creek stone fireplace.

A rugged-looking cowboy called out from behind a small bar to the right of the room. "Kat, happy Friday."

Kat smiled. "Happy Friday, Les." The ladies walked across the wide-planked pine floor.

Les stepped from behind the bar and gave Kat a hug. "Nice to see you, it's been a few weeks." His deep voice and thick western accent matched his rugged features.

"I've been *so* busy. Les, this is my friend Jill. She's new to town."

Les tilted his dark brown Stetson towards Jill, and his deep blue eyes met hers. "Ma'am, welcome to town, and The Nickle."

Jill nodded and smiled. "Thank you, Les."

Les said, "I have your table saved. Do you want to join me at the bar for a drink before it gets busy in here?"

Kat said, "Sure."

The two women slid a couple of dark wood bar stools out and placed their purses on the aged wood bar top, covered in buffalo nickels under a clear finish.

Jill looked down, and her gaze moved across the length and width of the bar. "This is awesome, Les. How many nickels are there?"

"Four thousand, three hundred and twenty. This is the original bar, which my great-granddaddy built back in 1889. We've added on over the years, but to me, this *is* The Nickle. I used to sit on his lap over there in the corner when I was a little guy. He tended bar till he was almost ninety years old."

Jill looked past Les at a wood-framed mirror that ran the length of the bar, its reflection dulled by antique glass. "I assume that's the original mirror also?"

Les glanced back. "Yep, it's looking tired, but I'll never replace it. I can only imagine the stories it could tell."

Jill panned the walls adorned with advertising tins from years gone by and animal heads, older than many of the customers that sit beneath them. "This is charming, Les. I feel like I stepped back in time."

"Thank you, Jill. Now, what can I get you ladies?"

Kat said, "I'll have the norm."

Les nodded. "Very good, whiskey and a splash of water with four cubes... and Jill?"

"Well, Les, in the spirit of this bar, I'll have what the cowgirl here is having, but hold the water."

"Be right back, ladies."

Jill leaned into Kat. "That is one sexy cowboy."

Kat whispered, "If I ever went back to men, he would be first on my list. Look at that ass in those jeans."

The girls giggled and stopped abruptly as Les walked towards them, drinks in hand.

"Two whiskeys, on me."

Kat said, "Thanks, Les, can you start up a tab, please? Dakota and Jake should be here soon."

Les said, "I haven't seen Dakota since the trial. She's gonna finally bring that man of hers into public,c huh?"

Kat leaned in. "They kinda been keeping it quiet, with his wife and all. That family still has a lot of healing to do."

Les lowered his voice. "Well, it's not hard to figure out, Kat. He's livin' on Jim's ranch, and everyone around here that's known Dakota since she was little could see how she looked at him during the trial. Hell, he saved her life."

Kat nodded. "I know, and it's not like his family lives in town. They wanted to wait till the press left and the story calmed down before they became more public."

Les looked past Kat. "My God, look at the prairie flower the wind has blown into my bar."

Kat and Jill turned to see Dakota and Jake walking across the room. Jill drew a slow, deep breath through her nose. Her insides fluttered as the pheromones of their essence coursed through her.

Les stepped from behind the bar and greeted them. He hugged Dakota. "Nice to see you, counselor. I thought you might have forgotten about us little people, being all over the news and all."

Dakota pulled back from his hug, still holding his arms. "How could I forget about the man who showed me how to tie my first lasso? How's your mom and dad doin'?"

"Cantankerous as ever."

"Les, you haven't met Jake. Jake, this is Les, the owner of the best bar in the west."

Jake held his hand out. "Les, Jake Michaels, nice to meet you."

"Jake, nice to finally meet you in person. Heck, after all that press during the trial, feels like I already know ya."

THE PYRES OF DESTINY

Jake chuckled. "Yeah, they didn't leave too many stones unturned, did they?"

Les shook his head. "No, sir, they didn't. Let me buy both y'all a drink."

The three walked to the bar to join Kat and Jill.

"Hey, girlfriends," Dakota said as she approached.

Kat and Jill stood.

"Jake, you've met Kat. This is Jill Boissonnette. She's new in town."

Jake leaned in and hugged Kat. "Kat, nice to see you again."

He extended his hand towards Jill. "Jill, Jake Michaels, nice to meet you."

Jill's eyes softened. "Jake, nice to meet you."

"Well, let's get this party started," Dakota exclaimed.

The group made their way to the table Les had reserved in front of the gentle burning fireplace. They settled in and placed their drink order with a server.

"So, Jill, what do you think of our little town?" Dakota said.

Jill smiled. "I love it. You all have made me feel at home in the short time I've been here."

Jake said, "Jill, your name is French. It sounds very familiar."

Jill smiled. "If you drink fine wines, you may recognize it. My family owns one of the oldest vineyards in the world."

Kat raised her brow and shot a quick glance at Dakota, who winked back.

Jake chuckled. "That would be it. Yes, I have sampled a *few* bottles of your family's wine over the years."

"Just a few, Jake?" Kat teased.

Jake squinted, cocked his head and smirked. "Maybe more than a few."

The four chuckled.

The server approached the table and placed the group's drinks in front of them. "Can I interest you all in appetizers?"

The group glanced at each other, and Dakota spoke up. "How does four orders of the smoked wings sound to everyone? They *are* the best."

The group voiced their approval.

Kat raised her drink. "A toast to new friends."

"New friends," the foursome cheered.

As the night wore on and the rounds of drinks quickened, the conversation at the table became increasingly comfortable and easy.

Laughter and a feeling of familiarity replaced the uneasiness of new acquaintances.

The server approached. "It's that sad time: last call. Can I get you all anything?"

"Boooo," Dakota said.

Jake put his arm around her and smiled. "Might I suggest Irish coffees?"

Kat chuckled and winked. "You need a little caffeine, Jake, for when you two get back to the ranch?"

Dakota patted him on the knee. "He already got it this morning. I'm going to bed."

Jake shrugged. "I guess the honeymoon's over."

The group laughed. Jill looked at the server, "Irish coffee sounds good."

"Four Irish coffees, it is. I'll be right back."

Kat said, "What's everyone doing tomorrow? The weather looks awesome. How does a hike in the Tetons sound?"

Dakota looked at Jake.

He nodded. "We're in."

Kat looked at Jill. "Tetons?"

Jill exaggerated a pout. "I can't tomorrow. I have to travel to Dallas for the weekend, but next weekend I'm in."

Kat said, "Business on the weekend?"

Jill nodded. "Unfortunately, yes. Some family stuff."

"Well, that sucks," Dakota said.

"I know, but I have a feeling we'll have plenty of time to do things." Jill looked at the group and smiled. "I'm thinking I may stay around here for a while."

The server returned with the coffees.

The band in the main bar finished playing, and a peaceful quiet followed as the lights brightened. The foursome finished their drinks and exchanged '*good evenings*,' calling an end to the night.

In the corner of the main bar, a newcomer to town adjusted the brim of his cowboy hat downward as Dakota's group passed. An ancient amulet hidden beneath his worn black duster gently vibrated against his skin. He lifted his head as Jill exited and swirled the last sip of his whiskey, his eyes narrowing.

It's been a long time, Love.

Jill crossed the Jackson Hole airport tarmac in the chill of the Wyoming dawn. She made her way up the stairs of the redeye flight to Dallas.

A stewardess greeted her at the door. "Welcome aboard, ma'am, enjoy your flight."

Jill smiled. "Thank you."

She settled into her seat and sent a short text message. A quick reply followed, after which she nodded, closed her eyes, and laid her head back.

A couple hours later, the airplane touched down in Dallas.

Jill collected her rental car and drove towards the Dibella ranch.

She pulled up to the guard house at the entrance to the ranch, and an armed guard approached her car.

She rolled down the window. "Jill Harris here to see Mr. Sellman."

The guard glanced quickly into the vacant back seat. "Yes, ma'am, he's expecting you. If you will please pull your car into parking area past the gate, one of our drivers will escort you from there." He signaled the guard shack to open the gates.

Jill followed the escort vehicle across the ranch, past the yellow taped-off, charred main house, to a stately stone colonial home. The escort vehicle stopped in the circular driveway.

Sellman stood on the front porch. A broad smile crossed his face as Jill stepped from her car. "You are a sight for sore eyes."

Jill sauntered towards him. "It's been a while, Howard."

The two met halfway and hugged. Sellman pulled away. "How have you been, Jill?"

She smiled and rolled her eyes. "Like you, it's been pretty fucking crazy, but I'm good."

He chuckled. "Crazy is an understatement. C'mon in. I have breakfast waiting."

The two made their way across the grand foyer to Sellman's office. They settled into a pair of opposing high-back leather chairs at a small, white linen-covered bistro table tucked into an atrium off on the back of the office.

Jill glanced down at two silver-covered plates flanked by mimosas. A crystal vase with fresh picked Birds of Paradise rested centered perfectly between the two settings. She raised a brow. "Very nice, sir."

Sellman lifted his glass. "Cheers."

Jill touched her flute to his, making a perfect musical ring. "Cheers."

Howard took a sip and set his glass down. He leaned back and took a deep breath. "I've known you for some time, and I know you didn't fly in on the spur of the moment to have breakfast. What's the urgency?"

Jill smirked. "Always right to the point, Howard. It's what I like about you. No, you're right. I'm not here on a social visit. I'll spare us both the idle chit chat. I ran into a gentleman in Wyoming, Dubois to be exact. He is, or shall I say *was*, under your employment. Does this sound familiar?"

Sellman shook his head. "No, it does not. I have no interests in that shithole after the Jake Michaels trial."

Jill paused, sipped her drink, and smiled. "Well, under great duress, this gentleman confessed that he was there to carry out a hit on Jake Michaels and Dakota Reynolds, a hit sanctioned by you. Does this ring a bell?"

Sellman's temples flared. "If it was true, what business is it of yours?"

Jill leaned in and locked her eyes on his. "I, and some very powerful people, have a vested interest in making sure both of them are unharmed. I am asking you to please abandon any further attempts on their lives."

Sellman's face reddened. "Our business relationship ended with the debacle at the ranch, and so did any business relationship I had with your people. *I* have a vested interest in making sure that murderer Jake Michaels and his half-breed attorney *do not walk this Earth one more fucking second. I will not* discuss this with you any further."

Jill sat back and glared at Sellman. "This is personal to you, isn't it?"

Sellman stood up. "I would like you to leave, Jill."

Jill raised her finger and motioned it downward. "*Sit down, Howard*, I'm not done yet."

Sellman jerked violently from his feet and crashed back into the chair. His eyes widened and his face paled as his body trembled from the invisible blow.

Jill slid her chair in front of his and leaned in. Her pupils dilated as she locked her soulless eyes onto his. "Do I have your *fucking* attention now?"

Sellman nodded.

"Now, tell me, why do you want them dead?"

Howard's lip quivered. "They killed my sons."

Jill straightened and her brow raised. "*Your* sons? They were Dibella's sons."

Sellman shook his head. "Only by name. He was infertile."

Jill paused for a second, then began to chuckle. Her chuckle turned to laughter.

Sellman barked, "What's so funny?"

Jill composed herself. "Your loins spawned two of the biggest pieces of shit I have seen in millennia." She stood up, walked towards the door, and paused mid-room to look over her shoulder. "Howard, forget about Jake and Dakota. Be smart, make the right choice, and live out your life."

Sellman stared blankly at the floor as Jill's heal taps echoed through the room as she exited. His fists clenched.

After several minutes, he stood and walked from his office to the front porch.

A member of his security force, positioned at the base of the porch, looked back at him. "Mr. Sellman, are you okay?"

Sellman looked in the distance as Jill's car wound its way across the ranch. "Yes, Rick, I'm fine, just a bit shaken by some bad news. Not that this ranch can endure much more."

Jill exited the ranch, drove a few miles, and pulled over. She stepped from the road into the cover of a wood line bordering the ranch, and dropped to her knees. She raised her hands to the sky and softly chanted, "*Hha-lom ya-rey ma-wet.*" The leaves overhead quaked as a cold wind rushed through them. "No, Howard, I will not take a chance on your pitiful vengeance altering my Destiny."

Sellman sat his desk and tried to steady his hands as he poured a glass of scotch. A chill raced through the room with an overpowering odor of flowers. He turned his head to look at the patio doors. They were closed. A movement at the edge of his peripheral vision drew his attention to a closet door, which slowly opened. The smell of burnt flesh, mixed with the putrid smell of rotting flowers, made him cover his nose. His eyes stayed glued on the door as it fully opened.

His entire body deflated as fear gripped him. "*Noooo.*"

The charred corpse of Vincent Dibella stepped from the darkness of the closet. His head remained down as he shuffled across the office.

Dread paralyzed Sellman as the ghost approached. His heart raced with each step forward his dead friend took. Vincent stopped a few feet from the desk and slowly raised his head. Sellman let out a blood-curdling scream as the two faces of the Dibella boys looked back him. A disembodied laugh filled the office.

"What's wrong, Daddy? Don't you miss us?"

The spirit shook its head violently and Vincent's charred face replaced that of his sons.

Sellman closed his eyes and dropped his head. "*Go away. Go away. I didn't mean to kill you.*"

"Howard, look at me," Vincent said in a calm tone. "Look at me, my old friend. It's okay."

Howard opened his eyes reluctantly and slowly raised his head.

The corpse leaped on the table, it's charred face inches from Sellman's, and let out a demonic scream. Dark green smoke rushed from its mouth.

Sellman gasped, breathing in the hot, suffocating cloud, and... silence fell upon the office.

The office doors shook violently. "Mr. Sellman, are you all right, sir? Mr. Sellman?"

The double oak doors burst open, and two security guards rushed across the office towards Howard.

Sellman's face was ashen, his mouth gaping, his eyes wide and fixed in fear. One of the guards placed two fingers on his neck. "He's got a pulse. Call 9-1-1."

Sellman's chest rattled as a wisp of black smoke filled his final exhale.

CHAPTER 31
FACES

Jake opened his eyes and stared at the ceiling. He slowly rolled to the side of the bed, placed his feet on the floor, and grabbed the sides of his head, and grumbled, "Oh man, I'm too old for hangovers." He stood up and stretched.

Dakota smiled as she watched him slowly move from a hunched position to fully erect. "What's wrong, old man, can't hang anymore?"

Jake shuffled across the cabin floor towards the kitchen, looked over his shoulder and smirked. "Hell no. Do you want some water?"

"That would be great. Then we'll go for a run and sweat last night out."

He shook his head and mumbled beneath his breath, "Life with a younger woman."

"What was that Jake?"

"Sounds good."

After returning to the bed with two bottles of water and two energy bars, he sat up against the headboard, downed his bottle, and exhaled forcefully. "That was much needed."

Dakota sat up and sipped her bottle. "So, did you have fun last night?"

"Yeah, Kat is a blast, and the new girl Jill is cool."

Dakota turned towards him. "I really like her. I hope she stays in town for a while."

"Yeah, but... did her face look familiar to you?"

She paused, thought for a second and shook her head. "No, does she to you?"

He squinted and nodded slightly. "Yeah, but I can't place her. Maybe I saw her in a wine magazine or something. Her family is a heavy hitter in that industry."

Dakota shrugged. "Could be."

He yawned deeply and sighed. "So, Miss Energy, what's our course this morning, and how far?"

She placed her hand on his thigh. "I was kidding. We don't have to run this morning."

"No, a run will help. Just give me a second to let this energy bar settle in and we'll go. But take it easy on me in the beginning."

She chuckled, threw her covers off, and quickly straddled him. "Hangover sex is the best. How easy do you want me to take it?"

After a quickie, the two lay back and stared at the ceiling.

Jake caught his breath. "Does that count as a run?"

"Nice try, Mister. That was our warmup."

He closed his eyes and smiled. "I knew you'd say that. Okay, how about we head to that waterfall you like to swim at? Maybe a polar bear plunge?"

"I would love that, but we won't be able to get up to it. The trail will be snow-covered and too dangerous along the cliff edge. We can run the canyon to it, though. It'll be pretty with the snow. That's about six miles down and back. Can you hang?"

He sat up, raised his hands overhead and stretched. "Yep, I'm loosened up know."

Webb Sadler shuffled through Cindy Fowler's autopsy photos, paused at a close-up of her twisted face, and stared deep into her eyes.

What could have scared you so bad?

His phone startled him from dark visions of Cindy's final moments. "Yeah, Steve."

"Webb, we just got word from Texas. Howard Sellman is dead."

"How?"

"No idea. Local medical examiners are on the scene now. But, one thing they reported back to us is that he had a terrified look on his face."

Webb glanced down at Cindy's photo. "Steve, have our ME's get on scene and work with the local folks. I'll get on a plane ASAP."

"10-4, Webb. Oh... one more thing... Sellman's security said a blonde female had just visited him. They said after she left, he appeared shaken."

Webb's brow tightened. "Do they have any video of her?"

"I'm working on that as we speak. From initial descriptions, she sounds like the blonde we saw at the ranch. I'll meet you on scene. I'm leaving DC in an hour."

"Okay. Is Fred flying out with you?"

"No, he got diverted to one of his own cases."

"Very well. I'll see you in about four hours."

Webb tilted Cindy's picture up and shook his head. "Who—or *what*—is she, Cindy?"

He stood up from his desk, grabbed his coffee, and walked onto the patio. He gazed across the sage- and pine-dotted high desert to the base of the Sandia mountains, and followed their snow-dusted, rugged peaks and deep canyon walls to the crest. He took a deep breath, filling his lungs with the crisp pine-scented air.

One of these days soon, we will see each other every day.

He raised his coffee to the crest in a mock cheer.

Webb and a local federal agent arrived at the heavily guarded entrance to the Dibella Ranch. When two Texas Rangers approached their black SUV, the local agent rolled down the dark-tinted driver and passenger windows, and he and Webb flashed their badges.

The Ranger on the driver side said, "Thank you, Agent Hess, we've been expecting you. Please pull through the gate. A Ranger will escort you to the scene."

Agent Hess and Webb followed the escort as they meandered across the property, looking out at the expanse Dibella had owned.

Hess shook his head. "Looks like beef paid well, sir."

Web chuckled. "*Too* well. Makes you wonder."

The duo passed the charred ruins of the Dibella residence, still abuzz with forensic units.

Agent Hess said, "I thought they ruled that an accident. I'm surprised forensics is still there."

"They're not there regarding the fire," Webb said. "It's part of another ongoing investigation connected to the Percovelli case. The fire opened the door for us to move about without a bunch of prying eyes."

Hess raised a brow, pursed his lips and nodded. "Smart. That whole Percovelli case seems like a shit storm. I have friends working on it up there."

Webb snickered. "Shit storm or Hell storm — not sure which one yet."

The lead car made a right turn past the grounds of the main house and arrived shortly at the congested lane to Sellman's residence.

The Ranger stopped his car and walked back to Hess and Webb. "Gentlemen, as you can see, there's not much parking space down there. No need for two more vehicles. We have a space saved for you. I'll radio down to our guys. Good luck."

Hess nodded. "Thank you, Ranger."

Hess maneuvered the SUV down the crowded lane. Both sides were soldiered bumper to bumper with investigation and first responder units from federal, state, and local departments. He pulled into the circular drive of Sellman's house, and a Ranger directed him to a spot in the grass island next to a stone fountain of a cowboy kneeling down and filling his canteen from a pool at the base of a small waterfall.

Hess put the truck in park. "That fountain probably costs more than I make in a year. I guess Dibella paid him well."

Webb stepped from the truck without a response. His eyes darted across the property. *Hmmm, amongst other income, I'm sure.*

He looked at Hess and extended his hand. "Agent, thank you for the ride."

Hess shook his hand firmly. "Do you need me to wait for you?"

"No, but thank you. I have one of my partners flying in from DC. We'll be here for a while. I'll leave with him when done." Webb broke his grip and turned towards the house.

As he approached the steps, an older gentleman stepped from the double doors onto the porch. "Webb Sadler, I heard you were coming down here."

Webb smiled. "After all these years, you still have that shit-kickin' accent."

The two men met halfway up the steps, shook hands, and hugged each other.

"Lou Jackson, I thought you retired five years ago."

"Well, Webb, I did. Then Maggie passed two years ago, and I got bored, so I do some consulting work with the Rangers."

"Lou, I'm sorry to hear that. She was a good woman."

Lou smiled. "Too good for a hell-raising cowboy like me. She gave me the best forty years of my life. How about you, my old friend? How has life been for you?"

"The Bureau's been my life. Unfortunately, I never met that right woman who could deal with my passion to be at their beck and call. In hindsight, at our age, I regret it now, but I can't change it."

Lou patted him on the shoulder. "Well, ole' boy, it's not too late. There's a lot of good women out there our age looking for companionship. You just gotta' step aside from this pile of cow shit we waded in for all these years."

Webb chuckled. "And *this* case is a big pile of cow shit. You have no idea, Lou. We'll talk over one of those Texas-size steaks and some cold beer tonight. So, whatcha got?"

Lou turned and headed up the steps. "It's the damnedest thing. You'll see."

Lou led Webb into an office, where Sellman's body remained sitting behind the desk, covered in a sheet. "We were told to leave the body in place till you got here, but figured the poor bastard deserved some dignity." Lou moved to the side of Sellman and pulled the sheet from him.

Sellman's twisted face and wide eyes looked to the center of the room. Webb's brow furrowed as he walked closer to the body, never breaking eye contact with the now too familiar death stare.

Lou said, "Something scared him to death, literally."

Webb hunched over the desk, lowering himself to Sellman's level, and looked into his bloodshot eyes. "Hmmm." He straightened up and turned towards Lou. "Did the folks that found him report anything strange?"

"They said they heard him screaming, forced the door open, and rushed to him. He had a shallow pulse for several seconds, and then exhaled a puff of black smoke and stopped breathing. They tried to move him to administer CPR while the paramedics were en route, but said he was stiff as a board. I got here well within time before rigor could set in, but he's frozen in place like he's been there for days."

Webb stepped around the desk and reached down to lift Sellman's arm. He yanked Sellman's wrist, attempting to break his death grip on the wood armrests, to no avail. He stepped back and looked at Lou. "He's ice cold. How long ago did they find him?"

Lou glanced at his watch. "'Bout four hours. I was on scene within an hour. His body temperature and lividity would say he's been dead much longer. I ain't never seen anything like it, except in cases of extreme cold exposure. It's eighty degrees outside, and that face.... Any thoughts?"

Webb walked over to Lou, leaned in, and spoke below the earshot of the forensic team in the room. "We'll talk later."

"Thank you," a familiar voice said from behind the two men.

Webb turned and flagged Steve across the room. "Lou, let me introduce you to one of my trusted colleagues, Steve Harris."

Lou extended his hand. "Lou Jackson, nice to meet you."

Steve returned the shake. "Nice to meet you, Lou."

Webb said, "Lou and I go back almost forty years. We went to medical school together."

Steve nodded. "I thought your name rang a bell, Lou. Webb speaks highly of old cases you two worked on. He said you were smart and left the Bureau, to stay put in Texas."

"Yeah, a good woman made me see things differently."

Steve smiled. "I got one of those back in DC. She's trying to make me see the same thing."

Webb said, "I keep telling him to listen to her before it's too late, but he's stubborn."

Steve glanced at Sellman. "What, and miss all this fun?"

Steve broke from the group and walked directly in front of Sellman's desk to look at him head on. He traced Sellman's hollow gaze and took several steps back, till his eyes met Sellman's perfectly. He looked at the distance from where he stood and the corpse, then turned towards Webb and Lou. "Whatever scared him stood right about here, maybe eight feet."

Lou said, "The two members of Dibella's security team that found him said no one entered the room after a blonde female guest left. Sellman escorted her out and returned to his office. 'Bout thirty minutes later, they heard his screams."

Steve said, "And they're sure she left the property?"

Lou nodded. "Yeah, they checked her out at the front gate. The head of the Ranch's security team is a retired Ranger and friend of mine. Dibella only hired the best. They're on point."

Steve looked back at Sellman. "Well, he saw, or *thought* he saw, something."

Webb said, "The two men who found him reported his last exhale expelled black smoke, and his body temperature and rigor would suggest he's been dead much longer than several hours."

Lou said, "Yep, he's stiff as an eighteen-year old's pecker in a whorehouse, and cold as a witch's twat."

Steve and Webb looked at Lou and chuckled.

Webb said, "It's probably best you left the FBI. HR would have had a field day with you these days."

Lou scoffed. "Yeah, no one has a sense of humor anymore. What do you boys think? Should we pry him out of that chair and get him to the morgue. Have y'all seen enough?"

Webb and Steve looked at each other and nodded.

Webb pulled a small camera from his breast pocket. "One second... let me get a couple pics."

Steve said, "Lou, where can I find the head of security. I know they're working on the video to get a look at this blonde."

"C'mon, boys, I'll introduce you to him."

As the trio left the office, Lou paused and motioned over a member of the coroner's office. "Bobby go ahead and get him on the meat wagon and over to the morgue. Let Doc know I'll be over there soon with two members of the FBI forensic team."

"Yes sir, Lou."

The trio walked from the office past the wide, marble, center hall stairs and into a small room to the rear of the home.

Lou said, "We'll be talking with Joe Fleming." He knocked on the door. "Joe, it's me."

The door buzzed open with a heavy metallic click.

Webb glanced at Steve. "That's heavy security for a camera room."

Lou pushed open the metal door and glanced over his shoulder. "It's more than a camera room, gents."

The men stepped into a much larger room than expected. Straight forward, a wall of cameras greeted them. To the left sat a massive oak desk, its face inset with a carved shootout between two cowboys. Two oversized brown leather chairs draped with multicolored horse blankets sat on either side of it. An antique oak and brown tucked-leather office chair sat behind the desk, perfectly framed by a wall decorated with old western rifles and side arms. To the right, modern assault rifles and shotguns occupied the length of the wall.

Joe stood and turned to meet the men.

After Lou completed introductions all around, he said, "Well, Joe, whatcha got on this blonde?"

"Damnedest thing, men... so far, every shot we have of her, she's either looking away from the camera or her hair blocks a clear view. But here's the fuck of it: at the gate, we have cameras that zoom in on guests for facial recognition. Those images are scrambled, as if blocked electronically."

Webb and Steve shot a quick glance at each other.

Webb said, "Did Sellman have cameras in his office?"

Joe shook his head. "No, he didn't want his guests to feel threatened or intimidated, or their business dealings recorded."

Steve said, "Do you know if she ever visited the ranch before? Maybe the main house?"

"Howard alerted us to her arrival and said she was an old friend, but none of the men that saw her recognized her. They said she was a piece of ass and they would *not* have forgotten her. Without the facial recognition pics, it would be near impossible to match her with visitors from the past. This ranch has seen thousands of people over the years. However, she was definitely off the property when we heard Howard's screams. Why the interest?"

Webb interjected. "We believe she may be the same person we have a heavy interest in from the Percovelli ranch. She slipped past us when we raided the place. We had the same issue with the cameras there. We were able to get a good look at her with our drones, only to have those shots lost to technical issues."

Joe spun around in his chair, his brow furrowed. "How would she know how to hack into Percovelli's, the FBI's, *and* our cameras and computers? On top of that, how could she do it so quickly? Almost in real time?"

Steve said, "We don't know, man. Our tech guys are baffled. We're thinking she wore some type of jammer. The only hole in that theory is, in our shots at the ranch, she was nude."

Webb took a deep breath. "Okay, Joe, please let us know if you come up with anything. We'll be in town for a few days."

Joe stood and shook both of the Feds' hands. "Will do."

Lou said, "Boys, should we get some lunch before we head to the morgue? I hate a good autopsy on an empty stomach."

Webb snickered. "You haven't changed a bit."

After Jill's plane touched down in Jackson Hole, she rented a car and drove back to town. She crested the hill on Main Street to see, in the distance, near her hotel, red and yellow flashing lights from multiple police and emergency vehicles.

"Shit," she mumbled.

She approached downtown and was met with a line of traffic backed up in front of a barricade. She inched closer to the officer signaling her to detour, and rolled down the window. "Officer, how do I get to the hotel? I'm staying there."

"Sorry, ma'am, there's been an accident there. Once our crews are done, you'll be allowed back in."

"What kind of accident, Officer?"

The officer waved his traffic wand. "Ma'am, please keep moving."

Jill rolled up the window. "Fucking Great!"

She picked up her phone and dialed Kat.

"Hey, you, how's Texas?"

Jill sighed. "I'm back in town but can't get to the hotel. They say there's been some kind of accident."

"Yeah, some out-of-towner died. My friend from there told me about it. One of the house cleaners found him. I'll fill you in... all kinds of rumors flying around town already. Why don't you come over to my place for dinner, and... maybe some special dessert?"

"Hmmm, what kind of dessert?"

"Use your imagination. See you soon."

Jill chuckled. "You little slut. Bye."

Sheriff Joe Kelly stared into the twisted face of the hotel guest. His eyes panned the room for any clue that would lead to the look of terror on the deceased.

Dr. Sanders clicked her final pictures of the corpse, stood up, and shook her head.

Joe said, "Doc, ever seen anything like this?"

Jessica stared at Mr. Smith's face. "No, Joe. Rigor, lividity, and body temp tells me he's been dead for over a week, but he was just seen by the staff two days ago. And that look... something scared the shit out of him, literally." She glanced at the soiled carpet to the side of his nude body. "There's no sign of trauma or a struggle. What did he see?"

Officer Cooper walked into the room and shouldered-up to Joe and Jessica.

"Joe, our Mr. Scott Smith, as he checked in with, is most likely an alias. The rifle in the closet has all the serial numbers erased, and the same with the handgun in his bedside table. By the looks of the rifle, he built it—all very expensive and very accurate parts. He was a professional."

Joe said, "What the fuck is a hitman doing here?"

Jessica said, "Maybe to settle a score." She walked to the window, pulled the shade aside, and nodded towards Jim and Dakota's law office.

Joe looked past Jessica. "Fuck, just what this town needs, another media circus. Chris, wrap the weapon and put it in the body bag. I don't want any onlookers seeing it. Have security give us a copy of their surveillance videos from the day he checked in till now. Let's see if someone paid him a visit. Run his prints through the system and see who this guy is. Jessica, let me know when the autopsy is done. For now, Mr. Smith had a heart attack."

CHAPTER 32
THE STRANGER

The Stranger stood behind the crowd of curious onlookers gathered around the perimeter of yellow caution tape at the hotel. Two men emerged carrying a stretcher with a black body bag. He tilted his head back slightly and softly inhaled. The familiar odor of pungent dead flowers and sulfur filled his nostrils. He squinted from beneath the brim of his worn black leather Stetson. Under the vinyl, hidden from the onlookers, he could see the twisted face of Mr. Smith, and nodded.

He stepped from the crowd and walked slowly down an alley to the edge of town. He paused there, made sure no one was in sight, and started up a steep twisting trail.

At the top of a granite rock face, stiff Wyoming winds caught his duster, trailing it behind him. In the dusk, his silhouette appeared as if he had wings. He watched below as the parade of emergency vehicles left the hotel, their flashing lights cutting through the birth of the night like beacons at sea. He turned from the commotion and, within a few steps, disappeared into the darkness of a pine forest.

His path turned and twisted below the thick canopy. Moonlight poked through the rushes of the tall, thinner tree tops, and cold winds howled as his journey continued upward. Beneath his feet, the sandy soil gave way to untouched snow. He paused and looked towards the heavens, and focused on a single star. He took a deep breath and continued his ascent.

In the distance, through the thinning woods, a clearing appeared.

He stepped from the edge of the woods and panned the high meadow. Beneath the silvery moonlight, its brown grasses danced side to side in the swirling winds. He moved towards the center of the meadow, pausing to pick up several small stones on his way. Once again, he looked towards the night sky, removed the pendant from around his neck, and briefly raised it upward. He placed the gathered stones in a triangle around him and laid the pendant at the apex, then raised his arms to his sides, and focused again on a single star in the Pleiades.

In an ancient tongue, he prayed. "Father, it is your will that I return to right the wrongs and end the battle. My Destiny is your plan. Grant me the power to do battle with our fallen."

With each word, snow-filled winds howled.

His prayer grew louder. "Grant me the wisdom to see through their lies."

The pines bent under deafening gales. Branches broke and were strewn across the field like arrows.

His gaze never left the darkening skies. "Grant me the weapons to pierce their flesh."

The snows whipped in a circular pattern around the meadow, forming a vortex, in the middle of which the stranger stood. Dark, menacing clouds covered the night sky with the exception of his star.

At the top of his lungs, he yelled, *"Grant me the power to follow my Destiny."*

A bolt of green lightning struck a small rock outcropping on the far edge of the field. Thunder shook the ground and the rocks exploded into the air, leaving traces of brilliant rainbow streaks. Then, the winds died, the ominous clouds gave way to clear heavens, and the blinding snow squalls turned to a gentle flurry.

The Stranger stepped from the triangle, retrieved his pendant, and walked towards faintly glowing coals strewn about the meadow. He knelt to examine the first one, and smiled. As it cooled, he picked up the transformed rock fragment and raised a razor-sharp crystal arrowhead towards the sky. "Thank you."

Rowtag stood on the cliff above the waterfall, watching the swirling storm at the edge of the Sacred Lands. His gaze traced the green bolt of lightning, and he felt the ground shake.

The ancient ones moved from the darkness of the forest into the field below and looked up at him. He stepped from the cliff's edge and descended through the night air to join them. They parted as he passed through them, and then began to follow.

He turned and raised his hand. "I will be back. For now, stay in the darkness."

He walked past the cabin and faded into the forest. As he approached the edge of the Sacred Land, he stopped, remaining hidden in the cover of the wood line. Under the moonlight, a Stranger moved about the meadow.

The Stranger paused his gathering of the arrowheads and shards strewn about the meadow. He must have felt a heavy presence, and slowly turned in a circle, panning the meadow's edge.

Rowtag nodded and stepped from the darkness.

The Stranger's eyes narrowed as he moved towards Rowtag, their glares locked. He reached within feet of the Sacred Land and stopped. The two stood yards apart, motionless.

Rowtag clenched his spear and slowly moved it to his side.

The Stranger peeled back his duster to one side and gripped the bone handle of a long knife hung from his belt.

Rowtag nodded, his mouth twisted in a wry smile as he pulled his spear back, turned, and walked back into the darkness.

He could feel the Stranger watching as he faded from sight.

No, my old friend, that's too easy.

CHAPTER 33
THE HIKE

Kat clenched the bedsheets as her breath quickened and her body arched, and she let out a series of moans and pants. She grabbed the back of Jill's head and gently pulled it away from her. "Please... you're... gonna kill me." She tried to catch her breath.

Jill looked up and smiled. "Nah, just to the edge and back." She moved slowly up Kat's drenched body, licking and kissing her until they were face to face. After a tender kiss on her lips, she rolled to the side of the bed.

Kat stared at the ceiling. "Of all the women, and the few men, I've been with, no one has done that like you. I guess what they say about French women is true."

Jill smiled. "I guess you've never been with an older woman. Eating pussy is like fine wine and wisdom—all get better with age."

Kat rolled onto her side and ran her hand over Jill's hard nipples and taught stomach. "Oh yeah, mid-thirties is ancient."

Jill chuckled. "I just look good for my age. You're a bit off."

Kat sat up. "Ya know, I know nothing about you, other than you come from a wealthy family. Who is Jill Boissonette?"

Jill stretched and smiled. "I'm forty-two thousand years old, give or take a few hundred years. I have walked amongst gods and mortals, and fucked both. I've seen the birth of your kind and will watch the demise of it. I have caused wars, pestilence, plagues, and famines with my womanly virtues... or curses, depending on who you ask. That's pretty much my story."

Kat's brow furrowed and she stared down at Jill in silence. Suddenly, she broke into laughter, then reached into her night side table and pulled out a joint. She threw her leg across Jill's waste, straddling her, and lit the joint. "Well, my ancient one, your womanly virtues are not a curse to me." She took a big hit, leaned over, and slowly blew the smoke into Jill's pursed lips.

They finished the joint and lay entwined with each other.

Jill stroked Kat's long hair. "To answer your question, I'm just a privileged rich girl who hit the lucky sperm lottery."

When Kat's text alert sounded, she rolled off of Jill and looked at the screen. "It's Dakota. She's asking what happened at the hotel and if you're okay?"

Jill said, "That's sweet of her. Yeah, I wonder what that was all about?"

"Yes, she's a dear. Let me text one of my cop bodies and see what happened. Only thing someone I know that works there said, was that they found a guest dead."

Jill raised her brow. "That's a lot of commotion for a dead guest."

Kat rolled her eyes. "Welcome to my town. You should have seen it during Jakes's trial."

"I was gonna ask you about that. I was out of the country for most of it and just caught bits and pieces."

"I'll tell you when I'm not so stoned. I don't want to leave out any details. It was fucking wild here."

Kat hit speed dial on her phone and placed it on speaker.

A male voice answered on the other end. "Hey, Kat, what's up?"

"You tell me, Officer. What's all the craziness at the hotel?"

"Are you alone?"

Kat winked at Jill. "Yep, just me."

"Okay, so they found a guess who appeared to have had a heart attack or something. But what's weird... they found him naked with a look of terror frozen on his face, like he saw a ghost or demon or something."

"Do you know who he is? Is he local?"

"No, not local. That's all I know. The higher-ups are doing their shit. You know peons like me are on a need-to-know basis."

Kat looked at Jill and shrugged. "Well, Terry, sounds like our town might have some more intrigue."

"Yeah, Kat, just what we need. It finally calmed down from the trial. Hey, gotta go, the Sarge is walking towards me. See ya."

"Okay, bye."

Jill said, "A twisted face like he saw a ghost or demon? That sounds a bit dramatic."

Kat rolled her eyes. "That's how the rumors start her. He probably had his mouth wide open. This should get good. By tomorrow, word will be around town they found him in a pentagram with blood strewn about the walls and his face carved up with satanic symbols. Just watch."

"Hey, before you call Dakota back, the weather is supposed to be beautiful for the next two days. Ask her if she has a break in her schedule and wants to go camping in the Tetons."

Kat thought for a second. "There's been a lot of early fall snow in the higher elevations. Where were you thinking?"

"We don't have to go into the Tetons themselves. I love the Gros Ventre area, maybe stay around Slide Lake?"

"God, it's been years since I've been out there. Let me call Dakota."

Dakota's voice responded, "Hey, you, whatcha' doin?"

Kat looked over at Jill and winked. "You don't want to know."

"Hey, Dakota," Jill said aloud.

Dakota chuckled. "Heeyyy, Jill. Never mind, I can figure it out. So, what's goin' on at the hotel? I heard they found some guy lying naked in a puddle of blood."

Kat looked at Jill and mouthed, *I told you.*

"I don't know, honey. All I know is some out-of-towner was found dead, supposedly from a heart attack. Rumors are already swirling. I didn't hear anything from my sources about any blood."

"Ugh, this town and their fucking rumors. Look at all the shit that swirled during Jake's trial."

Kat chuckled. "Yeah, my favorite was he had a pack of wolves in the mountains that were shape shifters, lying in wait to wipe out the town if he was found guilty. You didn't hear half of them 'cause you were tied-up in the trial. Pure friggin' small-town blabber."

Jill motioned Kat with a rolling hand gesture.

Kat nodded. "Hey, the weather is gonna be beautiful for the next two days. How's your schedule?"

"It's light and easily moveable, why?"

"Jill wants to go camping over to Gros Ventre."

Dakota paused for a second. "I know Jake has stuff to do with the network, so... girls only trip. I love it. God, it's been forever since I was over there."

Jill spoke up. "How does Slide Lake area sound, Dakota?"

"Perfect, Jill, I know of a couple great trail's there, pretty tough, so they don't get pounded like a lot of the others."

"That sounds great. Have Kat or you ever been to the hidden caves on the north side of Sheep Mountain?"

Kat said, "I've never been able to find them. Most people believe they're an old folklore, or were closed off when the landslide happened."

Dakota said, "Same here. My great grandfather tells stories of our Ancestors using them as hiding places during the wars, but I've never found them. I don't know of anyone that has."

Jill's lips pouted. "Well, damn, I was looking forward to seeing them. I love caves."

Dakota said, "Well, my great grandfather's stories always have some basis of truth. Doesn't mean we can't look for them. So, what time do you all want to leave tomorrow?"

Kat glanced at Jill and shrugged. "How's seven? It'll take us an hour or so to get to the parking area. Sun will be up by eight and we can start up the mountain."

Dakota said, "Sounds good. See you girls in the morning."

Kat set the phone down and glanced at Jill. "Are you getting hungry?"

With a sly smile, Jill said, "I just ate."

Kat laughed. "Food, silly."

Jake walked through the cabin door. "Well, I hear we have another mystery in town. Your grandfather just told me they found a John Doe in the hotel. He said Jay told him the guy had a look of sheer terror on his face."

Dakota chuckled. "I heard he was found naked with a terrified look. Kat told me he had a heart attack or something, but rumors already have him in a pool of blood."

Jake shook his head. "Poor bastard just got wheeled out in the meat wagon, and he's probably already died a hundred different deaths in town."

Dakota nodded. "Yep, that's our town. By the way, I know you're gonna be busy for the next several days with the network stuff. I'm gonna go camping over to Gros Ventre with Kat and Jill for a couple nights. Are you cool with that?"

"Of course. Have fun. Just let me know the area in case you all get too fucked-up and lost. With those two, I'm sure there will be weed and wine involved."

Dakota smiled. "I'm sure plenty of weed, but wine may be too heavy."

"No, being serious, just let me know. You know how crazy the weather can get."

She walked to him and gave him a hug and a kiss. "I know. We're going to Slide Lake and up Sheep Mountain looking for lost caves. I'm gonna head to the house and start packing. We're leaving at seven in the morning."

He smiled and patted her on the ass as she turned away. "Keep that sexy ass safe. I love you."

She looked over her shoulder. "I love you too. I'll text you a pic of the parking area, and text when we get camp set up, if there's service. See you on Wednesday."

Dakota stepped from her Jeep in front of Kat's house, took a deep breath of the refreshing morning air, and smiled.

"Hey, you," a voice called from the front porch.

Dakota turned. "Jill, good morning. It's gonna be a great day. Look at those blue skies."

Jill looked up. "No matter where I travel, the skies out here seem to have a blue all their own."

"I know. It's as if the Great Spirit created it and threw away the formula."

Kat walked onto the porch with her pack. "Well, bitches, let's find some caves. *Woo hoo!*"

The trio loaded up Dakota's Jeep and started their adventure.

Dakota said, "So, Jill, how was your trip to Texas?"

"It was good, short and sweet. I took care of business and got the hell out of there. I'm not a big city fan, and loathe traffic. I'm a mountain girl."

Kat chuckled. "Yeah, and then you come back to town and get stuck in traffic."

Dakota rolled her eyes. "The next great whodunnit. God, I love our town, but jeez, they can get the rumor machine going quick."

Jill said, "I thought he died of a heart attack?"

Dakota nodded. "Well, he did, but a good friend of mine on the force texted me last night and said there may be more to the story. They're waiting for confirmation on his prints to see who the John Doe is. They recovered a professionally-built, very expensive rifle at the scene."

Kat said, "It's hunting season. There are tons of high rollers coming into town with expensive guns. God, they love to reach for shit."

Dakota said, "Well... supposedly, this rifle had no serial numbers."

Kat pulled a joint out, lit it, and forced out between hits, "So... I guess... we have—or had—a professional hitman in town?" She passed the joint forward to Jill.

Jill drew a deep hit and exhaled. "I love this town more and more each day." She offered the joint to Dakota who held a hand up.

"I'm good right now," she said, "but thanks. Let me drive us there first."

Kat said, "It's my last joint. Sorry we won't have any more."

Dakota looked in the rear-view mirror at Kat and chuckled. "Yeah, maybe the last one you have rolled up. There's probably enough in your backpack to get half of Teton County stoned."

Kat laughed. "Yeah, I have enough that if we got pulled over by the park rangers, we'd all be on our knees sucking dicks to keep us from going to jail."

Jill looked over her shoulder. "Kat, when's the last time you had a cock in your mouth? High school, college? You'll probably skin the poor bastard. Dakota, don't get pulled over. She'll have us in jail for sure."

The girls all busted up.

During a break in the laughter, Kat said, "I'll have you girls know that I gave great blowjobs."

Dakota said, "For real, Kat, when was the last time you were with a guy?"

Kat looked up and rubbed her chin. "Hmmm...."

Jill said, "Oh my God! It was that long ago that you can't remember?"

Kat laughed. "No, I'm just fucking with y'all. It was three years ago. An absolutely gorgeous couple was staying in town, and checked into the gym for a week. After I got to know her a bit, she made it obvious they liked to swing. And girls, these two looked like centerfolds, only hotter. It was one of the best nights of my erotic life. Let's say each of them will remember my 'oral' skills for a long time. So, if I have to switch sides and take one for the team, that park ranger will know he got a blowjob."

Jill said, "God, I hope we get pulled over to watch 'Miss Blowjob' in action."

The girls busted up again.

Kat said, "Hey, Miss Virgin in the front seat, you might let the team down."

Dakota smiled. "Well, I'm the lawyer that will threaten the hell out of them. If that doesn't work, I can hold my own with a hard dick. I may have started late, but I'm making up for the time quickly. I can get Jake off in no time at all now."

Jill said, "Honey, you could get any man off in no time, most by just taking your clothes off."

Dakota pointed to a road sign ahead. "Okay, here's our turn. Enough of the sex talk. We're all gonna be in the mountains with no guys."

Kat and Jill looked at each other and busted out laughing.

Kat said, "Well, you can always join our team for the weekend. I won't tell."

Jill added, "Me either."

Dakota said, "I appreciate the invite, but I'll stay with dicks, thanks. Oh shit, speaking of dicks, the rangers have the check station open. Quick, roll down the windows and air the Jeep out."

Dakota rolled up to the small line at park entrance gate, where a young nerdy-looking Ranger was collecting fees.

Kat said, "Oh, we got this. Dakota, zip down your jacket a bit. Let's have fun with this young'in."

Dakota rolled up to the Ranger, made direct eye contact, smiled, and flipped her hair. "Good morning, Ranger."

The young ranger fumbled with his words. "Good... good morning, ma'am."

Kat rolled down her window and exaggerated her lean to show off her cleavage. "You're busy today, huh?"

"Ahh... ahh... yes, ma'am." The Ranger looked past Dakota and made eye contact with Jill.

Jill stretched and pushed out her chest. "Good morning, Officer."

The young ranger's glasses fell down his nose, and he pushed them up awkwardly. "Good afternoon... I mean morning, ma'am."

Kat said, "No need to call us ma'am. We're almost the same age."

The ranger looked down at his entrance passes. His hands fumbled to pull one apart from the stack. "That will be fifteen dollars, please. Where... where are y'all heading?"

Dakota smiled as she handed him the cash. "We're going to Lower Slide Lake."

The ranger said, "Be careful in the higher elevations with snow. Thank you."

The trio pulled forward and busted out.

Kat said, "That poor guy was shaking."

Jill said, "I bet he'll jerk off tonight."

Dakota said, "Aw, that was mean, but fun."

The girls drove through Grand Teton Park, past the small town of Kelly, and wound their way along the Gros Ventre River to the parking lot at Lower Slide Lake.

Dakota shot Jake a text of the parking area sign, along with: *I love you. Heading to Blue Miner Lake, taking the long trail.*

Kat tossed her pack over her shoulder. "Okay, ladies, let's get this party started."

The women hiked around the north side of the lake and stopped.

Kat said, "Based on the maps, we can take this old trail to the left, and it will eventually connect with the Blue Miner Lake trail. It's gonna be uphill for a while. What do y'all think?"

Jill said, "From what I read, some say the cave system runs from Dubois, through Sheep Mountain, and all the way to the Tetons. Old maps I looked at showed an entrance near the lake. Probably bullshit, but what the hell."

Dakota said, "Actually, there are caves and old mine shafts on my family's property behind town. Every one I've explored ended within a few hundred feet. There's too much seismic activity out here. But, maybe hundreds or thousands of years ago, they were all connected."

Kat stepped towards the old trail. "All right, the old trail it is. We're probably nine miles to the lake."

The trio meandered through pine forests, past wildflower meadows now in their winter slumber, and along rocky ridge lines.

Jill paused for a second and walked from the trail towards an opening in the high mountain forest. "Girls, look at this."

The hikers looked out over the valley below.

Kat said, "Isn't it amazing how different this area is from the rest of the Teton Mountains. The red cliffs remind me of Arizona or New Mexico."

Dakota cocked her head and stepped to the left for a better view. She pointed across the valley. "Look at the mountain to the right of the cliff, the one that drops lower than the others, right above the rush of pines halfway up. It looks like a cave mouth."

Kat and Jill followed her finger.

Kat said, "Oh yeah, good eyes. I see it."

Jill said, "Yep, I'm sure there are hundreds of them in these mountains." She stepped precariously close to the edge of the outcropping and looked down. "I betcha there are openings right below us."

Kat said, "Damn, girl, you're making me nervous. Get back from there. These rocks are not the most stable. Hell, a slide up here in 1925 caused the lake we parked at."

The group pushed forward. Their breathing became more labored as they ascended through nine thousand feet.

Dakota stopped for a second to take a sip of water. "Now... this is a workout."

Kat said, "Yeah, I'm sweating like a pig. That lake is gonna feel good."

Jill chuckled. "It's gonna be cold as hell."

Kat glanced between Jills legs. "Last I saw, there was nothing there to worry about shrivel factor."

Dakota smiled and shook her head. "You *are* a class act."

Kat chuckled. "Yeah, but you love me."

The three pushed on through a tall pine forest.

Dakota pointed ahead. "I think we're close. There's an opening ahead. I can see sage."

The group picked up their pace. They reached the opening, paused, and stood speechless. Below sloping meadows of gold fire weed, opaque green sage, and rushes of tall pines, a Caribbean-colored alpine lake shined like a jewel. The backdrop of red cliffs and rising, dark green alpine forests finished the poster card scenery.

Dakota said, "It's been years since I've been here. I forgot how beautiful it is."

Kat said, "I love this view. Should we set up camp here or down near the water?"

Jill said, "It's awesome up here, but it will be easier closer to the water, with putting out the fire and finding a nice flat spot for the tents."

Kat said, "Good point, plus we'll need rocks for a fire ring. After a dip, we may be happy to be close to a campfire."

Dakota said, "Okay, let's head down and set up camp."

The trio quickly set up camp a few feet from the water's edge.

Kat walked to the lake and bent down to feel the shallows. "Hey, it's not that bad."

Dakota said, "Yeah, in a foot of water. Wait till you get chest deep. Go ahead, strip down and dive in. It's just us back here."

Kat looked back. "If I do, y'all have to also."

Jill looked at Dakota and winked. "Okay, I'm in."

Dakota drew a deep breath. "Me too."

Kat dropped her pack, untied her boots, pulled off her top, and stepped from her pants. "You two better not be fucking with me."

Dakota said, "No, we promise."

Kat squinted at them, pulled off her bra and stepped out of her thong. She placed a foot in the water, then with reckless abandon, ran forward and dove into the azure blue lake. She surfaced looking away from the girls, gasped for breath, and looked towards the beach. "It's amazingly warm. Y'all are gonna be shocked."

Dakota looked at Jill. "Do you believe her?"

Jill half smiled and cocked her head to the side. "I don't know, but we made a deal." She dropped her pack and began to undress.

Dakota looked at Kat swimming around and Jill pulling her hiking pants off. "Oh, what the hell." She quickly caught up to Jill's state of undress. "Are you ready?"

The two women looked at each other, shrugged their shoulders, and stepped from their underwear. They mad a dash towards the water and, without hesitation, dove in.

Dakota surfaced, gasping for breath. "You bitch, Kat. *Holy fuck, this is cold!*"

Jill surfaced, and between catching her breath and laughing, she pushed out, "You cunt, how the hell are you staying in here?"

Kat started laughing. "Dakota forgot I do polar bear plunges every winter. Swim around. It will get warmer."

Jill and Dakota both made a dash from the water to the beach, struggling to find a towel in their pack.

Dakota said, "I hate her, we should have built a fire before jumping in."

Jill laughed between shivers. "I see why you two are friends. She's fun, but a bitch."

Kat stepped from the water and pranced across the rocky beach as if in the tropics. "That was refreshing, huh?"

Both women raised their trembling middle fingers while rushing to get dressed.

Dakota grabbed her phone. "It's almost one. That gives us about four good hours of sun to hike. Should we roll?"

Kat stepped into her pants. "Let's rock."

Jill pulled an old-looking map from her pack. "Based on this, there was an entrance on the south side of the lake. Looking at the rock formations up there, I could see that."

Kat looked towards the towering granite cliffs. "That looks steep from here, but we all have repelling gear, so I say let's go for it."

Jill said, "Based on this map, there's a trail that snakes along and behind the ridge line. I don't think we'll need the gear, but I guess it doesn't hurt."

Dakota moved closer to Jill and looked down at the map. "How old is that thing? It looks ancient?"

Jill chuckled. "Well, based on the date, which you can barely make out, it looks like 1890-something."

Kat walked over to examine the map. "The Henry Mining Company? Where did you find this?"

"I figured I would 'borrow' it from an old book I found in the town library."

Dakota said, "Oh great, we're probably cursed by a dead prospector or something."

Jill waved her hand forward. "Curses, shmurses... that's all bullshit, probably just like this map."

Kat pulled on her pack. "I guess we'll soon find out."

After several hours of strenuous hiking along cliff edges and around large granite columns, the group paused for a break.

Dakota took a deep sip of water and caught her breath. "So far, that map pegged the trail. Maybe we *will* find a cave entrance."

Jill glanced at the map and compared it to the features of the mountain. "Based on this, the cave entrance will be around a switchback, right past that rocky outcrop ahead."

Kat said, "The switchback will take us from the ridge line. How far into the pines does it show the entrance?"

Jill glanced down. "Maybe a hundred yards."

Dakota looked at the sun. "We have about three hours till sunset. Let's check it out. If it's there, we'll head back up here in the morning."

The group stepped onto the switchback.

Dakota said, "Okay, girls, this might be it, a few more yards."

Kat said, "I'll shit if this old map leads us to the caves people have been trying to find for years."

The trio slowed their pace as they surveyed boulder formations, many blocked by trees, shrubs, and tall undergrowth.

Kat said, "We should be right around it."

The hikers climbed around the rock formations, pulling back limbs and brush in hopes of exposing an opening.

After several minutes, Kat said, "Well, if it was here back in the 1800's, it's been closed off now. Or some old miner just played a joke on us."

Dakota took a few steps from the rocks and looked down at a game trail that made its way into thick brush. "Hold on, girls." She dropped to her hands and knees, and crawled into the thick cover. "There's old bear tracks," she called out.

Kat called out from behind. "Dakota, we don't want to fuck with a grizzly. What are you doing?"

Dakota paused and backed up slightly. She turned in the tight confines to face Kat. "Girl, you know they're hibernating now. I bet these tracks lead to a den, or maybe the cave."

"Yeah? And what happens if you're right and wake up a cranky bear?"

"I'll spray it and crawl like hell. Come on, let's at least go a little deeper and see if there's an entrance."

Jill moved next to Kat and knelt. "She's crazy."

Kat started to move forward, looked back, and smiled. "You have no idea. Before the attack, she had *no* fear. It looks like she's getting back to her old self."

Jill shook her head. "Oh well, what the hell."

The two girls followed Dakota's lead. After forty yards, the game trail became less dense.

They heard Dakota calling back back through the brush tunnel. "We found it. We *fucking* found it!"

Kat and Jill picked up their pace and joined Dakota at the mouth of a cave entrance about the size of a café table.

Kat said, "That's a bit small for a fattened-up grizz to get into."

Dakota looked at the ground, stepped to the right of the entrance, and took a few steps. "No, he or she isn't using this entrance. I bet if we followed the tracks, it would lead us to its den. Looking at the dirt in front of the entrance, there are some old tracks, maybe squirrel or badger, but not bear."

Jill pulled out a light and shined it inside the cave. "Girls, check this out."

Kat and Dakota followed the beam deep into an open cavern.

Kat said, "Jill, move it to the right just a bit. Doesn't that look like a passageway?"

Jill squinted, trying to adjust her eyes. "It does. Should we go in?"

Dakota said, "I think we save it for tomorrow. Let's head back to camp. I don't want to mess with that ridge in the dusk."

The excited trio agreed and made their way off the mountain.

As dusk gave way to night, the girls settled in around the fire.

Dakota leaned back in her camp chair. "These chairs were the best thing ever created. Remember when we were younger and you'd sit on the ground, or propped-up against your backpack?"

Jill reached into her pack. "Yeah, they weigh less than this bottle of wine."

Kat smiled. "Nice! Is that from your vineyards?"

Jill uncorked the ornate bottle, and notes of plum, cedar, and vanilla danced on the light winds swirling around the camp. "Of course. I can't increase the revenue of the competition. This is one of my favorite merlots from 1987. I hope you both enjoy it."

Dakota inhaled. "It smells delightful."

Kat pulled a joint from her cargo pants pocket. "This will smell delightful also."

Jill passed three tall glasses of wine around and lifted hers. "Cheers, bitches."

Dakota said, "Cheers to our new friend."

Kat, holding in her hit, forced out, "Cheers," before covering the fire ring with a plume of smoke.

Dakota's eyes widened. "Damn, girl, all that cardio gives you great lung capacity."

Kat laughed and passed the joint to Dakota. "Here, beat that hit."

The trio finished the joint and refreshed their wine. The conversation was relaxed and focused on the day's hike and the excitement of going into the cave.

Dakota stared into the dancing flames, then up to the clear night sky, and a peaceful smile painted the contentment on her face. "This is great. It's been a while since I did a girls-only camping trip."

Jill said, "It's been years for me. I haven't really had friends that I would want to spend time in the mountains with."

Kat said, "Really, Jill? All the people you know around the world, and you have no close friends? What about girls you grew up with?"

Jill shook her head. "The world of privilege is not what most think. It's often very lonely."

Dakota said, "I assume it's the same for finding a soulmate? You're so beautiful. How do you not have a dashing rich man or model girlfriend by your side? Surely, there have to be some good people in your circle around the world?"

Jill stared into her wine as she swirled it. "There was a man, a long time ago. We were friends since childhood. I adored him and he me. I was certain I would spend eternity with him. But our worlds drifted apart. He made a decision that tore my heart to shreds. After I rebounded, I buried myself in the family business and swore I would never be hurt like that again."

Kat scoffed. "Guys can be such dicks."

Dakota, sensing the mood turning somber, said, "Yes they can, but here's to their *hard* dicks."

Jill looked up from her wine, chuckled, and lifted her glass. "To their hard dicks. Use them and lose them."

Kat raised her glass. "Well, I won't cheer to hard dicks, 'cause I don't really care if I ever see another one. But, if y'all like them, cheers."

The group changed the subject. As the wine and weed flowed, their conversations became sillier and meaningless.

Dakota glanced at her phone, trying to focus on the time. "It's almost midnight. What time do you guys want to leave in the morning?"

Kat slurred, "It's about a two-hour hike or so, and it would be cool to spend time in the cave, if that was a passage. I say first light."

Jill nodded. "As much as I don't want this night to end, I say we get some sleep. I'm not sure about first light."

Dakota stood up and wobbled. "No, definitely not first light. Goodnight, bitches."

Kat rolled from the low camp chair and crawled towards her tent. Between laughs, she muttered, "Fuckin' wine! Goodnight, bitches."

Jill watched the two girls zip their tents shut, then stood and quietly strolled from camp to the lake. She moved a few rocks around and knelt on the shore. With eyes closed and arms outstretched, she whispered in an ancient tongue. Her body tensed as she traveled from the physical world to the gardens of the mountain mansion.

Dorian approached her. "How is our plan coming along?"

Jill said, "I have her on the mountain. Tomorrow we will enter the caves."

Dorian smiled. "Soon, our ancient journey will end, and a new one will begin."

Jill reached out and touched his arm. "We *will* inherit what is ours, Dorian."

Jill's body jerked. She opened her eyes and stared for several moments into the darkness of the lake. She reminisced about the past week in town, and a smile crossed her face as she thought about Kat, and Dakota, and their trip to the lake. Bringing *him* up again made her reflect on memories absent for so long, buried beneath the filth, perverseness, and depravity she'd wallowed in for millennia.

Is there a piece of humanity left in me?

She cleared her thoughts, took a deep breath, and returned to camp.

Kat cried out from her tent. "Oh, my God! My fucking head hurts."

Dakota's eyes sprung open as the sun peeked through the vents on her tent. She fumbled for a bottle of water and downed it, and a welcome smell caught her attention.

She rolled forward and unzipped the tent entrance to find Jill crouched over a morning fire. "Is that coffee I smell?"

Jill looked back. "Good morning, sleepy head. So much for first light, huh?"

Dakota fumbled for her phone. "Shit, it's almost eight o'clock. *Kat, wake up!*"

Kat and Dakota dressed quickly and joined Jill at the fire ring.

Jill smiled and shook her head. "You two look like hell."

Kat grabbed the sides of her head and nodded towards the two empty bottles of wine lying besides Jill's chair. "What kind of wine was that? I've never got that drunk off of four glasses."

"I told you, it was a very special vintage. We never released it for sale."

Dakota grabbed a second bottle of water and downed half of it. "I can see why you never released it. Damn, that shit had a kick. How do you look so good and feel so chipper?"

Jill pulled the coffee pot from the flame and chuckled. "Honey, I've been drinking our wine since I was a kid. I guess I have a tolerance for it. You should taste some of the older wines in our private collection."

Kat paused between chugging a bottle of water. "No thanks. I'm sure they're good, but I'll pass."

The trio made quick work of the coffee and breakfast to follow. Within the hour, they were on their way out of camp.

Dakota led the way with Kat and Jill following.

Jill thought about her visit with Dorian in the realm last night, and their plan. She knew Kat was a liability that could not stand in her way, and that there was a sharp incline ahead and a trail that hugged dangerously close to the edge of a cliff. She listened as her new friends laughed and joked, and her mind raced.

Now is not the time to be weak. It has taken millennia to reach this point. We have never been closer. Execute the plan.

She took a deep breath and shook her head.

No, not this way, not this time.

She starred at Kat's right knee and whispered, "Ssha-ma a-do-nai, hhul."

Kat buckled. *"Fuck."*

Dakota turned quickly and moved to her bent-over friend and Jill raced forward.

Dakota said, "Kat, what's wrong? Are you okay?""

Jill said, "What happened, Kat?"

Kat held her right knee and grimaced as she writhed in pain. "Oh, it's an old fucking injury. I guess I hit that rock wrong. *Fuck, fuck, fuck.*" She stood up and stretched her leg out. She put some weight on it and took a few ginger steps. "It'll be all right, but I can't make the climb. You two go ahead. I'll hobble back to camp and wrap it."

Dakota said, "No, we'll come back to camp with you and get you back to town."

Jill nodded. "I agree. Let's get you to a doctor."

Kat shook her head. "No, seriously, you guys, it'll be fine. I've tweaked this thing a dozen times over the years. A couple days of rest and a wrap and it'll calm down." She pointed her head towards a dead tree off the side of the trail. "Look, there's a perfect cane to help me get back to camp. Now go, and take some pics for me."

Jill and Dakota looked at each other, then back at Kat as she hobbled over to the fallen tree.

She broke a waist-high limb from it. "Look... perfect... now get out of here. I'll be fine. It's only a hundred yards or so back to camp." She turned and started to hobble back down the trail.

Jill said, "What do you think?"

Dakota shrugged. "She's stubborn as shit and will harass the hell out of us if we don't go."

Kat turned and looked back over her shoulder. "Sound travels well up here. I can hear you two. Now, start climbing. I'll have dinner ready when y'all get back."

Dakota shrugged. "Let's do it."

After several hours, Jill and Kat stood at the entrance of the cave. They reached into their packs and retrieved their headlamps.

Jill said, "How much rope do you have?"

Dakota pulled out a coil of braided orange nylon. "I have a hundred feet, how about you?"

Jill retrieved her rope. "The same, but I doubt we'll need it today for climbing in there. We can use it as a trail line. If this is indeed the cave system, we'll come back more prepared."

Dakota pulled out a cylinder of twine. "We won't even need the rope for a trail line. I've got almost twenty-five-hundred feet."

Jill raised her brow. "Wow, I'm impressed. You must have believed we'd find these caves."

"Well, I know there are caves all over these mountains. I wasn't sure we would find the 'Hidden Caves,' but figured we'd find a cave. Should we do this?"

Jill turned on her headlamp. "Let's do it. You lead."

CHAPTER 34
STRIKE FOUR

Officer Cooper knocked on Joe Kelly's doorframe.

Joe looked up from a report on his desk. "Come in, Chris."

"Joe, we have a fingerprint match on our Mr. Smith."

"Oh good, I assume he's not 'Mr. Smith'?"

Cooper shook his head and placed the report on Joe's desk. "Far from it."

Joe looked at the picture matching the prints and thumbed through the three-page file, skimming over bullet points on the profile. He glanced up at Cooper and redirected his attention back to the first page. "What the hell was the head of an international, private, paramilitary firm doing in town?"

Cooper shook his head. "And why did he check in under an alias?"

Joe's brow wrinkled. "And a professionally built rifle with no serial numbers? Chris, reach out to the FBI folks in Jackson. Has anyone else seen this?"

"No, I ran the prints myself."

"Good, let the Feds handle this one. They'll be a bit more covert about it. This place is finally getting back to normal. We don't need another media circus. Let's get his body turned over and out of town as quick as possible."

Webb sipped his coffee and looked at photos strewn about his desk, and the twisted faces of Cindy Fowler, Joseph Percovelli, and Howard Sellman stared back at him. A phone ring startled him. "Damn, I have to turn that thing down."

He looked at the number. "Hey, Steve, anything new with the surveillance from Sellman's people?"

"No, Webb, but we have another body. I just got a call from our Wyoming office. It appears Salvatore Ricci was found dead in a hotel room in Dubois. I'm forwarding photos taken at the scene to your fax as we speak."

Webb heard the fax. "They're coming over now." He watched the machine slowly feed the first picture out, starting from the top of Ricci's head. His eyes narrowed as the fax displayed more facial features. He remained speechless as the second and third photos finished printing.

"Steve, do we have the body?"

"No, the local morgue does."

"Okay, have our field agents arrange for the body to be sent to Cheyenne. Who is my point of contact in Dubois?"

"Sheriff Joe Kelly."

"Please reach out to him and let him know I'm arranging a flight into Jackson Hole ASAP. Text me his number, and have one of our local field agents standing by to pick me up. What the hell is this all about, Steve? That's four victims now in a matter of weeks."

"I don't know, Webb. Do you want Fred or me to join you?"

"No, you guys stay focused on what you're both doing, and keep me posted. I'll handle this myself, for now."

"Roger. Have a safe flight."

Webb added the Ricci photos to the group on the desk, stepped back, and panned over the twisted faces. "Whoever you are, this ends here."

Webb's plane touched down in Jackson Hole early afternoon. As arranged, a field agent met him. He called Joe Kelly to let him know he would be in town shortly.

Webb walked into the Dubois Sheriff's Station.

An officer at the front desk greeted him. "Yes, sir, can we help you?"

"Webb Sadler to see Sheriff Kelly."

"Oh yes, sir, he's expecting you. His office is the second one down the hall on the right. I'll let him know you're here."

"Thank you, Officer."

Webb turned and took several steps down the hall.

The sheriff stepped from his office to greet him. "Agent Sadler, Joe Kelly." He walked towards Webb with an outstretched hand.

"Sheriff, nice to meet you."

Joe turned towards his office. "Please come in. Can I get you something to drink—water, coffee?"

Webb smiled. "Actually, a black coffee would be great."

"You're in luck. I just put a fresh pot on. Please have a seat, make yourself at home."

Webb settled into a brown leather low-back chair before Joe's desk, and panned the office adorned with western motif, and proof of years of successful hunts mounted on every wall. "It looks like you've been in this office for a while, Sheriff." He admired a bull elk mount.

"Twenty-two years, and a total of twenty-nine with the Sheriff's Department. One more to go and I'm retired. How about you, Agent Sadler?"

Webb smiled. "Forty years with the bureau."

Joe nodded and handed Webb his coffee. "I thought you boys can retire after twenty-five?"

"We can, and I did. I made it six months and was bored to tears. Unfortunately, I never slowed down to marry, so there was nothing to retire *to*."

Joe nodded and slid a folder of photos taken at Ricci's death scene. "I guess shit like this can keep your attention for forty years. You ever seen anything like it?"

Webb hesitated. "No, I haven't."

"What do you suppose a guy like Salvatore Ricci was doing in Dubois, checked in under an alias?" Joe spun in his chair, unlocked a steel gun safe, and retrieved a rifle tagged *'evidence.'* He placed it on the desk. "And why the hell would he have a rifle like this, with no serial numbers on it?"

Webb's eyes narrowed. "I didn't see this in your initial report."

Joe shook his head. "No, as soon as I decided to turn this case over to the Feds, we elected to keep facts quiet. Small towns have a way of blowing things out of proportion."

Webb picked up the rifle and examined it. "Italian made, perfectly balanced, high end scope, Bartlein long barrel. Let me guess, 338 Lapua Magnum ammo?"

Joe nodded. "Six rounds recovered on scene. We found that a bit light if he was out here to go hunting."

Webb placed the rifle back on the desk. "I guess he wasn't planning on missing. Any prints on the gun except his?"

"No, just his."

Webb nodded. "I appreciate you deciding to let us handle this." He looked back at a picture of Ricci lying on the hotel floor. "Can I see the hotel room?"

Joe stood. "Sure, it's a short walk, if you don't mind stretching your legs a bit."

"Not at all. It's a beautiful day out there."

The two men walked briskly to the hotel, took the elevator up, and walked into the west corridor. Webb stopped halfway towards Ricci's room, and panned up and down the hall. "Plenty of camera's here. Have you looked at the footage to see if anyone came in or out of the room around the time of death?"

Joe held his finger to his lips, then motioned Webb forward. They entered Ricci's room, and Joe closed the door behind him. "I talk loud, and these walls have ears. The hotel has permanent residents. We have checked, and he had no visitors, including staff. As for the day of death, the body has our Medical Examiner baffled. We know he was alive two days before he was found, but the body displayed signs of advanced rigor and lividity, more like a week old or so."

Webb's brow wrinkled. "Hmm... interesting." He looked down at the area the body was found, where a chalk outline remained, then panned the room. He walked over to the window, pulled the blinds aside, and looked across the street. He closed the blinds and turned. "I'd like to see the body."

Joe nodded. "I'll call our M. E. right now."

"Also, Sheriff, I'd like to have any camera footage from the day he checked in, to the time of discovery, from both the corridor and the main lobby. Also, a list of all guests that checked in from a week before to right after Ricci did."

"No problem. It's the off season, so that list will be short."

"By chance, have you seen or heard of any strangers in town that may stand out?"

Joe thought for a second. "Only one that comes to mind is a striking blonde that's been seen in town hanging out with Kat Graziano, the owner of a local gym, and Dakota Reynolds, the attorney across the street. Word has it she's an heiress to a major player in the wine industry. She quickly joined the rich girl club when she got here."

Webb's ears perked, but he kept a poker face. "Where has she been staying?"

"Here in the hotel."

Webb nodded. "Okay, well, if 'Mr. Smith' died of other than natural causes, I'm sure his killer is long gone. Let's go look at this body."

The men made their way back to the station, retrieved Joe's cruiser, and took a short ride to the morgue.

A woman in a white lab coat met the two men as they entered the basement of the local hospital.

Joe said, "Agent Webb Sadler, meet Dr. Jessica Sanders."

She extended her hand. "Agent Sadler, nice to meet you."

Webb bowed his head slightly. "Dr. Sanders, likewise."

The doctor smiled politely. "If you gentlemen would please follow me to the prep area, we'll get dressed and head in."

The trio donned their lab coats, masks, and gloves, and entered the autopsy area.

Joe rubbed his arms. "Damn, Jess, you have it cold in here today."

"It's not me, Joe. Something's messed up with the system. Let's just keep our fingers crossed the meat boxes don't stop working. The last thing I need is a bunch of stinky corpses."

Webb chuckled. "How busy could you be in this small town."

Dr. Sanders said, "Agent Sadler, between an aging community and way too many alcohol and drug deaths on the reservations, my coolers stay full."

She walked the two men to a separate exam room, generic and sterile in appearance. In the middle stood a stainless-steel autopsy table. She pulled the sheet down on the body of Salvatore Ricci.

"Agent Sadler, have you ever seen anything like this?"

Webb leaned forward a bit and focused on Ricci's twisted face. "No, Doctor, this is very interesting."

She said, "I would love to cut into him, but I understand he's going to your M.E. in Cheyenne. Why do the Feds have such an interest, if I may ask?"

Webb straightened and without hesitation said, "Mr. Ricci has professional connections with our government and others around the world. We want to make sure this was indeed natural, and if not, kept under wraps for now."

Joe scoffed, "There's nothing natural about that face."

Webb reached down and pushed up on Ricci's wide-open jaw. "Hmm... frozen solid."

Dr. Sanders said, "Yeah, rigor and lividity is much more advanced than should be. My first thought was Mr. Ricci may have a strange pathogen or drug in his system that could have caused this."

Webb raised a brow and looked up from Ricci. "Doctor, I think that is an *excellent* hypothesis. I've seen enough. Our team will be here in the morning. If you would, please have him bagged and ready to go."

"No problem, and if possible, when your team is done with their exam, could you reach out and let me know what they find. I'm super curious."

Webb reached his hand out and smiled. "I promise, I will. It's been a pleasure meeting you."

The two men settled back into Joe's office.

"Agent, are you staying in town long?"

"Please, call me Webb, if first names are okay with you. Probably long enough to get the tape from the hotel and the guest list. It's been decades since I've been in Yellowstone. I might take a few days personal time and do some sightseeing."

Joe smiled. "First names are fine. I've heard Sheriff enough in my lifetime. I was starting to think it was my name." His smile turned to a grimace. "As for Yellowstone, sorry, but it's closed for the winter. The Tetons are open, but I do know a few of the Park Rangers at Yellowstone. If you decide to stay for a while, I can hook you up with them. They'll give you a great tour of the park void of tourists, providing we don't get a freak snow storm roll through. Then they'll be busy with snowmobilers."

Webb nodded. "That would be great, Joe. I appreciate it. I'll let you know. It's getting late, time for you to get home. Where can I get a good steak in town?"

"Well, the hotel does a good job. Where are you staying?"

"Down at the end of town at the Tumbleweed motel."

Joe laughed. "The Feds cutting back on travel expenses?"

"Why, is it a flea bag?"

"Nah, it's not bad, just not as nice as the hotel. Do you need a ride?"

"Thanks, but I'll walk. I should have a car waiting there."

Webb checked into his room. Before unpacking, he called Steve.

"Yeah, Webb, how's it going there?"

"Ricci had a sniper rifle, no serial numbers. His symptoms are identical to the other three. Also, our female of interest may be out here."

"The head of a powerful private international security firm with a fucking scrubbed sniper rifle, *and* our mystery blonde, in a small Wyoming town? Where the hell is this leading?"

Webb sighed. "I don't know with Ricci. As for the female, the sheriff described her as a striking blonde. She's telling people she's an heiress to a major player in the wine industry. She's also staying at the same hotel Ricci was staying at. The sheriff said she's been seen with the female owner of a gym in town, and the female attorney who represented Jake Michaels in the Dibella boys' case."

"Do we have a name yet of the blonde?"

"No, I'm waiting for a list of guests. But if it *is* our girl, why would she still be in town after Ricci's death... and not maintaining any anonymity? I doubt it's her—most likely a coincidence."

"Hell, at this point, we can't let any stone go unturned."

"I agree, and if it is her, why Ricci...? Wait, do me a favor. Reach out to Fleming and ask him if Ricci ever visited there, either with Sellman or Dibella. Also, scrub the files at Percovelli's place. See if Ricci's name shows up."

"What are you thinking, Webb?"

"Maybe a stretch, but Ricci's hotel room window faced the office of Dakota Reynolds. Also, the Medical Examiner here brought up a good point. Could the twisted faces and advanced morbidity of our victims be a result of a pathogen or drug given to them?"

"Biological agent?"

"It's a reach, Steve, I know, but an angle I never thought of, especially since toxicology reports on Cindy, Percovelli, and Sellman turned up nothing. But, we only ran panels on common substances."

Steve paused for a second. "Okay, let's assume Ricci did have recent contact with Sellman or Dibella, and had connections to Percovelli. Why is he in Wyoming with a sniper rifle? Was his target the attorney? Are we looking at a revenge motive? And, why does he suffer the same death as the others?"

"Dakota Reynolds crippled the Dibella empire. Vincent died in a *very* suspect gas explosion. We know his boys were connected to the Percovelli sex trafficking ring, and they're dead. Percovelli is dead, and his trafficking ring has compromised a shitload of powerful rich people connected to it. Now Ricci is dead before he can carry out a possible hit. The two common denominators are the attorney and our mystery blonde."

"Let's say you're right.... Why the massacre on the mountain? How did Cindy and Kelly fit into it?"

"They were working with us, and most likely were killed to make sure they couldn't finger any powerful players during a trial. Why Cindy's face was twisted, and the others on the mountain weren't, is a bit of a mystery, but it could lead back to perhaps she was administered the pathogen before leaving the ranch. One thing we can't *truly* determine is whether the facial contortion happened prior to death or post mortem."

"Webb, you're making my friggin' brain hurt. How the hell did you come up with all of this in the matter of a few hours in Dubois? Never mind, that's why you *are* the best. So, drawing the connections between the deaths, could we have two women working in tandem?"

Webb thought for a second. "You know, Steve, I *didn't* think in that direction. If I can remember correctly, the attorney was raped and filmed by the Dibella boys. Our blonde may have endured who-knows-what humiliation as she worked her way up the ranks with Percovelli. Maybe they're both out to right their wrongs, or maybe it's all coincidence."

"Let's say we have a duo of femme fatales, either working together or separately.... How did they know about and get to Ricci before he could pull the trigger?"

"I don't know. Before we dig deeper into this line of thought, let's see if Ricci had connections to Dibella and Percovelli. I'm gonna get an early dinner and poke around town a bit tonight. I'll talk to you in the morning. Have a good night."

Steve chuckled. "Thanks, I should sleep like a baby after all this shit you just laid on me."

CHAPTER 35
THE CAVE

Dakota tied an end of the twine to a thick vine at the entrance of the cave and placed the spool on a roller attached to her pack. "Are we ready?"

Jill turned her headlamp on. "Let's see how far this goes. I say we head towards the passage Kat thought she spotted yesterday."

"I agree. Hopefully, it wasn't just a shadow."

The girls panned the cave with their headlamps as they moved deeper.

After twenty yards or so, Dakota pointed. "There it is."

Their pace quickened on the sandy bottom as details of the opening became clearer. They stood at a slit passage in the granite walls.

Dakota stepped inside, spread her arms, and looked up. "I can reach the sides, and this must go up forty feet."

Jill followed her gaze upwards then looked forward. "I hope it's this big for as long as it travels under the ground."

Dakota said, "How the hell after all these years could someone *not* find this entrance?"

Jill shrugged. "Maybe it's like you said, and just one of many caves in these mountains, and *not* the legendary one."

Dakota chuckled. "Buzzkill, you just crushed my dreams."

Jill stepped past the opening. "C'mon, Indiana Jones, let's hope I'm wrong."

They meandered down the generic passage.

Dakota paused, took a drink, and looked down at her spool. "It looks like we're about a quarter-spool in, so maybe three hundred yards, give or take. Pretty boring so far."

Jill nodded, then cocked her head, squinted, and raised one finger. "Wait, do you hear that?"

Dakota concentrated. "No, hear what?"

Jill shined her headlamp up. "It sounds like a trickle of water, towards the ceiling on the right."

Dakota followed Jill's beam. "I don't see anything or hear it. Maybe around the bend up ahead?"

The spelunkers pushed forward, making their way around a sharp right bend, where a split in the passage greeted them.

Dakota said, "I can hear the water now. It sounds like its coming from the right passage. Which way do you want to go?"

Jill looked down at her compass. "If we go right, that would head towards the Tetons, which, based on myths, could lead us to the Hidden Caves. But we would have to drop deep under the valley to connect back to the mountains."

Dakota thought for a second. "And if the left passage follows the spine of the mountain, it could also lead there. I don't know. It's your call. Regardless, we can only go as far as our line allows us."

Jill said, "Good point. I guess we can head towards the sound of the water. If nothing else, maybe we'll find a subterranean lake. That would be cool."

"Oh my God, Kat would be *sooo* jealous. I could see her running and stripping as fast as she can to dive in."

"Yeah, she's not bashful, is she?"

Dakota chuckled. "Ah, no, she never has been, for as long as I've known her."

"Well, let's head right then. We'll go as far as the twine allows us."

As the two walked down the narrowing passage, tall ceilings gave way to head-high clearance. At points, the walls closed in enough to force the girls to turn sideways.

Dakota dropped to her hands and knees to avoid a rock wedged in the passage. "This is starting to become like work, and a bit more dangerous. This rock looks like it separated from the wall. But the water ahead sounds like a bit more than a trickle."

Jill followed Dakota under the boulder. On the other side, the two stood hunched over in the shrinking passage.

"What do you think?" Jill said.

"Well, we have plenty of twine. I say we push on for a bit more. The water thing has me intrigued."

Jill nodded. "Let's do it."

The passage took a less direct path and moved downwards through a series of switchbacks. Its bone-dry walls now seeped in places, and the sound of trickling water gave way to a pronounced babble, echoing from the passage ahead.

Dakota paused, turned off her headlamp, and refocused her eyes. "I see light up ahead."

Jill said, "Light.... How could light reach down here? It seems like we've been going deeper and deeper."

Dakota switched her lamp back on and looked at the spool. "I have no idea, but we have maybe a hundred feet or so of twine to find out."

The girls continued forward. They made a sharp left turn and stopped dead in their tracks at the edge of a cliff.

Dakota stood slack-jawed. "Oh... my... God." Her eyes fixed on a single beam of sunlight and a small waterfall from an opening in the cave's ceiling, hundreds of feet above them. Rainbow mist from the splash of water into the lake below created a dreamlike tranquility.

She pulled a flashlight from her pack and shined it past the tight area the sun beam illuminated. "Jill, look, the stream runs down another passage. I wonder if it feeds Blue Miner Lake?"

"Honestly, I think we're below lake level, but I could be wrong."

Dakota looked up at the sun-filled opening and shielded her eyes. "You might be right. My great grandfather said our ancestors told stories of an ancient river buried deep in the mountains that carried the waters of eternal life. They believed that, once white man came and spilled their blood on our lands, the waters were ruined forever."

Jill smiled. "I love the stories of your people. They are romantic, but always end with tragedy because of the white man."

Dakota chuckled. "You should meet my great grandfather. Sometimes, I believe he puts his *white man* spin on all the old stories of my people."

Jill said, "Well, aren't you half white?"

Dakota nodded. "Yeah, but since it's me, it's okay with him. Hell, half of his best friends are white. He just likes to bloviate."

Jill looked down at the water below. "Should we look for a way down?"

Dakota looked at her watch. "We have a few minutes. We need to take a pic of us standing in the water for Kat." She shined her light to the left and right of the cliff edge. "I think we can hug the wall to the left."

The girls shuffled along a remarkably wide ledge that followed the chamber's wall and gradually dropped to the lake.

Jill said, "That was almost *too* easy. Maybe your great grandfather is right."

Dakota bent over and waved her hand through the clear water, looked up, and winked. "Maybe."

Jill bent down next to her. "God, it's like ice. I'd like to see Kat jump in this."

Dakota cupped the water and slowly drew a sip. "It's got a sweet but mineral taste. Maybe we found the waters of eternal life."

Jill smiled. "Could be." She turned and walked along the bank. *Immortality... a curse the children of humanity are too weak to endure.*

Dakota said, "Hey, the sun beam is moving closer to us. Let's get a pic for Kat with it shining in the water behind us, then head out."

Jill slowly turned, closed her eyes, raised her hands to her side and whispered in an ancient tongue. "Ka-hhad leesh-kah."

Dakota smirked. "What are you doing, Jill, praying?"

Jill's whisper grew loader and demanding. "*Ka-hhad leesh-kah... ka-hhad leesh-kah.*"

"Jill, you're scaring the shit out of me."

"*Ka-hhad leesh-kah.*" The earth rumbled. "*Ka-hhad leesh-kah.*"

"*Jill, what the fuck?*"

Jill's incantation echoed off the cavern walls and the chamber rumbled violently. Waves from the once tranquil lake crashed on the shores, and the deafening thunder of falling rocks shook the ground and buckled Dakota's knees. Then... silence.

Dakota looked up, her eyes welled and lips trembling, as Jill's outline glowed against the pitch-black cave. "*What* are you? *Who* are you? What do you want from me?"

As Dakota watched Jill move towards her, her great grandfather's words raced into her mind. *'In their world, do not show fear. They pray upon it.'*

Jill made an upward motion. "Stand, Dakota, look about the cave."

Dakota struggled to her feet and panned the dim light of a green hue cast by Jill. A chunk of the cliff edge, from they'd descended to the lake, had broken off, and only a sheer wall remained there.

Jill stood feet from Dakota, her enchanting bright blue eyes now piercing as if looking deep into Dakota's soul. Her features were strong and clearly defined, as if chiseled from stone. A faint yellow aura emanated from her.

"Do you remember?" Jill said.

Dakota looked away from Jill's icy stare. Her body shook as her and Jake's hellish vision in the Cave of the Elders raced through her mind. She looked up, her voice calm and controlled. "Yes, I remember. What do you want? Are you going to kill me?"

Jill's eyes softened, her visage relaxed, and the aura disappeared. "No harm will come to you. As for what I want... that will be answered soon enough. For now, we have a journey to make. Follow me."

Dakota's steps fell heavy and forced as fear coursed through her body. A scene from her youth flashed before her....

On a warm summer morning during a visit to the ranch, she played down at the stream behind the barn. A low, slow moan caught her attention in the brush. Curious, as all young children are, she investigated. As she got closer, the brush moved violently. A mournful growl followed, and a young bear pulled itself forward using only its front legs.

She jumped back and ran towards the barn. "Woo Woo, Woo Woo."

Her grandfather, startled by her screams, dropped is work and ran towards her.

Dakota met him on top of the knoll and wrapped herself around his leg.

"Lomasi, what is it. What's wrong?"

Shaking and unwilling to release her clutch on his leg, she looked up. "A grizzly, Woo Woo, a grizzly by the big round rock, but he sounds hurt. He didn't chase me."

Woo Woo instructed her to stay in the barn. He grabbed a rifle from his horse pack and raced into the brush.

Dakota crawled up on his work bench and looked out a window towards the creek bottom. She saw glimpses of his red shirt as he moved towards the bear, then he stood still. The crack of a rifle startled her. After a few seconds, she saw his red shirt move back towards the barn. She jumped off the workbench and ran to greet him.

"Did you shoot him Woo Woo, or just scare him away?"

He bent down on one knee. "No, honey, I had to shoot him. He was hurt badly."

Dakota's eyes welled. "What was wrong with him?"

"He broke his back, most likely hit by a car crossing the road."

"With all this land, why would he cross the road?"

Woo Woo paused. "He probably could not resist the fat berries on the other side of the bridge. It was his weakness. All creatures great and small have them. It is how the Great Spirit wanted it."

Dakota wrapped her tiny hand around his thumb. "Woo Woo, do you have a weakness? I don't want you to die."

Woo Woo fought back a tear and wrapped his arms around her. "Yes, I have a weakness, but it won't hurt me."

Dakota snapped from deep thought, and a faint smile crossed her face.

Jill stopped at a slow but deep stream that emptied from the lake into a dark passage. She stepped along the banks into the darkness, and returned shortly with an ancient dugout. In the front of the hollowed tree trunk was a torch. She placed it in a holder and lit it. The faint smell of sulfur jumped from the flame as it came to life.

Dakota wrinkled her nose. "Jeez, that smells like fucking rotten eggs."

Jill looked back and smiled. "It will go away in a few seconds. Hop in."

Dakota snarled. "And if I don't? If we don't return to camp, Kat will have a search party here at first light, if not tonight. She knows where we are."

Jill bowed her head and shook it, then looked up and smirked. "Child, have you not seen my power? This cave has been sealed off. I know she'll have a search party. Given your stature in the community, it will probably be of a scope like nothing Wyoming has seen. Don't you think I've taken that into consideration? When Kat directs them to the cave, the passage we traveled will not exist." Her eyes glowed red. "Now, *get in the fucking boat* before I lose my patience."

A feeling of dread briefly paralyzed Dakota, except for her trembling hands. *You must stay strong to survive.* She took a deep breath and reluctantly stepped into the dugout.

Jill pushed the boat off and paddled into the current.

Dakota glared at the back of Jill's head. *Remember what Woo Woo said that morning with the bear: every creature has a weakness. Before Jake's trial, he said 'find and exploit your opponent's weakness.'* She narrowed her eyes and nodded lightly.

Jill turned. "Now relax. You're going to see things as we float that have eluded eyes since the beginning of your kind."

"What do you mean *your kind*? What are you, Jill, or *whatever* your name is?"

"You can call me Jill. I've used it for millennia. I'm like you in many aspects. I bleed like you. I loved at one time, like you. I crave companionship and touch like you. But, I am much older, much more powerful, much more evolved. I have no end of life like you."

Dakota shook her head. "Are you a god? A demon? An angel? A *fucking alien*? I don't understand. And what could you possibly want from a *'mortal'* like me?"

Jill chuckled. "No, definitely not a god, as you call them—far from it. It's complicated. As I promised, soon you will have your answers and understand your Destiny."

Dakota scoffed. "Destiny... I've heard that word too many times in the past year. Perhaps you know a spirit, demon, or whatever the hell he is, named Rowtag. He claims he *is* Destiny, or at least controls it."

Jill turned and half-smiled, then returned her eyes forward as she rowed to navigate a rock in the stream. "And where did you meet *this* Rowtag?"

"He guided Jake and me in the Spirit world."

"No, Dakota, I've never heard of him. There are things that have lurked in the shadows since the beginning, more than that I care to think of. Your Spirit world, as you call it, is just another dimension, one of many invisible to you."

"Well, how do you exist in both the Spirit world and the physical world?"

Jill paddled a few strokes without answering, then placed the paddle across the front of the boat as they drifted into a calm pool. She turned to Dakota. "I live in the physical world as you do. Over time, I have learned to move my energy into other planes. It's very complicated, and honestly, mankind is not advanced enough to understand the truth. It would topple religions and create panic like your world has never seen. The truth would bring the end of humanity."

Dakota huffed and mumbled, "Fucking riddles, just like Rowtag."

Jill smiled. "What was that?"

"Nothing. I said I'm getting hungry."

"I have jerky and trail mix in my pack."

"Thanks, but I have some smoked trout. Would you like a piece? I guess we can still be friends despite the fact you've kidnapped me for who knows what diabolical reason."

"We can be friends, and can continue after this. You're going to return to Jake and your life. There is nothing diabolical about our mission, trust me. It's far from it."

Dakota leaned forward with a piece of fish. "Here you go, and I'm not even gonna ask you why I'm here again. My *mortal egg shell mind* may not be able to handle it."

Jill chuckled and turned to accept the fillet. She took a bite of it and her eyes widened. "Wow, *that is* amazing, and you will understand soon enough. Would you like a glass of wine? Let's enjoy this trip."

Dakota took a deep breath, twisted her lips, and bobbed her head back and forth. "What the fuck, why not?"

The two made their way along the lazy river as it meandered through the subterranean labyrinth. Ancient stalactites with hues of blues, yellows, whites, and browns hung from the ceiling. Massive mounds and columns of stalagmites sprung from the floors, some joining their counterparts from the ceiling to form statuesque columns. Crystal formations, jetting from the walls, sparkled like diamonds under the torch light.

Dakota, feeling more relaxed against all odds, sipped her wine and ogled at the beauty surrounding her. "Well, you didn't lie about the scenery."

"I told you it was amazing. It's been a long time since I've been on this river. Up ahead, I want to show you something."

After a sharp right bend, a large cavern opened up. Jill directed the boat to the shore. "Hop out, let's stretch our legs."

Dakota looked down at her phone. *Almost six... Kat will be getting nervous.*

CHAPTER 36
THE SEARCH BEGINS

Kat looked towards the ridge line as the sun set over the mountains, hoping to see movement in the fading light. She glanced at her phone. "Fucking six o'clock... Dakota knows better." She stood and looked at the trail heading back to the parking lot, took a few steps putting a full load on her knee, and nodded.

She figured to use the heavier traveled trail out to the road, which was much shorter. There would be cell service once she crested the ridge and left the pines.

She prepared her pack for the three-mile night hike. "I'll give it till eight, and Dakota Reynolds, if I head out and you show up, I'm gonna kick your ass." Her eyes welled as she tested her headlamp and made sure there were spare batteries in her pack. She'd hiked with Dakota for years—something didn't feel right.

The last bit of light faded from the valley as night crept in. Her chance of seeing the girls descend from the ridge vanished into the darkness. She scribbled a note and placed it on Dakota's camp chair.

I've gone for help when you didn't show up by eight.

She sat and stared at the dim moonlit ridge, hoping to catch some movement, perhaps a falling rock from the ridge or a noise across the lake. Maybe she'd catch an echo of the girls' laughter or curses as they made their way along the dark rocky trail, or a glimpse of their headlamps. Time seemed to speed up as eight o'clock approached. She stood, grabbed her makeshift cane, and hobbled from camp.

The trail to the road was well traveled, making her walk painful but doable. She crested the much lower and less demanding ridge opposite of the one across the lake, turned off her headlamp, and allowed her eyes to adjust to the natural light. She panned the far ridgeline and the lake valley below in hopes of a flash of Dakota's or Jill's headlamp.

After several minutes, she checked the service on her phone, took a deep breath, and dialed.

"Sheriff's Office, Officer Adams speaking. Is this an emergency?"

"Janie, it's Kat."

"Hey, Kat, is everything all right?"

"I don't know. I'm out at Blue Miner Lake. Dakota, another girl named Jill, and I are doing some camping. Dakota and Jill left this morning for a cave we found yesterday up in Sheep Mountain and haven't returned."

"Dakota knows better than to be in the mountains at dark. Where are you right now?"

"I'm on my way out to Forest Road, on the Blue Miner Lake trail. I'm moving a bit slower than normal, 'cause my damn knee is messed up again. I should be on the road in the next hour or so."

"Can you go back and stay at camp in case they show up? I'm calling the Park Rangers. We'll have our search team out there also."

"Thanks, Janie. Hopefully, I'm wrong about this."

"Honestly, Kat, if it was anyone else, we would wait till morning, but Dakota is too experienced not to come off that mountain by dark. I'm sure she had ropes and headlamps in her pack, correct?"

"Yeah, we came out here prepared to explore a cave if we found it."

"What about this other girl, Jill? Is she experienced in the back country?"

"Yes."

"Okay, we'll be out as soon as possible. Do you have her grandfather's number?"

"I do, but can you reach out to him Janie. My phone is about to die."

"Wil do, Kat."

Janie sprang from the desk and rushed to the Sergeant on Duty's office.

"Hey, Norm, Kat just called. Her and Dakota and another girl were out hiking on Sheep Mountain. Dakota and the other girl, Jill, have not returned to camp."

Norm looked down at his watch. "It's almost nine. I hiked with Dakota when we were younger. She respects these mountains. What the hell were they doing on Sheep Mountain?"

"The three of them stumbled on a cave yesterday when hiking. Dakota and the other girl went back to explore it this morning."

"Why was Kat not with them?"

"She messed her knee up. She was on her way to Forest road via the Blue Miner trail. I told her to head back to camp in case they showed up."

"Damn, okay. Call the park rangers, and I'll reach out to Joe and see who he wants to send out there. And Janie, tell the rangers to move on this stat. Let me know if they give you any bullshit."

"Yes, sir, and Kat asked if we could reach out to Dakota's grandfather."

Norm nodded and gave a thumbs-up as he dialed the phone.

"Joe, it's Norm. We might have a problem."

Joe placed his beer on the table. "What do you have, Norm?"

"Dakota Reynolds, Kat, and another female named Jill—I assume that's the blonde that's been hanging around with Kat—were out on Sheep Mountain. Dakota and Jill have not returned to camp."

Joe glanced at his watch. "It's three hours past sunset. Dakota knows better. Get ahold of the rangers and get their search and rescue team out there, stat. Have our best team assembled. I'll be there in twenty minutes."

"10-4. Janie is calling the rangers. I'll get our guys together. Do you want to contact Jim White Feather?"

"Yeah, I'll contact Jim. I'm sure he'll have Jay Storm Walker meet up with us. Did Kat give any indication where Dakota may have hiked to on Sheep Mountain?"

"Kat said something about exploring a cave they found yesterday."

"Fuck, that mountain is loaded with old caves and mine shafts. I'll see you in twenty."

Joe pushed his beer aside, inhaled his dinner, and dialed Jim.

Jim, half-awake on his recliner, looked down at his phone. "A bit late for a fundraiser call, Joe. Tell me one of my clients is in trouble again."

"No, Jim, it's Dakota."

Jim sprang forward in his chair and slammed the footrest down. "What has happened?"

"Nothing, I hope. I'm sure you know she went camping."

"Yes, over by Blue Miner Lake."

"She and another girl didn't return to camp. Kat made her way from the valley and just called in."

Jim lowered his head. "She is a good hiker. Perhaps they got lost and decided to hole up for the night."

"Jim, I thought about that also, but you and I both know Dakota can find her way off a mountain. Kat said they went exploring a cave."

Jim paused, letting out a deep breath. "I'm sure you have reached out to the park rangers."

"Yeah, and I'm pulling in our best guys."

"Thank you, Joe. I will call Jay and Jake Michaels. We will be in town as soon as possible."

A moment later, Jake answered his phone. "Hey, Jim, a bit late for you, isn't it?"

"Jake, Dakota and the new girl Jill did not return to camp tonight. Sheriff Kelly said they went exploring a cave earlier today on Sheep Mountain. I'll pick you up in fifteen minutes. Have a pack ready."

"Damn, how do they know this?"

"Kat just called it in. We will find out more in town."

"Okay, I'll be ready."

Jim's hands trembled as he dialed Jay.

Jay responded, "What are you doing up so late, old man?"

"Joe just called me, Jay. Dakota and another girl were up on Sheep Mountain exploring caves. They did not return to camp tonight. He and the rangers are putting together a search team. Can you meet me at the Sheriff's Department?"

"Of course. I will be there in twenty minutes."

Anna walked from the bedroom, and when Jim turned to her, his look stopped her.

"Jim, what's wrong, who were you talking to this late?"

Jim's eyes welled. "It's Dakota... she was up on Sheep Mountain exploring a cave and did not return to camp tonight. I'm on my way over to town with Jake to meet up with Jay. Joe and the rangers are sending out a search party."

Anna took a deep breath. "Honey, I'm sure she is fine. She is experienced in the back country. Perhaps she got turned around on the mountain or in the cave, and made the decision to spend the night. It would not be the first time she has done that."

"It's not the mountain that I am worried about. It is the cave system up there. It is intertwined with old mine shafts. You know how dangerous they can be. Can you help me get my pack together while I change?" Jim brushed past her into their bedroom.

Anna looked up, closed her eyes, clasped her hands in front of her, and paused for a few moments to pray silently. "Amen."

She headed upstairs to a spare bedroom and grabbed Jim's pack, which he always kept mostly prepared. After a quick inventory, she paused and thought about the type of terrain he might encounter, then opened a closet and retrieved a second pack that he hadn't used in years.

He is too old to climb, but there will be no stopping him. I'm sure this stuff is dry-rotted.

She opened the pack, smiled, shook her head, and pulled out an unopened pack of fresh rope.

Always prepared, Jim White Feather, always prepared.

"Anna, did you find everything?"

She yelled down, "Yes, just looking for some fresh batteries for your headlamp."

"I have them in my office. I'll grab them."

Anna walked downstairs with both packs. "I found your climbing pack. Please, let that be for the younger guys."

Jim smiled and hugged her. "Why did you bring it to me?"

She looked up into his eyes. "Because I know you won't. Be careful, *please*, and trust that Dakota knows what she is doing. She has always been overly cautious. You taught her that way."

Jim nodded. "I love you. I have to go. I will keep you posted." He paused before the door and turned. "Please call your Dad so he hears it from us and not the gossip mill."

"Okay, now go, and remember you're not twenty anymore. Be careful."

She watched Jim leave the house then looked down at her phone, and at her daughter's number. *I'll hold off. Jim has not hit that level of panic yet, so I don't want to scare Dakota's mom.*

Jake and Honi waited on the cabin porch, watching as Jim's headlights bounced in the darkness as he drove down the lane. Jake looked down and said, "Let's go find Dakota, boy."

Honi cocked his head and whined in a tone mirroring his master's concern.

Jim rolled his window down. "Jake, I'm not sure the rangers will welcome Honi. His scent may stir the pack on the mountain and bring them in."

"I thought about that, but he knows Dakota's scent and will trail it. Plus, if we have to go into a cave, he can get places we can't. Besides, that pack should be off the mountains and following the elk herd towards their winter grounds."

Jim nodded. "I did not think about the herd moving towards the refuge by now. Good point."

Honi jumped into the pickup and muzzled up to Jim.

"Hello, Boy."

Jake threw his pack in the bed and hopped in. "What do you think? What do you know about the area they're at?"

Jim shook his head. "It's been about thirty years since I've been on that mountain, maybe more. It gets a lot of tourist traffic, so the trails are pretty easy to navigate. As for the caves up there, that concerns me."

"Why?"

"They intertwine with old mine shafts. As you know, we have a lot of seismic activity here, and those old shafts are unstable."

Jake blew out forcefully. "Well, I'm sure Kat will fill us in. I wonder why she wasn't with them?"

"I do not know. I was shaken when Joe called, and I did not ask."

Jim's phone rang. He hit the talk/speaker button on the steering wheel. "Yes, Jay."

"I'm pulling into the Sheriff's Department. How far out are you?"

"Jake and I just left the ranch, so twenty minutes or so. Have Joe brief you, and let his team head out. I will pick you up."

"Sounds good. They are grouped up in the conference room now. See you in a bit."

Webb pushed away from his makeshift office at the Thunderbird. His email alert sounded. It was from the hotel, and attached were two files. *Gonna be a long night.* He stood, moved his neck side to side, stretched his back, then grabbed his ice bucket, walked into the crisp night air and breathed in deeply. As he approached the small lobby, a group of teenage girls gathered around the front desk caught his attention.

Hmm... a strange place to hang out.

"Good evening, sir, is everything okay?" the handsome young front desk clerk asked.

Webb understood instantly the gathering, and smiled. He held up his ice bucket. "Yes, I just need some ice. Thank you."

The group returned to their chat.

The clerk said, "And I heard Dakota and that new woman in town are trapped in a cave up there."

A female in the group said, "Wow, and poor Kat can't do anything to help 'cause she broke her leg."

Webb's ears perked. He looked down at his bucket and decided to slowly add a few more scoops.

The clerk said, "I heard the Sheriff's Department and the park rangers are sending search and rescue crews out right now, in the dark. Tell me they aren't concerned."

Webb walked past the group. "I didn't mean to eavesdrop, but I heard you mention something about a search and rescue? I did that for years in the military."

The clerk said, "Oh yeah, two of the ladies from our town, Dakota and Kat, and a new woman were hiking on Sheep Mountain, and two of them didn't come back to camp."

A bubbly teenage girl added, "And they are lost in the caves."

Another girl interjected, "They *think* they are."

Webb shook his head. "I hope they find them. Caves can be dangerous."

The clerk said, "Why don't you go see the Sheriff and help?"

Webb said, "Well, I'm here on other business, and I'm sure the Sheriff's Department has plenty of competent people. You kids have a good night."

Webb walked towards the lobby door and heard the clerk whisper to the girls, "FBI."

He chuckled to himself and reached for his phone as the door closed behind him. "Steve, it appears Dakota Reynolds, the gym owner, and our mystery blonde went hiking. Dakota and the blonde did not return to camp. Search parties are heading out as we speak. I take it you've heard nothing from Fleming at the Dibella compound on Ricci?"

"He was off today. He said the name sounds familiar, but can't commit to him visiting Dibella or Sellman until he reviews the records tomorrow. What about the hotel guest list? Do you have a name on our blonde?"

"I just got an email from the hotel. I assume it's the register and video tapes. I needed to stretch and grab some ice, haven't had a chance to open them, but will shortly."

"Is it gonna matter, Webb?"

Webb's brow wrinkled. "What do you mean, Steve?"

"Think about our earlier conversation regarding the revenge narrative. With our girl's MO, I would say Dakota Reynolds *may* be in trouble."

Webb paused. "Let me look at what the hotel sent. I'll call you back."

He hurried back to his room and opened the attachments on the email. He scanned the sparse guest list, nodded, and scribbled on his note pad:

Jill Boissonette, 10/19, Scott Smith, 10/21.

He downloaded the camera videos and isolated the lobby the day and time Jill checked in. He leaned forward as a statuesque blonde moved gracefully across the lobby to the front desk. His eyes narrowed. "Got you, bitch."

Next, he jumped to the hall video two days prior to when Ricci was discovered, fast forwarded to all bodies moving in that hall, and zoomed in to see if Jill had visited that wing. At the end of the two-day video loop, the police moved into Ricci's room. There was no evidence of Jill stepping foot in that corridor. He sat back and tossed his pen down, then rewound the tape to the suspected day Ricci died and watched the hall activity a second time. Frame by frame, guests, workers, and Ricci himself moved about the hall, but not the mysterious Jill.

He sat back and sighed, but then something caught his eye. Ricci's door opened a crack, after several seconds it opened fully, and then it closed. He fast forwarded the tape. Thirty-one minutes later, the door opened and closed again with no one coming in or out.

Are you paranoid, Ricci, maybe hearing things? He watched the motion on the door for the next two days, but there was nothing. Ricci never left the room.

He picked up his phone and dialed. "Steve, did I wake you?"

"No, you're fine. I just dozed off for a second. What's up?"

"Our blonde checked in under Jill Boissonette. I'm running the name in our database as we speak. She matches the description of the female we saw on the drone video at Percovelli's."

"You mean the video that scrambled, leaving us with no proof but our word to place her there?"

"Yeah, but that doesn't concern me right now. I want resources out here to join the search ASAP. They're on Federal Park Land, so pull some strings. Call Captain Hollis and see if he can send Blake Roberts and Joe Running Horse down here. This is their kind of search."

"On it. What happens if this Jill chick is clean?"

Webb paused. "Then, no harm, no foul, but... she won't be. Call it a gut feeling. I doubt that's her real name."

"Can you place her near Ricci at all? Did the tape show anything?"

"Nothing, but I'm gonna send you an hour loop of Ricci's corridor and his room. Call me back and let me know what you see. It's on the way. I'll let you know when I get the report back on this Jill person."

While Webb waited for the FBI database to run its search, he googled Jill's name. Several women showed up on various social media sites, but their pictures were no match. One older news article from France caught his attention: *'Prominent Wine Maker's Daughter Gone Missing.'*

Webb looked at the picture and read the article. "Son... of... a... bitch! Are you kidding me?" He honed his attention on other articles. After nearly a year-long exhaustive search spanning most of Europe, the investigation ended with no resolution, and the case was eventually closed.

Webb's inbox dinged. The Bureau report listed forty-one females matching the name. He panned through each profile, but none matched this Jill's physical description. He leaned back in his chair and nodded, then got up, stretched his back, walked over to the kitchenette and poured a glass of wine. *Apropos, if I may say so.*

His phone quickly drew him back to the desk. "Yeah, Steve?"

"Hollis is fine. Blake and Joe will be there mid-morning."

"Good, I'll let the sheriff know we're bringing in a couple of our boys."

"What are you gonna tell him without raising a bunch of suspicion?"

"That we have an interest in Jill and her connection to Percovelli."

"Good call. Now, as for the tape, it looks like the door was opened to let someone come in or out — *twice* — but no one did. It's a bit strange. Maybe Ricci was hearing things?"

"Yeah, I found it odd. I got back the Bureau report. It has no matches to our girl, but I'm sending you a link right now. Take a second to read it."

Steve mumbled the first few words of the article, then silenced. After a couple seconds, he said, "Are you fucking kidding me? Look at that picture! It's almost thirty years old and she has hasn't aged. How is that possible? So, did she go AWOL from a family fortune to join Percovelli?"

"Or, Steve... was she abducted like who knows how many girls before her, and Stockholm Syndrome set in? As for the aging, plastic surgery does wonders."

"Webb, this case is spinning in friggin' circles. So, is Dakota in trouble? Or, do we have two missing hikers?"

"I don't know. Maybe this Jill found her way out when Percovelli died, and wants a new life here, new friends, a fresh start."

"If that's the case, man, why would she not go to the authorities and stop her family's anguish? Based on these articles, she'd be a very wealthy woman."

"Sins, Steve... maybe she can't face what she's been part of for years. Maybe she fears retaliation to her family from very powerful people she can finger. We won't know until we can interrogate her. As for money, I'm sure Percovelli paid her well. She probably has offshore accounts set up in shell companies."

"Say you're right, Webb.... Why use your real name, especially one as prominent as hers?"

"Prominent maybe in France, but did her name ring a bell to you?"

"No, I figured it was a Louisiana name."

"Exactly. Maybe a bit careless on her part, but it's clean on all databases, no red flags here in the states."

Steve exhaled forcefully. "Okay, boss, I'm gonna try and get some sleep. I should hear back tomorrow from Dibella's people on Ricci. I would tell you to do the same, but I know better."

Webb chuckled. "When you're my age, you'll have a tough enough time sleeping without this insanity. Goodnight."

Webb finished his wine, clicked off his computer, crawled into bed, and stared at the ceiling. A million thoughts raced through his head, but his gut told him something was drastically off balance. He glanced at the clock.

CHAPTER 37
WEAKNESS

Dakota stepped from the dugout onto a sandy shoreline and clicked on her headlamp. With her head on a swivel, she marveled at the enormity of the subterranean world illuminated before her. Stalagmites, ten feet or longer, were dwarfed by the height of the ceiling. The beam of her lamp faded into a black void as she directed it forward.

"This place is huge," she said.

Jill pulled the boat from the river and grabbed the torch. "Grab your pack. We'll spend the night here. Follow me. To borrow an American colloquialism, you ain't seen nothin' yet."

The two women had walked silently into the darkness for a couple hundred feet, when something on the cusp of Dakota's headlamp beam caught her attention.

"Wait, I saw something." She pulled her flashlight out and searched to her right. She picked up her pace as her target came into focus. Her eyes widened and heart raced. "Are you fucking kidding me?" She dropped to her knees and slowly ran her hand over the coarse fur of the perfectly preserved beast in front of her.

Jill sauntered over, giving Dakota time to admire the creature from an age long gone. "Magnificent, isn't he?"

Dakota looked up. "I always said that if cloning could bring back one animal, a saber-toothed tiger would be the one. So powerful and intimidating, yet majestic and graceful. He looks like he's sleeping. I can't believe how well preserved he is."

Jill knelt down, placed the torch in the earth, and turned her headlamp off. She petted the beast in the soft fur between his ears. Her head tilted, a relaxed smile crossed her face, and her eyes softened. In the torchlight, at that moment, she appeared to be somewhere else—*someone* else.

"They were so misunderstood," she said, her voice just above a whisper.

Dakota, taken back by the moment, moved from kneeling to sitting. She studied Jill, and said nothing.

Jill stroked the big cat with an almost familiar touch. Her eyes locked into the face of the beast, then she shook her head and snapped to her feet. "Come, let this creature return to his eternal slumber."

Dakota petted the tiger one last time and stood. "Thank you, that was amazing."

Jill nodded. "Wait until you see what's just up ahead."

The women moved a few hundred yards into the darkness.

Jill held her hand up. "Stay here for a few minutes. Let me make sure the bridge ahead is still there and safe."

Dakota watched Jill's torch bounce through the darkness then pause. A second lit torch appeared, then a third, and a fourth.

"Come forward," echoed from the torches.

Dakota moved towards the circle of light. As she got closer, she saw Jill kneeling next to what appeared to be a body.

What the hell?

She quickened her pace, crossed a natural bridge spanning a narrow dark abyss, and stopped dead in her tracks as she panned over a sea of bodies, all lying on furs. She walked gingerly towards Jill, looking down on each preserved corpse. Their brow ridge was stronger but not prominent, their noses broader but not dominant, their chin and forehead sloped back slightly. Their bodies were of medium height, and strong. Some were clearly older, many young. Men and women lay side by side, their hands intertwined. Babies lay across their mother's chest, and younger children cuddled against their parents.

Jill stroked the black hair of a female, maybe the same age as Dakota. Again, her demeanor changed, as with the saber-toothed cat.

Dakota looked down. "You knew her, didn't you? You knew all of them?"

Jill didn't look up. "Yes, her name was Ula."

"Their features are not Neanderthal, but not fully modern either. Who are they? What happened to them?"

Jill stood and gazed at the deceased, her tone solemn. "They came here when the continents were still fused. They fled their land in search of peace, and to preserve their kind from a threat like no other." She pointed to a far wall. "At that time, the cave opened to the valley below, providing them a panoramic view to watch migrating herds and potential threats. A massive earthquake shook the land and sealed them in. They had no escape. The head of the clan, Wula, Ula's father, fearing a long agonizing death of his people, mixed a potent drink made from poison they used to coat their spears with. They left this world peacefully."

Dakota looked towards the river. "Why didn't they follow the water to safety?"

"The river is a result of the ice age and thousands of years of seismic activity. It didn't exist at that time. This cavern ended not far behind where the river flows now."

"What threat were they fleeing from?"

Jill's jaw tightened and the veins in her forehead flared. "Genocide."

"Genocide from whom?"

Jill spun and walked away. "It's not important."

Dakota's eyes narrowed as she noticed a slight tremble in Jill's hands. *I found your weakness, bitch. It's the past.*

Jill paused for a few moments, took a deep breath, and faced Dakota. "Do you mind sleeping amongst the dead, or shall we head downstream?"

"Will you tell me more about them?"

Jill looked over the fallen, her eyes pools of sorrow. "Yes."

The two women sat at a small fire built in an ancient stone ring of the clan.

Jill stared into the fire. "I remember the first night I stayed here. I had met Ula in a precarious situation. I was moving through the valley below, and heard the growls of Dire wolves and panic in a female's voice. I climbed on a rock ledge overlooking a large pool in the river. Ula stood waist-deep trying to shoo the wolves as they paced back and forth on the bank. I drew my bow and killed both wolves. Ula looked up. At first, her eyes were thankful, but then she realized who had a saved her—a beast more dangerous than the Dire wolves."

"What was she fearful of?"

"My appearance. I was who they had fled from, or at least I looked like them. I placed my bow on the ground, raised my hands, and called out in her language. She moved from the water, her steps deliberate and her eyes never leaving me."

"How did you know their language?"

"I made it a point to learn the language of all the tribes that inhabited this planet. There is not a language I can't speak, then and now."

"So, she took you back to her people?"

"Yes, after I convinced her I meant no harm to her, or her clan. They were a very trusting race. Deceit, greed, lust and power — these were not emotions their brains had evolved to understand yet."

"If they were running from another tribe or race, they must have understood some bad qualities."

Jill looked down and shook her head. "No, they didn't. They understood love and family and, like any animal, preservation of their kind. It was their weakness, and ultimately the end of their race."

Dakota paused and looked at Jill's bowed head. "So, Ula brought you back to meet her clan, then what?"

Jill looked over at her corpse and smiled. "After the initial shock of her walking to the cave with me, she explaining to Wula how I saved his daughter's life, and they welcomed me."

"You said that your looks frightened her. Did you look different back then?"

"No, and neither did their enemy. Look at them. Our features are similar. They're just a few thousand years of progression, if you want to call it that, behind us."

Dakota locked her eyes on Jill's. "Who are you? What are you? Am I in a vision brought on by something you slipped me? Some kind of trip that lasts for hours? *Or* maybe this is all happening in seconds? Did I die on our hike up the mountain and land in some parallel universe?"

Jill chuckled. "No, this is very much real. As for who I am, as with Ula, I mean you no harm. Soon you'll find out the truth, but it's not my place to share that. Now, how about we catch a couple cave fish? You've never tasted meat so succulent. We'll have dinner, a glass of wine, and get a good night's sleep."

Dakota looked at her phone, which had no signal, of course, and which power was dwindling. "I didn't realize it's this late. Sounds good."

Jill stood. "Let's go fishing. Grab a spear from one of our camping partners."

Dakota watched Jill slide a spear from the grip of a young man lying several yards from the fire and start towards the river.

Almost eleven... I know a search party is being assembled. Woo Woo will call Uncle Jay. Jake will stop at nothing till I'm found.

Jill stared at Dakota while she slept. Shadows from the dying flame danced off her delicate features.

Soon, child, you will know your Destiny.

She quietly got up and crept towards the beach, where she stripped, removed the pendant from around her neck, and waded into the lazy river, slowly lowering herself beneath the icy waters.

After several moments, she returned to the surface. Her eyes emitted a glow like the embers as she sauntered from the water, dropped to her knees on the soft sand, and raised her arms to the sky. "Mina, Kimi, Aiyana, ha-lakh... hhe-nam... taph."

Mina took a hit of her joint as the moans and music of porn filled the dark living room. She rolled her head to the right and tried to focus her bloodshot eyes across the room on a guy lying on the couch stroking his limp dick.

Kimi walked from the kitchen and handed her a beer. She nodded towards the guy and chuckled. "I guess he wants more."

Mina said, "He did a good job, holding out for both of us. Should we help him, or kick him out, and look for another one at the bar?"

Kimi plopped down on the loveseat next her. "What a little slut you've become since leaving that mountain."

Mina took a sip of her beer and clinked the can off Kimi's. "Ah, I don't see you running from any cocks that come into this apartment."

Kimi smiled and looked over at the guy on the couch. "Not when they come packaged like that. He's hot."

Mina nodded. "Very, but let's say goodbye to him and find something different, maybe a surfer dude."

Kimi moaned. "Or two?"

Mina turned the porn off. "Hey, stud, leave that thing for another day. Grab your clothes and take off. We need to get ready for the night."

The guy stood up and approached the two girls with his dick in hand. "I know I can get it up again. Let's go for another round."

Kimi guzzled the remainder of her beer, grabbed his jeans from the floor, and playfully tossed them at him. "Beat it, Romeo, you have your story to talk about the rest of your life."

Mina stood up and paused, grabbed her lower abdomen, and leaned over. "Fuck."

Kimi said, "What's wrong, Mina."

Mina doubled over and wrapped both arms around her belly. *"Oh my God!"*

The guy said, "What the fuck's wrong with her?"

Kimi jumped up. *"Shut up and get the hell outta here."* She took a step forward and winced in pain. She tilted to the right and grabbed her lower stomach too. *"Fuck."*

The guy stepped back and fumbled trying to push one leg into his jeans.

"Go!" Kimi screamed. She then dropped to her knees, her breathing labored.

Mina crumbled into a fetal position as her cries of pain bounced off the condo walls.

The guy stumbled backwards as he hurried his second leg into his jeans and froze.

Mina's body tensed and veins flared across her taught body. She gasped for air, and then went limp. Dark, black blood flowed between her legs, and the smell of sulfur filled the air.

Kimi's own shallow panting and cries of pain intensified, then stopped. A puddle of tar-colored blood spread across the hardwood floor between her knees.

A black wisp of smoke lifted from both girls.

The guy's face twisted, *"What the fuck are you two?"* He grabbed his boots and denim shirt and raced from the condo.

Mina sat up. A relaxed innocence, gone since the mountain, softened her face. She hurried for a robe strewn across a chair, bent down next to Kimi, and wrapped a blanket around her.

Kimi looked down at the blood puddle, which slowly dissipated into the air. She closed her eyes and took a deep breath. "I feel like a dark spirit has been lifted from me." She looked at Mina and smiled. "There are those gentle eyes I grew up with."

Mina brushed the sweat-soaked hair from Kimi's temple. "I feel free, like a demon was exorcised. It's time to get back to our lives."

A tear fell down Kimi's cheek, accompanied by a light chuckle. "Do you think our cherries will grow back?"

"That won't happen, but we can certainly become stuck-up bitches and grow our hard-to-get reputation back again."

Aiyana stood at the cliff's edge, staring into the moonlit canyon below. She glanced back at a campfire and the couple she'd seduced on the trails earlier in the day. A battle raged inside of her, as the good medicine of her people held the most fragile advantage over the dark power of the mountain. She knew a leap would end the torment brought on by the shame of her insatiable vices, but... she feared the afterlife would doom her to an eternity of sinful deeds, and bring her back to walk the earth as a temptress.

Suddenly, she winced as a searing hot pain stabbed her above the pubic bone. She stepped back from the cliff edge, fell to her knees, bowed her head, and grabbed ahold of two small sage bushes on either side of her. Sweat flowed from her pores as the pain intensified, and blood soaked her inner thighs.

In the darkness, behind clenched eyes, an ancient warrior, aglow in white, drew an arrow — his target, a dark shadow moving with the speed of the wind towards him. The warrior's arrow found its mark, dropping the shadow in its tracks.

Aiyana's body relaxed, the pain subsided, and a peace coursed through her. She opened her eyes to see the stars shined brilliantly again. The smell of sage and pine rushed in, and the howl of wolves and the hoots of an owl echoed in her ears.

She stood, pulled her bandana off, and wiped the clotty blood from her legs. Then she walked into the glow of the campfire.

An attractive thirty-something female stood up and sauntered towards her, unbuttoning her denim shirt as she walked. "Shall we turn in for the night? I think my husband is ready to satisfy both of us again. It's amazing what that little blue pill does."

Aiyana smiled. "No, there won't be another round. I'm going home." She brushed past the woman, grabbed her pack, and walked into the darkness.

Jill drew in a deep breath as she returned to the physical world. She leaned over and splashed cool water on to her face, draped the necklace around her neck, redressed, and stood up. She gazed into the darkness of the lazy river, and then back at the dim light of the campfire.

No more pain, no more suffering for this failed creation. Destiny will soon be fulfilled.

CHAPTER 38
INTO THE DARKNESS

Jake and Jim jumped from the truck and hurried down the sidewalk to the Sheriff's Department. Sheriff Kelly's search team was exiting as they reached the steps.

Bill Wind Caller broke towards Jim with his hand extended. "Jim, we'll find her. Fortunately, Kat called it in quickly."

Jim gripped his hand. "Thanks, Bill. You have a good team assembled." He looked over his shoulder. "I don't know if you've met Jake or not."

Bill extended his hand. "I feel like I know you, but no I haven't. Nice to meet you, Jake."

"Nice to meet you, Bill."

Jim said, "Bill, Jake is bringing his wolf, Honi, with him. He knows Dakota's scent. It will not be a problem, will it?"

Bill shook his head. "I don't think so. We have our hounds ready to go for first light, but a wolf's nose and a familiar scent is hard to beat. Let me get going. I'll see you all out there."

Jim said, "Thanks, we will be right behind you. I want to talk with Sheriff Kelly for a second."

Jay said, "I will grab my pack from the truck."

Jim knocked on Sheriff Kelly's doorframe, where the door stood open.

The sheriff looked up, smiled and motioned him in. "Jim, my old friend, how are you doing?"

Jim half shrugged and took a deep breath. "I have had better days, Joe. You look like a train wreck, if you do not mind me saying."

Joe sipped his coffee and smirked. "I'm getting too old for sleepless nights."

"Well, thank you for putting together such a good crew as quickly as you did. Anna and I appreciate it. Could you do me one more favor?"

"Sure, Jim, what is it?"

"I know I will lose cell service out there. Could you from time to time update Anna? She is going to pick up Samuel, and we both know what a pain in the ass he can be a times. The last thing you need is him coming over here and camping out in your office."

Joe chuckled. "Yes, I *will* definitely do that. And *hell no*, I don't need him over here."

Jim reached over the desk and shook Joe's hand. "Thank you."

Joe winked. "Be careful out on that mountain."

Jake, Jim, and Jay pulled away from the commotion at the Sheriff's Department and followed the parade of first responder vehicles.

The Stranger stepped from the shadows of the alley across the street and watched the sea of strobe lights fade into the darkness as they crested the mountain outside of town. He walked a couple doors down to a small tavern, walked inside, and bellied up to the bar, keeping a few stools distance from some late-night stragglers.

A grizzled old barkeep walked up to him. "Howdy, what can I get ya?"

The Stranger said, "Evening, sir, a shot of your best local whisky and the most popular local draft you have."

The bartender smiled. "I appreciate ya helping our local boys stay in business."

The barkeep returned with the Stranger's order. "Here ya go. Let me know what ya think." He looked down at his watch. "It's about an hour before closing time. Do ya want me to run ya a tab?"

The Stranger took a sip of the whiskey, then threw it back. "That's smooth. Yes, a tab would be good."

The bartender pulled a whiskey bottle from beneath the bar and refilled the Stranger's glass. "That ones on me."

"Much obliged. A lot of commotion at the police station tonight. What's going on?"

"Hell, Mister, this used to be a quiet town once the tourists left for the season, but since the trial, it's been downright crazy. I guess a couple of our ladies were out at Sheep Mountain with a new woman in town. Dakota Reynolds and the new woman didn't come back to camp tonight. With her being somewhat of a celebrity around here, and her granddaddy's deep connections, they'll have half the county and the park service out there searchin'."

The Stranger swirled his shot and downed it. "The mountains can be a dangerous place at nighttime. I'd have to think these ladies are experienced hikers, growing up out here."

The bartender looked up, nodded, and grabbed a beer from the cooler below the bar. He placed it next to the Stranger. "Very experienced." He turned his gaze slightly and said, "Hey, Max."

A sheriff's deputy pulled a stool up and sat in front of the beer. "What a fucking shit show, Wilt. Give me a short one, please."

The bartender poured a shot of Jack Daniels. "Any word what's happening out on the mountain?"

"Nah, not yet. We'll know more once they get to Kat." The deputy tossed back his shot and chased it with a swig of beer. "It sounds like Dakota and that new one, Jill, went into the caves up there and didn't come out."

Wilt shook his head and poured another shot. "Now, why the hell would Dakota do a dumb thing like that? She knows better than to go into those caves. Hell, a little shake of the ground and her damn passage way could be gone. That's why they closed the mines up there a hundred years ago."

"I know, Wilt, that's what we were talking about as soon as we heard."

"Well, why didn't Kat talk some sense into her? Seems like she was smart enough to stay out of there too."

"She hurt her leg, and couldn't climb. Otherwise, I'm sure she'd be with them."

Wilt leaned over. "I heard the Feds are in town, staying down at the Thunderbird."

Max nodded and dropped his voice. "Yeah, it's about that guy they found in the hotel. Guess there's more to that story. Jessica told me the Feds are taking his body."

Wilt shook his head. "Damn town's going to hell." He looked over at the Stranger. "Another shot, Mister?"

The Stranger nodded. "And a beer, please."

Max glanced to his right. "Been in town long?"

The Stranger smiled. "Long enough to see all the commotion. I came out for some western peace and quiet. Sure picked the wrong week, I guess."

Max offered his hand. "Max Heller."

The Stranger obliged. "Moe Davidson, folks call me MD. Nice to meet you, Max."

"Likewise, MD. Where you from? I can't place that accent. You're dressed like a cowboy, but don't talk like one."

The Stranger chuckled. "Believe it or not, I was born out west, but my daddy traveled with his job, and I do too—never really called a place home. But I'm looking to settle down soon, maybe out here."

"You got a bride?"

"Widowed."

"Sorry to hear that."

"Thank you, but it was a long time ago. My career kept me on the move, so never remarried, but I'm still young enough to settle in with someone. Kids might be out of the question now, but a good woman would be nice."

Max swigged his beer. "Well, I'll tell you what, MD, our women out here know how to take care of a man. Maybe, you just might find the right one here."

Wilt looked up from cleaning the bar glasses. "You're a good-lookin' guy. If they get that new girl off the mountain, you should introduce yourself. She's a real looker."

Max said, "*Yes she is,* and I heard she's loaded, old family money from wine or something over in France."

The Stranger looked forward and half smiled. "Wine, huh? I might take you boys up on that... if she comes back to town." He glanced up at the old bar clock. "Well, it was a pleasure meeting you two. I'm sure we'll see each other again."

Wilt said, "Nice meeting you, Mister."

Max stood and shook the Stranger's hand. "Have a good night, MD. See ya around."

The rescue crews from town reached the Blue Miner Lake parking lot. Four park rangers stood at the beds of their trucks, doing final inventory on their packs. The lead ranger walked towards the Sheriff Department's team.

Bill Wind Caller stepped from his truck with his hand extended. "Charlie, nice to see you again. I figured you'd be out here."

Charlie took Bill's hand and patted him on the shoulder. "Good to see you too, if not under the best of circumstances." He turned and waved his men over.

Bill followed suit, and after formal introductions, he called out to Jay and motioned him over.

Charlie said, "Jay Storm Walker.... You brought the big guns out, Bill."

Bill said, "He's Dakota's uncle, not by blood, but a life-long friendship with Jim White Feather."

Jay walked in front of the other three rangers, pausing to shake their hands and exchange niceties, and approached Bill and Charlie. After a quick round of cursory greetings, he got right down to business, looking towards Sheep Mountain and into the clear night skies. "Weather is good. Let's go find these girls."

Bill laughed and said, "I guess *you* can get away with referring to these ladies as girls.... Anyway, the next two days look clear."

Jay said, "We will find them before that. Oh, Charlie, Jake Michaels, Dakota's boyfriend, brought his wolf with him. He is tame, and knows Dakota's scent. I hope that will not be a problem."

Charlie chuckled. "That wolf has diplomatic immunity in these parts. Do I have a choice?"

Jay smiled. "Not really."

Charlie slapped Jay's shoulder. "The pack out here is chasing the elk towards the winter refuge anyway, so he'll be fine. That would have been my only issue."

Bill said, "Okay, Charlie, why don't you take lead and call everyone together for a briefing? This is your park."

Charlie stepped to the middle of the small parking lot. "Guys, come on in for a second."

The search groups formed up in front of Charlie and Bill.

"Okay, I believe most of you know each other, and some may have worked together in the past. We'll head down the trail to the lake and meet up with Kat Graziano, the hiker who called this in. I believe a lot of you know her. She'll be a good asset. She's experienced and won't lead us on a wild goose chase up Sheep Mountain. Once we get out there, depending on what direction she sends us, I suggest we stay together while it's dark. We'll reassess once the sun comes up, if we don't locate the women before that. We have the pleasure of Jay Storm Walker joining us. For those that have not worked with him, watch and learn. He's one of the best."

The group paused, turned, and looked at Jay.

He raised his hand and nodded. "Kind words, Charlie, thank you."

Charlie continued. "Tonight, we also have a first for me, after nearly thirty years. Our search team will be using a wolf. I know all of you know of Honi, after the recent trial, and now you'll get to meet him. He knows Dakota's scent and will be more valuable than our canines at this point. He'll stay with Jim White Feather, Jay, and Jake Michaels. I'll let them take lead once we get on the ridge. Any questions?"

Mitch Haig, a ranger, raised his hand. "Cap, the initial report said they may be in a cave on the mountain. There was a report of some seismic activity earlier today. Do we have any maps of that cave system or mine shafts? We may need multiple access points."

Charlie nodded. "Mitch, that's a good point. I have the park service pulling together all geological reports and maps of both. For those of us that have lived here our whole lives, we know the myths of hidden caves around *all* these mountains. Hopefully, Kat points to a cave system or shaft that we have a map of. I'm praying that we find them *on* the mountain and not inside it. Anyone else?" He glanced around. "Okay, let's go find these women."

The group made final prep to their packs, checked their headlamps and flashlights, and performed cross checks with their radios.

Jake went back to the truck and retrieved Honi. The abnormally social wolf tugged him towards the group. "Calm down, boy, calm down."

The search teams moved towards Honi. Each took turns greeting him, and several bent down to love on him. After the slight delay, the group refocused and made their way towards the lake and Kat.

Kat kept the campfire low, so as not to ruin her night vision. She stood along the lake and stared towards the ridge, hoping to see a glimmer of artificial light. When the crunching of brush in the direction of the road caught her attention, she took a deep breath and headed back to camp.

The glint of multiple headlamps in the distance broke the darkness of the woods. She stood patiently and watched the search group crest the hills and move into the lower brush bordering the lake.

As they approached, the man leading the group extended his hand. "Ms. Graziano, Captain Charlie Trotter of the US Park Service."

"Captain, nice to meet you. Please call me Kat." She looked over his shoulder and saw Jim walk into the light of camp. She broke from Charlie, raced towards Jim and wrapped her arms around him.

Jim held her for a second as her trembling subsided.

"Woo Woo, I'm worried. She knows better than not to come off the mountain at night."

"Kat, she is smart, and did not come down for a good reason. We will find her."

She pulled away and wiped her eyes, drawing back a sniffle. "I'm probably overreacting. You're right. I guess sitting here in the dark by myself has my mind racing."

Jake and Honi walked up.

Kat gave Jake a hug and dropped to her knees to nuzzle Honi. "What are you doing here, big guy? You gonna help find Dakota?"

Honi's head cocked, and he looked into Kat's eyes and licked her face.

Kat gave him another hug and stood up. "Jake, you've been her knight in shining armor before, or how she says it, '*my brave warrior.*' Time for you to do it again."

Jake smiled softly. "We'll find her, Kat. Let's get back to the group so you can fill us in."

Kat approached Charlie. "How do you want to do this? Should I tell the group all at one time, or just you and you can share it with them?"

"If you don't mind, coming directly from you would be best. You can answer any questions they might have."

Kat nodded. "Okay, let me grab a map Jill had. She left it behind."

"What sort of map?"

"Hold on, I'll show ya." Kat pulled the map from her pack. "It's an old mine map. We didn't think much of it, but as we followed it across the ridge, we found it to be pretty accurate. This is the cave we found. I circled it."

Charlie examined the map. "Everyone, gather around please."

The group surrounded Charlie. "We have our first break, folks." He held up the map. "Dakota and Jill followed this old miner's map back to a cave circled on here."

Kat spoke up. "The cave is well hidden behind some dense brush, but there's a game trail through it. The game trail is not far from the main trail. We stamped it down pretty good."

Jake said, "Honi will scent her. We'll find it."

Charlie passed the map to Bill. "Everyone, take a quick look at this and let's get going. We have a great starting point."

The map reached Jim and Jay.

Jay examined it. "Hmm...."

Jim whispered, "What do you see, Jay?"

Jay whispered back, "The Henry Mining Company. Our people believed that, as they blasted the mountains, they released spirits. Elders who worked in the mines told stories of the ghosts of ancient people and beasts roaming the darkness. Eventually, they refused to work up there, and the mining company brought in Chinese labor from their railroad operation. Not long after that, the company went bankrupt and the mines were abandoned."

Jim shook his head and put his arm around Jay's shoulder. "How do you remember every ghost story of the Old West?"

Jay stepped forward and handed the map back to one of the rangers. He looked over his shoulder. "Not *every* one, Jim, just the ones the elders spoke of. They are not stories, but rather history to learn from. Let's go get Dakota."

Jim took a deep breath and looked towards the dark outline of the mountain. *Ghosts or not, Lomasi, we're coming for you.*

The rescue crews reached the ridge line and paused for a breather. Charlie glanced down at the map and ahead at the dim outlines of rock formations soldiered along the cliffs. He turned to the group. "Jake, bring Honi up and take lead from here. Based on what I'm looking at, we should be about a mile from the cave."

Jake moved to the front of the formation and bent down. "Okay, boy, where's Dakota? Find Dakota."

Honi's tail wagged, he let out an excited yelp, his nose dropped to the ground, and he raced forward.

Jake turned to the group. "When he was a pup, he and Dakota used to play hide and seek. He won't give up till he finds her."

The group pressed on, but their progress slowed as the nighttime trek along the cliff's edge turned precarious.

When they reached safer grounds, Charlie raised his arm. "Let's take a breather. It looks like we're about an hour or so from sun up. Grab a drink, eat something, take a load off. Based on the map, we're about a quarter mile from the cave."

Jake, Jim, and Jay grouped up.

Jake said, "Jay, what are your thoughts?"

"I was hoping to find them along the trail. Perhaps we still will. The caves worry me."

Jake nodded. "Yeah, me too. I know she packed climbing gear, so if they *did* decide to go exploring, she was prepared. I've climbed with her. She's good."

Jim said, "It is not her skills, Jake, but the caves themselves. They intertwine with old shafts. That is our concern."

Jake paused for a second. "Maybe that's a good thing, like the ranger said at our briefing. It can allow us multiple entry points."

Jay said, "Well, we will find out in the next quarter mile if we need to worry about that or not."

Charlie walked over. "How you boys holding up? That was a tough climb."

Jim chuckled. "You see Jay and I remain standing, unlike like the younger bucks, but not because we are such studs. We would never get back up, if we sat down."

Charlie patted Jim on the shoulder. "Hell, you two are probably in better shape than most of them. Jake, you ready?"

"Yes, sir, let's do it."

The group moved out. The trail was easy walking and they quickly closed in on the turnoff.

Honi paused at the exit from the main trail. He raised his nose into the wind, let out a serious of yelps, and darted out of sight.

Jake turned to the group. "He got a strong scent. That's what he does when he gets close to finding her." He raced ahead to catch up with Honi.

The group followed.

Honi stood at the entrance to the game trail waiting for Jake.

"Go ahead, boy," he said. "Go find her."

Jake dropped to his knees and crawled into the brush tunnel behind Honi, and the wolf's whines and yelps quickened his pace. He exited the game trail to find Honi steadfast at a cave entrance.

The wolf looked into the darkness, and back at Jake, his body trembling as he whimpered non-stop.

"Hold on, boy." Jake pulled a light from his pack and shined it inside the cave. "Okay, go, Honi."

The wolf dashed into the darkness.

Jake stepped in and shined his light, catching a taught piece of twine in its beam. He followed the twine, tied to an old root just inside the entrance, and quickly moved beside it. In the dirt, bordering the twine, were two sets of fresh boot prints, both smaller in size.

Distressful whimpers echoed in the cavern. Jake moved quickly along the guide line towards the back of the cave, then stopped dead in his tracks. In the light cast by his headlamp, he watched Honi dig frantically at the base of a large rock pile, behind which the twine disappeared. Jake walked slowly to his wolf, and shined his light about the rocks and towards the cave walls and ceilings.

"Jake... Jake," echoed through the cavern.

"Down here," Jake yelled back. "Follow the guide line."

Jim and Jay were the first to meet up with him.

Jake said nothing, just shined the light on the twine running behind the rock pile. One by one, the rest of the team grouped up at the blocked passage.

Jay stepped past Jake and examined some of the smaller stones, then shined his light on the walls and ceiling bordering the rock pile. "They are discolored, much lighter than the rest of the walls and ceiling. This cave-in is fresh. The twine looks brand new."

Jim lowered his head. "Can we be sure it's Dakota?"

Jake said, "There are two sets of boot prints along the guide line. Both appear to be women's sizes. And the way Honi is carrying on, I have no doubt, Jim."

Bill spoke up. "Jed, Harvey, go back to the entrance and see if we can get some photos of the boot prints. I'm not sure with all of us following the guide line it's possible. See what you can find."

Marsha Betts, a ranger and the only female in the group, stepped forward. "I'll go with you all and make sure you don't confuse my prints with theirs."

Jay looked back at the search group. "We're not moving these rocks from here, and who knows what lies beyond them. Charlie, how soon will the park service have the geo maps and mine surveys?"

"They'll have them this morning. I put a rush on it. Hopefully, they'll include this area. My fear is that the landslide of 1925 closed off *all* the entrances on the north slope."

Jim said, "Is it possible the mines on my land connect into this system?"

Jed Wilkes, a Sheriff Department search specialist, said, "Jim, it's possible, but that's at least sixty miles as the crow flies. However, I did a search about five years ago back at Chrystal Peak. I remember those mines headed towards Sheep Mountain. We didn't have to go too far in, found the missing couple pretty quick. Hell, that's maybe only eight miles or so from here. Back then, the shafts were in pretty good shape, pretty stable. That might be a way in."

Charlie turned his attention to the rock pile. He pushed on one of the medium-sized stones and shook his head. "Let's get out of here. Pat, you and Mitch are probably in the best shape. I want you two to get down off this mountain and head back to the office. Grab all the maps you can. Also, find out what the ETA is on our boys comin' from South Dakota."

Pat said, "10-4, Cap."

"The rest of us, I suggest we continue along the ridge. Maybe we find another entrance, or Honi gets a scent coming up through a vent hole. Bill, you have any suggestions?"

"Nah, Charlie, that sounds good to me"

"Jay, any thoughts?"

Jay shook his head. "No. Until we see the maps, poking around up here is as good an idea as any."

Webb woke with the first sign of daylight, rolled over and grabbed his phone.

"Good morning, Webb, did you get any sleep?"

"A few winks, Steve. How about you?"

"A couple hours."

"Steve, reach out to the park service in Yellowstone. Tell them I'll pick up Blake and Joe at the airport."

"Isn't that about a hundred miles or so?"

"Probably, but it's a beautiful drive. I may go to the search site with them. It's been a while since I've been back in the field on an active search. I want to be there when we find this Jill Boisonette."

"10-4, I'll reach out to their people. I should hear back in the next hour or so from the Dibella ranch. I'll let you know what they say about Ricci."

"Good. Let me jump in the shower. Their flight arrives at 10:18, correct?"

"Yep, Flight 2269 from Rapid City."

"Okay, call me when you hear from Texas."

Webb rolled out of bed, took a quick shower, and jumped right back on the phone.

"Sheriff's Department, Officer Kent speaking. Is this an emergency?"

"No. Sheriff Kelly, please... it's Agent Sadler."

"Yes, sir, one second please."

"Agent, you're up early."

"Well, Sheriff, you know us old folks don't sleep well."

Joe chuckled. "Yeah, and the 3 AM piss break always interrupts it. What's going on?"

"Just checking in to see how the search went last night?"

"They believe the girls are in the cave system on Sheep Mountain. They found boot prints and a fresh guide line."

"Good, so they can fine-tune their search."

"Well, that's where the positive news ends. It appears there was some seismic activity up there, and the passage way we believe they went down was blocked off. No telling how deep into the caves or old mines they were when this happened."

Webb paused and sat down on his bed. *How convenient, Jill Boisenette.*

"Webb, are you there?"

"Yeah, sorry, Joe, I got lost in my thoughts for a second. I wanted to touch base with you. I'm heading over to Jackson and picking up a couple guys from South Dakota. I'll probably join in the search. Do you want to ride with me and meet them? Were you planning on going to the search area?"

Joe settled back in his chair. His eyes narrowed. *Why are the Feds so interested in this Jill?*

"Thank you, Webb, but my second in command is on vacation. I need to handle some other shit here till he gets back tomorrow, but I have my best guys out there right now. If the search moves past today, then I'll probably be out there."

"Okay, hopefully I *don't* see you out there."

"I hope not either, but those caves are miles long, and the old mine shafts are dangerous. Be careful out there. It's some rugged country."

"Thanks, Sheriff, I will."

Webb crested Togwotee Pass, pulled over, stepped from his vehicle, took a deep breath of the pine-scented high mountain air, and nodded. He looked at the snow-capped peaks of the Tetons on the horizon, and for a second, all that was wrong with the world disappeared as visions of years long past raced through his mind. At this same spot, he could see his dad, pipe hanging from his mouth, with an old clunky camera trying to position his mom, his sister and him for the perfect picture. Their laughter filled the air.

He smiled as his eyes welled.

A phone call snapped him back to reality. He lowered his head for a second and collected his thoughts.

"Yeah, Steve."

"Ricci visited Sellman three times in the past year, most recently, ten days ago."

"Son of a bitch! And he checked into the hotel three days later."

"Yep."

"Good work, Steve. Do me a favor and take over coordinating getting Ricci's body out of town, then meet me out here. It appears that the Reynolds girl and Jill went into some cave system and seismic activity closed off their passage. This sounds like it could be a longer search than expected."

"Roger that. I'll see as soon as I can. So, Webb... where do we stand with Jill? What are your thoughts? Sellman, Ricci, and Percovelli all end up dead, and we can place Jill at all three locations the days of their deaths. Is she *protecting* Dakota? I'm fucking confused."

"I don't know, Steve, but one thing I *do know* is that I don't want her getting off this mountain."

"Agreed. I'll see you out there."

Webb ended the call and stared at the screen for a moment. He then turned to face the Tetons, hoping to catch the ghosts of simpler days one last time.

CHAPTER 39
DAY TWO

Dakota opened her eyes and stared up into the blackness of the cave, as visions of both dread and heroic rescues battled for dominancy in her thoughts. She rolled onto her side and glanced past the glowing embers of last night's fire at Jill. Her features appeared softer in the dim light, almost angelic.

Who or what are you? How do I fit into your plans?

Jill woke. "Good morning."

Dakota held eye contact. "Good morning, did I wake you?"

Jill smiled. "No. How did you sleep?"

Dakota sat up. "Considering it's the first time I've slept with a group of corpses from who knows how long ago, not bad."

Jill remained lying down. "About ten thousand years or so."

Dakota looked back at her. "Huh?"

"You asked how long ago. It's been about ten thousand years. Ice was retreating and tribes were migrating to warmer lands."

"And you walked among them? So, how old *are you*?"

Jill took a deep breath. "You're not going to give up, are you? I guess that's the attorney in you."

Dakota moved to her knees, grabbed a log, and scooted to the fire. She placed it on the embers and fanned it with an old hide strung between two long bones. "This works well. And *no*, I'm not going to give up until I understand why I'm in this *fucking land that time forgot*, with a beautiful woman that I can't decide is an angel or a demon or who knows what."

Jill sat up. "In your terms, I'm about fifty thousand years old. Where I come from, I'm still a young woman, *as* you see me. No, I'm neither an angel nor a demon, which are myths spun by the ignorance of your ancestors. I am just like you, just much more evolved. As I promised, you will *soon* learn the truth. We'll reach our destination this evening."

Dakota fanned the flames quicker and shook her head. "You're challenging every fiber of my intelligence."

Jill tilted her head to the faint calling of Dakota's and her names echoing through the cave. She glanced at Dakota, whose eyes remained fixed in deep thought, deaf to the faint yells from the surface.

Jill bounced up and said, "There, I've given you something to ponder. Let's get a move on so you can get the rest of your answers."

The two women packed out and walked to the river's edge.

Jill placed the torch in the front of the dugout and pushed the nose into the river. "Are you ready?"

Dakota turned and looked back into the darkness at the preserved snapshot from the past. "Do you miss all the people you've had contact with over the years?"

Jill nodded. "Yes, a few... very much, but most not at all."

The calls of their names became louder to Jill. "Hop in. I have more to show you."

On the surface, the search party moved about the rock formations dominating the ridge line. The calling out of the women's names echoed across the early morning quiet in the valley below.

Honi's gait was deliberate, his nose constantly lifted to the air. He looked back at Jake, his eyes confused, as if to say, *'Where is my hide-and-seek partner? It never lasted this long.'*

Jake bent down to reassure the wolf. "Where is she, boy? Find Dakota."

At mid-morning, the group came to the end of the ridge line and a cliff edge.

Charlie took a deep breath, looked over the valley, and turned to the group. "My thoughts are, men, that until we have maps, this is a crap shoot." He pointed north towards the next ridge. "We can move down into the valley and work our way back up that spine, hoping to find another entrance. What do you all think?"

The group followed his finger, each analyzing his suggestion.

Bill stepped forward and joined Charlie at the cliff edge. He panned the terrain and shook his head. "I think we need to see the maps. We need to know exactly when the seismic event happened yesterday, and where. This may help pinpoint how deep they may have been and how fast they could have been walking down there. Hell, the start of that passage looked pretty wide and clear, so they could have been scooting along."

Jim stepped from the group. "Dakota would have only gone as far as her guide line allowed."

Jake said, "If it's the same spool she had in her pack, and she didn't buy more, I think it was about twenty-five hundred feet. But, knowing her, she bought more, or Jill did. Maybe Kat will know that answer."

Bill said, "Jim and Jake, that's a great point. I suggest we head back to Kat, talk to her, and get our hands on those maps."

In unison, the group agreed and started their trek off the mountain.

Webb stood in Jackson Airport waiting for Blake and Joe's plane to disembark. He looked around at all the smiling faces of friends and family reunited in God's country.

I'm so tired of being in airports to begin or end heart-wrenching investigations.

"Webb," a voice called out.

Webb turned and smiled, and walked forward with his hand extended. "Joe, nice to see you again. Didn't think it would be so soon. Where's Blake?"

Joe smirked and rolled his eyes. "He's talking to a woman he met on the plane. He's not far behind."

Webb looked to the tarmac, where Blake and an attractive forty-something-year-old walked towards the arrival gate together. "Good lookin' woman. I didn't take Blake as a ladies' man."

Joe looked back. "He's not. I haven't seen a woman catch his attention since his wife and daughter were killed. That's been close to ten years now."

"Well, maybe it's time we all start thinking about life past this cesspool we made a career out of."

Joe nodded. "My wife and I talk about it often. When I was promoted to search, I was excited. I felt I could help families. Too many times, though, and more often than not, I had to deliver bad news. It gets tough to deal with sometimes, but I have two years left to retire."

"What about Blake? He's got to be old enough to pack it in if *you* only have two years left."

"He could have retired six years ago, but I'm glad he didn't. The loneliness would have killed him. This shitstorm we live everyday keeps him alive."

Blake stepped into the airport. He shook the woman's hand and watched her walk towards a twenty-something-year-old couple and their young son.

"Grandma," the toddler yelled as he ran forward.

Blake stood motionless for a second and smiled. He turned his attention towards the terminal and saw Joe and Webb smiling at him.

Blake approached Webb with a smile and outstretched hand. "Agent Sadler, nice to see you again."

"Likewise, Blake. Nice looking woman you were talking to."

Blake glanced towards her as she walked to Baggage with her family. "Yes, she is. She's an attorney from Sioux Falls and divorced. I'm gonna reach out to her when we both get home."

Joe smiled and patted him on the back without saying a word.

Blake said, "So, Webb, what's this about our blonde?"

"Let's get your bags and gear. I'll fill you both in once we're on the road."

After gathering their things, the trio exited the airport and started towards the search area.

Joe said, "Beautiful country. I did some training here years ago."

Blake said, "A lot more expansive than the other side of the Tetons, where we found the three girls. Speaking of which, Webb, how is that part going? Any more word on the mansion they spoke of?"

Webb said, "No. We believe they were drugged and taken to one of the many mountain homes around the area. Hell, they could have been in Montana, Idaho, Wyoming.... Who knows? So far, every owner has checked out clean, with no ties to Percovelli. Whoever had them, they dropped them off where we found them. They were most likely still high."

Joe said, "How are they doing?"

"From what we know, they seem to be doing fine. Mina and Kimi went back to college, somewhat celebrities, and Aiyana returned to her reservation."

Blake said, "Good, I assume they fared better than most of the ones Percovelli had kidnapped."

Joe said, "How is that investigation going, Webb?"

"Slow, Joe, very slow. None of the ranch workers are talking. Someone will crack. Maybe it will be our blonde, who has a name now: Jill Boisonette."

Blake said, "Boisenette... Cajun?"

Webb shook his head. "Joe, open up my briefcase and grab the folder on the top with her name on it. I have two printouts of an old news story. You and Blake take a couple seconds to read it."

Joe retrieved the folder and passed a copy of the article to Blake.

Blake read a few paragraphs and paused. "Are you fucking kidding me, Webb?"

Joe said, "Looking at the old picture and the one from the hotel, minus the hairstyle difference, she hasn't aged. How is that possible?"

Webb said, "Plastic surgery, I'm sure."

Blake said, "Why would a wealthy, attractive woman join an operation like Percovelli's? That makes no fucking sense."

Webb said, "Maybe she didn't... at first. Maybe she was abducted like the other girls, found she liked the sex trade, and moved up in the organization. Who knows? It makes no sense to me either."

Joe said, "Okay, let's assume you're right. Why is she in a small town in Wyoming? And now lost in the mountains with... oh shit, hold on... lost with Dakota Reynolds, the attorney that brought down the Dibella boys."

Blake said, "And we know those boys were connected to Percovelli. So, is she lost or is she here to settle a score?"

Webb pulled off onto a dirt road and parked. "Wait, this gets better." He reached into his briefcase, pulled out the Ricci file, and divided the death scene photos between Blake and Joe. "Look familiar? His name is Salvatore Ricci, the head of an International Security Firm. He was found a few days ago in a hotel in Dubois. They recovered a scrubbed, professionally-built sniper rifle from his room."

After several moments of examination, Blake said, "What's going on here? That's the same twisted, terrified face as we saw on Percovelli and Cindy."

Webb held his finger up, retrieved a photo from Sellman's file, and passed it to Blake. "And Howard Sellman, Vincent Dibella's attorney."

Blake glanced at the photo and passed it to Joe.

Webb said, "The common denominator: Jill Boissonette. We can place her at or near the scene of each of these people, the days of their deaths."

Blake opened the car door. "I need a fucking smoke."

Joe said, "So this Ricci guy... any ideas why he was in town?"

Webb looked at Joe in the rear-view mirror. "Only thing we can think of is he was there to do a hit. His room was directly across from Dakota Reynold's law practice. We have video footage of him at the Dibella ranch a few days prior to his death, and confirmed he met with Howard Sellman."

Blake bent over and looked in. "And they're both dead. What is our girl, the friggin' Grim Reaper?"

Joe shook his head. "Let's assume she somehow killed Percovelli, Ricci , and Sellman. Each one of them *would have* a motive to want Dakota Reynolds dead, but what about Cindy and the other people on the mountain that night? They had no connection to Dakota."

Webb threw his hands up. "No idea, Joe, other than Cindy and Kelly knew too much about Percovelli's operation, and the rest of the folks were collateral damage. I really don't know, but we need to find her. That's why I brought you two in. I don't know the local boys. I trust both of you. She *cannot* escape us again."

Blake stepped back into the SUV. "So, it would appear she's protecting this Reynolds woman. Based on the trail of bodies she's left behind, if she wanted Reynolds dead, she already would be."

Webb threw the vehicle into drive. "It would appear that way. As to why... who knows?"

Joe said, "Webb, the whole face thing.... What's your thought on that?"

"I've been wracking my brain, and the only thing I can think of is that it's some kind of biological toxin, one that we don't know about yet and that our panels can't detect. Ricci's body is heading to our labs, and we have Sellman's and Percovelli's. Hopefully, we'll find something common in their labs. I don't want to put Cindy Fowler's parents through an exhumation."

Blake said, "Hell no, they've been through enough."

Webb made a right turn. "Based on GPS, the parking lot should be up ahead about two miles. You boys ready to do some hiking and spelunking?"

Joe looked at the mountain tops. "Definitely not the Badlands, is it?"

Blake chuckled. "My smoking should mesh well with this altitude and climbing."

The trio pulled in amongst the group of emergency vehicles.

Joe said, "Damn! Park Service, Sheriff's Department, FBI... only thing we need now is the CIA."

Webb laughed. "It's still early. From what I understand, Dakota Reynolds' grandfather, Jim White Feather, has some clout."

Blake said, "Whoa, hold on! If it's the Jim White Feather I'm thinking of, ex-Special Forces Colonel, *hell yes*, he has clout. He's a highly decorated 'Nam hero. I've read about him. His childhood friend is Jay Storm Walker, a renowned tracker. They served together over there, and pulled off some pretty amazing shit. If Jay is here, we'll find these girls."

Webb said, "I worked a case thirty years ago with Jay. I believe he's long retired."

Joe leaned forward. "He taught a class I went to, probably ten years ago. I believe he's been running as a consultant on *very* select cases."

Webb said, "Well, let's introduce ourselves."

The three men approached two rangers leaned over a map draped across the hood of their truck.

Webb cleared his throat. "Officers."

One of the rangers turned. "Gentlemen, can we help you?"

Webb said, "I'm Agent Sadler, these are Detectives Blake Roberts and Joe Running Horse."

Both young rangers snapped straight up. "Yes, sir, sorry. I'm Ranger Mitch Haig, and this is Ranger Pat Wellen."

Webb said, "Relax, boys, this isn't the academy. Lookin' around, it appears the rest of your crew is on the mountain, correct?"

Ranger Haig said, "Yes, sir, they're on their way back to a camp at the base of it. We were just getting ready to take these maps out there."

Blake said, "Perfect timing. Give us a few minutes to grab our gear and we'll join you."

Ranger Haig said, "Yes sir."

Blake smiled. "Please, guys, drop the sirs. Call me Blake, and this is Joe and Webb."

"Yes sir... err... I mean Blake. Sorry sir."

Blake and Joe chuckled as they walked towards the truck.

Webb stepped behind the rangers. "Can you boys show me the map you're looking at?"

The two rangers parted, and Ranger Haig pointed to a ridge line on the topo map. "Right here is the cave we believe the girls entered. Unfortunately, there was some seismic activity. The passage we believe they went down has been blocked."

Webb nodded and peeled back the map to look at a survey below it. He examined the similar topo features. "Based on this, it appears there are several other cave entrances and mine shafts relatively close by."

Ranger Wellen said, "Yes, sir, the rest of the search party has been looking for another entrance, but they haven't found anything yet. They're on the way down for these maps."

Blake and Joe returned.

"Webb," Joe said, "we grabbed your pack. Is there anything else you need from the truck?"

Webb said, "Thanks, no. I just need to throw my briefcase in the back and lock it up. Take a look at these maps. The rangers will fill you in. I'll be right back."

Back at the truck, Webb leaned against it and dialed Steve.

"Yeah, Webb, how's it going?"

"Blake, Joe, and I are on site. The rest of the search team is coming down from the mountain. What I said earlier is confirmed. It appears the women *are* trapped in a cave system... by some well-timed seismic activity."

Steve paused for a second. "How convenient."

"That's what I thought, but I didn't say anything. How far along are you with Ricci's body?"

"It's handled. They picked it up about a half hour ago. I fly out at three my time, land in Jackson at five-thirty your time."

"Good, stay put in Jackson. It's a lot closer to the search area. Keep on top of the Medical Examiner. I'll reach out to you tomorrow. Oh, and Steve, bring your hiking gear and an explosive test kit."

"Roger that. You thinking what I'm thinking?"

"Well, let's not rule out anything with Jill. I don't know her motives, but we do know she's cunning. Also, tell our forensic teams *not to* cut on Ricci. I want every panel of known toxins that can cause death and paralysis run, including bio warfare shit. I want to make sure not a drop of fluid leaves his body. Have them test fecal and urine, or at least what's left inside him."

"Will do, Boss. See you this afternoon."

"Okay, have a safe flight."

Webb looked towards the mountain. *You're smart, Jill Boissonette, but I've been doing this too long.*

He rejoined the others.

Blake said, "Webb, the search team is off the mountain. Let's gear up and head out."

Webb picked up his pack. "Let's go."

Webb's group approached the women's camp, which now resembled a remote command center. Tents formed a neat circumference around the perimeter, and camp tables and chairs were grouped together to form a makeshift conference area.

As they passed the tents, they were met by a representative of the local contingent. After formal introductions, Charlie led them to the center of camp.

"Everyone, gather 'round please. I want to introduce you to Agent Webb Sadler from the FBI, Detective Blake Roberts and Detective Joe Running Horse from the Park Service in the Badlands. Each of these guys has years of experience in remote rescue and investigations. They'll be an asset to us. So please introduce yourselves, take a few minutes to get to know each other, and we'll regroup after Bill and I have a chance to look at the maps."

Jay whispered to Jim and Jake, "Webb Sadler is a heavy hitter with the bureau. I worked a case with him years ago. I thought for sure he was retired by now. There is something more to all of this."

Jim said, "Let's introduce ourselves. You take lead. I am sure he will remember you."

Jay approached Webb's back as he talked with Jedd Wilks. "Webb Sadler, I thought you retired years ago."

Webb broke conversation with Jedd, turned, and smiled. "Jay Storm Walker, I too would have bet you'd be sitting in a cabin high in these beautiful mountains somewhere, long displaced from this stuff."

The two men shook hands and gave each other a brief hug.

Jay chuckled. "And be bored to tears until the Great Spirit calls me home? Actually, this is personal to me. Dakota is like my daughter." Jay turned to his comrades. "Webb, this is Dakota's grandfather, Jim White Feather, and Dakota's boyfriend, Jake Michaels."

Webb shook each of their hands. "Jim, Jake, we *will* find her. I brought two very trusted men from the Badlands with me, and have one of my partners on the way out here."

Jim said, "Thank you, Webb, we appreciate all the help you can provide, but I must ask.... Why is the FBI so engaged, so quickly?"

Webb nodded. "A fair question." He turned and called two other men over. Once grouped up, he motioned the men to move away from the crowd.

After formal introductions, Joe said, "Jay, I took a class you taught years ago. Nice to see you again and work with you. You are a legend, sir."

Jay smiled. "I remember you, Joe Running Horse. You asked a lot of questions."

Webb lowered his voice. "Blake and Joe worked with me on the Badlands missing girls case. I'm sure you all heard about it—the press covered it well. As you know, that ended in tragic circumstances for three of the girls, two of which agreed to testify but never had a chance to. The woman, Jill, who is up there with Dakota, is a person of high interest. We know she worked for Percovelli, and she could be instrumental in closing the loop on an investigation that is being thwarted by very powerful people."

Jim said, "So that's why you were in town. What does she want with Dakota?"

Webb said, "No, I came into town over the man found dead in the hotel. His room was directly across from your office, Jim. A sniper rifle was recovered from the scene. During my investigation, I saw Jill on the hotel video. She fell right into our laps. We don't know what she wants with Dakota. It's very possibly nothing, and their being lost together could be purely coincidental. Or, it could lead back to the Dibella boys' connection with the Percovelli trafficking ring. Revenge is possible, or maybe she's protecting Dakota. We just don't know."

Jake's brow tightened. "Revenge, protection, coincidence... this is spinning in circles."

Webb said, "It gets more confusing, Jake. Again, please do not share what I'm going to tell you with anyone." He paused for just a beat. "Percovelli, Howard Sellman, and Salvatore Ricci, the man found in the hotel, all share three common denominators. One, they suffered a death that left their faces twisted in terror, something we can't explain right now, but we believe a poison toxin might be involved. Two, they were all connected to each other through business dealings, most likely tied into the trafficking ring. And third, Jill was the last person they saw alive."

After a moment of silence, Jim spoke. "I appreciate your trust and sharing these facts. Each of those men could want Dakota, Jake, and even me, dead. So, why would Jill, who we now know worked for Percovelli, appear to *possibly* be protecting us?"

Webb lowered his head and took a deep breath before looking up. "I wish I knew."

Jay said, "Webb, how do you want to handle this?"

"Let's blend in with the search. The most important thing is to find Dakota. When the time comes, Blake, Joe, and I will concentrate on apprehending Jill."

Jake said, "Does the Sheriff's Department or Rangers know about Jill?"

Webb said, "Sheriff Kelly and Charlie Trotter know we have an interest in her based on a connection to Percovelli, but I didn't elaborate. We'll leave it like that."

Charlie stepped to the middle of camp. "Okay, troops, let's pull it in. There are several openings plotted on the mine survey, not far from where the girls went in. Now, keep in mind these surveys are old, and as many of you know, the Park Service and mining company sealed most of the shaft openings years ago." He held up a map with red X's and traced his finger along them. "This is the ridge line we were on this morning. We walked right past these, so clearly mother nature has done a good job reclaiming them. Bill and I feel the openings in this immediate area will be a waste of manpower." He held up a second map. "Now, you can see where I've circled. This is a cave entrance, not a shaft, in the valley. It's about a half mile from the lake and about a half mile from where the women went in. We think this would be a good place to concentrate our efforts on. This map is dated October 2001, so not that long ago."

Bill spoke up. "With any luck, seismic activity has not closed this in. Does anyone have any questions or suggestions?"

The group looked amongst themselves and shook their heads.

Harvey Grimes said, "Let's go find these ladies. We got about six hours before the sun sets."

The search team geared up, set their GPS, and broke camp.

Kat, feeling helpless and useless, watched the group disappear into the woods across the lake. An uneasy feeling twisted her insides as the reality that Dakota and Jill were in trouble set in. She plopped on a camp chair, buried her head into her hands, and sobbed.

Anna pulled into to the assisted living complex.

Samuel paced back and forth outside his unit, keeping his eyes peeled for her car. He glanced down at his watch and shook his head as the sound of a vehicle turning down his lane caught his attention. He picked up his travel bag and stepped into the parking lot.

He got into the passenger seat and sighed. "Our ancestors told better time by the sun."

Anna rolled her eyes. "Dad, I'm eight minutes late."

"Hmm.... Any word on Lomasi?"

"No, in the last text I got from Jim, he said they were heading to Blue Miner Lake to meet with the search crew, and he will probably lose service. The waiting part is going to be the hardest."

"I will watch them through the eyes of an eagle."

Anna smirked and patted her father on the leg. "I hope so, Dad."

On the ride from town, Anna updated her father on the small details she knew, and said Sheriff Kelly would keep them informed.

Samuel said very little. He spent most of his time staring out the window in deep thought.

"Dad, are you okay? I know you're worried about Lomasi, but it's not like you to keep your thoughts to yourself."

After a long uneasy pause, Samuel said, "There is a force at work here, different than the one that invaded our lives before. It is neither good nor evil, light nor dark. It is unlike anything I have ever seen in the Spirit World. It is powerful, and I do not know how to deal with it. I cannot help Lomasi until I understand it."

Anna paused and chewed on her lip. "Well, Dad, maybe when you get to the ranch, your visions will be clearer."

"Perhaps. Perhaps."

Anna pulled up to the front porch. "Are you hungry, Dad?"

"No, I am cleansing myself." Samuel stepped from the car. "I will be up in the cave of our ancestors. They will guide me."

Anna seemed to consider trying to stop him from making the climb by himself, but she knew it would be wasted breath. She stepped from the car. "Be careful, please. Here, give me your bag."

The elder medicine man retrieved a ceremonial head dress, a deerskin pouch and beads from his travel bag, and then handed the bag to her. "Thank you, I will be down after I learn the truth."

As Samuel entered the cave of his ancestors, he thought about the last time he was here, and the shadow figure Jake had seen. The ancient Hebrew in which the Spirits spoke to Jake and Dakota had laid heavily on his mind. He had no explanation for it. Perhaps, *that* was the connection to the force he could not answer for. Today, he would talk with the Spirits of his ancestors. They would guide him.

He built a small fire, sat, and drew a circle in the dirt around himself. Next, he donned his shoulder-length headdress adorned with feathers of eagles, hawks, and owls, and draped the turquoise beads around his neck. From the deerskin pouch he retrieved a bone pipe and filled it with herbs.

"Cei3woono heeteniihi he'neexo3eehiiho."

He closed his eyes as a cool wind swirled about the cave. Whispers raced past his ears as he traveled back to the days of his father, then his father's father, and his father's father's father—to the days before white man walked the sacred lands.

His transition to the Spirit World complete, he opened his eyes and found himself standing in an expansive grassland area. Groups of moose meandered about nibbling on low growing willow tips. Elk herds grazed the flats for as far as the eyes could see. To the west stood the Teton Range, and to the east, Sheep Mountain... and Dakota. In the distance, at the base of the Tetons, gentle wisps of smoke rose from multiple points.

The nickering of a paint-colored horse to his right caught his attention. He walked slowly towards the animal with his arm extended and palm open. "Wooo woxhoox."

The mare stayed steady, her ears pricked in his direction.

Samuel reached her and gently petted her nose. When she nuzzled his shoulder, he nodded, grabbed ahold of her mane, and threw his leg across her back. The mare moved forward without a command. Samuel attempted to turn her towards Sheep Mountain, but had no control over his course of travel.

They moved with dreamlike speed across the grasslands without the mare ever breaking a gentle stride. They started across a wide but shallow river, and Samuel felt the mare tense halfway across. She became agitated and anxious, stopped dead in her tracks, and threw her head about wildly and neighed.

Samuel slid off the horse, and as soon as his feet hit the ground, the mare vanished. He looked ahead at a small foothill, behind which lay the source of the smoke. He glanced back at Sheep Mountain, confused about why the Spirits had led him farther from Dakota.

He crested the foothill and gazed over the village below. Tipis dotted the beaten-down grasslands that lay between the wide snaking river and the base of the towering mountains. Horses roamed freely about, and smoke rose from tipis and fire rings, but from the far reaches of the village to the tipis beneath him, he could see no people.

Once off the foothill, he reached the first cluster of tipis. He cupped his hands and yelled, "Hebee." Dead silence followed.

He cautiously moved to the entrance of a tipi. "Hebee."

No response.

He peeled back the tanned deer hide covering the entrance, and recoiled with the stench of rotting flesh. He covered his nose and mouth. The twisted face of a young woman, hugging two small children to her bosom, stared back at him. He allowed the flap of hide to drop, and moved to the next tipi, and then the next, and the next. Every single man, woman, and child, were frozen in profound terror, their posture cowered. Their weapons lay untouched, showing no sign of resistance.

He stepped to the middle of the village and slowly turned in a circle, thrusting his hands into the air. "Heeyou nuhu'? Tousinihiitee?"

A movement at the far end of the village caught his attention. He blocked the sun with his hand and squinted. A black silhouette waved him forward. With each step closer, the silhouette yielded no definition. *Is this the shadow figure Jake saw at the cave of my ancestors?"*

Samuel picked up his pace, but the Spirit maintained a distance, not allowing for interaction. It led him from the grasslands into a dark pass at the base of the mountain. When the Spirit pointed upwards, Samuel followed its finger to a towering twin pinnacle outcropping above the tree line.

He glanced back, and the Shadow Spirit had vanished.

The trek to the outcropping ascended over loose stones. Harrowing switchbacks with cascading frozen springs also made the climb difficult, and large ice puddles riddled a narrow path along sheer cliff edges. With each step, his heart pounded. He reached a shelf just below the twin pinnacles and looked out over the valley below. In the distance, across the vast grasslands, rose the mountain that held Dakota captive.

Why am I here, ancestors?

A warm wind cut through the frigid mountain air, and whispers floated on its gentle breeze. Samuel heeded the words of his ancestors and made the final climb to the base of the pinnacles. He moved between them, stopped in his tracks, and nodded. A long, thin, natural bridge spanned a dark slot canyon. Winds, filled with the final cries of those before him, howled from its depths. Buzzards perched ominously on the jagged cliffs, waiting patiently for the bridge's next victim.

The whispers of his ancestors then ushered him back to the physical world. He removed his headdress and beads, covered the small flame with dirt, and slowly made his way to his feet. He stepped into the warm afternoon sun, looked up, then back into the cave of his ancestors, and bowed his head. "Hohou."

Anna walked outside and greeted him on the back deck. "Did the Spirit World give you answers, Dad?"

Samuel nodded. "Not answers, but direction. I must speak with Jake. Please take me to the search area."

"Dad, it will be almost dark by the time we get there. I don't know if the search team will come off the mountain or not. I just spoke with Sheriff Kelly. He said the team was heading to a cave location behind the lake, about a half mile from where Dakota and Jill went in. They feel confident about it."

"They are wasting their time. I must speak with Jake. I will call Joe Kelly."

Anna sighed. "Go ahead, Dad. Do you have his cell number?"

"Yes."

Joe looked down at his cell phone, looked up at the ceiling, and forcefully exhaled. "Fucking great." He steadied himself and answered the phone. "Samuel, how are you, sir?"

"I will be much better if I can speak with Jim or Jake. Is that possible?"

"I just spoke with Bill about a half hour ago. They were heading into a valley area behind the lake. I'm not sure he will have a signal between the mountains. Is everything all right at the ranch?"

"Yes, Anna and I are fine. Your crew is wasting their time."

Joe shook his head and switched to speaker phone. "How do you know, Samuel?"

"The Spirits showed me."

Joe leaned back in his chair and placed a finger gun to his head, and pulled the trigger. "What did they show you?"

"A cave entrance in the Tetons, past Willow Flats."

"Samuel, you know that's probably thirty miles from where Dakota and Jill went into the caves. There is no way they could have gone that far. And who knows if that cave system runs under the valley and connects?"

Samuel paused. "Can you connect me with Jim or Jake, or not?"

Joe ran his hands slowly down his face. "Let me try to reach Bill."

"Bill, this is Joe. Over."

Static.

"Bill, this is Joe. Over."

"Yeah, Joe, I can hear you. Over."

"Is Jim or Jake Michaels near you? Over."

"Yeah, they're both out in front of me. Who do you want? Over."

"Jake," Samuel yelled over his cell.

Joe looked at his cell and shook his head. "Jake, please. Over."

"Who was that? Over."

"Samuel Red Hawk. Over."

Bill chuckled at Joe's slight change in tone. "Hold on, I'll get Jake. Over."

Jake's voice came through a moment later. "Yeah, Sheriff, this is Jake. Over."

"Jake, I got Samuel on speaker. Go ahead, Samuel."

"Jake, I have been to the Spirit World. I need you to come back to the ranch. They are wasting their time at Sheep Mountain."

"Jake," Joe said, "Did you copy? Over."

"Yes, Sheriff, I did. Samuel, what did the Spirits show you? Over."

"A cave entrance in the Tetons, past Willow Flats. I do not know what it means. The Spirits want you to go there."

Jake sighed audibly. "Let me check out a cave entrance we're heading to. If there is nothing there, I will come back to the ranch tonight. Over."

"You will find nothing. I will see you tonight."

"Samuel, Samuel."

Joe said, "He hung up, Jake. Over."

"Thanks, Sheriff, for patching him through. Over."

"No problem, Jake. I really had no choice. Over."

Jake gave the handheld back to Bill.

Jim and Jay had broken ranks and doubled back towards Jake.

Jim said, "Who was that?"

"Samuel."

"Is Anna all right?"

"Yeah, they're both fine. He said the Spirits showed him a cave in the Tetons, past Willow Flats. He said we are wasting our time here and the Spirits want me to go there."

Jim shook his head. "He knows there is no way Lomasi could have traveled that far, even if there is a connecting cave system."

Jake sighed. "I know, but do we dare ignore him?"

Jay said, "I would not. Jake, we have enough people here. If the cave entrance ahead produces nothing, go back and hear what he has to say."

Jim looked at Jay, then Jake. "Jay is right. We can handle this. Who knows what Samuel saw?"

CHAPTER 40
VISIONS

The search team crested the ridge line on the northeast side of the lake and stared down a steep pine-covered hill.

Charlie held his hand up. "Let's take five

folks. Based on the map, the cave entrance should be next to a small stream on the east side of that hollow."

Honi lifted his nose to the air. His ears perked and he let out a low whine.

Jake bent down next to him. "What is it, boy? Is it Dakota? Go find her."

The wolf broke from the search crew and rushed into the hollow.

Jake took a swig of water. "He caught her scent on the wind. I'm heading down."

The search crew hurried their packs back on and followed Jake down the slippery pine needle-covered hill side.

Honi's excited whines and barks cut through the silence of the dark hollow. Ahead of the team, Jake crested a small knoll to find Honi standing ankle-deep on a flat rock in the middle of a narrow rambling brook. His front shoulders sloped forward and his head focused into the water.

Jake dropped his pack and ran forward. Fears of finding Dakota lying dead in the stream made his legs heavy, and the distance between him and Honi seemed like miles. His heart raced.

This would kill Jim to find her out here.

Dread and adrenaline battled for control with each step. Then... relief and confusion rose, as the brook disappeared into a small opening in the ground. Jake dropped to his knees and looked into a dark abyss. His head blocked the sliver of sunshine that lit the cavern below. He pulled back a bit to allow light to filter in, and squinted, hoping to see some detail of the cave beneath him, but the depths were too great.

"Jake," echoed through the hollow.

He sprang up. "Over here, follow the brook down." He hurried upstream to meet them.

Jim rushed to the front of the crew. "What do we have, Jake? Is there an entrance?"

Jake nodded. "There is, but it's small and appears to be well above a cavern. I couldn't see much without a light, but Honi definitely smelled her."

The group raced forward.

Bill pulled a high-powered flashlight from his pack and dropped to his knees. He pushed some moss aside and stuck his face and light into the hole. "Dakota, Jill... Dakota!"

His calls echoed in the cavern below.

Charlie said, "Can you see anything?"

Bill glanced sideways and shook his head. "No, nothing. From this angle, all I can see is water below us."

Jay said, "Honi scented her, so there is soil down there, probably banks."

Charlie rifled through maps and surveys. "I don't see anything to indicate another entrance within a mile or so from here, and that's too small to get into."

Bill shined his light around the hole. "Below the dirt is solid granite, maybe three feet thick. We can't expand the opening."

Jed said, "We could blast it."

Bill sat up. "I don't know, Jed. No tellin' how weak this roof could be. I'd be scared we cave the whole thing in, and hell, maybe send tremors down any passageway the women may have taken."

Charlie said, "I agree with Bill, blasting could be dangerous."

Mitch nervously spoke up. "We could drop a small drone down there and look around."

The group turned and looked at him.

Charlie smiled and nodded. "That's a great idea, Ranger. It's about three hours before dark. Can you make it to the trucks and back before then?"

Ranger Wellen stepped forward. "I can, sir, no problem."

Charlie paused and glanced at the approving nods of the search party. "Go for it. And be careful."

"Yes sir."

Ranger Pat Wellen dropped his pack, grabbed two protein bars and a bottle of water from it, and said, "I'll see you all in about two hours, maybe less."

The group watched the young ranger jog away.

Harvey said, "To be young again."

Jim said, "He is a good kid, and broke all kinds of track records in high school."

The crew heard heavy, steady crunching coming from the rim of the hollow.

Jake glanced at his watch. "Damn, one hour and fifty-five minutes. That's a hell of an effort."

Pat jogged up to the group, dropped the drone backpack, and bent over to catch his breath. "Under two hours... told you."

Charlie sidled over and patted him on the back. "Good job, son."

The rest of the group followed.

Bill said, "Okay, let's get this thing underground."

Mitch opened the drone pack, made a couple simple assemblies to the small unit, and hit the power switch. "She's ready." He walked over and measured the drone to the hole. "It's tight, but I can fly her through it."

The group stood back and watched Mitch surgically navigate the tiny drone through the tight opening.

He looked back at the group, took a deep breath, and wiped beads of sweat from his brow. "She's in the cavern. Gather round and watch the monitor."

The drone dropped into the darkness, and its lamp lit up the subterranean world, quickly proving what Jay had said about solid land.

Charlie said, "Mitch, take it down to the banks. Let's see if we have footprints."

"Roger."

Mitch piloted the tiny drone along the sandy banks, foot by foot.

He zoomed to the right and said, "There we go!"

Bill said, "Two sets. Our girls are moving."

The group exploded into cheers.

The drone zoomed out a bit and followed the prints along the bank, until they disappeared into a passage.

Jay said, "They are following an underground stream... smart."

Jim nodded. "Charlie, can we get a survey or map that would show this water?"

"I'll reach out to the Geological Survey's Water Resource Division. I'm sure they *have* to have *some* surveys of the area's aquifers, or a hydrologist's reports."

Jim patted Charlie on the back. "Good, thank you."

Bill stepped in front of the group. "Great work, everyone. Let's get back, get rested up, and be ready to hit this first thing in the morning."

Kat watched the sun set, bringing another night over the mountains as the orange and red vests of the search team dotted the far banks of the lake. She sprang to her feet and anxiously counted the group, and her head dropped. She hobbled along the banks towards the group as they made the turn towards camp. To her surprise, their chatter sounded upbeat.

She reached Jake and Honi first. "Good news?"

Jake nodded. "We know they're alive and moving downstream along an underground river. The drone showed footprints about a half mile from where they went in at."

Kat glanced towards the heavens and whispered, "Thank you." She redirected her attention to Jay and Jim as they joined Jake and her. "Okay, what's next?"

Jim said, "Charlie is contacting the Park Service to get geological reports on ground water here. Hopefully, this underground river system is plotted and we can determine where it may empty."

Jay said, "If we are lucky, the girls will find another passage or feeder stream and a way out."

Kat smiled. "God, I hope so. You guys look exhausted. C'mon, let's get you all back to camp and fed."

Jake said, "Jim, Jay, are you both sure you want to stay out here tonight, or do you want to go back with me and get a good night's sleep. I'll be back here at first light."

Kat said, "Where are you going, Jake?"

"Samuel said he needs to talk with me. He had a vision. Do you want to go back, Kat, and get some fresh clothes and maybe a real shower, versus that polar bear plunge you do every day?"

Jay interjected. "Jake, Jim and I will stay here. Samuel will insist you follow the Spirit World in the morning."

Jim said, "Appease him, Jake. I think we all have learned a lesson regarding his visions. Besides, you will not be far past here, and can rejoin us if his sight leads you nowhere."

Kat said, "Jake, I'll stay. I like helping with dinner for the team and getting you all off in the morning with fresh coffee."

Jake chuckled. "You'll make a great wife someday."

Kat rolled her eyes. "We'll see about that. The altitude must be messing with you."

Jake readied his pack and approached the weary search team, which had settled in around the fire. "Are you all sure no one needs to go back to town tonight?"

Each member looked up and shook their head.

Charlie stood and handed Jake a handheld radio. "If you find *anything*, reach out to me immediately. I don't know if we'll be in range, but I've instructed any ranger that can hear you, to provide any support possible until they can reach me and we can join you."

Jake said, "Thanks, Charlie, good luck tomorrow. I'm sure I'll be back out here sometime in the afternoon. And please, if *you* find something, *please* relay it to me."

"I will. Be safe."

Jim and Jay walked Jake to the edge of camp.

Jim said, "Jake, do not let Samuel's visions send you on a wild goose chase. If it appears he saw something that simply does not exist, like a mountain, a body of water, a landmark, etcetera, do not hesitate to abandon his directions. We know Dakota is beneath us and moving. We need you and Honi back here."

"Okay, Jim, I'll use my best judgment."

Jim nodded and walked back to the fire.

Jay said, "Jake, I heard you in the lobby during the trial speak in the ancient language of our people. Be smart with what Samuel gives you. You have a Spirit guide. Use him if possible."

Jake patted him on the shoulder. "I will, Jay, thank you. You and Jim be careful. You're not twenty anymore."

Jay smirked and nodded towards Jake. "And I don't see many twenty-year olds with crow's feet. You also be careful."

Jake winked. "Good point."

Samuel stepped from the front porch as Jake's headlights shined up the long drive. He had been patiently waiting at the kitchen table since dinner.

Jake parked and jumped from the truck. "Good evening, sir. Nice night, huh?"

Samuel motioned him forward. "No time for small talk, Jake. Come."

Jake shrugged and smiled as he followed Samuel up the porch steps.

Anna greeted him at the front door with a hug. "Jake, how is Jim? The sheriff called and filled us in on the footprints. That's positive news, right?"

Samuel raised his hand. "Stop. There will be time for questions in a few minutes. I need Jake to concentrate on what I must show him. Jake, come to the kitchen table."

Jake waited for Samuel to turn, then rolled his eyes, nodded, and whispered to Anna, "He's fine, and yes, good news."

Samuel grumbled, "I'm old, not deaf." He hunched over a topo map spread across the kitchen table. "In my vision, the Spirits led me through Willow Flats, right here." He circled the wide area and traced his steps on the map. "Past the flats, I crossed this river and crested a small knoll. On the other side of the knoll was a village of death, in these grasslands."

Jake interrupted. "A village of death?"

"Yes, every man, woman, and child lay in their tents, their faces twisted in terror, their bodies frozen in a cowered position. They saw evil and could do nothing about it."

"Is that something I need to worry about, Samuel?"

"I believe so. I believe the Shadow Spirit showed me that to warn of the evil that may exist in the mountain."

"Shadow Spirit... like the one I saw up in the cave?"

The medicine man nodded. "It may have been the same one. It was warning us and we did not know that."

"Okay, sir, sorry for interrupting."

"No problem. You need to be aware of every detail the Spirits showed me. Past the village, the Spirit led me into a short dark pass, right here. At the end of the pass, maybe a few hundred yards, on the right side of the mountain stood two granite pinnacles. You need to climb to those pinnacles. Behind them is a narrow natural bridge that crosses a deep slot canyon. The wails of souls that have failed to cross this bridge rose from the depths. The keepers of secrets perched along the jagged cliffs, and glided in the swirling winds of doom. Across this bridge is a cave. It is *here* the Spirits have guided me to. It is where you must go to find Lomasi."

Jake straightened and paused, and his gaze traced Samuel's outlined path on the map. "Did the Spirits not allow you to cross the bridge?"

"No, they brought me back to our world."

"What do you think the significance of caves is? Dakota and Jill are trapped in one. Your vision showed you another. The Shadow Spirit... *Damn, damn!* It's been right in front of me and I didn't see it."

"What, Jake? What has been in front of you?"

"Dakota and I have seen the path of two souls that live within us. The Spirit at the cabin showed us their journey, but never the end. Now, the cave you saw will perhaps finish their story."

Samuel pulled a chair out slowly and sunk into it. His head drooped, and his always steady hands trembled slightly. He said nothing.

"Samuel, are you okay?"

"Jake, you must go at first light. Do not allow the essence of those inside Lomasi and you to control your Destiny. Be cautious of the tongue of those you encounter. Those that speak in the ancient language, not of our ancestors, cannot be trusted. I must rest now."

Jake watched a hunched-over and fragile shell of the medicine man shuffle towards his bedroom.

Anna said, "Dad, are you all right?"

Samuel slowly raised his hand. "I am fine. I need to sleep now. A battle is coming."

Anna shook her head. "He gets himself so worked up with his drug-induced visions. After all these years of this battle he warns of, you would think, as an educated man, he would see the error of his thoughts."

Jake rolled up the map and shrugged. "Who knows, Anna, maybe one day he'll be right. I'm gonna head down to the cabin and get some rest. I want to head back out before dawn. Goodnight."

"Goodnight, Jake."

The Stranger pulled a seat up at the bar.

Wilt walked over. "MD, good to see you again. What can I get ya?"

"Wilt, I'll have the same as last night. Much quieter tonight I see."

Wilt nodded. "Yeah, normally is on a Thursday."

Sheriff Kelly bellied up next to the Stranger. He dropped his hat on the bar and plopped onto his stool with an audible exhale.

The Stranger glanced at the badge on his hat. "Tough day, Sheriff?"

Joe looked into the mirror at the Stranger. "You can say that."

Wilt approached with the Stranger's drinks. "Run a tab, MD?"

"Sounds good, Wilt."

Wilt looked at Sheriff Kelly as he popped him a beer. "Joe, you look like something the damn coyotes dragged through the desert."

Joe held up two fingers an inch apart. "And a short one, Wilt. Yeah, it's been a tough two days with this search, then to top it all off, Samuel Red Hawk called about some medicine man mumbo jumbo. Just what I fucking needed."

Wilt chuckled and pulled a bottle of tequila from the top shelf. "One of the best Vets this state ever saw, but he sure did go hog wild on the medicine man stuff when he retired. How's the search going?"

Joe slammed the shot and chased it with a deep slug of beer. "We know the women are alive and moving through a cave on Sheep Mountain. A drone confirmed that. Looks like they're travelin' along an underground stream."

Wilt said, "Dakota's smart. She knows to follow the water downstream. Hopefully, it spills out from underground somewhere. So, what did Samuel want you to do?"

"He wanted Jake Michaels and his wolf to head over to the Tetons past Willow Flats."

Wilt's eyes widened. "Willow Flats? That's damn near thirty miles from where y'all are searching. Ain't no damn way those girls traveled that far already. What's Michaels gonna do?"

Joe put a big dip of tobacco in. "Come on, Wilt, does he have a choice? Samuel will ride him, and me, like a cheap whore till he at least appeases him. But hell, who knows, maybe there's an entrance over there the old boy remembered about when he was stoned on that stuff he smokes—maybe from an old Indian myth or something."

The Stranger put a twenty on the bar, stood up, and tilted his hat. "Have a good night, Wilt, Sheriff."

Wilt said, "I'm sorry, MD, where's my manners. Sheriff Joe Kelly, this is Moe Davidson, or MD, as he likes to be called."

The Stranger reached his hand out. "Sheriff, my pleasure."

Joe nodded and looked into the Stranger's ice blue eyes. "Joe Kelly, nice to meet you, MD. You visitin' or movin' in?"

MD smiled. "Looking to retire, Sheriff. Jackson Hole is too rich for my blood. I like this town so far, so maybe moving in."

"Well, welcome. It's normally a bit quieter this time of the year. I'm sure you heard about the search."

"Yes sir, Sheriff, it's all over town. Nice to meet you. I'm sure we'll see each other again."

"Likewise, MD."

Joe watched the mirror as MD left the bar. "More and more strangers showin' up here, Wilt."

Wilt poured another shot of tequila. "Well, you heard him, Joe. Normal folks can't afford to live on the other side of the pass no more."

Jake woke well before dawn. He sat at the kitchen table with a cup of coffee, the topo map Samuel had given him, and a calculator. After several calculations, he was satisfied with the amount of climbing rope in his pack. He ran through one last inventory of his gear, then retrieved a 9mm pistol from the bedside table, along with two full clips.

"Well, Honi, not sure what we'll run into in this cave, if there is one, but we'll be prepared."

At first light, Jake and Honi arrived at Willow Flats. A dirt road, not shown on the older topo map, allowed them to travel the perimeter of the flats. After a mile or so, the grounds to the left gently inclined to produce a knoll. Jake pulled along the berm, unfolded the map, and checked his GPS.

"Damn, Honi, Samuel was dead on so far. Let's go, boy."

The two walked up a short path and were met with a sign warning:

Removal of any artifacts is strictly prohibited.

A quick rush of adrenaline coursed through Jake. He picked up his pace, crested the knoll, and stopped. As far as the eye could see, a rolling terrain of golden grasses danced in a gentle breeze. A river, wide and slow, glistened with early morning rays as it meandered through the flat land. He closed his eyes, raised his face to the early morning sun, and drew in a deep breath, savoring the pristine air.

"Okay, boy, so far so good. Let's see what kind of signal we have."

"Jake to Charlie, come in, Charlie."

"Jake, this is Charlie, how do you read? What's your twenty? Over."

"Loud and clear, Charlie. I'm standing on a knoll off Willow Flats. It appears maybe an old Native American village is below me, based on an artifact sign. Over."

"Jake, I know the location. Where are you heading? Over."

"To the right of the grasslands and into the mountains. Samuel claims there's a cave up there, past some twin pinnacles. Over."

"Jake, I've been back there a few times. I don't know of any pinnacle rocks or caves that part of the Tetons. Maybe some small stuff, dens or bat caves, but nothing ever plotted on maps. Over."

Jake looked down on the map and shrugged. "I don't know, Charlie, so far what Samuel said has been spot on. Maybe he just saw a familiar place in his vision. Over."

"Roger that, Jake. Be careful, and if things don't pan out quickly, please head back. I'll have the water surveys by nine a.m. sharp. Over."

"10-4, Charlie. I'll know in about an hour or so. Over."

Jake and Honi stepped from the knoll into the grasslands. They'd walked several hundred feet when an icy wind raced past them.

Honi let out a low slow growl, and when Jake looked down at him, he saw the hair on his back standing and his tail lowered.

"What's wrong, boy?"

Honi's eyes locked onto something in the distance, and his growls turned to snarls. He hunched and slowly crept in front of Jake.

Jake pulled up his binoculars and traced the wolf's stare. A flash of something upright and dark moved into the pines to the right, several hundred yards ahead. Jake drew his sidearm, chambered a round, and slid it back into the holster.

"Kind of late for a bear. Maybe the warmer weather held this one from hibernation a bit longer." He reached down and stroked Honi's head. "It's okay, calm down, boy."

The wolf calmed with Jake's touch and tone, and he moved forward again with a confident stride, his eyes still fixed to the edge of the pines.

They approached the area where the figure ducked into the woods.

Honi stood firm, his lips curled.

Jake looked down at fresh pile of bear scat. "Honi, come, it's a bear. You know what a bear smells like. *Come here*."

The wolf moved forward.

Jake pointed down. "Bear, Honi, bear."

The wolf smelled the scat and relaxed.

Jake shook his head. "Dummy, you're scaring the shit out of me." He unfolded the map and checked his GPS. "Well, that's a coincidence, but it looks like the bear is heading the same direction we are."

The two made their way through the pines and into a dark pass. Ahead, the crashing of brush, then the sound of loose rocks, caught their attention.

Honi broke for the noise.

"*Stay, Honi!*" Jake commanded as he reached for his sidearm. He followed the commotion and caught a glimpse of the hind end of a large black bear scamper towards an outcropping above the pines, and he relaxed. "Good boy, Honi, good boy."

The duo made their way through the relatively short dark pass. Jake opened the map and looked up the mountainside for twin pinnacle towers. He pulled up his binoculars to get a better look above the tree line. After a minute or so, he dropped his glasses and leaned up against a boulder.

"Well, Honi, looks like we may have gone for a nice hike this morning."

The harsh grating call of circling ravens caught his attention.

He nodded and smiled. "The keepers of secrets.... Come, Honi."

After a tricky climb over loose rocks from an old slide, they reached a shelf just above the tree line. Jake panned the outcroppings and cliffs, then plopped down on a boulder, took a deep draw of water from his canteen, and filled a divot in the rock for Honi.

"I don't know, boy, so far Samuel's vision has been spot on, but I don't see these pinnacles."

Honi cocked his head and wagged his tale as if knowing what Jake talked about. Then movement in the cliffs above and behind Jake caught his attention, and he jumped up and snarled, his eyes locked towards the sky.

Jake, knowing Honi hated birds, turned nonchalantly, but then sprang up. He slowly reached for his sidearm. "Shhh, Honi, easy boy."

Jake's eyes locked onto a grizzly perched on a shelf a hundred feet above them. The bear's body was relaxed, his eyes gentle. He darted a glance down at Honi, and did a double-take.

The wolf sat back on his hind quarters, his eyes as calm as the bruin's above them.

Jake watched the bear saunter along a narrow ledge and disappear around a jagged cliff face.

At that moment, the vision of Mingan and Hurit flashed before him. He knew this rock ledge... he had been here before.

CHAPTER 41
THE PYRES

After a strenuous but benign climb, Jake and Honi reached the landing the grizzly had stood on. Jake walked to end of the shelf and looked at the narrow ledge along the cliff. He bent over slightly and stared into the depths of a dark slot canyon. "Well, Samuel, so much for pinnacles and a fucking bridge," he mumbled.

Jake tied off one end of his climbing rope to a piton he drove into the granite wall just before the cliff edge. He looped the rope through his harness and shuffled out along the two-foot-wide ledge.

Honi cautiously place two paws on the ledge.

Jake raised his hand and barked, "*Honi, stay, stay.* I'll be back for you."

The wolf backed up, dropped to his belly, and whined.

Jake turned towards the granite wall and shuffled forward as winds howled from all directions, challenging his balance. Every four feet or so, he drove a piton into seems of the rock wall and strung a guide rope through them. He reached a blind bend after five pitons. Just as in Dakota's and his vision, below him was a landing.

He doubled back to Honi.

"Okay, boy, let's get your harness on."

Jake pulled several feet of rope from his pack and cut it into lengths. He threw the first length over Honi's shoulder.

Honi grabbed an end of the rope and went into a tug of war.

Jake chuckled and let go of the rope. "No, Honi, this is not game time."

The wolf walked back with the rope and laid it down. When Jake reached for it, Honi snatched it up and tugged.

Jake rolled his eyes. "Okay, we'll play for a bit."

After several minutes, Honi sensed Jake was not in the mood and got bored.

"Now, can I do this?"

Jake tied one loop around the wolf's chest and back, a second around his hips, and two joining both loops long-ways down his back. He hooked a carabiner onto the makeshift harness and gave it a tug.

"Looks good, boy. Let's do this."

The climbers approached the ledge, and Jake hooked both their harnesses onto two short slide ropes attached to the guide rope he ran along the wall. Step by harrowing step, they made their way to the blind turn and dropped to the landing below.

Once there, Jake removed Honi's harness. "You're a brave boy, yes you are." He reached into his pack and tossed his excited companion a piece of dried trout.

Jake looked towards a tall cliff face on the west side of the landing. *That's where Mingan and Hurit entered the cave.* In the real world, tall lodgepole pines blocked his view.

"Okay, boy, let's go find the cave."

The two meandered between rows of pines. Thirty yards or so in the distance, a break provided a clear view of the streaky gray and pink granite face. A low howl caught Jake's ear. He paused, tilted his head, and shrugged. They stepped from the pines into a clearing dominated by the silver-green patchwork of sagebrush and alpine grasses.

"Son... of... a... bitch."

Lying prone, covered by years of growth, were the fallen heaps of two pinnacles. Jake walked between the toppled granite columns, and with each step forward, the howl grew louder, deeper, and more foreboding. He stopped at the foot of a natural bridge spanning a deep narrow canyon. Across the moaning abyss stood the cave of Samuel's vision. His brow wrinkled.

"This is not the cave in Mingan and Hurit's journey, but that was the cliff edge. Could our visions be intertwined?" He stepped back and moved a few yards along the slot canyon's rim to get a side profile of the bridge. "Well, Honi, it looks sturdy enough."

He returned to the bridge and shuffled a couple feet out, but a sudden updraft from the canyon caught him off guard. He threw his hands out to steady himself, and jumped back. The raspy hiss of several vultures poached on the cliffs seemed to mock his attempt.

He held up both middle fingers and yelled, "You're not getting a free meal that easy." He shook his head and said to Honi, "Okay, boy, we're not walking across that without ropes."

He drove a piton into a large chunk of the fallen pinnacles, tied a rope off, threaded it through his harness, and stepped to the foot of the bridge. The swirling winds below wailed with the cries of lost souls before him, and the thundering wings of vultures, launching from their perches, echoed along the cliffs. The sky darkened briefly as the birds of death moved into their circular flight pattern.

Jake shielded his eyes and looked up. "Sorry to disappoint, guys, but I'm a bit smarter than those before me."

He lowered his center of gravity, looked back, and ordered Honi to stay. Step by step, he then shuffled forward, battling gusts from all directions. Every two feet, he drove a piton and threaded his rope through it. The howl of whirlwinds reached a near deafening level as he reached the halfway point, their gale forces rocking him from all angles. He dropped to his hands and knees and pressed forward, inch by inch. The other side grew closer, and suddenly, the winds died, the howls from the canyon below silenced, and the hoard of circling vultures settled back onto their perches.

He stood up several feet from the other side and took a deep breath. "Did I pass the test?"

He drove his last piton and cautiously turned back for Honi. He braced for hell as the middle of the bridge approached, fearful the dark Spirits of the abyss would up their game, but only calm breezes greeted him.

After tethering Honi to the guide line, the two made an uneventful trip across the bridge.

Jake paused at the small entrance of the cave and pulled his handheld out.

"Charlie, can you read me? Over."

Static.

"Charlie, can you read me? Over."

Static.

"Yellowstone, can you read me? Over."

Static.

"Well, Honi, they have a good idea where we are. They'll see our ropes from the air if we get lost."

He donned his headlamp, turned it on, and bent over to enter the cave. His lamp illuminated a bedroom-size cavern with one passage to the left. He moved to the center and slowly panned the granite walls adorned with sporadic petroglyphs of bison and elk. The faint echo of dripping water from the passage caught his attention.

"Come, boy."

The claustrophobic passage twisted and turned while steadily descending, and the gentle babbling of water grew louder with each step. A faint flicker of light at the end of a straight stretch of the labyrinth caught Jake's attention.

Honi stopped and raised his nose.

Jake turned his headlamp off to assure it was not a reflection. "What could that be, boy?"

As the two moved forward, the light became brighter. Shadows danced off imperfections of the passage walls, and a faint smell of burnt oil filled the air. Jake unbuttoned his holster.

What the fuck could this be?

After the two made a sharp left, Honi whimpered and dropped to his belly, and Jake stood motionless, his jaw slack.

His eyes locked onto two Native American elders. Their waist-length, flowing headdresses, and their chests of beads ending with talismans, announced their status. They sat motionless on carved wooden thrones, flanked by a pair of spears adorned with eagle feathers. Behind them, sage bushes protruded from small rock ledges above a gently bubbling spring. Torches, evenly spaced around the chamber, illuminated walls covered in cave art more akin to murals than petroglyphs.

The elder on the right rolled his hand slowly, motioning Jake forward.

Jake looked into the eyes of both elders. "I know both of you. I've seen you in the Spirit World. You are Mingan's great grandfather, and you are Hurit's father. But I'm not in the Spirit World, or am I?"

Askuwheteau shook his head. "No, you are not in the Spirit World. It has led you here."

Jake paused and panned the painted walls. A dark nightmarish landscape of a burning village caught his attention. He moved closer to examine it, and glanced towards the elders.

Chogan blinked slowly and nodded.

Jake followed the scene before him, and then the next.

In reverse, a familiar story unfolded. He stopped at the last scene, the day Mingan and Hurit left their respective villages for the Sacred Mountain. He thought for a second, then turned to the elders.

"My vision ended before the burning village. Why have Mingan's and Hurit's souls not rested? Why do they live inside Dakota and me?

Can you help me find her?"

Askuwhetean smiled. "You want all the answers *now*, just like Mingan. You are a worthy host. We will tell their story."

Chogan stood and walked to a village scene besieged by weather. "Rains, foul to the nose and bitter to the tongue, drenched the land this night. Thunder shook the ground with each thrust of their hips. The sins of their flesh changed the world they knew."

Jake said, "In my vision, a Spirit showed them their future was to unite both their peoples and rule together."

Askuwhetean moved from his throne to Jake, and placed a hand on his shoulder. "Yes, they were tricked by that Spirit. Their lust for each other blinded them. For generations, only those that came from the mountain knew of the other tribe. It was a secret we guarded. It was a promise the first people of our kind made to the Great Spirit. It was his will that the Land of the Sunset and the Land of the Sunrise *never* come together."

Chogan turned from painting. "They came from the mountain, anxious to share their plan. Hurit approached our village holding a bundle of the sacred bush above her head. Crowds gathered around them, joyous their next leader had returned. They cheered and hailed her as she made her way through the village. Her mother and I stood beside our tent, watching as she approached. Our smiles were but a mask to protect our people.

"She rushed forward at our sight, proudly holding in front of her the sacred bush. We hugged her and announced to the people their future had returned from the mountain. She stepped inside our tent, bursting to tell of her adventures on the mountain. Inside, the elders were gathered. Her grandmother asked to know of her adventures. She could barely contain herself. Her excitement to proclaim Mingan as her husband and to unite our peoples gushed like a raging spring river.

"The elders hung their heads and wept. I crawled from my tent as the pain of a thousand snake bites coursed through my body. Her mother's wails silenced the celebrations in the village. I struggled to my knees and, as tears burned my cheeks, ordered her to be taken away and imprisoned." Chogan dropped his head and shuffled back to his thrown.

Jake welled up. The pain in Chogan's voice, after thousands of years, shook him. He knew this story would be tragic.

Askuwhetean moved to a mural of Mingan and his wolf. He patted it as if petting the animal, and slowly turned and smiled.

"Mingan walked into town, his stride confident as normal. He yelled out, '*No eagle is powerful enough to keep its feather from the leader of the Land of the Sunrise.*' As with Hurit's village, celebration filled the air.

"I greeted him at our ceremonial tent, as was common to our people. Inside, he professed his love for Hurit and their plan to unite our tribes. When a single tear befell my cheek, he asked why I was so sad. My answer was simple. '*I have heard the grieving cries of your father, and his father, and my father, and all the fathers before them. Your arrogance, and the sins of your flesh, has cursed our people.*' I left the tent, and ordered him to be taken."

Jake pondered for a moment. "So, what became of them?"

Chogan said, "Two moons passed, and my people demanded answers. The truth was not an option. With each rain, the virtues the Great Spirit had blessed us with slowly eroded. Man began to steal from man. Women lay with the men of other women. Blood-colored clouds covered the sun, and our fields wilted. Our hunting became more difficult. I prayed to the Great Spirit for guidance, but my pleading fell on deaf ears. On the first night of the third moon, a Raven came to me in a dream. I was to meet Askuwhetean at the base of the Sacred Mountain in three nights."

Jake looked towards Askuwhetean. "Did your people suffer the same fate?"

The elder turned from the painting, his eyes glazed in a frozen stare. "A dark Spirit walked the paths of my village. My people's punishment was greater. With each morning, wails of grief filled the air. One by one, my people took their own lives—men, women, children. The dark Spirit spared no one. At night, the cries of their souls carried in the wind. I could not stop this Spirit. It was more powerful than my magic. Like Chogan, I too was visited by the Raven and directed to the Sacred Mountain."

Chogan walked behind his throne. He stepped over the spring and drew back sage bushes covering another painting. "Come closer."

Jake's eyes narrowed as the details of the cave art became clearer. At the base of the mountain, the two elders stood with a powerfully-built figure, his headdress framing a black abyss. "Rowtag."

Chogan nodded. "Yes, the Spirit of Destiny. The Spirit World has introduced you?"

"Yes, he's the Spirit that showed us Mingan and Hurit's journey, but left Dakota and me with no ending, no answers."

Askuwhetean interjected. "He will not give you an answer, but only a choice of paths, as he did Chogan and I that night."

Chogan continued. "Rowtag showed us the bleak future of our people. He showed us great suffering, a world with no guidance, a land with no reverence for the Great Spirit."

Jake said, "Did he *not* show you a second path?"

Chogan nodded. "Yes. We were to punish Mingan and Hurit for their crimes against the Great Spirit. Our crops would be bountiful again, our hunting lands abundant with buffalo and elk."

Jake's head drooped. "A difficult decision, but a necessary one."

Askuwhetean moved to the middle of the cave, and he panned the story laid out on the cavern walls. "So we thought."

Jake said, "What do you mean?"

"Rowtag, without giving us a clear answer, stepped into the darkness as soon as the second path was shown. Chogan and I deliberated for two days and two nights. We thought about sparing our children and banishing them from their people. We would send them to battle the Six Evils that led them astray. If they failed, their death would satisfy the Great Spirit. If they won, their victory would satisfy the Great Spirit. Either ending would hopefully restore prosperity to our people."

Jake paused for a second. "A third path Rowtag did not show you. That sounded like a viable option. What confuses me is that, in my vision, Rowtag showed the Six Evils entombed. He said it was his Destiny to never allow them to walk this earth again. How did they escape their imprisonment and trick Mingan and Hurit? Why did Rowtag allow this?"

Chogan said, "We do not know. Perhaps your journey will answer these questions."

Jake took a deep breath and looked towards Askuwheten. "Please continue."

Askuwheten nodded. "Confident in our decision, we returned to our villages. We met with Mingan and Hurit, informed them of our judgment and the *one rule* we would impose, should they return from the mountain victorious: their tongues would never speak each other's name again. The people of the Sunrise and Sunset would forever be divided, as the Great Spirit intended."

Jake said, "Rowtag said their souls have wandered the land for millennia, in search of each other. I assume they failed on the mountain?"

Chogan stepped to a small ledge and pull aside the sage. "No, they never made it to the mountain." A wall painting glowed with two lone pyres burning along a river. "They refused our rule to stay apart. Their love for each other and desire to unite our people clouded their judgment. The Spirit's magic was too strong.

"We anticipated their resistance. On the eighth night of the third moon, Askuwhetean and I climbed to the highest hill outside our villages and fired a flaming arrow into the night sky. The next morning, our children were restrained, gagged, hooded, and thrown across a horse like a dead animal. We told our people they angered the Great Spirit and were being taken to the Sacred Mountain for judgment."

Chogan paused to clear his throat. "We traveled for two sunrises. I begged Hurit to reconsider, until my voice was but a whisper and my tears ran dry. Over and over, she pleaded with me, convinced that her Destiny and the Destiny of our people was clear, and that the old ways of our people cursed the Great Spirit." The elder's hand trembled and he fell silent.

Askuwhetean interjected. "At the river, flowing beside the Sacred Mountain, we placed our children on stakes facing each other. We prayed to the Great Spirit for their souls, and to spare our people. We offered them one last chance to save themselves, but they never spoke. Their eyes locked on each other as the Pyres were lit. When the flames danced at the flesh of their feet, they screamed each other's names. It would be their last words. We drew our bows, and ended their lives before they suffered an agonizing death."

Jake's gaze dropped to the black sands of the cave. "In a dream... Dakota and I died. Mingan's and Hurit's souls rose from us and reunited. Rowtag brought them back from eternity. He told them their punishment had been served, but yet did not free them. He said they would be called upon again by him, and casted their souls back into Dakota and me."

Chogan said, "What else did he tell you?"

"He said Dakota's and my Destiny would not be fulfilled until we destroyed the evil that Mingan and Hurit's indiscretions set free. I assume that evil is the Six. We have seen them in visions, twice. Now you speak of them. Did Mingan and Hurit release them into the physical world? How can they move between the Spirit world and ours?"

The two elders looked at each other, and nodded.

Askuwhetean said, "As night fell and the bodies of our children smoldered, Rowtag walked from the shadows. He stood in the river between both Pyres, raised his arms to the sky, and spoke in a foreign tongue. The top of the Sacred Mountain glowed with an orange hue, the ground shook, and the river stood still while he prayed. He stepped from the water, motioned Chogan and I towards him, and spoke. *'Beneath the ashes of the forever wandering lies their Destiny, and two to follow. The seed of the ancient ones has been planted.'* He turned and vanished into the darkness."

Chogan motioned Jake towards the bubbling spring and knelt. "We sifted through the hot ashes of our children, choking back the smell of their burnt flesh. Our hands blistered from the heat. In a dark pile of Hurit's ashes, I saw movement." Chogan reached shoulder-deep into the spring, and gently pulled his arms from the pool. Cupped in his hands was a fetus. "*This* is the Destiny of Mingan and Hurit, and the *'two to follow'* whom Rowtag spoke of."

Jake's brow wrinkled and he shook his head. "I don't understand."

Askuwhetean said, "The night Mingan and Hurit united in the flesh, they were not alone. The Six used powerful magic. They took Mingan's likeness and lay with Hurit. Their seed blended with his. Our children did not know this."

Jake raised his hands. "How the hell could a fetus survive the flames, and for thousands of years without being in a womb? In fact, how have you both survived in this cave? Are you Spirits?"

Chogan said, "No, we are human, as you are. The blood of the Six that coursed through the Child's veins shielded it from the flames. The Waters of Eternal Life has sustained the three of us till such time as our Destiny can be fulfilled. That time has come. Your Destiny lies cupped in my hand. It is what the Six have yearned for since before our people, and the people before them, and the people before them."

"What? My Destiny is to *deliver* their child to them? I don't get it?"

Chogan smirked. "No, the Six knows not of the Child. At the time of its delivery to the world, they were still weak. They did not have the power of sight to reach beyond the mountain. We pulled the Child from the embers and wrapped him in sage and feathers of the Sacred Eagles. This blocked his life force from the Six."

Jake's temples flared. "Then *what is* my Destiny?"

Chogan placed the Child back into the spring. "When we returned to our villages, the punishment of Mingan and Hurit had satisfied the Great Spirit. Our crops grew, herds of beasts roamed the grasslands, and the virtues of our people returned. But unknown to us, on the mountain, the Six grew stronger each day."

Jake interrupted. "So Rowtag lied?"

Askuwhetean said, "No, he did not lie. We asked how to punish Mingan and Hurit, and save our people from the wrath of the Great Spirit. That he answered. We did not ask him what was to follow."

Chogan continued. "The Six rode from the mountain with an unholy fury. Mingan's and Hurit's deaths infuriated them, and their vengeance knew no limits. Our spears and arrows could not pierce their skin. They started with the settlements farthest from the main village, raping our women, torturing and killing our men. The children, they spared at first. They sent them ahead to warn the next settlement of the hell coming for them.

"The Raven came to Askuwhetean and me once more. We were directed to flee our villages and retreat to this cave with the Child."

Jake nodded. "So, what does the Six want? How do Dakota and I play into this, besides being the hosts of Mingan's and Hurit's souls?"

Chogan glanced towards the spring. "A Child, born of the pure essence of Mingan and Hurit and their kind."

Jake stood silent in deep thought. "After thousands of hosts, how could their essence still be pure? Why did the Six simply not choose two more of your people, once they discovered Mingan and Hurit were gone?"

Askuwhetean said, "When Mingan and Hurit were in the mountain, the Six altered their essence, purified it. This would allow for many hybrid offspring. The Rains of Punishment, which the Great Spirit showered the land with, forever tainted the human race, *all* but the hosts carrying our children's essence. The Six have chased those hosts for millennia, never able to find them together, until now."

Jake's tone grew defeated. "They found us in the Spirit World, didn't they? They have Dakota."

Chogan walked towards Jake. "What has protected us has also condemned us. We cannot see beyond what our eyes show us. We cannot risk visiting the Spirit World for answers. If they have seen you in the Spirit World, your essence shines like the sun to them in the physical world."

Askuwhetean said, "They understand the weaknesses of love. If they have her, they know you will come for her. At that time, you will have to make a decision. Do you complete *their* Destiny, or end it?"

Jake looked up and shook his head. His eyes welled. "How do I kill something that can move between two worlds, which has been around longer than our kind? How do I kill immortality?"

Silence fell about the cavern. The complexity of Jakes's question offered no easy answer.

Chogan spoke up. "You make a deal with them. Offer them the Child in exchange for Dakota and the souls of Mingan and Hurit."

Askuwhetean leapt from his throne. "*A deal*, Chogan? You want him to bargain with the evil that forced us to execute Mingan and Hurit? That wiped our people from the land? An evil that has moved around this world and, for tens of thousands of years, spread hatred, greed, and lust? An evil that has mocked the Great Spirit and forced the reset of humanity several times? One that has toppled countries and stirred wars? We *have not* stayed guard over the Child all this time only to turn him over. It *is not* what the Raven ordered us to do. It *is not* what the Spirits of our ancestors would have us do."

Chogan fired back. "What is your answer? How does he destroy what weapons cannot? Perhaps, the Six are not meant to be destroyed. Why has the Great Spirit allowed them to spread their carnage and spew their hatred since the beginning?"

Again, the cavern fell silent.

Jake said, "Even if they agreed to an exchange for the Child, it appears Rowtag controls Mingan and Hurit's eternal Destiny, not the Six. He directed Dakota and me to eliminate the Six. Those were *his* terms for Mingan and Hurit to finally walk side by side."

Askuwhetean lowered his head, inhaled deeply, and walked to one of the two sacred spears flanking the elder's thrones. He drew the first from the ground, and then the next. He moved towards Jake, stood in front of him, and drove the spears into the sand on either side of him.

Chogan said, "Askuwhetean, you know what that means?"

Askuwhetean nodded. "Yes, Chogan, it is time. We have watched this world fall from grace. We have walked on streets that, once, the great herds roamed. Our skies have turned dark with the soils of industry. I am ready to hold my wife's hand again. I am ready to stand on endless plains beneath clear skies, and drink from clean flowing water."

Jake's eyes narrowed. "You mean the both of you have not been *solely* in this cave since moving the Child here?"

Chogan said, "No. Like the locust, we venture from this subterranean world every so many years. It was important we understood how the world was changing, in the event the Great Spirit called upon us to lead a battle against the evil that grips the earth. That request never came."

Jake said, "So how do the spears play into all this?"

Askuwhetean said, "They have shielded Chogan and I from the eyes of evil, as they have every leader of my people since the Great Spirit created us. Once they leave this cave, the Six will hunt us down. They will finish their revenge on the *last* of the People of the Sunset and the People of the Sunrise. The spear heads are made from rock sent from the heavens, a gift from the Great Spirit. It not only shields evil, but can kill it."

Jake pulled a spear from the ground and examined its razor edges. "But there are only two spears and six of them."

Askuwhetean said, "Use the Child as a distraction. Strike swiftly and mercilessly. The Six have never sustained lasting wounds from the weapons of humanity. True pain and blood flowing from their bodies will stagger them."

Jake looked at both elders. "There is no other way, is there?"

Chogan gently shook his head. "Make your attack swift and your blows lethal. Fulfill our children's Destiny and yours. Spare us from an agonizing death by their hands."

Jake said, "Where do I find them?"

Askuwhetean pointed to the murals. "The Sacred Mountain is the highest of the mountains we stand in now. Ascend the western face, above the clouds. You have been there in your visions."

Jake gazed at the mural, paused, and looked back. "If I'm successful in defeating the Six, and spare you their vengeance, will you continue to drink from the Spring of Eternal Life?"

Askuwhetean looked toward the spring. "I drank from it the final time this morning."

Chogan Said, "No, I will hold the hands of my wife and daughter again."

Jake nodded. His eyes soft, he pulled several feathers from the spears and moved to the spring. He plucked a few sprigs of sage from the rock ledges above it, dunked a shirt from his pack in the cool water, and filled his canteen. He reached into the spring and gently retrieved the Child.

Honi joined him there, gently sniffing the Child.

Jake wrapped the Child in the damp shirt, then the feathers and sage, and nested him in a safe area in his pack.

He returned to the spears, secured them in a crossed fashion behind his back, and faced the last of the People of the Sunrise and the People of the Sunset. "Askuwhetean, Chogan... thank you. I will see you again when my journey in this world is over."

The elders bowed their heads and slowly settled back into their thrones.

Honi whimpered, as if sensing the great sadness.

Jake reached the exit of the cavern, hesitated for a second, and began to turn. Suddenly, the cave went black and a wisp of oil smoke ran past his nose. He stopped, smiled, and nodded.

"Come on, Honi, let's find Dakota."

Jake and Honi exited the cavern, secured their harnesses, and shuffled across the bridge.

As they walked between the fallen pinnacles, Jake shook his head. "Samuel, one day I hope I have your gift."

He moved to the edge of the landing, panned the majesty below, then focused on Sheep Mountain in the distance. He pulled the handheld from his belt.

"Charlie, this is Jake. Over."

Static

"Yellowstone, this is Jake Michaels. Over."

Static.

"Piece of shit." Jake shook his head. "Okay, Honi, let's get down off this mountain."

Below, from the darkness of the pines, the Stranger looked up. His eyes narrowed, and he focused on the crossed spears behind Jake's back.

He tipped his worn leather Stetson, nodded, and said, "Well done, Jake Michaels."

CHAPTER 42
THE BRIDGE

Dakota stepped from the subterranean river and paused. A feeling of freedom embraced her as she stood naked on the banks where her ancient ancestors may have once stood. The flames of the morning campfire danced in crystal formations springing from the walls and draped from the ceilings, bathing the cave in the light of a million prisms. She inhaled the aroma of fresh coffee. Movement from Jill's tent rushed her to wrap a towel around herself.

Jill stepped from the tent and sauntered towards the water. She dropped her towel a bit prematurely.

Dakota could not help but admire the gracefulness of her body moving through the dreamscape cavern.

Jill, apparently feeling Dakota's stare, exaggerated an overhead stretch and yawn. "Good morning."

Dakota's eyes darted upwards. "Good morning. That coffee smells great. Kind of surreal as we stand in this prehistoric world, isn't it?"

Jill chuckled. "It is. How was your morning swim?"

"Cold as hell but refreshing."

"Well, today we'll reach our destination. The waters there are as warm and soothing as a vintage wine."

Dakota, taken back by Jill's first clue of their destination, paused and chose her words carefully. "So, we're leaving this underground world?"

Jill walked past her and stepped into the water. "Eventually, yes." The splash of her dive ended the conversation.

Dakota walked towards camp and smirked. *These mountains will be crawling with search teams. Game over... soon.*

Dakota dressed and sat at the campfire. She poured herself a cup of the aromatic brew and, while contemplating her next move, a bright flash of light from above caught her attention. She moved her head into several positions until the flash duplicated itself. She looked down at the wispy smoke rising from the campfire and smiled. After a quick glance towards the water to ensure Jill was not coming, she stood and performed her morning stretches. With each movement, she inched towards Jill's chair to confirm the glint of sunshine was not visible from her angle.

Jill stepped from the river and walked towards camp, in no hurry to wrap herself. She reached the fire, toweled off, and finally covered up as she sat down. "That smells so good."

Dakota poured her a cup. "It's amazing. Where did you get it?"

Jill took a sip. "It's from a small village in Columbia. Every time I go there, I grab some. We can't get it in the States."

Dakota took a sip. "Well, it's amazing. You need to get me some next time you go. I mean... if I'm still alive and we're still friends."

Jill chuckled. "Nice try, Counselor. I know you want to understand what this is all about, and soon you will, but I will tell you this. Your journey, your Destiny, has nothing to do with death. In fact, it's all about life. We will emerge from this underground world as nothing more than two females lost in a cave, who were smart enough to find their way out. Yes, I will bring you back coffee. In fact, maybe Jake, Kat, you, and I can all go there."

Jill's voice and body language gave Dakota no indication she was lying. Her answer gave her hope, and added to her confusion. "Well, I've never been to Columbia."

Jill smiled. "Good, let's break down camp and hit the river. We only have four hours or so to go."

Dakota said, "Do you want any more coffee?"

"No, or I'll be pissing all day."

Dakota stood and doused the fire with the brew, sending a puff of smoke upward. From the corner of her eye, she watched the plume lift towards the sliver of sunshine.

Jake reached his truck and tried the radio again.

"Charlie, this is Jake. Over."

"Jake, this is Charlie. Anything on your end? Over."

Jake unfolded his topo map and traced his finger along a creek. "Roger, Charlie, I found a cave with some old wall drawings. They showed a river that seemed to appear at the base of the Grand Teton. I assume it flowed from underground. The tribe that drew it showed them fishing. They also drew falls downstream, and eventually a large lake. Above the river scene, they drew a cave on the south face of the mountain. Over."

Jake shrugged, hoping his story was convincing. The truth of two elders thousands of years old, and a fetus that survived the flames of a funeral pyre, really was not what Charlie or the search crew needed to hear.

Charlie paused. "Sounds like several streams up there that empty into Jenny Lake. What's your thought? Over."

"Have the hydro surveys given us any direction? Over."

"Negative, Jake. There is water flowing everywhere beneath us. No telling which direction the women may have traveled. Over."

"Do the maps show this far out from Sheep Mountain? Over."

"Negative. Over."

"10-4. It may be worth getting them. If you have nothing else, I'm gonna head to the south face. Who knows? Maybe an old medicine man's vision will help us. Over."

"It can't hurt. I'll get hydro surveys of that area. Over."

"Roger, Charlie. If I don't find anything, I'll head back your way. It's probably an hour or so to the base of the mountain. If the old cave drawings are right, it's maybe a two-hour climb to the cave. That puts me there around one. Over."

"Okay, Jake, be careful. Keep us in the loop. Over."

"I'll try. I couldn't reach you until I came off the mountain. Maybe I'll have better luck on the south face. Hey, is Jay or Jim nearby? Over."

"They're about fifty yards to my right. I'll grab them. Over."

"That's fine, Charlie, don't worry about it. Just pass this info on. Over."

"Will do. Again, be careful. Over."

Jake double-clicked the handheld and reached for his phone.

"Anna, is Samuel nearby?"

"He's right here, Jake. Do you have any news?"

"Nothing that we would understand, but Samuel may."

"Here he is, Jake."

"What did the Spirits show you?" Samuel asked.

"Two elders from thousands of years ago, maybe tens of thousands of years. They claim they're human, not Spirits, kept alive by a Spring of Eternal Life. Is that possible?"

Samuel paused. His deep breath was foretelling. "I have only known the Spring of Eternal Life to be a myth. Did they say what tribe they were from?"

"The People of the Sunset and the People of the Sunrise. Dakota and I saw them in our visions, in the story of the two souls that live inside us. That makes me believe they were Spirits, but I was not in their world. I was in ours."

"What did they direct you to do?"

"I have a fetus with me, maybe two months old. They called it the Child, and said it was the offspring of the souls in Dakota and me, and of evil beings, from before mankind. They called them the Six. I assume they are who Dakota and I saw in the cave above the ranch, the ones that spoke in ancient Hebrew."

"I know this story. Our ancestors spoke of an abomination, born of man and Gods, but it was lost when the Great Spirit punished the people and flooded the earth. What are you to do with this Child?"

"Return him to the Six in exchange for Dakota."

The medicine man mumbled in his native tongue. The repetitiveness, tone, and urgency worried Jake.

"Samuel, are you okay."

"Jake, I must rest now. I need to visit the Spirit World for answers. I do not know what the end story of this Child is. I must assume it was never spoken of after the Great Floods for a reason. Keep the Child from the evil ones. Find another way to rescue Lomasi. I must go to the cave of our elders, sleep before them, and pray for direction."

"Samuel... Samuel...."

"It's me, Jake," Anna said. "He looks worried. What's going on?"

"Visions, Anna, I hope—just visions and myths. I'm heading to another cave out here. I spoke with the search team. They're getting more maps to investigate underground water sheds. Hopefully, Dakota and Jill follow the right one."

"Okay, be careful. Bring her home."

"I will. I promise."

Jake ended the call and dropped his head. Samuel's demeanor worried him. He pulled the two spears off his back and looked at their razor-sharp metallic stone heads. "Whatever Destiny has meant to be your target, I hope your edges find it."

He unloaded his pack, shared several smoked trout fillets with Honi, and they jumped in the truck. A hundred yards down the road, he passed an old Willy's Jeep with Montana tags parked near a small bridge. "Nice old Jeep. Bet there's some great, late season trout fishing in that stream, Honi."

Honi's ears perked.

Jake laughed. "Yeah, I remember the first meal I ever gave you. You haven't stopped eating them since."

The Stranger stepped from a thicket on top of the knoll separating the road from the grasslands. He watched Jake's truck disappear around a curve, then looked to the clear blue mid-morning sky and nodded.

"Listen carefully to the voices carried on the wind. They will tell you secrets."

He jumped into the Willys, unfolded a map of Grand Teton Park, and tapped his finger on the south face.

"Soon... this ends."

Charlie made his way through a rush of thick laurels to Jim and Jay, and called them over from their search team.

"Guys, I just spoke with Jake. He said he found a cave with old drawings. It showed another cave on the south face of Grand Teton, and a river or stream that flowed from the base of the mountain. He said the water continue past some falls and into what I assume would be Jenny Lake. Do either of you know any caves up there? I've been all over that side of the mountain in my climbing days, and I don't recall any caves of any significance. At least, none that would warrant drawings of them."

Jay and Jim looked at each other and shook their heads.

Jim said, "Like you, Charlie, I have climbed the South Face. I do not recall any caves."

Jay squinted and dipped his head slightly. After several moments, he held up a finger. "I remember a story my great grandfather once told me of a cave on the south face. A sacred grizzly lived in it. The grizzly angered the Great Spirit, and the cave entrance was sealed. The grizzly never walked the earth again."

Charlie looked at Jay, and gathered his words so as not to offend him. "Well, sounds like it was closed off way before that area was ever mapped."

Jim said, "What's Jake's plan?"

"He's gonna take a couple hours and head up the south face to the area the cave supposedly exists. He said it was about halfway up. As you both know, that's not a bad climb, mostly rope-free."

Jay said, "What are your thoughts, Charlie? It looks like we are striking out here."

Charlie took a deep breath and looked towards the Tetons. "Jake suggested we get some surveys of the mountains. If he comes up with something, *anything*, we'll split the crew up and send half over there."

Jay nodded. "Sounds good."

Jim said, "Is it possible they could be moving that fast beneath us to reach the Tetons in a couple days? They would need a clear unobstructed path. I find that near impossible, even if they follow a river. They surely would come across a shaft, a cavern with an above ground entrance, like we just found — something that would keep them from continuing to go deeper underground. Dakota is smarter than that. She knows search crews are crawling all over Sheep Mountain by now."

Charlie shrugged and rolled his hands over at waist level. "I really don't know what to think. I thought for sure we would find them by now, or at least a way into the caves."

Jay patted Jim on the shoulder. "You are right, Jim. She *is* smart and has a plan. We just do not know it. Let's keep looking and wait for Jake."

Jim nodded. "Thank you, Charlie, for the update."

Charlie looked Jim in the eyes. "We'll find her." He winked, turned, and walked towards his group.

Jay watched Charlie move from ear's distance. "Jake is fabricating a story. He found something he could not share with Charlie, something a white man, and *most* of our people nowadays, would not understand."

Jim looked towards the Teton Range, and his eyes narrowed. "I climbed those mountains for years. There are no caves on the south face, at least not now." He half smiled. "But a sacred grizzly story?"

Jay raised his brow, his face relaxed. "Ah, more entertaining than seismic activity, right?"

Samuel opened his eyes, sat up, and slowly threw his legs off the bed. He moved to the window and looked towards the sky. The noon sun told him his nap had been short, but his mind told him it was much needed. His mind had been blank in the dream world, the Spirits having chosen silence. He knew the answers he searched for would be found only in the cave.

As he shuffled into the living room, each step loosened his old legs.

Anna looked from the kitchen. "Did you have a good nap, Father?"

Samuel nodded. "Much needed, Anna. Jake is up against powers he *cannot* face alone. I must talk with our ancestors. They will help him."

Anna smiled. "Are you hungry? Would you like some lunch?"

"No, thank you. I must not have white man's chemicals in my body when I go into the Spirit World. They cloud my visions. Unless you have fresh prairie turnip and bison?"

"Sorry, Father, I'm out of both."

Samuel shook his head. "Then I will eat when I come down."

Anna watched her father traverse the hill for the second time in as many days. His tone and demeanor worried her. She'd never seen him this distracted from the real world.

She walked into his room and looked at his Alzheimer's medication. The prescription date was eight days ago for thirty pills. She poured them into her hand and counted twenty-two.

Lack of medication is not the issue.

There was something else, something she'd never dealt with, something he was not sharing with her. His caregivers and doctors at the assisted living home always kept her abreast of any changes in his mood or condition, but they had not reached out to her. Perhaps, the stress of Lomasi's disappearance had taken a sudden toll on him. Jake's call seemed to concern him more than Lomasi being lost.

Maybe he would come down from the cave at peace, satisfied with what the Spirits showed him.

Samuel approached the cave entrance. He lit a sprig of dried sage and gently waved the smoldering plant as he moved to the center of the cave, whispering a prayer in the tongue of his ancestors. He moved the stones from the fire ring used yesterday, placed them in a circle several feet from the west wall of the cave, and settled to his knees between the wall and the fire circle. Next, he shielded himself from dark Spirits with a perimeter of pine cones. Four arrowheads were pressed into the dirt, marking the positions of north, south, east, and west. He used the sprig of burning sage to start a small fire.

From a leather satchel around his waist, he retrieved a single row of beads finished with a raven skull. With the beads pressed to the sky and eyes closed, he paused for several seconds, nodded, and placed them around his neck. He settled into a sitting position, his back resting against the cave wall, and lit his pipe.

The disembodied whispers of his ancestors circled the cave.

He opened his eyes and drew in a deep breath. Warm western breezes blew through his black hair, and the sun kissed his taught skin. He moved forward through swaying grassland, void of the aches and pains of his aged body left behind in the cave.

On the banks of a gentle river, a young maiden stepped ashore.

He smiled and quickened his pace. "Talisa, Talisa."

The maiden turned, her eyes wide. "Samuel." She quickly pulled her buckskin dress over her wet body and ran into the knee-high grasses.

The two young lovers embraced, and Samuel spun them in a circle as they kissed passionately.

Talisa placed her hands on either side of his face and looked deeply into his eyes. "My husband, I have missed you so. The Great Spirit has finally called you home and to my side."

Samuel's eyes welled. He allowed her to slowly drop to her feet. "No, my love, not yet. Our Lomasi is in trouble. I must seek help from our ancestors."

Talisa's head fell. "The Great Spirit called me home too soon, Samuel. I wish I could have been there when she was born, and be there now to help her and you."

"My beloved, it is not a good world anymore. Soon, I will be joining you."

Talisa smiled, ran her hand through Samuel's flowing black hair and down his shoulder, and held his hand. She slowly stepped back from him, their eyes locked and fingers touching to the last moment. "My husband, I look forward to the day we stand side by side again."

Samuel watched Talisa fade from him. He dropped to his knees, buried his hands in his face, and sobbed.

"Samuel," a stern voice commanded. "Stand."

Samuel pulled his hands away. His gaze met the knees of a Spirit lurking over him, and he panned upwards. A large rattlesnake skull hung about the Spirit's neck, dwarfed by a massive chest. A flowing headdress fell past powerful shoulders, its feathers framing a skeletal face. In one hand, the Spirit held a spear adorned with eagle feathers.

As Samuel stood, his mind raced. *The circle of pine cones should have protected me from dark Spirits. How is this entity in the same land as my beloved Talisa?*

The medicine man regained his composure and barked, "*What is your name*, Spirit? Why do you hide your identity with a mask of bones?"

The Spirit said, "My name is not important. The sins of our people have torn the flesh from my face, and my eyes dried to dust from tears spilled through the millennia."

Samuel paused. "I am seeking answers of life for the virtuous, *not* the sinner. Why do you greet me?"

"The answers you seek are not of the virtuous. The one you seek to protect is in the grasp of original sin and the truest evils."

"You said your flesh has been torn from your face by the sins of our people. Are the ones that threaten my great granddaughter our kind?"

"No, medicine man, they are from a time before our kind, before this land flowed with grasses, and rivers ran deep and mountains high."

"How do I do battle against them in the Spirit World?"

"You cannot. They move at will between the two worlds. They cannot be trapped in either. Our magic has no power over them, nor do our weapons."

Samuel's temples flared. "Then why have my ancestors sent you?"

"To give you the answers you prayed for. You cannot help Dakota. It is *her* Destiny, not yours." The Spirit turned and walked away.

Samuel yelled, "I never told you her name, Spirit. How do you know it?" He darted forward and reached to spin the Spirit, but his hands passed through air as the entity vanished.

He dropped to one knee, dug a handful of the earth, and held it to the sky. "Great Spirit, please give me the sight I ask for."

"Samuel," a soft voice said behind him.

He lowered his head. "Talisa, I cannot bear to look into your eyes again. It will tear my heart in two."

"Samuel, turn and look at me, please."

He stood and slowly turned. His eyes met hers.

"Lomasi has many years ahead of her. A warrior will save her. Go back to the world and give Anna a hug. Our time to walk hand in hand is near."

Samuel's eyes stared into the flickering flame as the afternoon sun shined into the cave of his ancestors. He stood, and looked upon the art of his father, and his father's father. The heavy heart he had carried into the cave was now lightened. He moved to the exit, turned for one last look, and smiled.

The search teams emerged from the woods into a clearing at the end of their respected grids. Charlie held up his hand and whistled, motioning them to regroup on him.

Webb, Joe, and Blake huddled before moving.

Joe said, "Webb, what are you thinking?"

"I don't know, Joe. Blake, any ideas?"

Blake shook his head. "We need to find a way underground. If those women find a way to the surface, and Jill gets word that the Feds have joined the search, she'll be gone again."

Webb nodded. "I agree. I wonder if Michaels is having any luck."

Joe said, "I doubt it. Jim and Jay would have headed his way already if there was any inkling of a clue."

Webb said, "All right, let's see what Charlie has in mind."

The searchers circled around Charlie and Bill.

Bill said, "Okay, team, we'll break for a few. Grab yourself some lunch, take a load off. Charlie and I were looking at a one of the mining surveys. About a half mile west of here, there's an entrance. Who knows if it's open or not, but it's all we got right now."

Charlie stepped forward. "Jake Michaels radioed earlier. He found some old cave art depicting an underground river flowing from the south face of Grand Teton, and a cave midway up." He threw his hands in the air. "I don't know of any cave entrances up there, but I'm sure thousands of years ago there may have been. Regardless, he's there and gonna check it out before heading back."

"Charlie, this is Station Twelve, come in. Over."

Charlie held up a finger. "Excuse me for a second."

"Station Twelve, go ahead. Over."

"Charlie, a group of hunters flagged one of our guys down, and reported smoke rising from below a small rock outcropping off or SR 10 at Willow Flats this morning. Over."

"Smoke? Please continue. Over."

"They said at first it was just light wisps, and figured it was some geothermal escape. Crazy part is, they've hunted there for years and never seen it before. A few hours later, one of the men posted up near the smoke, said a large amount escaped, then nothing. He said it smelled of wood and, oddly enough, coffee."

"Did you say coffee, Station Twelve? Over."

"10-4, coffee. We have a unit heading out there now. Over."

"Roger, Twelve. Keep me posted. Over."

"Will do. Over."

Charlie rejoined the search team. "Okay, men, a group of hunters reported smoke escaping from the ground over near Willow Flats. As we know, that's not uncommon around here. What *is* uncommon is it had the scent of wood and coffee. They also said it varied in intensity, then was gone."

Jim stepped forward. "Coffee, Charlie? Do we have a survey of that area? Willow Flats is near Jake."

Charlie knelt and unrolled a map. "Everyone, gather around, please. Okay, this map ends about nine miles from SR 10, right here. Bill, hand me that water survey we looked at earlier." He laid the water survey halfway up the topo map, and pointed at a blue line that ran off it. "This water runs towards SR 10. We need topos and hydros to confirm. Mitch, call HQ and have them send a unit out there ASAP."

Jim said, "Charlie, why not move our search over there?"

"We may, Jim. Let's wait till the rangers update us and we see the maps. We need to determine where that underground water flows *to*. I don't want to guess its direction and end up five miles off course."

Blake whispered to Webb and Joe, "We need to get the fuck over there. We're chasing our tails here."

Jay stepped forward. "Would you mind if Jim and I broke off and headed over there?"

Charlie looked up and paused. "Jay, I trust your experience. If you feel you need to go, by all means, head out."

"Thank you. I would like to take Agent Sadler and his men with me also." Jay slowly blinked.

Charlie cocked his head and squinted, and Jay nodded slightly. He understood Jay's body language—knew he couldn't talk. "That's fine, Jay. Hopefully, we'll all be over there soon enough."

Jay said, "My gut tells me you will."

Charlie said, "Let's all head back to camp and wait for the maps."

Jim and Jay, along with Webb, Blake, and Joe, gathered their belongings at camp and headed for the parking lot.

Webb said, "Jay, thank you. I didn't want to say anything while we were out with the group."

Jay smiled. "I heard Blake back there and agreed with him. We *were* chasing our tails on Sheep Mountain."

Blake said, "Was I that loud?"

"No. Fortunately, my hearing is one of the few things I still have."

Joe said, "Shit, Jay, you and Jim didn't even break a sweat on that mountain. I'm gassed, and a hell of a lot younger."

Blake pulled a smoke out and lit it. "Yeah, me too. My lungs were screaming. What the fuck?"

Jim said, "We are just used to the altitude. All three of you did well."

Webb said, "Jay and Jim, this is your world. What do you make of the coffee and wood smell in that smoke?"

Jim said, "Underground fires can happen out here, and geothermal escape is common. It is a bit strange, though, that local hunters that know the area reported it. That tells me this was a new and unique situation."

Jay said, "I've smelled different odors from beneath the ground. Coffee is new, but that is not what caught my attention. It was the intermittent smoke, then nothing. It sounded like a campfire to me."

Blake said, "What doesn't add up to me is... say Dakota *is* in trouble.... It seems strange they would be camping and drinking coffee, like they're on some *fucking* expedition."

Webb said, "Maybe she's not in trouble, or... at least confident her circumstance is not grave."

Jim said, "Or perhaps, both girls are keeping their cool and executing an old survival plan, to follow water downstream."

Joe said, "Above ground, that normally works, but I don't know about below ground."

Blake took the final drag of his cigarette and field-stripped it. "Hell, they don't need to follow the water. All they have to do is lift their noses and smell for shit. That'll get them to the surface fast."

Joe shook his head and tapped Blake on the shoulder. "My partner, a man of eloquent speech."

The group chuckled.

When they reached the parking lot, Jim looked at Webb's rental. "That will be tight for five of us and gear, Webb."

Webb glanced at his cell phone. "One of my guys is in Jackson. Hopefully, I have service."

"Yeah, Webb," came over the speaker.

"Steve, where are you?"

"I'm in Jackson with one of our guys. The first panel of tox results on Ricci should be over soon. What's up?"

"We may have a lead on our girl. I need you to meet us not too far past the airport. I'm gonna hand the phone to one of the local boys for directions."

"Sounds good, Webb."

Webb handed the phone to Jay. "This is another one of my guys, Jay. Please tell him the fastest way out here."

After Jay did so, he handed the phone back.

Webb said, "If you guys want to take my car, I'll wait for Steve. Just leave me directions."

The four other men glanced at each other, and all shrugged.

Jim spoke up. "That is a good idea, will save us about an hour or so of daylight."

Webb said, "Okay, you boys get going. I'll see you soon."

Jake reached the turnoff to the southern side of the mountain. He traveled several hundred yards and hit an unbreachable gate. A sign read:

Road closed for the winter.

"Are you fuckin' kiddin' me?"

He unfolded a park map and examined the trailheads. "Okay, Honi, looks like we have to cover the next mile and a half on foot."

The two walked quickly to the base of the mountain. Jake pulled up his binoculars and panned the smooth granite faces and jagged cliffs, paying specific attention to ridge lines, ledges, and landings for any indication of a cave entrance. Snow pack distorted finite features as he followed the cliffs to mid-point and above.

"I don't know, boy. I can't see any indication of an entrance. Let's get climbing. Maybe it's just hidden from the ground."

Steadily, the duo reached a quarter of the way up the mountain. Well-worn trails had made the first part of the journey unremarkable. Jake retrieved his glasses again and surveyed the cliffs just above the snow line. On his second pass from east to west, a movement caught his eye. He zoomed in, and a flash of tan slinked along a ledge and vanished.

He lowered the binoculars, unstrapped his sidearm, and mumbled, "That's the last thing we need is a friggin' mountain lion." *Wait... where did it disappear to?*

They cautiously pressed upwards, taking advantage of well-worn switchbacks etched into the mountain over centuries. On a landing a hundred feet from the snowline, below the ledge, the mountain lion crept along, and their good fortune of a benign ascent ran out.

Jake moved from one side of the landing to the next, his hand blocking the sun and snow glare. *Is it really worth it?*

He pulled his handheld out. "Charlie, this is Jake. Over."

The response came a few seconds later. "Yeah, Jake, loud and clear. Over."

"I'm just below the snow line on the south face. No signs of an entrance. Over."

"Roger, Jake. I tried to reach you earlier, but no luck. We have another possible lead. Over."

"What kind of lead? Over."

"Some hunters saw and smelled coffee-scented smoke rising from an outcropping earlier this morning near Willow Flats. Over."

"Did you say coffee? Over."

"Roger. I'm waiting for more maps of the area. My gut says our girls are staying the course along the water. Jim, Jay, and the Feds are heading there now to investigate. Over."

Jake paused and glanced at the ledge above him. "10-4. I'm going to go another hundred feet or so up. I caught a glimpse of a lion on a ledge, but I lost it. Maybe there's a small cave entrance up there. If I don't find anything, I'll head down. Over."

"Ah, Jake, I would leave it alone. A lion on his or her turf is a losing proposition. Even if you find a cave, it's probably a den. Man, the last thing you want is an angry momma with cubs. Over."

"I thought about that. I'm armed, but certainly don't want to kill anything. I'll give the tracks a look. Maybe it was just hunting sheep. Over."

"Roger. Touch base when you can, and I'll do the same when I get the report back from Willow Flats on the smoke. Over."

"10-4. I'll be on ropes the next hundred feet, but I'll try to call when I reach the ledge. Over."

"Be careful. Over."

Jake double-clicked the radio, took his pack off, and retrieved his and Honi's harness and climbing gear. "Well, boy, this should be fun."

They climbed the first twenty feet on a rush of loose, broken rocks lying between two behemoth boulders. Jake drove a piton into a crevice in one boulder, pulled his rope through it, caught his breath and looked down at Honi.

"Show off! I wish I had 4 legs."

Suddenly, a familiar but recently dormant feeling coursed through him. He quickly knotted the rope and leaned back against one of the boulders.

The high noon sun faded, and darkness covered the mountain. Two tiers of birds, eagles on top and ravens beneath, circled to the west of the landing, their wing tips barely missing a sheer rock face. One by one, the ravens ascended to the eagles, until both flocks soared as one. Their flight quickened, round and round—white, brown, and black feathers blurred together. From the whirlwind, a hybrid bird rose to the center. It glided to the boulder opposite of Jake and perched, its size imposing but not threatening, its red eyes intense but not menacing.

The bird leaned its snow-white head towards Jake, its midnight black beak inches from his ear, and whispered, "Cebisee cei3woo hooxuu3iin."

The darkness slowly faded as Jake's spell ended. He shook his head to clear the fog, took a sip of water, and looked towards the sky where the birds circled.

He looked down at Honi, and the distressed wolf's body weight was pressed firmly against his master's legs, his eyes locked onto Jake.

"I'm okay, boy, I'm okay. Been a while since that happened, huh? Let's get up to that ledge."

Foot by foot, the two climbed and clawed their way over loose stones, up and around jagged boulders, and along precarious shelves, until they reached the snow-covered ledge.

Honi immediately pressed his nose into fresh cat tracks, and let out a low, deep growl. His lips curled and the hair on his back stood up as he crept forward.

"*No*, Honi, stay. *Come*."

The wolf looked back at Jake, and again ahead at the tracks, before heading the commands.

Jake crept along the ledge in the opposite direction of the lion's prints. The ledge narrowed with each step, to the point it faded into the mountain. Winds swirled upward from the cliff bottoms as he leaned forward, his feet digging into the loose gravel edge.

The bird spoke of walking Spirit bridges. Did I interpret this right?

He dropped to his belly and inched out over the edge. His heart pounded as he stared into the dizzying depths of the canyon bottoms. He shuffled back, sat up, took a deep breath, and glared at the towering rock face.

Honi moved to his side.

"What the fuck was the bird trying to tell me, boy?"

Jake stared forward, his eyes fixed on the south face.

Spirit bridges... walk Spirit bridges....

A distant hollow growl of a mountain lion snapped him from his thoughts. The thunderous sound of a thousand beating wings and high-pitched chirping echoed across the mountainside.

Honi jumped up, turned, and looked to the sky.

Jake reached for his sidearm, moved to his knees, and spun. His gaze darted to where he'd seen the large cat earlier, but the ledge was clear. The deafening sound of wings and chirping grew closer, and suddenly, from the east side of the ledge, the sky turned black. A colony of bats raced around the cliffs and overhead. Jake followed their flight to the far west side of the south face. They quickly funneled into a narrow pattern and vanished into the rock.

He stood up and nodded. "Where there's bats, there's caves."

He looked at the cliffs below him. A different perspective made everything clear. His eyes followed a ledge that appeared to empty into the sky, but he knew better. The ledge *was* the bridge, one that had started Mingan and Hurit's faithful journey.

A bridge that will connect the Spirit world and this world. A bridge to Dakota.

"Let's go, Honi. Time to find Dakota."

The two descended twenty feet to a ledge, tracing the precarious path as Mingan, Hurit, and Wahya had millennia ago. They dropped to a small landing tucked behind jagged cliffs, hidden from the world below. Jake paused to scan the nooks and crannies of the gray rocks surrounding the landing. Their color made for an ideal place for a mountain lion to lay in wait for its prey.

Step by step, with his sidearm drawn, he inched towards the mountain face where the cave entrance should be.

Honi's nose stayed buried in the snow, his eyes fixed forward as he tracked the big cat.

Three quarters of the way across the landing, the cat's tracks made a sharp left for the mountain wall.

Jake held his hand up. "Whoa, boy."

He stepped a few feet forward and followed the tracks behind a large boulder. They reappeared on the opposite side of the boulder in remarkably wider spacing, and headed towards an outcropping on the eastern side of the landing.

He thought for a moment, and chuckled. "Big bad mountain lion scared of some bats. Come, boy."

Jake quickened his pace. Behind the rock, a head-high fissure split the granite wall. He shined his light into the darkness and nodded.

"Charlie, this is Jake. Over."

Static

"Charlie, Yellowstone, this is Jake Michaels. Over."

Static

He took a deep breath, made sure the handheld's location beacon was switched on, and placed it atop the boulder shielding the cave entrance. He then pulled his headlamp from his pack, tested it, and placed it on his head.

"C'mon, boy, time to follow Destiny."

CHAPTER 43
THE PURSUIT

Jill glanced back at Dakota. "Around the bend is your Destiny. Are you ready?"

Dakota paused. Her stomach tightened. *Now is not the time to show weakness.* She smiled and playfully flipped her hair. "How does my hair look?"

Jill chuckled. "I don't think you can have a bad hair day."

With each stroke of their paddles, Dakota grew more anxious. *Who or what will be waiting for me? What do they want? She talks about life, not death.*

As the bend approached, light reflected in the still waters of the river ahead.

Jill removed the torch and doused it in the river. "We don't need this anymore."

Dakota's muscles tensed and her mouth dried as she gripped her water bottle and took a deep swig. Her breathing quickened. Destiny was a few boat lengths away. The light around the bend intensified. Then....

The truth.

The boat drifted to a standstill at the mouth of a large underground lake. Torches, spaced evenly on the walls, lit the crystal cavern. She gazed upon the familiar dreamscape.

Jill turned. "Welcome. Beautiful, isn't it?"

Dakota's anxiety calmed. "Yes, where are we?" *Don't lie, bitch! I've been here before in the Spirit World.*

"We are beneath the Tetons, in the basement of my family's mansion."

"Your family's mansion? I've been all over these mountains. I don't know of any mansions in the park."

"We're not in the park. We own over a thousand acres on the Idaho side. Let's paddle to shore. I'm ready to get out of this damn thing."

Dakota made several paddles and paused, causing the front of the boat to list right. "Jill, if we were coming to your property, why didn't we just drive here? Why kidnap me?"

Jill pulled her paddle from the water. "Honey, you haven't been kidnapped. There is no ransom. In a day or so, we're going to walk out of here, together with Jake. Our journey will be over. It was imperative we did this as we did. Jake needed to follow a spiritual path and understand his Destiny also."

Dakota gripped the paddle. "What does Jake have to do with this?"

Jill resumed paddling. "You'll learn everything soon, I promise. For now, can we *please* get to shore? I'm ready for a warm bath, some real food, and a glass of the best wine you ever had."

Dakota obliged. As the shore approached, she looked to the gilded bridge. Beyond that sat a feature she hadn't seen in Mingan and Hurit's journey—an ornate marble and gold altar. *Hmm... a new addition since their tryst down here a gazillion years ago.*

"Jill," a male voice called from the shadows on the far right side of the shore.

Dakota's head snapped in his direction.

A statuesque man sauntered across the sand with a bottle of wine and three glasses. Jill jumped into knee-high water and pulled the canoe ashore. "It's my brother. Leave your stuff, we'll get it later." She dashed towards the man and wrapped her arms around him.

Dakota stepped from the canoe and walked slowly towards the siblings.

Jill looked back. "Don't worry, he doesn't bite. Well... unless you're into that kind of stuff."

The man chuckled and extended his hand. "I assure you, I don't bite. My name is Dorian. Welcome to our home, or should I say basement."

Dakota detected a unique accent in his deep, rich voice. His piercing blue eyes, dark black hair pulled tightly into a ponytail, and perfect features left no doubt he and Jill were related. She looked at the two, standing side by side, and her eyes narrowed as she retracted her hand.

Jill said, "What's wrong, Dakota?"

Dakota took a step back. "There was always something about you, Jill, something I couldn't put my finger on. *Now*, in this place, standing next to your brother, it hit me. Both of you were entombed here at one time — in fact, across that bridge, past the altar, in a room to the right. Then, I saw *him* in a visit to the Spirit World. He was one of five riders in a hellish landscape. He approached me and spoke in an ancient Hebrew tongue, but I didn't see you. I assume you were lurking in the shadows, or perhaps continuing to slaughter helpless people in the village."

Jill glanced at her brother.

Dorian smiled. "The Spirit World, as you call it, can be manipulated by fears and fantasies, hidden in the darkest recesses of our mind. Truth and fiction can be blurred. Tell me, Dakota, why were we imprisoned here?"

"You were punished by the Great Spirit for sins against humanity."

Jill slowly waved her arm, palm up towards the gilded bridge. "Please, show us the room we were imprisoned in."

"Jill, don't take me for a fucking fool. I've seen your powers. I'm sure that room was destroyed thousands of years ago."

Dorian said, "Dakota, did you have a Spirit guide in your visions? One that told you of our '*sins*' against humanity?"

Jill held up a finger. "Let me guess. His name was Rowtag?"

Dakota paused. "How did you know that?"

Jill smirked. "We know him as Mastema. He is, or shall I say, *was* one of us. He didn't agree with our vision for humanity, or this planet, so we banished him. He swore he would spend eternity battling us and protecting mankind from our plan." She held up the eight-pointed cross dangling beneath her denim shirt.

Dakota darted a glance at Dorian's half-open white linen shirt, and the same amulet lay across his muscular chest, which she spent a second too long fixed on.

He said, "We stripped him of his amulet, damning him to impotency. He would never walk in the physical world again. His power is nothing more than words cast in dreams."

Dakota looked back at Jill. "And *what is* your plan, Jill? What would be *so* important that you would damn one of your own kind?"

Dorian interjected. "Soon, child, you will learn everything. First, you need to meet the rest of our family, rest, take a shower."

Jill grabbed the wine and glasses from Dorian. "And sample an elixir from grapes long extinct."

Jim, Jay, Joe, and Blake reached the area near Willow Flats where the hunters had reported seeing the smoke. A young Park Ranger walked towards their truck as they parked.

Blake stepped out first and lit a cigarette. He took a few steps toward the young officer and held his hand out. "Detective Blake Roberts."

"Officer Pete Anson. Nice to meet you, Detective."

Joe, Jim, and Jay approached.

After formal introductions, and the young officer gushing about meeting "Mr. Storm Walker," Jay smiled and nodded over the young ranger's shoulder. "I assume that's the hunter that reported the smoke?"

"Yes, sir, one of them. His name is Mr. Olden. The rest had to go to work."

Blake took a drag of his smoke. "Let's have a talk with him."

"Yes sir." Anson turned and walked quickly towards the hunter.

Blake looked at Jay. "Remind me to get a few autographs from you. I can sell them for big bucks to these young Rangers out here. I thought that kid was gonna piss his pants."

Jay chuckled. "I wish I would have that effect on women."

Jim patted him on the shoulder. "Maybe thirty years ago, old man."

Jay said, "Never count an old Indian out. We have good medicine."

The group chuckled then walked towards the hunter.

Officer Anson introduced the group to the hunter.

Blake took a deep drag from his smoke and field-stripped it. "Okay, let's go check this out."

The men walked several hundred yards to a small outcropping positioned atop a knoll overlooking marshland.

Olden pointed to a crack between two rounded stones. "That's where I saw the smoke and smelled the coffee. A few wisps for a while, then all of a sudden, a plume, then nothin'—as if someone doused a fire."

Jay bent down and stuck his nose to the crack, then his ear. He retrieved a flashlight and shined it through the slit. "I do smell a faint odor of burnt wood. The opening is too small to see anything, but I hear water moving."

Jim walked behind the outcropping, and pressed his foot into the soft turf at several locations. "It's solid underneath."

Joe said, "I have an idea." He pulled a pen light from his pack and a roll of twine. He secured the twine to the light and passed it to Jay. "Will this fit through the crack?"

Jay looked up. "It just might." He moved the light into different positions and angled it just right to force it through the crack. "You're not getting this back out."

Joe huffed. "It's two bucks."

Jay knelt holding the roll of twine. "Here, you have younger eyes than me."

Joe changed positions with Jay and pressed his eye to the crack. Yard after yard, he lowered the pen light into the cavern. He paused, cantered his head, let out a few more feet, and nodded.

"There we go, men. I'm over top what appears to be a fire ring." With a pendulum motion, he moved the light side to side, then back and forth. "There are tracks of some sort down there—hard to make out any details—and a stream."

Jim said, "Joe, can you tell what direction the stream is moving?"

"Hard to tell with just flashes of light. It's pretty still water."

Jay said, "Hold on. Blake, can I have a cigarette, please?"

"Sure, Jay, didn't know you smoked."

Jay smiled "Not since Nam, at least tobacco." He winked and pulled a small piece of fiber from the filter. He moved next to ponding water in the marsh and dropped the piece of filter between the reeds. After a slight movement of the fibers, he pointed towards the Tetons. "Water does not flow up hill."

The group followed his finger to the mountains.

Jim said, "I'll call Charlie, tell him to move the search towards Jake."

Blake nodded. "I'll update Webb. They should be here soon."

Jake and Honi entered the cave. Jake scanned the walls for drawings, and shrugged. *Maybe that was just in the visions.*

They moved deeper, making a slow, steady descent. Several hundred yards in, a split in the passage caused them to pause.

"Hold on, boy, let me think." He closed his eyes and dropped his head, desperately grasping for a clue from Mingan and Hurit's journey. "Fuck, I can't remember. I *do* remember the walls glistening with quartz." Both passages jumped to life under the beam of his flashlight. "Shit, that's no help." A quick glance at his compass showed the path dead ahead was true north, the other west. "Let's go north."

After several hundred feet, Jake stopped. "No wall paintings, no luminescence... I don't know, boy. It looked like the landing, but this *does not* look like the cave system. We should have hit water by now."

Jake drew a sip from his canteen and poured a bowl for Honi. He opened a topo map and examined it.

Mingan and Hurit met Rowtag on a cliffside, not far above the underground lake. This topo shows no details to support this.

His eyes panned past the South face to the western slopes. "Damn, Honi, how did I miss this? The People of the Sunrise and People of the Sunset... east and west. C'mon, boy, we need to go back and make the left turn."

The Stranger jumped from the ledge onto the landing, and looked at Jake's and Honi's prints in the snow.

The static of Jake's radio broke the mountaintop silence.

"Jake, this is Jim. Over."

The Stranger paused and ducked into a rock alcove to the left of the ledge.

"Jake, this is Jim. Over."

No response.

"Jake, if you can hear this, we are heading your way. Over."

The Stranger listened for a response, then stepped from cover.

"Jake, do you copy? Over."

No response.

He crept along the rock formations on the western side of the landing. After several more attempts of radio messages, and no response from Jake, he moved towards the cave entrance.

The Stranger closed his eyes, recalled Jake's voice from the knoll, and picked up the radio.

"Jim, this is Jake. Over."

"Jake, we believe the girls are heading to the mountain. We found another campsite along the underground river. Over."

The Stranger nodded slightly. "Roger, Jim, I'm on a landing to the west of the south face, about halfway up, and heading into a cave. Over."

"A cave? Then Samuel was right. Over."

The Stranger's eyes narrowed. "10-4. Over."

"Okay, Jake, I know we'll lose you below ground. Leave your radio outside the cave and turned on. We'll follow the ping. Over."

"Roger, Jim. Over."

The Stranger stared at the radio for a second, then glanced at the edge of the landing. He lifted his arm to heave the handheld, but stopped. He set the radio back on the boulder and entered the cave.

Jake's and Honi's prints in the soft cave soil left no question which direction they'd gone. At the split in the passage, he paused. The soil gave way to a combination of gravel and flat stone. He bent down to examine the ground for any indication of their direction, and from the right passage, a faint voice lifted from the depths. He darkened his headlamp, backed quickly into the shadows, and grasped the talisman hanging around his neck.

"Well, Honi, we should be reaching the split soon."

Honi lifted his nose to the air, paused, and let out a low, slow growl.

Jake undid the strap on his sidearm and shined his light up the passage. The first thing that came to mind was the mountain lion.

He knelt next to Honi. "Shh... quiet, boy."

Jake turned his ear to the passage ahead, and after a minute or so, Honi relaxed. Jake patted him on the back and stood up. "Okay, it's gone, boy. Let's go."

The Stranger quickly back-tracked to the entrance, and tucked himself into the rocks bordering the landing. Removing his necklace and disappearing into the realm would be a last resort. The end of the mission was within his grasp, and the risk was too great.

Jake and Honi turned at the split and started a much steeper descent. After several hundred yards, the compass pointed due west. The bone-dry walls began to show evidence of water, and the smell of moisture assured Jake his decision to abandon the other passage had been the correct one.

The Stranger glanced at his watch. Over and hour had passed since he'd returned to the landing, and the ascent to the surface only took thirty minutes.

He took a swig of water and returned to the cave.

Dakota followed Jill and Dorian across the small, humpbacked, gilded bridge. With each sip of the ancient wine, a feeling of enchantment lessened her anxiety. She panned the mystical dreamscape, where sparkling quartz walls, and crystal formations dangling from the ceiling, shimmered like icicles on a Christmas tree.

Dakota paused. "So, tell me, what's the altar for?"

Jill looked back. "Human sacrifices, of course."

Dorian, with a straight face, added, "Virgin blood keeps us youthful."

Dakota's eyes narrowed.

The siblings held a serious look for several seconds, then busted into laughter.

Jill said, "Many years ago, when we had faith in the heavens, our family held services down here. Now, come and show us this room we were 'entombed' in."

Dakota took a sip of wine and raised it up. "I'll admit, you had me for a second." The minute they turned, she saluted them with a middle finger.

Past the altar, the trio entered a hall. Dakota looked intently at the torchlit passage.

Was it up here, or past the marble room with gold statues? I can't remember. Probably both are gone by now.

At the end of the passage, they stepped into a large circular room filled with hand-carved, long tables atop glazed tile. Provincial marble bistro tables, akin to those found on French sidewalks, lined the perimeter. Art work, spanning centuries, hung from the polished granite cave walls. Crystal sconces, matching the huge chandeliers above, lined the perimeter of the room.

Jill walked to the one visible exit. "And this goes to an elevator to the main house. So, you see, your *'tomb room'* is our conference and entertainment area."

Dorian smiled. "Rowtag always did have a flair for the dramatic. You're not the first to which he portrayed our home to be a house of horrors."

Dakota's eyes followed the solid rock walls. "How can he control our visions in the Spirit World?"

Jill walked over to her. "Watch, hold your hand out. This won't hurt."

Reluctantly, Dakota extended her hand.

Jill gently held it and looked to the ceiling. "Ge-shem."

A warm, gentle, vanilla-scented rain fell on Dakota. She licked the sweet drops from her lips.

Jill said, "A-tsar," and let Dakota's hand fall.

The rain stopped, and Dakota looked down to find her clothes dry and no evidence of water on the tile floor. Bewilderment overtook her.

Jill said, "And that's in the physical world. Imagine what we can do in your *Spirit World*."

Dakota said, "So, your kind can control people's thoughts?"

Jill nodded. "To the point of insanity."

"How much of this is real? How do I know I'm not in one of your created worlds in my own head?"

Dorian walked forward. "You don't. Do you feel as if you are?"

Dakota pulled up her shirt and looked at a scratch she received walking to the cave with Kat and Jill. She ran her finger along the fresh pink skin that replaced a scab. "If I was in a dream world, I don't believe this would heal. So, no."

Dorian smiled and turned. "Let's go up and eat. I'm sure you're starving."

Webb and Steve arrived at the coffee-scented smoke area, and Webb made introductions.

Blake filled the new arrivals in on the latest developments.

Webb glanced at his watch. "When is Charlie and his crew due over at the mountain? We got about three hours of daylight."

Jim said, "They should be getting there in about thirty minutes. Charlie was waiting for two more water surveys to pinpoint where the stream flowed into the mountains. We should arrive the same time they do."

Webb looked at the crew. "Let's go find these ladies."

Webb's group arrived at the blocked gate ahead of Charlie. They pulled their vehicles next to Jake's truck and jumped out.

Jay said, "Charlie will have the gate keys. That will save us some time. The road should be good. The White Owl is late this year."

Blake's face twisted. "Who the hell is the White Owl?"

Joe chuckled and patted him on the shoulder. "You have not paid any attention to me over all these years, have you, partner? White Owl is the winter bringer of snow."

Blake shook his head and lit a smoke. "I have a fuckin' hard enough time with the changing English language and slang." He made air quotes. "LOL, WTF, BTW.... Can't we just speak words anymore?"

The group chuckled.

Jim looked up the road. "Here they come."

The group turned.

Jay said, "Good hearing for an old man."

Jim raised his brow. "*Selectively* good. Ask Anna."

Charlie jumped from his truck, and fumbled with some keys as he walked to the gate. "Good news, gents, the hydro survey shows the river running from the flats and right below Grand Teton."

Jay said, "Where's your crew?"

"I told them to hold tight and wait for my call, get rested up and be ready to relieve us if this turns into a multiple-day event underground."

Jay looked up at the mountain. "Good call, Charlie. Do you have Jake's radio pinged?"

"I do." He unrolled a map and motioned everyone in. "The signal is coming from the east side of the south face... right here." He tapped the map. "Jake said he's at the snow line."

The group turned their attention to the mountain.

Jim said, "That is not far up, maybe an hour climb or so."

Blake shook his head and lit another smoke. "This is all the cardio I missed for the past ten years and ten going forward."

Charlie said, "Ya know, Blake, I was gonna comment on that. How do you smoke and stay up with us?"

Blake held his pack of smokes up. "They're ultra-lights."

Joe shook his head as the group laughed; Blake's levity in stressful situations was always well timed.

Charlie walked to his truck. "There's a parking lot about a mile or so down the road. That will save Mr. ultra-light a few steps."

The group reached the parking area at a convergence of trailheads near the base of the mountain. They geared-up and gathered.

Charlie said, "The south face trail is the steepest but most direct, and fastest to Jake's location. Stretch out and let's get climbing."

The search party reached a flat area and paused.

Charlie caught his breath and panned his binoculars upward to the snowline. He paused and zoomed in. "I see Jake's ropes running from the next shelf to a ledge at the snowline, just as he described. Have your guns ready. This is big cat country."

Jim and Jay raised their field glasses.

Jay lowered his voice. "Samuel had this pegged."

Jim took a deep breath and lowered his binoculars. "So far, yes."

Webb gazed across the valley below. "Pretty country, isn't it?"

Joe nodded. "I wish the Badlands had mountains like this."

Blake chambered a round in his Glock and stepped beside Joe. "You two tourists ready to climb Everest?"

Joe looked up. "Can you imagine? Right now, we're at maybe nine thousand feet, and panting like dogs. What's eighteen thousand feet like?"

Blake shook his head. "No idea, but *I do* know one thing. I'll take my chances with a Yetti, versus a pack of hungry mountain lions blended into those rocks up there."

The group pressed upward to the last shelf below the snow line.

Charlie shielded his eyes from the high sun and surveyed the climb.

Jay tugged Jake's ropes. "I may have approached it a bit differently, but this will work."

Charlie glanced at Webb. "You boys okay?"

Joe gave a thumbs-up.

Webb said, "That ledge looks like it falls off the world up there."

Blake patted him on the back. "Should be a perfect picture for you two tourists."

In single file, the group clawed their way to the snow-covered ledge.

Charlie lifted himself over the ledge's lip and dropped to one knee to catch his breath. One by one the group joined him.

Blake, struggling to catch his breath, glanced forward. "Are you... fucking... kidding me? That must be... two feet wide, *max*."

Joe chuckled. "Remember that climb we did on the Anderson case. That was a white knuckle one too."

Blake stood, looked down, and out at the blue skies Jake's guide rope appeared to end at. "At least I could see the fucking ground below me. That looks like a path to the heavens."

Joe said, "Well, if you fall, you'll be closer to your maker."

Blake scoffed and pointed down. "That's where he's sending me. This will be the closest I'll ever get to him."

Charlie said, "Let's hook in and get off this ledge." He took a couple steps forward past a bare area and hit snow. He held his hand up, leaned over, then turned to the group. "Jake didn't say he had someone with him."

Jim stepped forward. "What do you mean, Charlie?"

"There's two sets of boot tracks, and Honi's."

Jim glanced back at Jay, who shrugged.

The group pressed together and looked at the tracks.

Webb said, "Someone is on to us. We need to move quickly. I can't have Jill alerted and slip through our fingers... *again.*"

Charlie nodded. "Let's go."

The group hastened their pace, each step deliberate, a few borderline-careless. Against sporadic, shifting gusts and blowing snow, they reached the end of the ledge and dropped to the landing. Each readied there sidearms and raced along the footprints.

Charlie was the first to turn around the large granite boulder blocking the cave entrance. "Okay, here's Jake's radio. Gear up. Let's go in."

Dakota, Jill, and Dorian stepped into an elevator straight from the era of downtowns and department stores, long lost to malls. Dorian pulled the black folding metal cage across the opening and closed the cabin's ornate, art deco door.

Dakota looked at the gawdy, shiny stainless steel and wood interior. "I've only seen these in old movies."

Dorian pushed main on the ivory buttons set into a brass control panel.

The old people mover lurched upwards, and Dakota grabbed for the mahogany hip rail. "Damn, you could have warned me."

Jill turned and smiled. "Sorry. Yeah, the take-off is a bit dramatic."

The elevator came to smooth stop after a minute-long ascent.

Dakota said, "How many stories did we just climb?"

Dorian glanced backwards. "Approximately ninety-five, a bit more than the Empire State Building."

The doors opened to a marble foyer. Dorian led Dakota and Jill down a short hall adorned with small brass sconces casting a warm glow off its oak walls. The hall emptied into a grand study.

Dakota took several steps forward, and her jaw dropped as she panned the two-story room. Rich mahogany shelves, lined with books bound in all colors, ran floor to ceiling on three walls. A massive stone fireplace, surrounded by a half circle of ten high-back leather chairs, dominated the fourth wall. To the left of the fireplace, a set of narrow wood doors, inlaid with family crests, towered three quarters of the way to the ceiling.

She moved to the west wall and slowly walked along it. A dark leather-bound book caught her attention, and she ran her fingers along the gold leathers embossed on the spine.

She glanced at Jill and Dorian. "May I?"

Jill nodded. "Of course."

Dakota slowly opened the cover. "*First Edition Don Quixote*? Is this real?"

Dorian said, "Of course. Come, let me show you a special collection we are very proud of." He sauntered to the middle of the east wall with Dakota in trail, slid an attached platform ladder several feet down the shelves, and motioned Dakota to climb up. "The top shelf across this wall contains books rescued from the libraries of ancient cities before they were burnt to the ground. Books are wisdom, wisdom is power. We shared this wisdom with humanity once... well before it was ready to receive it. Now, it stays safe with us until such time humanity can accept the truth and not be drunk by its power."

Dakota slowly scanned the ancient bindings, embossed in a language foreign to her. "Thousands of years have passed since then. We *have* evolved. Surely, we're capable of such truths now."

Jill said, "No, but soon. *This* is part of your Destiny."

Dakota stepped from the ladder and faced Jill. Her temples flared. "*What?* Have I been chosen to deliver the new *fucking gospel* to humanity? I'm getting bored with this Destiny bullshit already. *Please*, stop talking in riddles and level with me. *Why... am... I... here?*"

"It's far from a gospel," a stern male voice spoke from across the room.

Dakota turned to see a couple, eerily similar in looks to Jill and Dorian, walking between the medieval entrance doors of the study.

The female closed the doors and stood in front of them.

The male moved with an air of confidence across the marble floor towards Dakota.

His intense blue eyes, locked on hers, sent a familiar chill up her spine, but she refused to look away as he stopped an arm's length away.

"A gospel is the work of humanity, to explain what they could not explain." He pointed to the ancient books on the shelf. "*There* is the truth, the answers your kind have sought since The Grand Architect of this Universe breathed life into your species."

Dakota paused. The mention of a creator caught her off guard. "And this '*Grand Architect*,' did he create your '*species*' also?"

The man's eyes narrowed. He paused for a second, and a faint smile softened his features. "Forgive me. I did not mean to come on so intensely." He extended his hand. "My name is Josef."

Dakota looked down. "If you don't mind, I'll skip the handshake. I've seen what your sister's touch can do."

Josef turned and motioned the female from the doors. "This is my other sister, Jordana."

Dakota watched the female move across the floor with the grace of goddess.

Jordana's warm smile put Dakota at a bit of ease. "Dakota, nice to meet you. Jill speaks highly of you."

Dakota nodded. "Nice to meet you. My feeling for your sister was mutual, until she kidnapped me."

Jill and Dorian moved to the sides of their siblings.

Jill said, "We had this conversation. You have not been kidnapped."

Dakota looked at the group. "Where are your other brother and sister? Then I'll stand in front of the dreaded Six, for the second time. And Jill, if I'm not being kidnapped, let me leave now."

Jordana said, "You will meet them soon. They are indisposed at the moment." She glanced at Jill and smirked. "The Six... I see she has met Rowtag."

Jill rolled her eyes. "He never tires of that story, does he?"

Jordana nodded. "Or that foolish name, Rowtag."

Josef interjected. "Dakota, you will soon leave here, perhaps as early as this evening, And with you, a clear understanding of *your* Destiny and *ours*. Jill will show you to the kitchen, then your room. Please, eat and relax."

Jill gently tugged on Dakota's hand. "Come, my brothers and sisters are amazing chefs. Then you can bathe in warm mineral springs that fill our tubs."

Jill and Dakota exited the grand library.

The siblings watched in silence, then Jordana moved to the doors and closed them.

A narrow section of the bookshelf swung open, and David and Adah emerged from a torchlit rock passage.

David said, "Jake and the wolf are ascending towards the lake. As we suspected, there's a search party in trail. They're several hours behind him."

Jordana said, "How many, Brother?"

David said, "Seven."

Josef said, "Shall we eliminate them?"

Adah moved towards the group, nestled up to Josef, and kissed him gently on the cheek. "My brother, the warrior... always quick to kill. I believe they pose no threat. Once Jake reaches the lake, I will erase any prints he and the beast have left behind. The others will never find their way through the labyrinth."

Dorian nodded. "I agree, there is no more need for bloodshed. We have seen enough in our lifetime."

Anah said, "I assume Jill is readying the girl?"

Jordana said, "Yes."

Dorian faced his brothers and sisters. "Millennia now gives way to hours. The altar is ready. Our time has come. Let us prepare ourselves."

CHAPTER 44
THE BALANCE

As Jake and Honi traveled deeper into the mountain, mineral water seeping from the cave walls filled the air with an earthy, faintly sweet smell. Jake panned the passage with his headlamp looking for any recognizable feature to confirm he was tracing the journey of Mingan and Hurit.

He paused and took a deep breath. "I don't know, boy... no luminescence, no cave art. Are the Spirits sending us on a wild goose chase?" He took a sip from his canteen and shook his head. "Let's trust them. We have no choice."

Several hundred feet ahead, they reached an intersection of three passages. Jake shined his flashlight up a narrow passage to the left, down the much wider opening to the right, and finally forward on the path they had been following.

"Fuck!"

He reached for his compass, took several steps forward to each opening, and examined their headings. He snapped the compass shut and shoved it in his pocket.

"Who knows, Honi? Each of these passages could twist and turn back and forth. None of them look familiar." He pulled his pack off and took a seat on the fine cave soil.

Honi followed his lead.

Jake examined each opening again, drew a deep breath, forced it out, and laid back. His headlamp illuminated the ceiling above, and his eyes fixated on the rocks in the narrow beam as he drifted into deep thought.

A moment later, he sprang to a sitting position, startling Honi from a nap, and chuckled. "Sorry, boy, didn't mean to scare you."

He jumped to his feet and focused his headlamp on the fine cave soil. He identified the footprints of the usual suspects that would inhabit this dark world. The passage forward and the narrow passage to the left each showed footprints in both directions. The wider opening to the right, however, indicated no movement into or from its darkness.

Jake retrieved his pack. "Let's go, boy. There's a reason no critters use this one."

The passage became increasingly difficult to traverse as fine soil gave way to mossy, slippery rocks. Pooling water graduated to a gentle trickle on the right. With each step, the passage morphed into a subterranean slot canyon, so deep that Jake's headlamp beam disappeared into darkness overhead. He knew this was not the passage Mingan and Hurit had traveled. He hedged the flowing water would end into a much larger body of water, perhaps the dreamscape lake where Mingan and Hurit started their fall from grace.

After a harrowing hour of descent, the passage leveled and the gentle trickle of water gave way to a small stream. Sandy soil replaced the mossy rocks, and familiar luminescence sparkled on the walls. Jake smiled and nodded. He turned off his headlamp, allowed his eyes to adjust to the blackness, and looked downstream. In the distance, a small glimmer of light stood out like a single star on a dark night.

He flicked his headlamp back on. "Let's go, boy. Let's find Dakota."

The Stranger reached the intersection in the cave. He looked at Jake's and Honi's footprints in the fine soil and nodded, then walked in several circles, then crisscross patterns, leaving no clear direction of Jake's prints. Last, he stepped into Honi's prints, erasing them.

That will slow them down.

He held the amulet around his neck.

Soon, my love, you will not hide behind this power. Your weakness will be your end.

The search party paused at the first intersection in the cave.

Charlie motioned Jay forward, and shined his lamp on the multiple footprints in the dirt. "What do you think?"

Jay examined the faint prints for several seconds. He took several steps into the right passage, then returned to the left. "It appears they looped back from the right and headed that way."

Jim said, "Who could be with them? Jake made no mention of having help with him."

Jay shook his head. "No idea."

Blake said, "Who says the other person is there to help him? Maybe Jake is being followed. Have there been any new faces in town, Charlie?"

Charlie threw his hands up. "Hell, since the trial, the town has had all kinds of new faces, then add hunting season into the equation.... It's impossible to identify any one individual."

Steve said, "Did anyone notice the old Willys parked about a half-mile or so down the road before the gate?"

Charlie said, "I did, but didn't pay much attention to it. This is a popular area for late season trout fisherman. Plus, we never suspected Jake would have company. Let me get out to the landing and try to radio headquarters. I'll have a unit drive out and check the plates real quick. Go ahead, I'll catch up to you all, won't take but about fifteen minutes or so."

Webb said, "Go ahead, Charlie, we'll wait."

Charlie rushed from the cave to the landing.

"Dispatch, this is Charlie. Over."

Static

"Dispatch, this is Charlie. Over."

"Charlie, this is Vicky, go ahead. Over."

"Vicky, there's an old Willys Jeep parked along Teton Park Road near Cottonwood Creek picnic area. Do we have a unit near there? Over."

"One second, Charlie... yes, Unit Fourteen is over near Taggart Lake. Over."

"Great, have him run an MVR on it *ASAP* and radio me back. Over."

Several minutes passed. Charlie paced back and forth on the landing.

"Charlie, this is dispatch. Over."

"Go, Dispatch. Over."

"The plate is registered to a Doctor Maurice Davidson of Helen, Montana. He's clean. Over."

Charlie nodded. "Roger, Vicky. Thank you. No further action needed. Over."

Charlie rushed back to the group. "The plate belongs to a Doctor from Helen, Montana. I'm sure he's here fishing, as we suspected."

Jay said, "Okay, let's assume Jake is being followed. We need to get moving."

Jill pushed back her high-backed leather chair from the grand mahogany dining table, and rubbed her belly. "I'm stuffed. Did you enjoy the food?"

Dakota pulled a linen napkin from her lap, blotted the sides of her mouth, and placed it on the table. "I couldn't eat another bite. That was the best Wellington I've ever had. Are you fattening me up for the kill?"

Jill chuckled. "Yes, we love our sacrifices to be well fed. It makes their blood much richer."

"Well, mission accomplished. So, now what?"

Jill stood and motioned Dakota to follow her. "Come, let me show you to your room."

The women walked up a wide, gently-turned white marble stair, its veins rich with gold. They passed several rooms and stopped.

Jill said, "Here, you swing the doors open."

Dakota hesitated for a moment, then slowly pushed open the highly polished ebony doors. Across the spacious room, a wall of windows framed the Tetons and valley below. She sauntered across warm hardwood floors, ran her hand across sheer silk curtains draped around a high bed, and stood at the windows, marveling at the view of the valley below.

Jill said, "Beautiful, isn't it?"

Dakota nodded, her eyes not leaving the first sunshine she had seen in days. "Yes."

"Check out the bath. It's through the double doors to your right."

Dakota walked to the doors, Jill in tow, and opened them both simultaneously.

Three walls of windows greeted her. A large stone tub in an irregular shape spanned two walls of windows. Water gently bubbled in the middle.

Dakota glanced at Jill. "It looks like a hot spring."

Jill smile and nodded. "It was fashioned after one of my brother Josef's favorite springs in France. The water is pumped from the mineral springs below. I'll leave you now. Enjoy a bath, relax, and do sample the wine my brother Dorian provided from his private collection. I think you'll find it... enchanting."

Dakota watched Jill pull the doors shut as she exited, leaned over and ran her hand through the warm water, then walked to a window facing Dubois. She gazed to the heavens as her eyes welled.

What have the Spirits... or Demons... delivered me into? Am I paying a price for taking Jake from his life? Am I leading him to his punishment?

Jake and Honi quickened their pace as the light in the darkness grew brighter and the smell of fresh water filled the passage. After several hundred yards of a gently sloping gradient, they stood on the shoreline of a small pond. Rays of sunlight from fissures in the cave's roof pierced deep into the clear waters. Tiny fish shimmered like specs of gold and silver in their beams.

Jake nodded and smiled. He took one knee and patted Honi on the back. "*This* I recognize, boy. Up ahead will be a large lake and a bridge. The Spirits have led us back to where this all began." He reached behind his neck and retrieved the two spears. "Time to right the ship and end this for Dakota and me. Let's go."

The stranger quickened his pace, reached the area of mossy rocks, and paused. He squatted and pressed his hand into Jake's footprint left behind in the wet spongy carpet. His eyes narrowed.

Where are they leading you, Jake?

He resumed his descent, his pace as quick as possible given the treacherous footing.

Upon reaching the transition area from rock to soil, he bent over and cupped a handful of water from the frigid stream. As he raised his head, a glimmer of light caught his eye. He stood, his hand braced on the sword handle at his side.

This ends soon.

The search party moved deeper below the mountain, their pace as quick as possible given the conditions afoot and age of the group. They reached the three-way intersection and paused.

Jay examined the rambling footprints in the soft soil, took a deep breath, and pointed towards each passage. "The prints go back and forth to each entrance. I do not see Honi's at all. Whoever is down here with Jake must know we are following. We need to travel a few feet into each passage."

Blake said, "Can we take five?" He pulled a smoke from his pocket.

Webb said, "Good idea, but Blake, I wouldn't light up. I'm not sure which way the smoke will move down here. We can't alert whoever is following Jake."

Charlie held out a tin of snuff. "Here you go."

Blake pushed the cigarette back into the pack and nodded. "Good point, Webb. Thanks, Charlie, been a few decades since I did that. I'll pass. That shit will kill ya!"

Joe chuckled and patted Blake on the back. "You're one of a kind, partner."

Jim said, "I'll look up the left one."

Charlie said, "I'll look dead ahead."

Joe moved towards the largest opening on the right. "I'll check this one."

After a minute or so, Jim returned. "The soil ends a few feet into the passage and turns to rock. There are no prints."

Charlie returned soon after. "No human prints down there, just some small critters."

Joe emerged and held up a small tuft of hair. "This is canine, I assume the wolf's."

Jim and Jay looked at the fur and nodded.

Jim said, "Yes, that is Honi's color."

Webb said, "Good job, Joe."

Charlie tossed his pack on. "Let's move."

Dakota stood in front of a wall-length beveled mirror above the three-bowl marble sink. She leaned in, stared at her reflection, and muttered, "You look like hell." She glanced across the room to a Hollywood-level makeup area then back at the bath, and shrugged. "What the hell, I'll play your games. Jake will end this soon enough."

She dropped her clothes at the sink and sauntered across the marble floor to the bath. *I'm sure you have cameras in here, you pricks. Here's an eyeful.* She bent over and uncorked the gaudy wine bottle. A rich fruity aroma followed the cork, then a hint of an earthy undertone. She poured a glass of the deep red, swirled it and pulled it to her lips. An intense rush of berries and smoky chocolate awakened her taste buds. She raised her brow and took a deeper sip of the elixir, turned to the center of the room, and defiantly lifted the glass in a cheer. "I know you're watching."

She settled into the bath, and the warm bubbling waters massaged her tight muscles. She leaned back against the smooth rock wall and closed her eyes. For a moment, she imagined this bath was the hot spring at the cabin, and her anxiety gave way to thoughts of a simple, magical time. She reminisced about the first time she watched Jake undress and step into the spring with her. A smile crossed her face, remembering how bashful he was. Then Christmas time on the mountain, and the red and green light sticks she'd dropped in the spring to watched Jake's nakedness through the bubbling waters. She snapped her eyes open, and a tear trickled down her cheek.

Why did the Spirits bring us such joy, and now this? What do they want from us?

The Six gathered in the library.

Two grotesquely hunched and crooked figures draped in dark, hooded robes emerged from the hidden passage behind the book case.

The taller of the two spoke up. "Jake Michaels is at the pond. He will reach the lake soon."

Adah said, "Thank you, Balam."

Josef walked over, looked down to waist height, and laid his arm on Balam's shoulder. "Soon, my brother, you will walk tall and erect again. Gone will be your tail and sores. Please assemble the rest of our siblings and ready the altar."

Balam said, "Yes, Brother, it will be nice to look you in the eyes again, to step from the shadows and feel the sun on my face."

Adah said, "David and I will go down, erase Jake's and the beast's prints, and help with the preparation."

Josef said, "Jill, please see to Dakota. Make sure she drank the wine, and ready her for the altar."

Jill nodded. "Yes Brother."

Jordana watched Jill exit. "She has become close to the girl. You can see it in her eyes. I have not seen that weakness since we first found her. Will she fail us?"

Dorian shook his head. "I do not believe so. Her reward is too great. The stakes are too high. She would never betray us."

Josef said, "She will complete her transformation tonight. This is something she has yearned for millennia. I am not worried."

Jordana nodded. "I trust your judgment, Brother. The time is here. I am going to prepare. I will see both of you at the altar on the hour."

Josef and Dorian turned and faced each other.

"Josef, our Destiny is here. Soon, what is rightfully ours will be handed to us. *He* can no longer stop this."

"Brother Dorian, *His* creations have spilled much blood. Their tears stain the earth, and for what? A planet *He* has turned his back on... a planet *He* has flaunted in our faces as punishment for our transgressions."

Dorian nodded and chuckled. "Transgressions... born only from desires we were created with. No, Brother, this had nothing to do with punishment. This is how *He* answered to the One, how *He* covered *his* mistake."

Josef extended both hands and placed them on the sides of Dorian's shoulders. "I will see you at the altar, Brother."

Jake and Honi walked along the shore of the small pond and followed the outflow to the start of a dark passage. Jake shined his headlamp into the blackness and smiled.

"There they are, boy, just like in the vision." He reached into his pack, retrieved a lighter, and lit the first of a long row of torches hanging on the passage wall. One by one, he lit each torch as he passed. "This will help us get out quicker if we need to, Honi."

After several hundred yards, the duo reached the confluence of the stream and a large lake. Its waters shimmered with the torchlight from the passage.

Jake shined his headlamp into the darkness, beyond the illuminations of the torches, and refocused the beam to the right side of the vast cavern. "There we go, boy. Let's light this motherfucker up."

"Jake Michaels," a voice boomed from the darkness, its tone familiar.

Startled, Jake gripped both spears.

On the far side of the lake, a circle of torches sprung to life, and the glitz of a gilded object caught his attention. Jake lifted his binoculars, then slowly lowered them. His eyes narrowed.

"Rowtag, we meet at the gold bridge, after many lifetimes have passed," echoed across the water.

Silence befell the cavern.

One by one, torches danced to life around the lake. Into the light, a small wooden boat, resembling an ancient Viking ship, glided across the still water. Two small, hooded oarsmen piloted the craft with precise strokes.

Jake stood motionless as the boat edged its stern to the shoreline.

The fur on Honi's neck stood up as he snarled and lowered his front into a defensive posture.

One of the hooded oarsmen hobbled to the right of the boat and lowered a small ramp. "Calm the beast. We mean no harm," he said, his voice feeble and raspy.

Jake's gaze darted between the two unimposing figures. He reached down and placed his hand on Honi's head. "Easy, boy, it's okay."

The wolf slowly uncurled his lip and relaxed his posture.

"Who are you?"

The oarsman said, "My name is Morox. Please, come aboard. Leave the beast."

Jake shook his head. "No, he stays with me."

On the far side of the lake, a figure draped in white moved into the light of a large altar. "Let the beast pass, Morox," the figured commanded.

Jakes eyes narrowed. *That's not Rowtag.*

The stern order had fallen on his ears as if the figure stood an arm's-length away, not hundreds of yards across the water. He paused for several moments, then moved forward, his steps cautious, his hand resting on the sidearm at his hip.

When he reached the ramp, Morox stepped backed to the center of the boat.

Honi snarled and stepped in front of his master. Jake bent down and whispered a command in the wolf's ear, and Honi moved to the side.

Jake stepped onto the ramp, and the small craft dipped dramatically to one side. Jake paused.

Morox said, "Move forward. It will right itself."

As Jake and Honi stepped from the ramp onto the craft, its ancient boards creaked beneath their feet.

Morox drew the ramp up and assumed his oarsman position. Slowly the boat turned and made its way towards the opposite shore.

Jake stood quietly, his eyes fixed on the altar. The splash of oars on the glass-top lake echoed in the still of the cavern.

When the boat reached the halfway point of the lake, Jake saw three figures, dressed in flowing white gowns, emerging from a passage to the right of the altar. The distance to shore was close enough to make out some distinctive features—three dark-haired men, and one female with platinum blonde hair.

Jake nodded. *Four... Jill will be five... and I'm sure there's another....* *The Six.*

The Stranger stepped into the grotto. He tilted his head back and closed his eyes, allowing a beam of sunlight from above to warm his face. He looked down at Jake's and Honi's tracks, followed them to the pond then around the right bank into the torchlit passage. A brushing noise caught his attention, and he quickly stepped back into the darkness. The noise grew closer, and wisps of fine dirt clouded the torchlight from the passage. The Stranger settled deeper into blackness, his eyes fixed on the dimming light of the passage.

A figure appeared, her hands moving in a fanlike motion, swirling the dirt ahead of her.

His nostrils flared, and a vein pulsated in the middle of his forehead as the smell of putrid sweet flowers filled the cavern. "Adah," he whispered.

He stood motionless, watching Adah clear all evidence of Jake's and Honi's prints.

She returned to the entrance of the passage, inhaled deeply, and blew forcefully down the torchlit hall. She then reached into the pocket of her white gown, and placed a neckless and amulet around her neck before disappearing into the dark passage.

Fresh air quickly replaced the sickening floral smell. The Stranger waited several minutes before creeping back into the sunlit grotto. He drew his sword and ran his hand across the razor-sharp stone blade. His eyes focused on the passage Adah had retreated into.

Soon your beauty will fade.

The search team reached the slick moss-covered stones in the passage, and the hazardous footing greatly slowed their descent.

Jim watched as Charlie paused and held his hand up. Charlie focused his flashlight down the steep grade ahead, up at the dramatic vaulting of the narrow cavern ceiling, and looked back at the group. "How is everyone doing?"

Jay stepped next to him and shined his own light down the emerald-colored path ahead. "That is steep." He shined his light overhead and traced the ceiling as far as the beam would allow. "Eventually, this will even out. The water will flow into something."

Blake chuckled. "Yeah, into our graves."

Joe brushed past Blake and patted him on the shoulder. "Trust me, partner, the mountain Gods don't want your soul entombed here for eternity."

Blake scoffed. "Gods... I think more like devils. This is what I picture Hell to look like, minus some molten rivers. I'm sure that's up ahead."

Webb bent over and stretched his back, and slowly moved back to erect. "These rocks are brutal. Charlie, will we need ropes ahead?"

Charlie shrugged. "Not sure they'll help much. We just need to take it slow and hug the walls best we can. I'm with Jay: this will even out eventually, my guess is onto a stream bed."

Jim leaned against the damp wall and took a deep breath. The slippery footing and uneven rocks were taking a toll on his knees, but quitting was not an option. He trusted Jay's and Charlie's assessments of the subterranean landscape.

"We need to press forward," he said. "I have to assume Jake, and whoever is following him, are hours ahead of us."

Charlie pulled a set of trekking poles from his pack and adjusted them. "If you guys have poles, now would be the time to use them. Let me know when y'all are ready."

The group followed Charlie's advice. They began the knee-breaking descent, poles in hand, pace at a crawl.

A knock on the bedroom door snapped Dakota from her daydreams. "Who is it?"

"It's Jill, can I come in?"

Dakota downed the rest of her wine and stood in the bath. "One second."

She pulled a neatly folded thick spa robe from the bath's edge and stepped from the warm water. "Come in."

Jill walked through the bedroom to the bath. "Did you enjoy the bath... and the wine?"

"Yes, they were *both* much needed."

Jill smiled. "Good." She moved to a walk-in closet in the bath and emerged with a semi-sheer, flowing white gown. A gold border ran along the plunging neckline, and a matching gold, braided tie hung from the hanger. "Isn't it beautiful? It's made of the finest silk available."

Dakota glanced at the gown. "It's a bit sheer, don't you think. Where's the rest of it?"

Jill said, "This is all of it. Don't be bashful now. I've seen some of your magazine shoots. Go ahead, dry off. Feel free to use the makeup. Within the hour, you'll realize your Destiny... and your freedom. Now hurry. My brothers and sisters are waiting. I'll meet you in the kitchen."

Dakota watched Jill exit, then held up the sheer gown and dropped her head.

What do they want? Are they going to use me in some fucked-up ritual? An orgy? Great Spirit, what does this all mean? Jake, where are you?

Dorian and Jordana crossed the gilded bridge as the boat inched closer to the shore. Jake stood fast in the middle as the oarsman lowered the ramp, his gaze locked on the approaching siblings.

Morox hobbled down the ramp, paused, and looked back at Jake. "Please, come ashore."

Dorian said, "Yes, Jake, come ashore. We will let Dakota know you have arrived."

Jakes eyes narrowed and adrenaline coursed through his veins.

This, Jake, is what you're trained for.

He took a deep breath, stepped down the ramp, and walked across the soft sand towards Dorian and Jordana. He held his head high, shoulders squared, and pace confident.

Dorian extended his hand when Jake came within reach. "My name is Dorian, and this is my sister Jordana. Welcome to our home."

Honi moved to Jake's side and let out a slow, low growl.

Jake said, "Easy, boy, it's okay."

He hesitated for a moment. His instincts told him to refrain from shaking, and his training told him to grip Dorian's hand.

Show no fear, Jake. Look him in the eye.

Dorian's hand was firm, his flesh warm. An oversized vein bulged in his powerful bicep. Then he broke his grip.

"Let's skip the formalities," Jake said. "Where is Dakota?"

Jordana stepped forward, her hand extended. "My name is Jordana."

Jake froze for a second. Jordana's eyes mesmerized him, her beauty intoxicating. Her hand was soft and warm, and as her enchanting eyes locked on his, he felt something simultaneously evil yet angelic about her.

He regained his composure and broke the grip.

Jordana half smiled and stepped back. "Dakota is up in the main house. She will be joining us shortly. Now, please follow us across the River of Life."

Dorian and Jordana turned and walked towards the gilded bridge.

Jake paused to survey the area, and followed. He looked into the crystal waters as he reached the hump in the bridge, and nodded.

It's all making sense now.

He stepped from the bridge into the bright glow of the ambulatory.

Dorian nodded to his right. "These are my brothers, Josef and David." He glanced over Jake's shoulder. "And behind you is my sister, Adah."

Jake half turned.

Adah sauntered from a dark passage into the light. She approached him, her mystical blue eyes locked on his, raised her brow flirtatiously, and smiled. "Welcome." She then turned and walked to Dorian's side.

Jake panned from right to left. "So, I stand in front of the dreaded Six, or shall I say five. I assume Jill, or whatever her name is, will be joining the party?"

"I wouldn't miss it for the world."

Jake looked past the altar.

Jill and Dakota stepped into the light.

"Jake!" Dakota cried out, and raced forward, leaping from the ambulatory into the soft sand.

Jake met her and the two embraced.

Dakota buried her head into his shoulder and sobbed, her body trembling. "I'm so sorry, Jake, I'm so sorry."

He calmed her. "Shhh, love, it's not your fault." He wiped the streaming tears from her cheek and leaned in to her ear. "I have what they want."

Dakota pulled her head back and looked into his eyes.

His face relaxed as he nodded slightly and whispered, "Play along with them."

Jake turned towards the Six and took several steps forward, hand in hand with Dakota, with Honi by their side. "What do you want from us?"

Dorian stepped forward and paused. He opened his arms to his side, palms up, and raised his head, tracing the cavern's perimeter. "Many millennia ago, in this cavern, our Destiny was created. Your kind, in their ignorance, took that from us."

Jake squeezed Dakota's hand. "How could our kind take anything from you? We are mortal."

Dorian chuckled. "Don't play me for a fool. We know Rowtag, or Mastema as we know him, showed you Mingan and Hurit's journey to this place. That night, a child was conceived along these banks."

Josef stepped forward. "That child was burned at the stake while in his mother's womb. His veins coursed with our blood and that of Mingan's and Hurit's."

Jake paused. "So how do Dakota and I fit in?"

David said, "As both of you know, the essence of Mingan and Hurit live inside of you. It is pure."

Dakota said, "If this *is* true, how, after all these lifetimes and hosts, could their essence still be pure? What are you going to do? Sacrifice us and bathe in our blood?"

Jordana stepped from the ambulatory, sauntered in front of Jake and Dakota, and stared at Dakota's nakedness beneath the sheer gown. "No, tonight is a celebration of life. Tonight, your kind will once again lay with our kind. Our seed will combine, and a child of pure essence will be conceived—a child you will carry and give birth to."

Jill walked to Jordana's side. "This child will unite our races, as it should have been from the beginning?"

Jake barked, "*No.* You are not touching her."

Dorian laughed. "What, are you going to kill us? I see two spears on your back." He clapped his hands.

From the shadows behind the altar emerged a horde of small, hooded creatures, each with grotesquely distorted shapes similar to the oarsman.

Jake mumbled, "Oh no, attack of the munchkins."

Dakota lowered her head but couldn't hide her smile.

Jake shook his head. "No, I would be a fool to raise arms against you."

He undid the latch from around his waist, slung his pack over his shoulder, knelt on the sand, reached into the pack, and retrieved a soaked shirt wrapped in feathers and sage.

He stood and raised the offering into the air. "The Child did not die."

Jill and Jordana spun and looked at Dorian.

Dorian paused, looked at his sisters, and back at Jake. "Bring it to me."

Jake gently passed the makeshift swaddling to Jill.

The Six gathered as Jill laid the Child on the altar. She carefully removed the feathers and sage, unfolded the shirt, left to right and up and down, and stared at the fetus. Blood pumped through its veins beneath transparent skin, assuring them the Child was alive.

Dorian leaned in close to the Child, stood up, and looked at Josef. He motioned towards the horde. "Morox, come over, please."

Morox hobbled to the altar, his head at eye level with the Child.

Dorian held his hand out. "Morox, your knife, please."

Dorian turned to Jake and glared as he wiped the knife across his gown.

Jake yelled, "Do not kill that Child. *It is yours!*"

Dorian turned back to the Child, placed the knife across its midsection, and drew the blade across its flesh. He offered the knife back to Morox.

Morox lifted the knife towards his face, and his serpentine tongue darted from his hood across the blade. He then fell to his knees, his body convulsed, and his agonizing shrieks echoed through the cavern.

Then, silence.

Slowly, Morox pressed to his knees. His torso grew straight, and the hood, his prison for millennia, tore across his expanding body. He peeled the garment away and stood naked at the altar. The scales that had covered his body disappeared. His formerly crippled, frail stature vanished with the scales, and he now stood erect. Muscles bulged beneath tight skin, and his head, patchy with tufts of hair and oozing soars, was quickly covered by flowing black locks.

The Six stood speechless.

Morox smiled. "My brothers and sisters, once again I look you in the eyes."

Dorian looked down at the Child. The small knife wound had healed completely. "Quick, move the Child to the Waters of Eternal Life."

Jake took a step forward. "I have given you what you want. Now, let us leave."

The Six looked at Jake without a response.

Josef tapped Dorian on the shoulder and motioned him to step behind the altar. "What do we do with them, Brother? They are of no use to us anymore."

Dorian paused and glanced at Morox. He watched Adah place the Child into the cool waters beneath the bridge, then focused on Jake and Dakota.

"Josef, the fetus has not grown since falling from Hurit's womb. We need a child that can walk with us, learn from us, and inherit what is his."

Josef placed his hand on Dorian's shoulder. "Brother, the Child can heal us. We can remove these amulets and walk freely on the earth again. This land is *our* throne for eternity. Do we need an heir?"

Dorian drew a deep breath. "Do you not want children, Brother? Is that not why we fell from grace? Why we made the ultimate sacrifice? What we have waited for, imprisoned in this mountain, for tens of thousands of years?"

Josef looked his brother in the eye and nodded. "Yes."

Dorian smiled and turned towards the altar. "Prepare the ritual."

Adah and Jill walked towards Jake and Dakota.

Jake stepped in front of Dakota, drew the two spears from behind his neck, and slammed them defiantly into the sand. "*Stop!* There will be no ritual. *This is over.* I have delivered your Child back to you. There does not need to be bloodshed."

Jill looked at Adah, then at the two spears planted point-down in the sand, and laughed. "Seriously, Jake? Two old spears against all of us? Let me show you something before you make a huge mistake."

Jill lifted the amulet from her neck and dropped it to the ground. She raised her arms slowly towards the cavern ceiling, leaned her head back, and whispered several words in the ancient language. The ground shook beneath Jake's and Dakota's feet, and a fissure opened in the sand. A nauseating stench rose from it, along with the wails of disembodied souls, and filled the cavern.

"Look down," Jill commanded.

Jake and Dakota looked into the pit. Faces, twisted in agony and too numerous to count, stared back at them.

"Here is your choice, Jake. Do as we ask, and both of you will leave this mountain together. Resist, and when we are done with Dakota, that will be your eternity." Jill waved her hand over the cracked ground and sealed it.

Jake turned and locked his eyes on Dakota's. A tear fell down his cheek. "I can't have them touch you."

Dakota wiped a tear from her eye and lifted the same two fingers to do the same for Jake. She smiled. "Tonight, my love, our tears are joined in pain, but will again be joined in happiness. We will grow old together, and this night will fade. We have no choice."

Jake nodded and looked at Jill. "Can you use your magic, so we forget this night?"

Jill glanced back to Dorian, who returned a nod. "Yes, we will do that."

Jake dropped his head for a moment, then looked up at the altar. "Okay."

Adah stepped forward. "Dakota, come with me to the Waters of Purity."

Dakota held Jake's hand to the last moment as she drew away, her eyes locked on his. She followed Adah to the shoreline of the lake.

Adah dropped to her knees, bent over, and placed her hands on the surface of the lake. She made opposite circles in the calm water. "Ka-vas, ba-sar, be-khan, beyn"

The waters sparkled with the colors of the rainbow as Adah turned back to Dakota. "Please, disrobe and step into the water to cleanse your flesh, child."

Dakota looked back at Jake, her lips trembling. She dropped her silk gown to the sand and walked into the lake, her head fixed downwards.

Jake drew a deep breath and looked towards the altar. All eyes were fixed on Dakota's nakedness. Dorian, Josef, and David dropped their robes, and their dicks stood hard against their stomachs. Jordana and Jill draped a black silk cloth, embroidered with cryptic scarlet text, across a stone bed.

Jake's hands trembled as he looked at the two spears in the ground, and back at the altar. His mind raced with attack scenarios... all impossible to survive.

How did Chogan and Askuwhetean expect me to defeat such powerful foes? Is there magic in the spears they did not show me?

Dorian said, "Dakota, step from the water and join us on the altar. Adah, prepare Jake."

Dakota moved from the lake and paused in front of Jake, and the look in her eyes clearly indicated she'd seen something in Jake's eyes. She hugged him tightly, her body trembling, and whispered, "Please, don't do anything crazy. You can't beat them. I can't lose you."

Jake pulled back slightly, smiled, and gently gripped both her shoulders. "Trust the Spirits... I love you."

Adah said, "Go, Dakota, he will soon join you."

Dakota crossed the gilded bridge and stepped onto the marble altar.

Jill escorted her to the bed. "You will soon know pleasure like never before. Relax and accept your Destiny. Lie back."

Adah moved in front of Jake, her enchanting blue eyes locked on his. "Hold out your hand."

Jake did as instructed, and Adah's grip sent a feeling of arousal coursing through him.

Adah stepped back. "Remove your clothes and step into the lake."

"*Enough*," echoed through the cavern.

All eyes focused to the darkness on the far side of the lake.

From the shadows, the Stranger emerged. He walked into the dim light on the far shoreline. "Release them."

Dorian motioned Morox over. "Take care of this distraction, quickly."

Morox sneered. "Gladly. My blade has missed the sound of slicing through flesh."

The Stranger pulled his black Stetson off and dropped his duster to the ground. He reached behind his head and pulled his necklace and amulet from his neck, grasped it for a second, looked up, nodded, and dropped it to the ground.

The cavern trembled lightly, and the Six darted glances at each other.

The Stranger stepped onto the lake. His black-ringed armor emitted a light blue glow in the dim light.

Dorian commanded, "Morox, stand down. An old friend has come to the party."

Jake watched as the Stranger made his way across the lake, his strides long, his posture confident.

The Spirits have delivered.

He glanced back at Dakota and winked.

The Six and their horde stood silent.

Josef shouldered to Dorian. "Always the fool, he has been. It appears Adom comes alone. My arrow will fall him before he reaches the shore."

Dorian shook his head. "No, let Lilith have her vengeance." He stepped to the front of the ambulatory. "Adah, join us, please."

Adah stepped in front of the ambulatory. "I thought he was dead."

Dorian held his hand up and said nothing.

Adom reached the shore, and Jill's gaze locked on him. She spun and faced Dorian, her eyes wide.

He returned a slow nod.

She turned back to Adom and stood motionless, her eyes narrow and breaths deep.

Adom returned the icy gaze. "Hello, Lilith."

Jill moved towards him, and with each step closer, the veins in her temples pulsated. She reached arm's-length and paused. "Adom, my *loving* husband, I was told you were killed in a colonization millennia ago."

Adom smirked. "Sorry to disappoint you."

Jill moved her eyes across his broad shoulders, down his torso, to the belt wrapped around his waist. She shook her head slightly and half smiled. "Two swords, a spear, a bow, and a quiver of arrows, all of ancient metal.... My foolish husband, we have evolved past any harm these can do. *Still* blind to their orders, I see, *always* the good soldier, *never* questioning them."

Adom said, "As you once did also."

Jill nodded. "Yes, I did, until you chose them over me, and abandoned us."

"No, Lilith, I chose to carry out our mission, a mission you agreed to, knowing the risks, a mission *I rejected from the beginning*. Has time wiped your memory of this? No, *you* abandoned us."

Jill paused, stepped back, and turned away for a second to compose herself. She fixed her eyes back on Adom's. "When I lost our first child, I trusted the Makers would heal me. But after our second and third, it was clear they could not. With each child lost, my heart broke, but I had you. Then, they sent replacements, younger women that never saw battle. These women, healed of the imperfection, were shielded from the gravity on this forsaken planet. And *you*... you followed their orders. *You* chose *her* over me, just as the other men did. I begged you to leave and return to our home, but you pushed me aside."

"No, Lilith, I did not push you aside. Those women were *not* sent to be our wives, they were sent to breed, to carry out the plan, to *colonize* this planet and *save* our race. The other women accepted this change. They welcomed children from their husband's loins, and raised them as their own. You could not, *would* not."

Jill's face reddened. "You expected me to lie in bed and listen to her moans as you *fucked* her? Watch her belly swell with your child after *I* watched our children slide down my legs in a bloody clump?" She tilted her head back and breathed deeply.

Adom, seeing her eyes well and lips quiver, dropped his head for a second. "The morning I woke and discovered you were gone, I left the colony and my unborn child behind. I searched for you *endlessly*. Days became weeks, weeks became month, months... became years. Finally, I gave up. I assumed you had perished, and my heart broke. I returned to our home, never to take another woman, my life devoted to battle across the heavens, hoping, praying that I would die and be reunited with you again."

Jill's face softened. "When I left the colony, I wished for a quick death. I moved about the tribes of earlier creations and the abominations of the Maker's failed attempts to seed this world. I gave my body, *over and over*, to secure food, shelter, and safe passage." Her eyes narrowed and jaw tightened. "With each thrust of their cocks and putrid breaths on my back, sorrow turned to rage. Vengeance on the Makers and the colony fueled me to live. My heart turned black, my soul empty." She turned towards the Six. "Then I met my brothers and sisters. They taught me their magic, empowered me with immortality. And tonight, after millennia, I have repaid them. I delivered what they need to realize their Destiny, to make strong a weak race the Makers have walked away from."

Adom said, "And what of *your* Destiny? What does immortality hold for you? Will you bear children? Will you love again? I saw the tears in your eyes and the tremble of your lips. I know the woman I once loved is buried beneath all this hatred."

Jill moved to within inches of him, and ran the back of her hand down his face. "I will *never* love again. You took that from me. I have killed you a million times in my dreams, all slow and agonizing deaths. Tonight, I will let you live for a bit, and watch us cleanse the offspring of the colony, *your* offspring. Then, I will drive my hand deep into your chest and rip your heart out as you did mine."

Adom fixed his eyes on hers and with a swift movement, drew a knife from the sleeve of his armor and buried it between her ribs.

Jill's eyes grew wide and she gasped. A look of surprise and pain overtook her face.

Adom held onto her as her legs buckled, drew her in close, and whispered in her ear.

Her eyes softened and a look of peace relaxed her face.

Slowly, he lowered her to the ground and laid her on her back, her eyes glazed and breaths shallow.

Jake flinched as deafening shrieks from the horde filled the cavern.

Adom drew his bow and an arrow, aglow with green, whistled past Jake's head, finding its mark in Josef's eye, falling him in a heap on the tabernacle.

Dorian dropped to his brother's side, looked closely, and yelled, "He's dead. The Makers forged his weapons. *Drop your talismans! Harness our power!* Morox, *kill him!* Adah, you and David stay back. Don't let the girl escape."

The horde, led my Morox, jumped from the tabernacle, swords, spears, and bows drawn. Their blades, tips, and points glowed brightly in yellow.

Dorian and Jordana stayed back and observed from the edge of the tabernacle.

Adom rushed past Jake yelling, "Get the girl and get out of here. I'll distract them."

Jake paused. He glanced at Morox and his minions as they raced forward, then up at Adah and David standing guard in front of Dakota, their swords drawn. He drew his spears from the sand. "Honi, come."

Adom met Morox and the horde at the gilded bridge. A lightning-fast draw of his bow and release of two arrows at once crumbled Morox as he crested the hump in the bridge, but the horde kept coming, crawling over Morox's body like an army of ants. Adom drew two swords from his side and raced forward. The horde's arrows and weakly thrown spears bounced off his armor, and one by one, with speed and agility, he sliced his way through the onslaught of hooded foes. Cries of agony echoed through the cavern as sprays of blood painted its sands.

As Adom quickly slaughtered his minions, Dorian reached his hand up and drew an ivory-handled, golden, long blade from thin air. He turned to David and Adah. "Our Destiny will not be taken from us. Don't let her escape."

He and Jordana jumped onto the sand and raced towards Adom.

Jake and Honi advanced in the shadows along the left flank of the battle. Jake watched Adom thin the horde as Dorian and Jordana advanced.

"I can't," he muttered. He raced from the shadows with one spear drawn backwards, and yelled *"Hey!"*

Jordana turned, and Jake let the spear fly.

With supernatural speed and aim, it flew over the horde's head and struck Jordana in the torso. The force lifted her off her feet and drove her yards backwards. The spear head passed through her and dug into the sand, impaling her body feet off the ground. She screamed in agony as her arms and legs flailed in the air.

Dorian turned to the writhing of his sister.

Jake looked at Adom, who recognized his chance and raced forward, using the hump on the bridge to give lift to his jump. He drew his sword back in mid air and yelled.

The leader of the Six turned his attention from his sister, and in that moment, Adom's sword passed through the top of Dorian's chest and out the middle of his back. Dorian stumbled back and fell to his knees. He rocked back and forth, his arms listless at his sides.

Adom looked at Jake and winked. "Go get her." He turned his attention back to Dorian, drew the sword from his chest, and readied it to decapitate.

Dorian looked up, his eyes glassy, his body limp. "Wait... my old... friend," he labored.

He paused.

"Why... Adom, after all this time... do the Makers send you back?"

"Judgment, Dorian, for you and the rest of the Fallen. To end the suffering of my beloved Lilith. To stop the tears of the Creator. And most of all, to protect this colony from an evil that girl would have given birth to."

Dorian coughed blood, spraying Adom's boots. He took a rattling, deep breath. "Evil, Adom? We would have birthed the perfect species—all the knowledge and power of our kind, and the flesh of your kind. It was the original plan."

"And you *saw* the abominations from earlier attempts. We were *never* meant to mix our kind. The Creator, *your Father*, ordered you to stand down, but your lust for flesh and quest for power blinded you. The Makers pleaded with Him for millennia to end your carnage here, but He would not kill His own children. He had faith that, one day, you and your brothers and sisters would find your way again. But tonight, you were going to upset the scales of the Universe. It was time for you to face your judgment."

Dorian smirked. "This colony is lost, Adom, and *you* know it. The Makers know it, and *my Father* knows it. They are so easily manipulated by greed, power, and lust. Their morals are lost. Despite all the cleansings, all the warnings, they do not give head. We were here to save them, to cleanse them and breed imperfections out of them."

"Let her go," Jake commanded, as he stepped from the shadows onto the far side of the tabernacle.

Adom glanced over Dorian's head towards the tabernacle. He drew his sword back and looked into Dorians's eyes. "Peace be with your Soul."

With a swift blow, Dorian's head tumbled to the sand.

Movement in the corner of his eye drew his attention.

Jill pulled her way through the sand, elbow after elbow, inching closer to the Waters of Eternal Life.

Adom moved towards her, at all times keeping an eye on Jake. He placed his foot on her back, forcing her body flat against the sand. Lilith looked up out of the corner of her eye as he raised his sword overhead.

Their eyes met, and Adom paused and said, "We will walk together in the gardens again, my love. They promised me mercy on you."

Her eyes softened, and she blinked slowly.

He nodded and drove his sword through her back, staking her to the sand.

He then raced stand side-by-side with Jake and Honi.

David jumped behind Dakota and pulled a sword to her throat. "Take another step, Adom, and I will toss you her head. Drop your weapons, both of you."

Jake and Adom, each with weapons raised, paused.

Honi reared on his haunches, prepared to attack at Jake's command.

"*Do it*, David ordered, with Adah at his side. "And calm the beast."

Adom dropped his sword on the tabernacle, unbuckled his belt, felling his second sword to the ground, and laid down his bow.

Jake followed with his spear.

Adom glared. "Now what, David? Dorian's head lays separated from his body. Josef's blood flows across the tabernacle like a river. Lilith and Jordana are staked to the ground. Your minions lie in pieces at the foot of the bridge. Your reign of carnage on this planet is over."

Adah chuckled. "My dear, foolish Adom, always the follower, always the soldier—traits I found admirable when I watched you and Lilith fight together across this universe. When the Great Wars ended, the Creator laid your bounty at your feet. Lilith and you could have grown old together in paradise, but that was not good enough for either of you. The Makers asked for one last mission, and neither of you could say no. *You* tempted Destiny. *Look* where it led both of you—your beloved staked to the ground by your own sword, your final breaths to be taken on a planet forsaken by the Creator millennia ago. And for what, Adom?"

Adom paused, his icy stare darting between Adah and David. "And what did you achieve, Adah? Your brothers and sisters lie dead. You have been imprisoned on this mountain since the last cleanse. Your Father has wept every day for tens of thousands of years. Your mother passed, broken and grief-stricken. The good names of you and your brothers are a curse now. All for what? Lust, greed, power?"

David snapped, *"No, Adom!* Those are traits *only* your kind fall to. It is what made Lilith such a good soldier for us here. Her hatred of you and the Makers and the Father burned like a cauldron inside her. This world was her playground, to live out every dark, twisted fantasy possible, and punish this race. She relished the powers we granted her to manipulate the course of history, all to make this day possible. Now, you get to watch as we right the course."

David turned to his sister. "Adah, gather their weapons and throw them in the lake. Put the beast to sleep."

Jake and Adom watched their weapons whirl overhead and soar toward the lake. Their splashes echoed in the cavern as as Adah passed her hand in front of Honi.

He let out a small whimper as he settled to his belly, his eyes droopy.

David moved Dakota to the head of the altar. "Disrobe."

Dakota's eyes locked on Jake as she slid one shoulder from the silk gown, then the next. She paused, holding it tight to her breasts as her gaze darted between Jake and Adom.

David grabbed the back of the gown, ripped it from her clenched fists, and forced it past Dakota's knees. He pulled his ceremonial robe over his head and bent her forward, pressing her face against the shrouded altar.

Dakota felt his hard dick bounce off her ass as he positioned himself. Her mind raced back to the night Jake rescued her.

The Spirits sent him that night, and they will give him the power tonight. He will save me.

"Adah, prepare him," David commanded.

Adah stepped in front of Jake and Adom. "Jake, remove your clothes. Adom, how fitting you watch as we change the course of this race. *All* you have sacrificed for it, *all* you have given to the Makers, and soon... *all* for naught, after a couple thrusts in her."

Jake looked over her shoulder, his eyes narrow and locked on David. "Fuck you, bitch!"

He shoved her aside, dashed forward, dove towards the body of Josef, pulled the arrow from his eye, and thrust it over Dakota's head, burying it deep in David's throat.

Jake looked back as Adah spun towards her brother.

With lightning speed and a flawless move, Adom reached into his boot, sprung forward, yanked Adah's head backwards by her golden hair, and drew his blade from ear to ear.

Her body crumbled to the ground, twitching, spraying blood across the marble tabernacle.

Dakota stood and looked down on David, his breathing labored as blood gurgled from his throat. She looked at his erect dick, smiled, reached down and grabbed the sword by his side. With a quick slice, she sent his member across the tabernacle.

David writhed in agony as blood sprayed across both their naked bodies.

She drew the sword overhead, but paused. "No, I'll let you bleed out, you bastard."

Jake stepped behind her and draped his jacket over her shoulders. She spun and buried her head against his chest, and her sobs echoed in the still of the cavern.

Jake held her tightly. "Shhh, it's over now. It's over."

Adom walked past Jake and Dakota and stood over David, watching him gasp for air like a fish out of water. He knelt and stared into David's eyes. "Once, a long time ago, we did battle side by side, my old friend. Where did it all go wrong? Where did the hatred for your Father come from?"

A tear fell from the corner of David's eye, and with the shallowest of breaths, he pleaded, "End it."

Adom shook his head. "No, you deserve to suffer."

From the shadows to the left of the tabernacle, a familiar *thwang* drew Adom's attention. He sprang to his feet as Jake lurched sideways.

A second *whoosh* followed, and Adom recoiled with the thud of an arrow against his armor. "Get down," he commanded.

"Nooooo," Dakota screamed.

Adom grabbed David's sword and raced past Jake and Dakota into the shadows. An eerie silence fell about the cavern.

Dakota knelt next to Jake, cradled his head, and looked down at the arrow buried in the side of his chest. His shirt quickly soaked with blood, and she reached down to pull the arrow from him.

He grabbed her hand. "No... I'll bleed out." He coughed forcefully, spewing blood upwards.

Dakota's eyes welled at the gravity of the situation. "You can't leave me, Jake. Hold on, my love. I'll get you out of here."

Honi woke from his slumber and walked towards his fallen master, head low and eyes sad. He dropped to his stomach and laid his head across Jake's shoulder.

Jake placed one hand on Honi's head as his other hand tightly grasped Dakota's hand. His breathing grew shallow and he struggled to keep his eyes open. "As the seasons pass... I will be with you in the mountain wild flowers, the warm summer breeze blowing across the plains, the yellow of the fall aspens, and the winter snow. Tell my children I love them. Tell Alex to forgive me, that this was my Destiny, and it could not be changed. Take care of Honi."

Dakota shook her head as tears streamed from her eyes. "No, Jake, stay with me. The Spirits sent you to me. You can't go. It's not our Destiny."

Adom emerged from the shadows, his armor soaked in blood. He stepped over Jake and Dakota.

Dakota looked up, her body trembling and lips quivering. "Save him. *Save him, please...* with your magic. Help me get him to the surface. We can call for help."

"I am a warrior. My magic is taking lives, not saving them. There is a search party behind me. They will have supplies."

Dakota looked back at Jake. "Did you hear that, baby? Help is coming. Stay with me."

Dakota looked back at Adom. "Who are you?"

"I am a man, searching for his own Destiny." He turned, stepped from the tabernacle into the sand, and disappeared into the darkness.

Jake's hand fell limp in Dakota's as the rise and fall of his chest slowed.

Dakota's cries filled the cavern. "Stay with me, Jake. Stay with me."

In the sand, on the banks of the Waters of Eternal Life, Jill thought back in time. Memories of a time when she once loved danced before her eyes. Memories of Adom and her, as young children filled with dreams, brough a smile. Memories of his touch and the warmth in his eyes when he looked at her sent a feeling of calm through her body. Slowly, as her life faded, so did her hatred.

She looked towards Dakota, whose cries tugged at her heart, then down at a stream of blood flowing from her body towards the Waters of Eternal Life. With the last bit of energy in her body, she reached out and cupped the sand, damming the blood from the Sacred Water. Her eyes closed, and peace befell her.

Jake's eyes closed. He clenched Dakota's hand, then his body relaxed.

Honi stood and lifted his head to the sky. Mournful cries bounced off the walls of the cavern, across the lake, into the grotto and towards the night sky. The wolf looked at Dakota, his eyes blank and soulless, his muzzle soaked with tears. He dropped his head below his shoulders and lumbered towards the darkness.

"No, Honi, don't you leave me too." Dakota sobbed as her body rocked back and forth.

"Dakota," a deep familiar voice called out from the darkness behind the lake.

She looked up to see a glow moving across the water. As it got closer, a human form took shape. "*Rowtag, come!* Hurry, please!"

Rowtag paused when he reached the beach and he gazed about at the carnage.

"Hurry!" Dakota pleaded.

Rowtag stood at Jake's head.

"Please, you brought us here. Please save his life. I beg you."

Rowtag remained silent as he knelt and placed his hand on Jake's forehead. He then muttered several words in the ancient language of the Six.

Dakota watched for life to spring back into Jake.

Rowtag stood. "His Destiny is complete. His soul will rest and wait for you."

Dakota leapt to her feet. "*No,* you bastard! You *will save* him! You sent us on this journey and we trusted you. Look around. There is nothing but fucking death. Was this your plan? And your lies... how are you here in the real world?"

Rowtag's icy stare locked on Dakota. "Lies... no. If I had shown you the truth, you would have never followed the path you were destined for. Embrace what you cannot change, and accept what you will never understand."

"*No!* Enough of your fucking riddles." She raced towards the spear that impaled Jordana and kicked it below her body, snapping it in half, and pulled the head from the ground. She walked towards Rowtag, the razor sharp point held in front of her. "I *will* send you to hell with the rest of them. Save him or die."

Rowtag chuckled. "Weapons cannot hurt me. Do you not think many have tried before you?"

Dakota screamed and lurched forward, sinking the spear deep in Rowtag's massive chest.

Rowtag stood strong against the blow, drew the spear head out, and looked at it. "Sent from the Makers... impressive."

Dakota stepped back. "*What* are you? *Who* are you?"

Rowtag turned and walked away. He paused at Jill's body, drew the tip of his spear across the sand, and opened the dam holding back her blood. The crimson trickle meandered across the sand and dripped into the Waters of Eternal Life, which turned crimson then quickly cleared.

He nodded, then glanced over his shoulder towards Dakota. "I am the Balance."

THE MIDDLE...

WATCH FOR BOOK THREE IN THIS "CALL OF DESTINY" SERIES TO RELEASE IN LATE 2026 OR EARLY 2027.

Acknowledgements

Thank you to my wife Lorri for her unwavering support of my writing career. Sharing a world and characters that take up hours every day of your spouse's life can be challenging.

Thank you, Evolved Publishing, for your continued support.

Thank you, Dave Lane (aka Lane Diamond), for your patience as I hone my craft. I could not ask for a better editor and writing coach.

Thank you to the men and women of the National Park Services, especially those in Yellowstone and Grand Teton Parks. You are the stewards of God's Country.

Thank you to those who are fighting to stop the senseless slaughter of the American Grey Wolf.

Thank you to Richard Tran for the absolutely amazing cover art.

Finally, I stand humbled before the Grand Architect that sculpted the majesty of the American West. It is the inspiration behind the Call of Destiny series.

ABOUT THE AUTHOR

Like many new authors, I said for years I wanted to write a book, but life, careers, and other necessary evils seemed to always derail that goal. Then, four years ago, on a road trip out west, I found the spark that ignited *The Temptation of Destiny*, and now *The Pyres of Destiny*.

My journey began in Hazleton, Pennsylvania. After high school, I joined the U.S. Coast Guard, spending the better part of eight years busting holes in the sky on C-130s. After the military, my career path meandered through the financial services industry, auto industry, bar industry, and construction management.

A two year stay in New Mexico, The Land of Enchantment, inspired me to open the ongoing story line up to span multiple states, and take readers on another roller coaster ride in *The Pyres of Destiny* (as *The Temptation of Destiny* did).

In my downtime, I enjoy hiking and other outdoor adventures with my wife. Hunting, fishing, and doing everything possible to stay from falling into the "status quo," fuels me.

When it's time to wind down this adventure we call life, I hope to be sitting in a cabin high in the alpine forests of the Rockies, spending the days with my wife, children, family, and friends, reminiscing about the blessings this life afforded us all.

D.M. Earley

For more, please visit me online at:
Website: www.DMEarleyAuthor.com
Goodreads: D.M. Earley
Facebook: DM Earley
Twitter: @DMEarleyAuthor

MORE FROM EVOLVED PUBLISHING

We offer great books across multiple genres, featuring high-quality editing (which we believe is second-to-none) and fantastic covers.

As a hybrid small press, your support as loyal readers is so important to us, and we have strived, with tireless dedication and sheer determination, to deliver on the promise of our motto:
QUALITY IS PRIORITY #1!

Please check out all of our great books,
which you can find at this link:

www.EvolvedPub.com/Catalog

Thank you!

www.ingramcontent.com/pod-product-compliance
Lightning Source LLC
Chambersburg PA
CBHW030848030726
47495CB00005B/1423